Erin Pizzey founded Women's Aid, a refuge for battered wives. Her struggles to get The Refuge established and accepted were successful after the intervention of a personal letter from the Queen.

She was born in a castle in China, and spent a footloose childhood in Africa and the Middle East, before being educated in convents.

She is well known for her non-fiction, most recently the highly controversial *Prone to Violence*, written with her second husband, Jeff Shapiro, and its predecessor, *Scream Quietly or the Neighbours Will Hear*, as well as the autobiographical *Infernal Child*. She has written regularly for magazines such as *Cosmopolitan* and has completed a second novel, *In the Shadow of the Castle*. With her husband, Jeff, she is now living happily in New Mexico, where her interests are reading, writing, cooking and gardening. *The Watershed* is her first novel.

The Watershed

Erin Pizzey

CORGI BOOKS

THE WATERSHED

A CORGI BOOK 0 552 12462 1

Originally published in Great Britain by Hamish Hamilton Ltd.

PRINTING HISTORY
Hamish Hamilton edition published 1983
Corgi edition published 1984
Corgi edition published 1984 (three times)

This book is set in 10/11 pt Mallard

Corgi Books are published by
Transworld Publishers Ltd.,
Century House, 61-63 Uxbridge Road,
Ealing, London W5 5SA.

Made and printed in Great Britain by
Hunt Barnard Printing Ltd, Aylesbury, Bucks.

Contents

Seven out of ten married men are said to be unfaithful to their wives. This book is dedicated therefore to those seven out of ten married women who have suffered this pain.

I would also like to dedicate this book to my sister Kate Grierson, who paid our mortgage while we wrote the book, to Mr Gutteridge and the Midland Bank, who had enough faith in us to allow us an overdraft, and to Peter Lavery, who rescued the synopsis from a filing cabinet where it had languished for two years.

Rachel had been born and raised in a world run by women. It had been a safe, secure and nurturing childhood. She hadn't realized she was motherless until she heard the cleaning lady tell the cook: '. . . the poor motherless little thing, she'll have to spend the rest of her life in bed.' She was resigned to the bed part of this comment because it had been explained to her by the family doctor – one of the few males in her life – that she had contracted rheumatic fever and had a very high temperature, that it had affected her heart, and that therefore she must stay in her bed for many long months. So it wasn't too much of a shock to contemplate the rest of her life in her orderly, pretty bedroom; it was the news that she was 'motherless'. Certainly at the all-girls' primary school she attended she knew that the other girls had mothers and fathers, but since she was a bit of a blue-stocking and found most of the girls embarrassingly silly she kept to herself and assumed that, while others had mothers, she somehow had inherited her two aunts. The three of them lived in seclusion in a large, rambling Edwardian house in the Devon valleys.

Rachel was eight at the time of this information concerning her mother. Rachel was a thin, long child with big hazel eyes and thick, strong black hair in two plaits, the ends of which she chewed.

She didn't look very different now at thirty-six. She was still thin with big feet and hands, and her hair was still thick and black. The nurses had plaited it for her and she was sitting in the high white bed with the sheets folded neatly round her, chewing furiously at the end of her plait, waiting for visiting time so that she could see her children. She had been in this hospital for nearly two weeks – ward 6-B, ironically called 'Hope' ward – the ward for all the flotsam and jetsam of female failures, the depressives, the neurotics, the divorced, the aborted, the anorexics. Beds full of women who used the hospital as a refuge.

Rachel, unlike the others who moaned and schemed to get out, knew that for her she was in the safest possible place. It was indeed where her husband had always promised her she would end her days – in a mental hospital. But with her last shred of sanity she also knew it was her choice, either to stay forever in the confines of the walls of the hospital or to metamorphose into a new self. The metamorphosis would require a 'letting go' of all her years and then a rebuilding, the outcome of which no one could predict. If she failed, she could well end up like so many middle-aged women unable to pick up the pieces, wandering the streets with shopping bags full of rubbish, each piece a symbol of the distorted past.

Her husband had the children. He had organized her committal on the grounds that she had been found wandering and unconscious. 'Possibly suicidal' the committal papers stated. She hadn't been able to put up much of a fight. Both her aunts were dead. She had no other relations. Her husband had a widowed and despotic mother who was only too happy to move in with and to look after her adored only son and his children in their comfortable home in Richmond.

What did Rachel have to offer? Not much at this point in her life, but if she took the risk and let go, she could come out the other side. Who knew? Her psychiatrist had explained that to put her to sleep for a period of three weeks would allow her exhausted body and nervous system a chance to revitalize. For so many years – as many as she had been married – she had been running like a hamster on a treadmill round and round her married cage. Other women had seen their married situation as their goal in life, but she, a disobedient and recalcitrant rodent, had always secretly wished to get off. But she had no just cause in view – no reason to call a halt to the endless monotony of life with her successful and outwardly excellent husband – until the day he decided it was safe enough to confess to a lifetime of affairs with other women. Some of them had been major, lasting for a year or two, some of them casual with chambermaids or air hostesses on his travels.

When he confessed, the pain of his betrayal brought instant tears. She felt her jaw dissolve and crack open, and to her embarrassment she was crying like a small child. Her mouth hung open and she dribbled. She felt her nose start to run, the sounds were baby sounds, 'Ma ma, ma ma'. He had the grace to look ashamed. They were in bed on a Wednesday morning. But his urgent and subconscious need to destroy her, as he systematically destroyed all women who came his way, was greater than his conscious desire to care for her. Besides, his current mistress had given him a cast-iron ultimatum. 'Either you tell her or I will'. And he was afraid that Rachel, on hearing of his infidelity from another woman, might well take the matter to court. This way, catching her off guard, after a night of love-making, his killer instinct assured him that he had the greater chance of success.

Rachel was thinking of that moment when the bell sounded and the visitors surged towards the beds. She saw him with the children in tow striding purposefully towards her. He loomed over her and kissed her on the forehead. Judas, she thought, the eternal betrayer. At that moment she made her decision. She would agree to the sleep therapy. Three weeks of oblivion. It was her own particular watershed, and from now on her path through life would have to be re-channelled. She began the course of drugs that night, and like Alice in Wonderland she fell into a very deep black hole, where she could feel herself drawn back through time into her early memory of Aunt Emily's big warm soft-nippled breasts.

Book One
Past Tense

1

Aunt Emily was small and fat. Her eyes were a particularly intense brown. She smelled, like many fat people, of a moist dampness reminiscent of cornfields after the rain. Or maybe it was her powder, kept in a large, blue, Victorian glass jar with a huge powder-puff, which she applied liberally to her person every morning after her bath. Rachel's earliest memories would be morning images of being about four and running from her room across the polished pine corridor to her aunt's bedroom. She had to reach, standing on her toes, to turn the solid brass knob that filled both her hands as she pushed to gain entry. There, every day for all the years she lived at that house, she would see the same scene. Between Aunt Emily's bed and the spare bed would be a mahogany Georgian breakfast table. Prepared by Irene the cook, breakfast was brought to Aunt Emily by Rachel's other aunt, Aunt Bea, which was short for Beatrice.

She thought of Aunt Bea as secondary to Aunt Emily because Aunt Bea lacked the pillowed warmth and intimacy of Aunt Emily. There was no mystery about Aunt Bea's lean shape. Her shoulders were wide and her arms sinewed. There were no magic crevices or shadowed valleys in the distances between her breasts and her knees – a distance all the more exciting in Aunt Emily's case because modesty forbade her ever to appear totally naked. Both aunts could only be seen in nightgowns or in their sensible vests and serviceable knickers. However, untidy careless Aunt Emily was always lacking essential buttons and the child would find herself secretly moving towards the bare inviting flesh, and running her urgent fingers towards a gentle mound, and then feeling an exquisite, relaxed contentment flow through her little body as she lay quietly beside her aunt.

Touching Aunt Bea was always an effort. True, her aunt kissed her every night, 'Good-night, child,' she would say, but she was apprehensive of Rachel, and sometimes a little short with her when she found her yet again folded into Aunt Emily's body. 'Haven't you got anything else to do?' she would say. However, breakfast was a time of trinity between them. The breakfast-set was a practical blue and white. All her life, Rachel, who later inherited that particular set of china, was to have her morning tea from the pot that signified those days of her childhood.

Aunt Bea would sit on the spare bed already having dressed herself and walked her two dogs. She favoured boxers, both bitches, who were the prime objects of her affection after Aunt Emily whom she treated like a spoiled amiable child. Aunt Emily poured the tea, and in doing so leaned forward, and that magic moment of the hot, yellow liquid arching from the spout of the teapot into the cool, waiting porcelain cup was shadowed by the swell of her breasts as they escaped the constraint of her nightdress. Flushed with concentration, she would poke her pink tongue from between her teeth and Rachel, the observer, would breathe deeply the smell of the toast and the marmalade, and share the animal warmth of that morning moment.

During breakfast, Rachel sat on a child-size wheelback chair with a matching little table. She was not expected to talk at this point because Aunt Bea was going to discuss the day's business with Aunt Emily. This was the only time of the day that there could be any possibility of disruption between the two women. Rachel, whose love for Aunt Emily was so passionate, felt far more deeply disturbed by the slightest impatient quiver of Aunt Bea's nostril than did Aunt Emily, who, when faced with an unpleasant financial piece of information or with an obligation she did not wish to fulfil, would turn a bright shade of red and throw up her hands and declare the world an unfit place to live in. In fact, Aunt Emily continuously vowed to depart this world, thereby leaving the little girl in a state of terror. Though she was secure in the fact that Aunt Bea would love and protect her in her own fashion, the loss of Aunt Emily was unthinkable. However, usually the day's affairs were taken up with Aunt Bea's appointments as a Justice of the Peace – an honour she held most dear – or with Aunt Emily's hospital committees, various bridge evenings, and the odd sherry party.

These women were from a generation that saw most of their brothers and their potential suitors lost in a war. They then watched their married sisters and brothers in their turn lose their sons in a second war. Certainly, for Aunt Bea marriage had never been an option. Without ever saying as much, she thought little of the male world and was always full of stories of the deviant and delinquent men who came before her judicial bench and of their atrocities to their wives and children. She relished their sentencing, and would silence Emily, who would timorously suggest that maybe she had been a little harsh, with a 'Don't be so wet, Emily. He'll have to learn a lesson.' Emily would brighten up and agree that, of course, Bea was right.

Money was very rarely discussed at those morning meetings, except if Aunt Emily had been particularly extravagant and had bought an outrageously expensive dress, or if, a more likely possibility, she had seen something for Rachel. 'You spoil the child,' Aunt Bea would say with a sigh.

'I know I do, dear, but she's all we've got.' And 'all we've got' would sit back in her chair, luxuriating in the exclusivity of her indispensability.

Money was not a problem for those two women. They each had a trust fund until their deaths, with sufficient capital sensibly invested to survive even the most socialist of governments. Once a year an elderly gentleman would come from as far away as Exeter to the house, knock on the door, wipe his feet carefully on the coconut mat, and then enter the drawing-room where the two aunts would be waiting to receive him. Solemnly, he would explain about their shares and their dividends, while Aunt Emily poured the tea from the Rockingham teapot, and Rachel passed the sandwiches and sponge cake politely between the three of them.

Her duties over, Rachel could sit in the background and watch her Aunt Bea question the elderly gentleman sharply about their financial state, because she took *The Times* every day and was extremely worried at the state of the country. Aunt Emily, not listening to a word, would nod when she felt it was appropriate and, if questioned on a point of understanding by Aunt Bea, would busily inspect the state of the teacups. It was a yearly event and one that was made remarkable by the fact that a man had taken tea at the house. Because all the members of the house were female – from the cook to the cleaning lady to even the dogs – several hours spent in the company of so alien a creature left Rachel much to think about.

'Did I ever have a father?' she would ask Aunt Emily. She would never address so intimate a question to Aunt Bea. On the few occasions she so forgot herself as to ask Aunt Bea about herself, Aunt Bea would start like a horse. Her eyes would widen as if she could not believe what she had heard, and the silver-grey tight curls that clamped to her head would shake ominously. 'Nice girls don't ask questions,' she would reply.

With business over, it was time for Aunt Bea to play her daily round of golf. She was well known for her golfing ability; her handicap was eight. The downstairs mantelpiece in the study was lined with trophies, a source of great pride to Aunt Bea, who would supervise the cleaning lady whose job it was to polish them and to hear yet again how each one was snatched from the jaws of a competitor to the roar of approval from the onlookers with an ecstatic Aunt Emily looking on from her perch on a shooting-stick.

Clearing away the breakfast tray, Aunt Bea would stand and shake any stray crumbs to the floor, and then bend rigidly from the waist to pick up the heavy tray. Rachel could see the expanse of her heavy lisle stockings disappear into the elasticated tops of her navy-blue knickers, all neat and tidy and about as interesting as a wet Sunday morning after church – quite unlike Aunt Emily, whose stockings were usually insecurely clamped to her leg with over-stretched elastic garters because she refused to wear stays.

Aunt Bea would then leave with an instruction to Rachel 'not to stay too long'. When the door shut behind them, Aunt Emily and Rachel would giggle like small children. Rachel would leap on to her bed and they would roll and tussel like two puppies at play. As Rachel got older their play would become more furious until Aunt Emily would call a halt, and they would lie side by side puffing and panting with Aunt Emily awash with perspiration.

Now it was time for Aunt Emily's bath. She would leave the bed and go to the adjoining bathroom, where the shiny brass taps hung over the huge ball-and-clawed Victorian bathtub. Shouting comments to Rachel over the hiss and the steam of the taps, she would adjust the temperature of the bath and lay out the large white fleecy towel on the triple-railed wooden towel rack. Rachel, having moved into the damp form on the bed left by her aunt, would watch the ritual through the door.

Once the bath was sufficiently full of water, Aunt Emily fetched a large, crystal, glass-stoppered bottle from the marble washstand. The bottle contained oil that Aunt Emily ordered from London. As she explained to Rachel, the oil came all the way from India. Certainly the smell was sweet, musky and mysterious. Once the oil met the hot water, the vapour filtered from the bathroom across to Rachel. Wide-eyed, she would watch her aunt slip off her bed jacket, exposing her plump bare arms. Before closing the door between herself and the child, she would put her hands to her hair to pull it all into a knot on the top of her head. Over the bath hung a large bevelled mirror. The frame was gilded, and the carvings on it depicted ebullient angels and naked nymphs, and satyrs in a merry chase eternally in pursuit of each other. Aunt Emily, with her thick white arms forming a graceful arch exposing the deep hollows of her downy armpits, would smile into the mirror at Rachel, both of them smiling in a perfect moment of complicity.

Then the door would shut and Rachel would close her eyes and imagine her aunt removing her nightgown, lifting the fine white lawn garment up over her head, and for a moment her breasts rising to the strain of the arms, and then her flesh sagging back to its familiar folds as she let the nightdress drop to the floor beside the bathtub. Rachel could hear the sound of the water moving against the immersed body. She imagined the loved and trusted nipples that would never be hers expand in the heat – a phenomenon she had discovered for herself when lying against her aunt in the cool of the winter, which turned the gentle yielding mounds into tight buttons.

As she grew older, her imagination fired her mind with all sorts of fantasy. She travelled with the soapy flannel into all the forbidden nooks and crannies of Aunt Emily's form. Roused by the images, lulled by the musky smell escaping from under the door, the child would strain to hear the sound of her aunt rising from the tub. Imagining her drying herself, rubbing her pale skin pink from the friction of the towel, vulnerable and exposed as she bent to dry her legs. The child would count the seconds till her aunt would put on her bathrobe and open the door: 'nine, ten, eleven, twelve'; the door would swing open and Aunt Emily would walk purposefully into the room. Her face would reflect her preoccupation with the new day's events. 'Run along, Rachel,' she would say, 'it's time you got dressed.'

The bubble burst, the moment gone, Rachel would skip back to her room, secure in the knowledge that the evening would bring another tryst with Aunt Emily who would tenderly bathe her. Now she would ready herself for another day's activities around the house and gardens that hid in the gorse two miles from any main road and seven miles from Upottery, Devon.

2

While Rachel was growing up in her secluded world of women, some fifty miles away, outside Bridport, Charles was fighting for his little life. Bridport possesses an attractive high road but is very definitely a poor relation to nearby Lyme Regis, Charmouth, or Uplyme. The town sprawls in an ungainly fashion like a loose woman with her skirts spread wide. The little bungalow that was Charles's home for his early years crouched balefully alongside others of exactly similar design in a long row on the edge of a rather derelict field used by the local children as a play-area, and by the dogs as a public convenience. Charles's mother had great pretensions.

When she finally stopped shaking the walls of the little cottage hospital with her screams and took a surreptitious look at the naked baby held out to her by an exhausted midwife, the first thing she noticed was Charles's swollen and blue penis. She shut her eyes immediately at the disgusting sight, and then upon reopening them she was aware that her new-born son was also the proud prossessor of a spectacular pair of multi-coloured testicles. 'Do they always look like that?' she asked the nurse in horrified tones.

The nurse laughed good-naturedly, 'It'll all go down . . . baby boys often come out with swollen genitals. Mind you, he's going to be well hung. Someone's going to be a lucky lady.' It was all too much for Charles's mother – she who had only ever seen her husband without clothes, and had never much appreciated the sight. 'Girls are so much neater,' she murmured to herself as she slipped off to sleep.

The baby was put into the nursery where he screamed and scratched his face all night. Charles's mother didn't hear him. She dreamed of her dead mother who would have approved of her daughter producing a son as her first grandchild. He would also inherit the family secret, which was that they were Jewish, heavily disguised as Welsh. This was why in a family peppered with names like Morris, Sidney and Max, Charles's mother had changed her own name from Ruth to Julia, and now carefully had her first son baptized Charles Rupert Alexander Hunter. Hunter was the name of her blond, blue-eyed husband whose roots were deeply embedded in the Dorset soil. He never really knew why she chose to marry him and she never told him. If the family secret could never be told, it could at least be genetically eradicated. All the girls of her family were to marry blond, blue-eyed men.

Julia was born into a large family who were crammed into a dingy house in Hammersmith. Originally her parents had come from Poland with few possessions and a passion to do well for their children. Julia's mother never really made the transition from one world to another. The woman's English was always gutteral and so fractured that she made few friends among the cold, inhospitable people around her who resented 'foreigners'. Julia's father, from the moment he set foot on English soil, decided that he would completely obliterate their past. That is why he chose to live well away from any Jewish area. Their surname, 'Markovitz', was changed to 'Grey' and he never again attended synagogue.

The change of identity was easy for him. He was an excitable, temperamental man who was out to make a fortune. But for his wife it was an angry decision. She was forbidden to talk Yiddish to the children, and the candles were never lit again on the Sabbath. In return, she grew more and more isolated and bitter. She had a child every eighteen months until Julia was born – the seventh child – and then mercifully her exhausted womb collapsed in protest and she had a hysterectomy.

Left at home all day and friendless, she obeyed her

husband to the letter as far as religion was concerned, but nobody could eradicate her cultural right to matriarchy. In short, she was a tyrant in the house and the scourge of her children. Her husband soon found his feet, and put his little bit of capital into a small chemist shop on Hammersmith Grove. He was a convivial man who liked his customers. Soon the local people came to him with their ailments, and he would advise and bully them into good health. 'Health is all you've got – if you haven't got your health, you haven't got nothing.'

It was just after such a speech that he dropped dead in his shop. 'A heart attack,' said the doctor, '. . . too much time advising others.' The doctor looked severely at the small crowd that had gathered. You could have heard a pin drop. Those who had defected from the doctor's surgery guiltily felt around their chests. The surgery was crowded that night.

The local people were sad because they had come to trust the odd little man with his quick wit and smiling face. They offered condolences to his wife. She remained passive and silent, thanking his old customers with a nod of her head, but she did not invite them in when they called at the house.

As far as Julia was concerned, it was an emotionally bankrupt childhood. Once her father died, her mother virtually excluded the outside world from the family reality. The children attended the local school, but as they were so close in age they stayed together and they knew without even being told that their friends would not be welcome at their house. Julia had two brothers, and Max, the eldest son, took over his father's role in the family. Their mother set his place at the head of the table, and his wish was her command. Eventually, he became such a bully that the others hated and feared him. His mother, cut off from any social relationships, turned more and more to Max for comfort and reassurance. 'My Max,' she would say, 'someday you'll be hearing from him.'

Fiercely protective of her children, she would see them off to school in the morning, after they had obediently eaten a huge breakfast. Then she would labour round the house until their return. Forbidden to speak to them in Yiddish, she would put all her memories of home into her cooking. She had been so brainwashed by her husband's paranoia about their Jewish origins that she felt sure that if they were discovered observing any part of their religious rituals, someone somewhere would have the power to order them from their house and they would become refugees again.

She comforted herself with the rich brown smell of kasha cooking permanently on the back of the stove. Indeed, the smell of kasha would be with Julia for life. For her, her childhood was a mean memory of little money, threadbare carpets, and children sitting round an old oak table listening to their mother urgently bidding her children to excel at everything – 'to be somebody'. For the girls, she had mapped out unrealistic marriages to noble-born sons of great English families, and for the two boys business futures as professional men. 'A dentist or a doctor yet,' she would say at the end of still another long rambling lecture. She seemed to think that if she rehearsed their futures daily like a catechism it would become real – like the cinema.

She had one passion in life which she shared with the children – the cinema. Every week they would go to the local Palace Cinema and sit in a long row: Max next to his mother and on down to Julia, the youngest, who sat at the end. If anyone kissed too long on the screen, their mother was liable to take offence and storm out trailing her children behind her. As films grew more explicit, the children saw less and less of an entire film, until they could only recall fragments. They got round this problem by pooling their meagre pocket-money and sending Julia for half-price to see the whole production. She would then come home and fill in the ending.

This practice taught Julia three major things in her life. One was how to be devious, the second was that sex was disgusting, and the third was that real life was never as good as the cinema. In order to escape her mother's ever vigilant eye, Julia told her that she was taking Wednesday afternoon games. She told the games' teacher that her mother had excused her games in order to do needlework, and the needlework teacher was told that she was excused needlework in order to do games. Then she spent the afternoons in the cinema.

It was during a particularly riveting moment in a murder drama that Julia felt someone take her hand. She was so wrapped up in the moment of possible death of her heroine that she disregarded the hand enveloping hers until she felt her own small hand being firmly wrapped round a stiff sausage-shaped object between the thighs of the person next to her. She glanced sideways. It was a man. She closed her eyes in terror.

He was breathing thickly and she could hear him muttering under his breath. His hand held hers firmly against his genitals and he forced her to rub backwards and forwards. To her, his moaning and mumbling filled the cinema, but another quick look showed her that all along the row people were glued to the screen. She had no idea of what would happen next. Would they sit like this until the end of the film? She stole a look at his face. He sat with his head slightly tilted back. The flaps of his raincoat covered her hand and his erection. His mouth was pursed, the lips tightly bunched together – just a little sound bubbling from the puckered centre. He had big ears, she noticed. His hand movements increased, and she could feel an increasing wetness on the palm of her hand.

Suddenly, without warning, he left go of her hand and put his hand behind her neck. He wrenched her head down towards his lap and ejaculated with full force into her face. Just as quickly, he let her go and slumped back into his chair. She was terribly confused. Her eyes were full of sticky liquid, and the stuff was dripping down her chin. She tried to wipe it off on her sleeve. She wanted to vomit, believing that he had urinated on her. But she knew she could go now.

As she got up to leave, she could hear him saying softly, 'Thank you . . . thank you . . . nice little girl . . .

thank you . . .' She ran up the aisle, tears washing down her face. Just before the door, she was dreadfully sick – all over herself and over an elderly woman on the end of the last row. The old lady was furious; holding Julia firmly by the arm, she frog-marched her to the usherette and the trio went to the public lavatory to clean up the mess. Julia was so distraught that the usherette took pity on her and helped her wash and dry her face and her clothes. Still Julia cried, so the usherette offered to take her home, but that made things far worse, as Julia contemplated her mother's reaction on hearing of her deceit.

Julia realized at that moment that she had been defiled. She knew that what had happened in the cinema was what many of the children were whispering about in the playground. The event in the Palace Cinema effectively made Julia frigid for the rest of her life. Indeed, she could never bear a man's face too close to her own, which explained her hysterical outburst every time she was in the dentist's chair.

Shocking as Julia's experience may have been, it must be remembered that it was not an unusual baptism for any young girl alone and easy prey to predatory men. Indeed, it was that year that the local park-keepers were obliged to remove many of the splendid bushes that lined the pathways near her home for fear of the child-molesters who would haunt the playhouses the children made in their branches.

Julia was unable to tell anyone, not just because of her mother's anger at her delinquency but also because sex, or the subject of sex, was never mentioned in her house. When each of the girls in her family reached their menstruation time, their mother would give them a packet of sanitary pads and a pale pink elastic waistband with hooks. At the same time, they would receive rather torturous looking items of clothing which they were informed were brassières. Along with these items, they would get a lecture which went something like this: 'Now that you have some blood, you can have babies. Never see a boy alone. Never sit on a lavatory seat that is not your own. If you have a baby and you are not married, you will kill your mother. Always wear your brassière or your chest will fall to your knees. Never touch yourself "there" or you will grow a large vegetable between your legs and everyone will know what you have been doing . . . besides, you will be blind.'

This last piece of advice was only delivered to the two boys. As far as Julia was concerned, all she wanted out of life was to marry a blond, blue-eyed young man who would take her away from the dull grey streets of poverty-stricken Hammersmith, and would give her a pretty house to care for and two lovely fair-haired daughters who would not inherit her nose. That was why Charles, her first-born, was something of a shock.

He looked exactly like a small monkey after his birth. He had a mass of tight black curls, huge ears, a large nose, and big feet with prehensile toes. When the nurse brought him to Julia for his first feed, he lunged at his mother's bared nipple with such ferocity that she pulled herself away and covered her breasts with her arms. 'Come now, dearie,' said the nurse, who was in a hurry, 'you've got a good little feeder there. Just give it another try.' Julia, who had made a vow to be a perfect wife and mother, tried again. This time they connected. The little boy's mouth pulled and sucked at her. It created a terrific tension and a pain in her uterus. She complained to the nurse, who told her that it would retract her expanded womb and hasten her return to a normal size and shape. Julia decided that this was worth all the discomfort, the cracked and sore nipples, and the leaking milk. She had been mortified to see huge purple and grey marks welling up on her hips and breasts – she, who was so careful to take care of her porcelain-doll-like self. After the first week, she even found she had grown attached to the picture of herself as the young nursing mother. She would sit in her bed surrounded by flowers and bowls of fruit from her family in a swan's-down jacket nursing Charles, smiling at the nurses as they passed. 'A proper little mother,' the nurses would say to each other, 'not like some.'

'Not like some' referred to the woman in the next bed to Julia who flatly refused to breastfeed her little baby girl, and who smoked whenever she escaped the matron's eagle eye. Julia had never had to spend seven days in close proximity to a woman who so clearly represented all that was truly dreadful and ignoble in a woman's nature. This woman was coarse and vulgar. Her language was crude and she farted in her sleep. This last outrage upset Julia more than anything else. In her family, if the need should ever arise to pass wind, you were expected to leave the room – or sit on it until the wind passed. But to allow great blustering thunderous explosions to rend the night air was more than Julia could bear. She finally broached the matter very delicately with her.

'I see your stomach was a little upset last night?' she inquired gently.

The woman, whose name was Mona, frowned. And then her face broke into a huge grin. 'Farting, you mean? Do it all the time. Don't you ever fart?' She asked Julia very seriously.

Julia shook her head. By this time, they had established some sort of rapport between their daily struggles to clean, feed and care for their babies in the hospital. Secretly, Julia envied Mona her little blonde blue-eyed girl, while Mona, who had hopes for a boy as this was her third child, admired Charles.

'He's lovely, he is. He's going to be big – look at his feet and his little willy.' Poor Julia froze when she watched Mona bending over her son. Mona would tickle his belly and then slide her fingers down to Charles's penis and gently tug at it. It made Julia feel sick, especially as Charles would kick his legs enthusiastically. Julia very soon decided that she would not risk Mona turning Charles into a sex maniac at the tender age of seven days old, so she kept him firmly wrapped in a shawl.

William, Julia's husband, had played such a minor part in the birth of the baby that his presence for an hour every evening was almost like the presence of a stranger visiting a friend. William was a handsome man. A full six feet, and possessing periwinkle blue eyes, he was extremely attractive to look at. Actually, he had been the first thing Julia saw when the train pulled into Bridport station. Julia's family were taking a holiday. They chose Bridport because it was unfashionable and therefore cheap. Julia was nineteen. Her brothers and sisters had brought a variety of wives and children with them. Only Julia and her sister Mary were unmarried. But from the moment Julia saw William, she knew her days of waiting were over. When William saw Julia framed in the carriage window his heart gave a great lurch. They were a very 'foreign' looking family, but he was immediately attracted to her fragility. In Bridport, he'd grown up with big, heavy-boned land girls, the daughters of the local farmers who milked the cows and stood together in groups at the local dance halls laughing noisily. They had thick thighs and care-worn hands which were rough to the touch. Their talk was of farrowing, or of milking. He had always been a bit afraid of them. His innocence about girls came from the fact that, apart from the usual dirty talk at school, he had no experience at all of living with women. His mother died giving birth to him. He was a late baby and an accident. His two older brothers and their father cared for him with the help of an aunt in the early years, but once he was of school age the aunt stopped coming by and the house became a masculine stronghold.

At sixteen, he went to work for Mr Fursy, the local chemist, and there he was to remain for the rest of his life. By the time he was twenty-one and saw Julia that first day in Bridport station, Mr Fursy had made it clear that William would inherit the business. William had a future and prospects. For Mr Fursy, William was a godsend. Mr Fursy was an elderly bachelor, and he lived for his shop. He liked the slow, quiet, gentle boy, and they worked side by side, often late into the night, mixing the powders and the liquids. No new-fangled storage drawers in his shop. No, it was all exactly as his father had left it to him: shelves of glass and marble interspaced with shining mahogany cabinets, deep drawers faced with walnut, and glowing brass gas lamps hanging in clusters from the ceiling. William was to keep it that way. To him, it was the most romantic place in the world. It was to become a refuge from an increasingly dissatisfied and angry wife. But from the moment he saw Julia, he was enslaved, and he continued to love her faithfully and without complaint all his life.

3

Julia and William were married a year after their first meeting. Julia's mother approved of William who, after all, followed in her husband's profession; and even if he lacked other connections, he did have fair hair and blue eyes. William's father seemed pleased to have at least one son off his hands. The other two seemed destined to remain bachelors for the rest of their lives. Had the old man looked at the firm set of Julia's pretty little mouth and the frown on her face when she visited his house and observed the men at the table with their elbows spread and their belts undone, belching comfortably into their thick steaming cups of tea, he might have been alarmed. William felt her disgust and resolved to be sensitive and attentive to this beautiful creature from the metropolis.

Just before they were married, Julia's mother had an embarrassing conversation with Julia which condensed into a traditional mother's warning to her daughter. 'Sex is what they all want. If you give them enough, they won't stray. If they look at other women, it's your fault. Even if you don't like it, never let them know.' This advice had been passed on to Julia's mother by her mother, and in turn Julia would pass the message on to her daughter. So far, Julia had had little trouble coping with William's amorous demands. They saw very little of each other and most of the courtship was conducted by post. She lived in Hammersmith with her mother, and he came to visit on four occasions. He looked dreadfully out of place in the streets of London. His clothes were ill-cut, and his best boots were designed for hard country walking. But even as she grieved over his provincial ways, she reminded herself that they were to rent a small bungalow with two bedrooms, a sitting-room and a kitchen. It even had a modern bathroom. No longer would the bath be situated in the kitchen. She couldn't wait to be mistress of her new household and escape from her increasingly critical and invalid mother.

Because William had no mother, the wedding was a very quiet affair. Julia's relatives all attended, as did William's two brothers and his father. It was a civil ceremony, because Julia's family had never attended the churches in the area. William's father and two brothers were very uncomfortable in their suits and thick hairy wool shirts. Julia's family, who were all beginning to go up in the world, appeared at ease and sophisticated to the travellers from Bridport. William noticed what a tight-knit family they all were. They seemed to know each other's business right down to the last penny or idle piece of gossip.

'Aunt Jessie couldn't come . . . Uncle Ron's been at it again,' one sister would say to the others. A ripple of comprehending nods, a roll of the eyes and a smug smile would indicate that they all got the message. Aunt Jessie had failed again to control Uncle Ron's drinking. In this family, like most families, the women were all-powerful. They were raised on old proverbs such as 'the love of a good woman can change any man.' If your husband didn't change and failed to become a pale phantom of his former self, always attentive at family gatherings and ready to nod approvingly at anything his dear wife said, then you were a failure. If a husband was unable to keep up with the family's rapacious need for new cars, holidays, and kitchen equipment, then he was a failure. Above all, the veneration of the Family was paramount in the eyes of the blood members.

Uncle Ron was the family black sheep, and in later years his erratic behaviour was a great source of comfort to William, who felt suffocated and smothered by the huge family gatherings. Although he would never offend Julia by voicing his dislike of these events, he would make a point of spending a few minutes with Uncle Ron in the back garden of the house in Hammersmith. Ron, always slightly drunk, would complain bitterly about 'the Family'. 'The old dragon,' he would say, referring to Julia's mother. 'She took her boys' balls, and the women of that family . . . they're all going to be like her.'

William was a little horrified at such treachery, but even he could see that Max and the younger brother, Michael, were totally subdued in the presence of their mother and sisters. 'You know,' Ron said, on one of William's pre-nuptial visits, 'your Julia's the toughest of the lot.'

William protested at this, but in his heart he knew Ron was right. He watched her organize the rest of the family. When their many arguments erupted in screaming and shouting matches, it was little quiet Julia who, hands on hips and eyes ablaze, always had the last word. He found her passion strangely exciting, he who had always lived in a world of quiet countrymen without women. He believed, in his romantic way, that when they were together and alone they would share that passion in their most intimate moments and Julia would never again need to scream and shout. He comforted himself with the fact that she had to hold her own in the quarrelsome, noisy family interactions, and he became increasingly impatient for the day when she would belong to him alone.

William married Julia on 14 October 1942 at the Hammersmith registry office at 10.00 a.m. Julia wore a white silk dress with matching shoes and a cream straw hat that dipped over her left eye. She carried a bunch of white freesias in her hand, and she was very nervous. Standing next to her, William was even more nervous. His eldest brother was waiting beside him with the ring, and mentally William was going over the programme for the day. 'After the ceremony, we go back to the house. After the food, we say good-bye and get into the car.' William's father had lent William his Austin Seven for the honeymoon. 'Then we drive to Brighton . . .' his thoughts strayed.

'Do you William John Anthony Hunter take this woman . . .'

'I do,' said William so fervently that the whole congregation jumped. Julia smiled. She enjoyed the feeling of power she had over this big handsome man. She looked at him rather like a cat looks at a cornered mouse.

She smiled. '. . . I do,' she said in answer to the registry official's question. William kissed Julia with all the sincerity and joy he felt would be theirs for a lifetime. Julia returned his kiss in a perfunctory fashion. The thought of the wedding night was becoming large in her mind. So far, she had managed to avoid thinking about it, but now, with the ceremony over, it would be a matter of fact in a very few hours. Julia pulled herself out of William's arms and turned to see to her guests. Time enough to face that ordeal later, she told herself firmly. The family comes first.

The food was already laid out at Carthew Villas. Julia's mother had baked for days beforehand. The sisters all provided dishes of their own, a source of much competition among them. Max opened the wine and the beer and they all toasted the health of the bride and the bridegroom.

Secretly Julia would have liked to have had sherry served on round trays, especially as several of her teachers had been invited to the meal. Julia had once been invited to the teachers' private sitting-room with the other students who were leaving school, and she always remembered the fire in the grate reflecting on the silver goblets won by members of the music society. She also noticed the graceful Georgian tables and the rich carpet which made such a contrast to her meagrely furnished home. When she was offered a sherry by a mob-capped maid, Julia resolved that she too would own a room just like that. Even if she could never have a maid, a silver serving tray and a bottle of medium dry sherry would be a lifetime's ambition.

As she moved round the dining-room, talking to everyone in turn, she was uncomfortably aware of a glint in many of the curious pairs of eyes. Although the sisters never discussed their private lives with each other, much could be gained by their often throw-away remarks.

Usually pregnancy and breastfeeding were a respite from the demands of their husbands. Whenever one or other of the sisters announced a new arrival, the others looked relieved on her behalf. Julia intended to have a baby as soon as possible anyway, but even when she approached her older sister, Melissa, a few weeks before the wedding in a joking attempt to discuss the subject of sex, she was brushed off with the comment, 'Well, if you want a baby, you'll have to do just like the rest of us – grin and bear it.'

This was cold comfort for Julia. She felt even more isolated and vulnerable once she had kissed all the members of her family good-bye. She and William drove for several miles in silence, both of them panic-stricken at what lay ahead of them. Julia had chosen a guest house in Brighton, recommended by Max who knew about such things. Max had arrived at a stage in his life when he could holiday in such places, and Julia was determined that anything her brother's family could do, she would do better.

They arrived in Brighton at about five o'clock. High tea, they had been told, would be served at six o'clock. It was raining. Julia suggested they drive along the sea-front. It was deserted. The sea was a desolate grey, and it pounded the shore in an uncomfortable reminder of what was to come. Hastily removing her gaze from the scene, Julia announced it was time to find the guest house. On arrival they had to endure congratulations and jokes about newlyweds from their jovial proprietor, but Julia felt she could detect a hint of compassion in the landlady's eyes as she looked at her and said, 'We've given you the best room. It faces the sea . . . I hope you'll like it.'

Julia didn't think she'd like anything of what was to come. She had contemplated telling him it was her time of the month, but then she reminded herself that she couldn't use that excuse indefinitely. 'No,' she said to herself, 'once I'm pregnant, it'll be bad for the baby, so

I may as well get pregnant as fast as I can.' Fortunately for her, William, like most men of his day, would never consider reading a mother and baby book, so the myths and folklore created by the women of the family were passed along to their men. Most of the matriarchal myths were about times and situations that excluded sex. Julia would rely very heavily on this information for the rest of her life, but now they were approaching the bridal bedroom with a bathroom to the side.

It was a pleasant enough room. It did indeed look out on the sea, but Julia pulled the curtains firmly shut. It was altogether too animal a sight. The sea seemed determined to suck the pebbled beach dry, and the rhythm of the demanding waves discomforted her. William seemed much less ill-at-ease. Delighted with the time he could now spend with his beloved new wife, he made little jokes and was anxious to help her unpack. The thought of a man handling her intimate underwear was too much for her to bear. 'I'll unpack later,' she said, and fled to the bathroom to wash her face and hands.

High tea was served in the dining-room of the guest house. Julia had suggested that William ask the proprietor to serve a bottle of champagne with their meal. William was quite happy to order such an expensive luxury, even though he had no idea whether he would be able to stomach wine. Julia had never tasted champagne, but it was all part of her relentless ambition to rise like a phoenix from the ashes of her poverty-stricken childhood and to take her rightful place among the middle classes.

As they faced each other in the little dining-room, Julia looked at William. In a few hours from now, they would be doing the unmentionable and unimaginable act that would create the child which would be her passport to a new world. Logically she accepted that she herself would probably not achieve much more than good social standing in Bridport. But she felt certain that her son, with her guiding hand, would capture a major position in society, and that her daughter would marry a peer of the realm. Whatever had to be endured to achieve these ambitions would be endured with good grace. 'Why are you smiling, darling? Are you happy?' asked William, taking her hand gently in his. He was radiant in his love for her. Never would he hurt her. Julia came out of her reverie. She squeezed his hand. 'Of course I am, darling.' She smiled again.

The proprietor came forward with the bottle of champagne, and because he was unused to opening such a bottle (his clients normally asked for beers or ciders) he mishandled the cork. The champagne exploded over the table. Julia sat transfixed as the long green neck of the bottle, with a stream of creamy bubbles erupting on to her lap, transposed itself to what she had been forced to touch in the awful moment in the Palace Cinema. Caught between the memory of the past and the knowledge of what was to be in the future, she felt a rising sense of panic. William was laughing and mopping the table with his napkin. He looked at her stricken face and cheerfully reassured her, 'There's lots left, Julia.' He assumed she was upset over the great waste of money.

Julia shook her head. 'I'm all right now,' she said. 'It was just a bit of a shock.'

William filled her glass and then his. He raised his glass to her and made a toast. 'To our future together,' he said, going pink at exposing such emotion.

'To our future,' said Julia, putting the wine glass to her lips.

William enjoyed his first glass of champagne enormously. The bubbles delighted him as they would a small child. Julia could not bring herself to swallow a mouthful. Indeed, for the rest of her life, she never touched champagne. William was concerned that she did not drink from her glass. Julia said she didn't care for the taste. She never told him why. This meant that William had the rest of the bottle to himself. Not being used to alcohol, he became slightly tipsy, which in turn suited him because he had been feeling nervous.

Now he relaxed and began to tuck into his dinner. It was good English food – roast chicken, stuffing, boiled and roast potatoes with cauliflower. For dessert they had trifle with sherry and thick cream. Julia picked a little bit here and there; she had no appetite. The more William talked of their future together and laid plans for the shop and the bungalow, the more trapped she felt. Maybe in her hurry to get away from her mother and her bleak environment, she had chosen the wrong man. Certainly none of his plans included moving up in the world. They all centred around her and the little bungalow. While she dreamed of a detached house and membership to the Bridport Golf Club, he talked of mackerel fishing and his plans for an allotment. Julia gave up on William as a partner for her ambitions at this precise moment. Even before the marriage was consummated, she relegated him to the background. He would have to be her prop while she created the conditions for her children to fulfil her dreams.

'Let's go upstairs,' William said, eager to hold her in his arms.

'You go ahead,' she said. Calm had descended in her soul. 'I must ring my mother to tell her we are safe.'

'Of course,' said William. Having never had a mother, he was all his life to respect Julia's account of how 'real' families behaved.

He went upstairs and busily occupied himself with the business of unpacking his new clothes. He was particularly proud of his new pyjamas. He decided to put them on before unpacking the rest of the case in order not to embarrass Julia or himself. It would take a little time, he was sure, before they would be intimately comfortable together. He was quite wrong. He never saw his wife naked in his lifetime. He put this down to her innate modesty which, like all her vices, he created into a virtue. He pottered around the room, putting away his shoes and placing his new check slippers under the bed. He was sitting on the bed gently bouncing up and down to test the springs when Julia came in.

'Everything all right, love?' he said.

'Yes,' she said. 'Everyone's gone home and all the cleaning up has been done. I think I'll take a bath,' she said distractedly, collecting various items of clothing from her suitcase. 'I won't be long.'

She wasn't very long. Indeed, she realized that prolonging the wait for the moment to arrive was more uncomfortable than bowing to the inevitable. She re-entered the bedroom with as much of a warm smile on her face as she could muster. William looked at his new wife with undisguised admiration. Her loose hair made her face more gentle. She wore a pale pink nightdress embroidered with daisies with a matching peignoir. She looked younger than ever. A tremendous surge of tenderness came over William. He rose to his feet and put his arms around her small body. He felt her tension and resistance. 'Don't be afraid, my love,' he said. 'I'll not hurt you.' Awash with emotions that he had never felt before, he was carried away by the conflict between his gentle affectionate nature and an urgent need to achieve sexual satisfaction.

Julia was luckier than most women of her time. William was by nature gentle and sensitive, so the ordeal for her was less traumatic than for her friends. No one had ever told her how painful it would be. The pain came as a shock. It took her so by surprise that she concentrated on clenching her teeth in order to stifle her urge to scream. William, at this stage, was oblivious to everything. Once he had managed to penetrate her, he felt as though he were sliding down a long dark tunnel on a cushion of liquid that eventually exploded. He was catapulted into the universe. He rolled off her, pulling her into his arms and holding her tight.

'That was lovely,' he said. He was amazed. He had never once imagined that making love could be such a delight. He brushed her hair back from her face and saw she was crying. 'Did I hurt you?' he asked anxiously.

'Only a little,' she said. 'It's all right. It will pass.'

Full of love and unaccustomed champagne, he fell asleep. As soon as she felt his breathing deepen, she slipped out of bed and went into the bathroom. She filled the bath with cold water and gently eased herself into it. Opening her legs she saw slight traces of blood, and she hoped he hadn't damaged her. She felt bruised, and resented the feel of his sperm in her body.

She sat for a long time with her chin on her knees. She was no longer a virgin and there was no going back. 'For better or for worse, until death us do part,' she said to herself.

4

'We mustn't lose touch with each other,' said Mona very seriously to Julia on the day they were both to return home with their babies. Julia's immediate response was to purse her lips and to refuse, but over the days she had become fond of Mona. Her mother would never have approved of this large laughing gypsy of a woman, but Mona saw through Julia and all her pretensions, making Julia feel quite comfortable in her company. There was a feral animal quality about Mona's body that Julia found oddly exciting. The woman had an olive skin with shining black eyes. When Mona laughed, Julia was struck by the pinkness of her gums and by the evenness of her strong white teeth. Living next to her in the shared intimacy of a ward, Julia became comfortable with her presence. It was both mocking and protective.

One day, after Mona had been visited by Sid (who, Julia thought, was possibly the father of the baby, but was certainly not in any lawful relationship with Mona), Julia got up the courage to ask her, 'Do you really like all that pawing and kissing?'

Mona was lying on her back in bed. It was a hot day. She looked at Julia and then she laughed. She raised her strong arms above her head and stretched. She gave off a musky smell; the hairs under her arms were thick and tangled. 'I've always loved sex and the company of men,' said Mona. 'Sid's good to me and we have a nice time together, but I'll never belong to any man. I'd get bored.'

Julia did not know where to look. The room was filled with the electric excitement of a woman ready to make love. Mona said, 'I can't wait to get home. Cook some decent food, drink some cider, and go to bed with Sid . . . How do you feel about going home?' She looked quizzically at Julia. Julia blushed. 'You don't like being in bed with your husband, do you?'

Julia looked down at her hands. 'Well, at least he has to wait for six weeks,' Julia said. 'I wish I could get to like it, but quite honestly I find the whole thing disgusting, repulsive. I hate him for doing it to me, and I hate myself for not liking it.' That was the most honest moment of Julia's life.

Mona looked a little nonplussed. She had spent ten days with Julia. The first few days she had been angry with her because of her patronizing attitude. After that she had begun to realize that Julia was a very insecure, vulnerable young girl. She had no natural mothering ability. The way she handled the baby made Mona wince. The way she responded to her kind husband's attempts at affection made Mona wonder how she ever managed to conceive a child, and Mona ended up feeling very sorry for Julia.

When she saw Julia's relations, she felt even more sorry. The sisters arrived accompanied by Max. Max exuded bonhomie and newly acquired wealth. His shoes were too bright, his collars too full, and his hands supported too many large gold rings. Mona, gypsy by birth, was immediately attracted to the glint of the gold. Max, sexually deprived by his wife, was immediately attracted to Mona. For all his faults, Max was a lively and likeable man.

Julia's sisters settled themselves on the chairs by the bed and began a close inspection of their nephew. Max settled himself strategically on the other side of the bed and began an even closer inspection of Mona, who lay languidly outstretched on her bed. Her breasts were full of milk and her eyes full of erotic promise. Max felt a tide of lust starting to rise from the soles of his feet. It crept up to his knees and threatened to overwhelm him altogether. He quickly dropped his eyes, crossed his legs, and cleared his throat. 'Lovely boy,' he said, his voice clotted with emotion.

Julia was surprised. It was not like Max to be enthusiastic about a baby. She looked at her sisters. 'Very like Father,' was the general verdict about the baby. 'But never mind,' said Mary. 'Babies do change.' Julia looked at Charles. He was obviously not going to be an English gentleman. Thank God her mother was dead. At least he wouldn't pick up any of those awful Yiddish expressions. Neither would he learn any of her funny foreign ways.

Meanwhile, the sisters were deep in gossip. Uncle Ron had offended his sisters by refusing to contribute to their mother's funeral costs. The family was outraged. They had planned to erect a white marble tombstone over both their parents who now lay side by side in the Hammersmith Graveyard. Once the marble was in place, they all secretly felt it would be the end of an era. The children who were born in England could now think of themselves as English. There would be no smell of kasha or chicken soup.

'Uncle Ron never liked her anyway,' Julia reminded them.

The sisters looked startled. 'How can you say that?' said Mary.

'Because,' Julia replied very firmly, 'Ron has always been an outsider. He doesn't believe in family life.' She added, intent on making as much of an impression as she could on the other sisters: 'He is said to see other women.' Max looked shocked. He thought he was the only one who knew about Ron. They used to exchange information on the sly at family gatherings while the women washed up and the men stood around the sitting-room making conversation.

Julia didn't know if this last piece of news was actually true, but now that she had her child in her arms she had time to consider the facts. Her mother's death had made little impression on her. She had been very heavily pregnant at the time, and was unable to travel to the funeral. Although she cried upon receiving word that, like her father, her mother had died suddenly and without warning, she knew that she would now make a bid to step into her mother's shoes. Particularly where

Max was concerned. William was not going to be any kind of social asset to her, so she would need Max to stand by her side and to advise her on her upward journey.

As the family now said good-bye to her in the maternity ward, she pressed Max's hand and said, 'You will help me, Max, if I need you, won't you? Now mother's dead, I'm going to need someone to turn to.'

Max was very flattered, but also he was mesmerized by Mona. Bending down to kiss Julia, he caught Mona's eye. 'I'll be down to see you just as soon as you've settled back home,' he said loudly. Julia sat back complacently. Things were going according to plan.

'Randy sod, your brother,' Mona said after they had all left.

'I don't know what you mean,' Julia said.

'I know you don't.' Mona snorted with laughter. 'None of your sisters do either!'

'We weren't brought up that way,' said Julia. At that moment Charles woke up and loudly demanded his feed.

'Filled his nappy, I should think,' said Mona. 'Here, I'll change him. No point in you throwing up before you feed him.'

Julia did indeed feel totally nauseated when she took the baby's nappy off. God knows what I'm going to do without Mona, she thought. Suddenly the hospital felt like a secure place, and the thought of the little bungalow frightened her. How was she going to cope with a new-born baby and a husband who didn't understand anything apart from his work and the allotment?

William arrived several hours later to take her home. He had borrowed Mr Fursy's car for the event. Mona had already left, and Julia had been on her own in the now quiet room with Charles. Julia was in a dreadful panic. Because she was the youngest in her family, she had no knowledge of childcare. She had never even held a baby in her arms. To be sure, her sisters had raised children, but Julia had never been truly interested in any of them. She had seen herself as the 'intellectual' member of the family. She had always been a little disgusted at the mess and mucous that seemed to surround small babies. Here she was now, about to devote years of her life to bringing up Charles, and she would invest every ounce of her determined character in the child. As much as she comforted herself with her dreams and ambitions, she also grieved for herself.

No one had ever explained to her that most women were cut when they were giving birth to a child and, even though in all the commotion she had not felt the cutting, she remembered with rage and shame being stitched by a brutal midwife who insisted she should feel no pain. Each stitch was like a red-hot knife-thrust, and there were eight of them. She howled each time. Inwardly she cursed William who had been waiting meekly in the visitor's room. Lying on her back, strapped to the table with her legs splayed apart, she felt like a huge obscene beetle. Every time she remembered the event, tears would pour down her face. She never quite forgave William. Somehow, even though there was no question of his being in attendance, she always held it against him that he was not there to comfort and protect her when she most needed him. This grudge would join all the others she amassed against him.

She sat gingerly on the bed, for she was still sore from the stitches, holding Charles in her arms. By now, she had established a far closer bond with her baby than she had thought possible. It was not a maternal bond, because she found that much about the baby disgusted her, but it was a feeling of ownership, of power over this helpless little creature who needed her to survive. Also, she now had an ally in life. Charles would return her care and years of mothering with his own reward. His career would reflect Julia's diligence in his studying. His marriage would express Julia's choice of a daughter-in-law. His children would learn at Julia's knee all the wisdom she would have accumulated by then.

Her reverie was broken by William who knocked shyly on the door. 'Come in,' she said with a hint of impatience. William opened the door. She looked at him. His honest face showed a measure of alarm at the idea of taking his wife and new baby to their little bungalow. Like Julia, he felt safe while they were both in the hospital, but now it was time for him to take charge of the situation, and William did not feel up to the whole proposition. Julia knew exactly what he was thinking. She always knew what William was thinking. She controlled the familiar sinking feeling in her stomach. It was no good expecting William to take the lead. It would never be any good. She would have to be strong for both of them. She calmed herself, and then, with a sweet smile, she indicated the waiting suitcases.

With Charles in her arms, she made her way out of the hospital, saying good-bye to the nurses as she went. Matron made a special point of wishing her well. 'You have a fine boy there, Mrs Hunter. He will be a credit to you.'

What a lovely young couple, Matron thought as they drove off.

Matron would not have been so sanguine had she witnessed the scene in the bungalow at about ten o'clock that night. Julia was trying to feed Charles, and because she was tired and upset by the move home there was not sufficient milk. Charles became agitated and began to scream. William stared helplessly at both of them. If this was fatherhood, it was about a million miles away from his fantasy of a bonny baby bouncing on a contented mother's knee. Julia had banished him from the bedroom while she fed the child, but he could hear the baby screaming and her increasingly exasperated response.

He knocked on the door and she called for him to enter. Her face was flushed and furious. Charles had betrayed her. He had showed her up as something less than perfect in front of her husband. Julia had to be perfect. Every good mother breastfed her child, and Julia was the perfect wife and mother. Therefore she would breastfeed.

The days and nights passed for Julia in a haze of exhaustion. She was not a natural breastfeeder. To breastfeed takes a calm and accepting temperament. Julia found the sitting still tedious at first. Gradually, however, mother and child settled into a routine, and she began to find Charles's sucking curiously erotic. Like many first-time mothers, she spent a lot of the night getting out of bed to go to his cot to check his breathing. She moved the cot closer and closer to her side of the bed, and then, after a particularly anxious night, she asked William if he could sleep in the guest-room. 'Your snoring disturbs the baby. Besides, I can't hear him breathing.' William was hurt, but he accepted his banishment with good grace. Little did he know that he would not gain entrance to his wife's bed for another two years. With William safely tucked away next door, Julia enjoyed a very private life with her small son.

William would wake in the morning, make his own breakfast, and then bring her a cup of tea. He would take a peek at Charles who was usually asleep, and then, kissing his wife on the forehead, he would leave for work. Once the front door slammed behind him, Julia would relax against her pillows and wait for Charles to wake up. Her morning breasts would be achingly full of milk. As the minutes ticked away to the eight o'clock feed, she would wait, running her fingers along the swollen blue veins at the side of her breasts. The baby's first stirrings in his sleep brought an unbearable tension to the erect nipples, and then she would lift the still drowsy child into her arms. The baby, sniffing the scent of warm sweet milk, would suddenly snap his eyes open and his gums would work convulsively as he rooted around the breast. Once he found the nipple, he would slide his tongue under it so that the suction would be even greater. He would take the milk from his mother at first in hurried gulps. She would encourage him with little cries and whimpers.

The relief of pain and tension and the pull of his mouth on her nipples gave her a highly charged sexual feeling. This feeling was quite new to her. Certainly it was nothing like the feelings she experienced with William, who occasionally tried to take her nipple in his mouth in an embarrassed fashion. At those times she felt he looked foolish, and she became embarrassed for them both. This feeling with Charles went far beyond any romantic vision she might have had when she used to think about breastfeeding. It was a very intense animal feeling. Her body felt a great heat, and she sensed a curious melting inside. She looked forward to feeding times immensely. There was nothing in her baby book to explain this feeling. The instructions on baby care were very clinical and primitive. She had no one to share notes with. Maybe, she resolved, if she bumped into Mona she could tentatively ask if this feeling was normal.

The feed over, it was time to get up and dress the baby. Getting up was an unhurried, pleasurable time for both mother and child. First Julia would bathe and dress herself, and then it was Charles's turn. She was getting used to his genitals. They were considerably less swollen now, but she could never quite bring herself to clean under his foreskin. She decided to have him circumsized. 'Much cleaner,' she said to herself. The only chore that marred their happy existence was when she held him out over the pot. Her book, a bowdlerized version of Truby King, warned all mothers that babies must be 'held out' as soon as they reached six weeks. Failure to do so would flaw the child's character for life and lead to dreadful physical complications. Julia was not a patient woman, and if Charles failed to perform, her displeasure was evident. Even worse, if he failed to perform and later filled his nappy she took it as a personal insult. The subsequent changing of the nappy would be a rough and scolding affair, with much cajoling and bullying. In later years she could boast to whomever was listening that Charles was potty-trained by twelve weeks.

Once up and about, the rest of the day followed a very simple routine. The bungalow was small, but Julia could take all morning with obsessive cleaning. She came from a home where to sit for more than ten minutes was considered idle. All the women of the family except Mary maintained spotless homes. Julia found the sight of a room polished and shining a reflection of how she felt about herself. Try as he would, William could never meet her high standards. Every morning she would enter the kitchen and find stray crumbs or a teaspoon that had escaped his anxious eye. Often he would have to endure a lecture on the best method of washing dishes. Gradually, he did less and less around the house until she ultimately possessed the place as her domain.

In the evening after the meal, she would allow him to dry the dishes. This made her feel that they were a happy couple performing a mutually agreeable task together. She would boast about how good William was to her to the envious sisters. Even Mary was married by now, and she would say, 'I wish my Joseph was like that. It's down with the food and straight to the public house for him.' Julia would think about her own good fortune as she vigorously polished the little house and planned the food for the day.

After the lunch-time feed, it was time for Charles to have his day's outing. The pram was a Silver Cross. What was good enough for the Royal Family was good enough for Julia. She would put on her gloves and her coat with the musquash collar, and push the huge pram down the long bleak road towards the shops. So far she had made little or no effort to get on with her neighbours. She considered them 'common'. Her mother had infected all her children with the notion that they were a social cut above most people, so it was almost impossible for Julia to make friends. She did occasionally bump into Mona. She could never really admit to herself that she was lonely or that she often took a route into town that might possibly mean that she could see Mona.

Usually, Mona would be pushing her battered old pram full of groceries and the baby. Tugging at her skirts would be the other two girls, and Mona would greet Julia with a happy wave of her hand and a ribald inquiry. Sometimes she would ask after Max. But often she would be in the mood to spend a little time with Julia and they would discuss their child-care.

Mona would try to encourage Julia to go with her to the bag-wash. The bag-wash house was a huge room full of steaming machines. There all the women would meet with their week's washing combined in a huge white laundry bag with a drawstring at the neck. All the bags were thrown into machines that hissed and boiled. After a suitable amount of time the bags were retrieved by their various owners who then sorted out the contents and pushed the now clean clothes through the huge iron mangles. Children of all ages ran riot in between the machines. The steam made the women's faces red and their hair lank with sweat. The whole scene had a nightmarish quality, but it was the focal point of many women's lives.

Julia went once and was appalled by the sight of so many red-knuckled women. It was all too visceral for her. There was a man's drawers draped over an ironing board lying in casual intimacy next to a pair of pink stays. The women's conversation was shockingly sexual. 'Had your leg over this week, Lil?' asked a toothless old crone.

Julia left at this point. She complained to Mona that it was thoroughly unhygienic to share the water with other people's dirty linen. Mona laughed. 'A few germs never hurt no one! Anyway, I wanted you to get to know people. You can't live all by yourself.'

'William comes home for his lunch and then he's back by six in the evening. I find plenty to do. Charles takes up a lot of time, especially now he's beginning to creep.'

William had not counted on returning home for his lunch every day, but he knew his young wife was lonely. Before his marriage, he had been in the habit of having his lunch in the pub next door. There he would meet his friends and play a game of darts or two. However, Julia preferred to have him home for lunch, so, obedient to her wishes, he went home and gradually he lost most of his friends. It was the same story at night. Julia felt that public houses were also 'common'. She didn't actually refuse to let him go out; she simply made it clear that none of her family frequented such places. If he did stop off on the way home, he noticed that she would fall silent for the rest of the evening and sit in her chair by the fire with a small sad smile on her face that made him feel guilty because he knew he had put it there.

Charles grew up in the cramped little house with an exclusive relationship with his mother. For the first two years of his life she breastfed him. As soon as he was on solid food, she discontinued the daily feeds, but at night she indulged herself in her favourite occupation. The feed over, Charles would collapse at her side, his stomach distended with milk, and he would fall into a deep untroubled sleep. As for Julia, satiated and pleasantly tired, she would fall asleep and dream of a bright future with Charles at her side. But as Charles grew older and more demanding, she realized she would have to give up the feeds. It got too difficult when the child would climb on her knee and reach down the front of her dress for her breast. 'Num num,' he would say. Her refusal would infuriate him and he would cry loudly.

Also, William was getting very restive in his lonely room next door. It was difficult for William to decide what was really happening in his marriage. He had no family of his own to consult. His father and two brothers still lived on their own without the company of women. As far as William could make out, his wife was an exemplary mother to his son. He did try to be a good father, but the boy seemed to resent his presence and would cry or run to his mother when William tried to play with him. Julia recognized that William was becoming very upset with her family arrangement, so she decided that the time had come for Charles to have his own room and for William to return to the marital bed.

It was a dreadful shock for Charles to find himself summarily banished from his mother's bed. Like everything she did, Julia did it swiftly and thoroughly. One night there was the familiar orgiastic breastfeeding routine, and the next night Charles was in his cot in a strange room with no late-night feed. He howled and screamed himself to sleep for many nights. Julia told William that the child had to learn to sleep on his own. William was only too happy to agree, now that he had his bed back. Not only did he have his bed back, but he was also allowed to make love to Julia. There was no sudden conversion on Julia's part to sex, but Julia had decided that it was time she had a daughter.

As before, Julia bore William's sexual advances with fortitude. She would allow him to climb on top of her, she would then open her legs sufficiently wide to just let him in, and then wait for it all to be over. When he tried to talk to her in moments of passion, she would murmur words of encouragement to him. 'Anything,' she would say to herself, gritting her teeth, 'anything, just to get it over with.' When William climaxed convulsively on top of her, she often would be reminded of the man in the cinema. She despised William in those moments. To be prey to an emotion that resulted in such a lack of control that he would gasp and moan and sometimes, to her acute embarrassment, raise his voice and shout! 'Shh . . .' she would say, putting her hand over his mouth, '. . . the neighbours.'

When it was over, William was very attentive for the next few days. He would do little things to please her, like bring her flowers, and he would sing around the house. She soon learned to ration him just enough to keep him happy, so that his thoughts would not stray. As far as she was concerned, sex was one of the unpleasant chores of life and she did it as competently as she did the washing or the ironing.

Pictures of Charles show him in lace dresses at the age of two. His black curly hair fell in ringlets to his shoulders. Even William remarked that he looked a little sissy compared to the other toddlers down the road. Julia sniffed at this and pointed out the different standards of the neighbours who allowed their children to play in the streets and run unwashed and unshod in the summertime. William remembered his own childhood with similar frivolous freedoms, and was grateful to his wife for her ability to better their family.

When Charles was three, Julia found she was pregnant. With a great sense of relief she informed William, who was delighted but also sad because he knew that this was the end of their intimacy together. Ever after, when he would ask, she would occasionally consent, but only if she had a request in mind. William soon learned not to ask too often, and took to his allotment where he grew magnificent vegetables. He became a very quiet and introverted man. He still loved his wife with a passion, but he knew that his passion offended her, so he was content to lie side-by-side with her, totally overshadowed by her domineering and neurotic nature.

From the moment Julia knew she was pregnant again, her attitude changed towards Charles. She took him to the local barber and had his hair cut short. Then she went to the local co-op and bought him shorts for the summer and long trousers for the colder days, to replace the lace dresses of his earlier years. Once home, Julia occupied herself with making clothes for the new baby.

She was not well during this second pregnancy. She had always been short-tempered, but now she found the antics of a three-year-old boy more than she could bear. She became very sharp with Charles and then, as her stomach grew heavier, she began to hit him when he disobeyed her. It was all very confusing for Charles who had always been the most important thing in his mother's life. Now she had really very little time for him. For much of the pregnancy she lay in her bed, in between bouts of obsessive housework.

William was no help to Charles, as Julia had always kept them apart. So now, when Charles needed his father, there was little or no communication between them. Sometimes Julia would smother Charles with kisses as in the old days, but then she would push him away or lock him out in the back garden to play for hours by himself, while she preserved the cleanliness of the house.

In due course, Elizabeth was born in the same hospital where Charles had been born. Aunt Mary, who was childless, left her husband and hurried to stay with Charles for the ten days that Julia was in the hospital. Charles liked having Aunt Mary in the house. She was much more relaxed than his mother, and he was allowed forbidden treats, like food out of tin cans and sweets to eat at odd hours of the day. Aunt Mary let him climb on the furniture, and even let him play out in the street with the other children. Of all the aunts, Mary was his favourite. She was the least snobbish, and would often embarrass her sisters by long reminiscences of their drab childhood days in Hammersmith. Aunt Mary shared Charles's room with him. Every morning she would call Charles into her bed. There they would sit together while she told him stories of her life with her husband. Her husband, Joseph, ran a small general store that sold everything under the sun. One of their games was shopping at Uncle Joseph's. Aunt Mary missed Joseph a great deal.

Charles liked getting into bed with Aunt Mary because, unlike his mother who smelled of carbolic soap, Aunt Mary had a fascinating mixture of odours. Sometimes she would smell of the cut grass in the back fields. Other times it would be smoky, like the fire in the sitting-room. She also used a talcum powder that smelled of lilacs. He loved to bury his head in her soft breasts. Aunt Mary really loved Charles. She would hug him and kiss him all over his face, and then tickle him until he yelled for mercy.

He realized that her body felt different from his mother's. Even when he was tiny he could sense the tension in his mother's caresses. He could feel the possessive, highly charged emotional demands she made on him. When he was much younger it made his stomach tense, and often he had to be taken to the doctor for stomach aches. The doctor never guessed. He saw Mrs Hunter as an excellent mother, even if she did seem a little over-protective.

Also, Aunt Mary didn't mind his 'dinkle', as he called it. When he played with it in the bath, she didn't slap his hands or tell him it would fall off. That had been a frequent nightmare for him. His mother was constantly nagging at him for touching himself. The more she nagged, the more nervous he got, until she would lash out and hit him. 'You'll wake up one morning and it'll be gone,' she would say. 'Don't be so dirty.' Charles went to sleep every night with his hand firmly anchoring his dinkle to his body. He wasn't taking any chances. In his nightmare, someone would enter his room with a pair of scissors. All his life he was to sleep that way.

He asked Aunt Mary if dinkles fell off. 'Lord no,' she said. 'If they did, there'd be precious few children about.'

It was an interesting ten days for William. It was all quite proper for Mary, as his sister-in-law, to stay in the house and to care for them both. What he hadn't reckoned on was the contrast between the two sisters. Julia had always complained of Mary's slovenly ways, but she was obliged to ask for her help in the end because the other sisters were all busy with their growing families. William, after the initial embarrassment of sharing a bathroom with a strange woman, really began to enjoy Mary's easy-going attitude towards housekeeping. No longer did he have to feel guilty about using an ashtray. It was not whisked away as soon as he had put out a cigarette. He could eat his tea on a tray in front of the fire instead of sitting down to a properly laid table which was a mine-field of possible social faux-pas.

By the fourth day of her stay he would garden after work and then sit in the kitchen in his vest. Mary never so much as batted an eyelid. The boy played outside and did not everlastingly whine. William even took Charles to the allotment and showed him the growing vegetables. Charles was so pleased to be allowed to run up and down the rows of sprouting green-beans and carrots, without fear of his mother's reprisals, that he fell on purpose several times into the thick, rich, Dorset earth. When William took him back to the house they were laughing, and when William apologized for the mess Mary laughed and said, 'That's how boys are. You want him to be a man, not a sissy.'

There was an uncomfortable silence between the two of them. William remembered what a struggle he had with Julia to get the boy out of girlish baby clothes, and he recalled the nights of near-arguments he had with her to get his hair cut.

'You're right, Mary,' he said later that night. 'I've been thinking about Julia. She doesn't like the boy to be rough or ill-dressed. I worry for him when he goes to school. But she gets so upset if I talk that way.' William was slow to express himself and uncertain if any discussion of Julia might be construed as a criticism of her.

Mary laughed at his apprehensive expression. 'Our mother couldn't hold much with boys. She always said she would rather have girls. She took to Max when Dad died, but before then she brought the boys up as if they were girls. They had to sew and cook and clean the house. They played games like us, and she never let them out with the other boys. Julia will do the same. As for her getting upset, don't let that bother you. Julia always rules the roost with her airs and graces. She's too clever by half. Just you tell her when you want something done your way. Don't mind the tantrums.'

William gave a half-hearted shrug of denial, but in his heart of hearts he knew Mary was right. The boy was so much more normal these last few days. William felt such a surge of fatherly love towards his little son that he promised himself he would buy a football and take him out to the field and teach him how to kick.

When he came home one lunchtime with a football, Charles was wild with excitement. He, who had so wistfully watched from the front windows as the other boys raced up and down the road, followed by the smaller children of his own age, now was the proud possessor of his own football. William took him out on the green, and amid the cigarette packets, the old paper bags, and the dog mess, father and son played football.

It was a pity that Charles had to mention it to his mother that evening at the hospital. She was immediately angry with William.

'How could you let him play in that dirty place? He could get all sorts of diseases. Really, William. I don't know what you were thinking of.'

William was unwise enough to try to argue. 'The other children play out there all the time.'

A very determined look settled on Julia's face. She knew intuitively that she was losing her grip on her husband. All the years of nagging and denial of his rights were being undermined by her loose sloppy sister who would let him slip back into his old bad habits.

'I suppose you've been sitting around in your vest again,' she said. William hung his head. 'It won't do, William. We won't have a future if we don't work at getting ahead.'

'I know that, Julia . . . I won't do it again. Please come home soon, I do miss you.'

For William the easy-going atmosphere in the house with Mary was proving too threatening. He was frightened of the feelings of freedom and escape he felt. All would be better when Julia returned and put everything back in order. She would tell him how to behave so that he didn't let her or the boy down.

Charles, who had been playing at the foot of the bed with a loose end of the blanket, shook the flap fiercely at his mother and said, 'I'm a ghost and I'm coming to haunt you – whooooo!'

'Who taught you that nonsense?' said Julia sharply.

'Aunt Mary. We've been playing ghosts in bed in the morning.'

Julia's nostrils flared. The thought of her son in bed with anyone but herself was anathema. This was the first betrayal. 'You mean you get into bed with Aunt Mary?' she said in a deceptively quiet tone of voice.

'Every morning we play "ghosts",' babbled the unsuspecting child.

'Go and wait outside. I want a word with your father.'

Charles could hear them arguing through the door.

He sat on the chair in the brown-soup-coloured corridor and waited. It was the first time he had ever heard his father answer back. Charles hoped his mother would stay in the hospital forever. That way he could visit her every day, but he preferred to live with Aunt Mary and his father. His father came out flushed and worried.

The two then went to the baby nursery to see Elizabeth, who waved her fists at them through a glass partition. William's face cleared, and he beamed at Charles. 'That's our baby girl,' he said. 'She'll be home soon and then you can hold her.' Charles tried to look suitably impressed. Actually he would rather have had a tricycle than a sister.

Julia discharged herself the next day and returned home with the baby. Mary was summarily dismissed, and William was told to borrow Mr Fursy's car and drive Mary back to Joseph in Purley. Mary didn't wait for Julia to arrive at the house. As soon as she had been told by an embarrassed William the night before, she smiled philosophically, 'That's Julia all over. Can't let anyone be. Well, that's an end to your freedom.' Then she suddenly became very serious, and taking William's hand in hers she warned him, 'Watch Julia with that son of yours. She'll make an egghead and a softie of him. You mind Michael?' William nodded. He did indeed mind Michael, with his high-pitched giggle and his funny friends.

'If you need me, just ask,' said Mary. 'Send the lad to stay with Joseph and me. We could do with the company. The family's not much for seeing us these days now that they're so grand.' William nodded.

They were both sitting by the fire. William had his shirt on in deference to Julia's orders, but they had shared an illicit dinner of fish and chips. William had eaten two pickled onions – even if he farted in his sleep he felt Mary would not think the less of him. The glow of the fire lit up Mary's bare legs, free from the discomfort of stockings. Her legs were white and lumpy with fat calves mottled with red and purple spider-like veins. Julia possessed perfectly shaped legs; he had never seen them without stockings. But, he thought, looking at Mary sitting opposite him, I wouldn't care if Julia's legs looked like Mary's, if only Julia loved me.

Every so often during their married life together he would get these lonely desolate moments. It was as if he lived in a glass case most of his life. Within that glass case, he preserved his illusion of their mutual love for each other. Just occasionally, as in the friendly warmth of Mary's presence, his illusion would shatter and he would find himself naked and alone.

Quickly he brushed aside the moment. Hurriedly he got to his feet and said good-night. Alone in bed that night he comforted himself. Of course Julia loved him. She just wanted what was best for them all. But Mary had a point about the boy. William would try to spend more time with him.

5

'It's no good crying, Emily,' said Aunt Bea firmly. 'Rachel has got to go to a boarding school where she can be with other girls her own age and make friends. She is far too isolated here.'

'But she's all we've got,' sobbed Emily, her shoulders heaving. Rachel, who had graduated from the child's wheel-back chair to a place at the little breakfast table, looked on in alarm. There had been talk about boarding school for weeks. But Rachel had a unique way of insulating herself from real life. She learned it from the hours she had spent in bed suffering from the rheumatic fever. It was partly the enforced isolation for nearly two years of her life which gave her inner resources that were to last her in good stead for the rest of her life. Also she lived so completely in Aunt Emily's woman's world that she was oblivious to everything outside it.

'It's no good blubbing, Emily. You'll just upset the child,' said Aunt Bea, who detested emotion. 'Rachel, dear, we have decided that you should be a boarder at St Anne's Convent. We have an appointment to see the nuns next week.'

'I haven't decided anything,' Aunt Emily said, but Aunt Bea would not be moved. Rachel felt very torn between the two aunts. On the one hand, she loved her life in the comfortable house with cook and the dogs and her aunts; but on the other hand she was beginning to feel the need for friends. During her long days in bed after the tutor had left, she read all the books she could get her hands on.

Aunt Emily would trundle off in the little car to the

local library every week. Fortunately she had no inclination to educate Rachel, unlike Aunt Bea whose tastes ran to Jane Austen and Thomas Hardy. No, Aunt Emily would consult the assistant librarian who was just out of school, and together they would find Enid Blyton adventure stories and *Greyfriars. What Katie Did* was another favourite. *Heidi* and *Swallows and Amazons* fired their imaginations. Then on the way home Aunt Emily would stop for a cup of coffee at Anna's Tea Shoppe. Next door at the newsagents', she would pick up Aunt Bea's copy of *The Times*, then *Beano, Dandy,* and *Film Fun* for Rachel. The comics were a secret between the girl and her aunt because Aunt Bea would never have approved. Rachel loved to lie in her bed on library day and in her mind follow Aunt Emily's progress through the town. As her life was so severely confined by her illness, she visualized the outside world with infinite detail. She would see the thick pine railings that fenced the books in the library from the general public. She remembered, as a small child, the excitement of passing through the barrier, past the big desk, noticed by at least two librarians with spectacles resting on their noses. She remembered the rich thick smell of the books themselves, and the delicious dilemma of choosing the books. She could imagine Aunt Emily puffing a little as she stretched and bent, searching the shelves for new arrivals.

Then, with her arms full, she would make her way across the polished echoing floor to the desk again. Here she would pass on information about Rachel's health to the librarian. They were all very sympathetic. Indeed, the youngest one had once offered to come and read to Rachel. It was a horribly embarrassing experience for Rachel, as she hated anyone to read anything to her.

For Rachel a book was a secret experience. To pick it up, to hold it, to feel the weight of it and then to smell it – the smell would tell her where it had been and how long it had been around. Then she would open it slyly as if the printed words might leave their pages if incorrectly handled. Then, having checked the title pages for information on the book, read the dedications, and looked at the date for return, she would dive straight into the first chapter. Submerged in the story she would remain oblivious to the world until the end. The closing pages would find her beached on her bed, exhausted and triumphant. For that space in time, she had fought the good fights, adventured the adventures, outwitted the wicked, and triumphed with the triumphant. She became a phenomenally fast reader.

The advent of the assistant librarian in her bedroom felt like sacrilege. The librarian may well have chosen her profession for a need to keep things in neat order, for it was certainly not out of a love of books. Her reading voice was high-pitched and whining. She meant well, but Rachel could not help but imagine that it was her pink moist nose and her slightly buck teeth that had led her to choose *Alice in Wonderland* to read aloud to Rachel.

' "I'm late! I'm late!" ' she read, turning the page in a flurry of nervousness. Rachel decided that a fainting spell followed by a threat to be sick was the only way out. The librarian was decidedly relieved, for she had not expected such a mature nine-year-old. There was something curiously ambivalent about Rachel's external childishness and her other self which was that of a continually watchful adult. It was a quality that would attract people to her all her life. It also meant that she could slip into a child's world at will, indeed, in her later ill-fated marriage, it was her consolation.

It was the librarian who unwittingly set off the whole idea of boarding school. On her way downstairs she had passed Bea who inquired after the reading session. 'She should be with other children her own age. She's far too grown up. She needs to play. It can't be good for her all alone like that, poor little thing.'

Aunt Bea stopped in her tracks and considered the matter. In fact, she had been feeling concerned about Rachel for many months. She realized that Rachel was no longer a child. At nine she was tall for her age, and quite thin. Her hair grew thick and glossy; indeed, during those two years she was confined to her bed, her hair sometimes seemed the only living part of her except for her big, alert, shining eyes. In her own way, Aunt Bea cared for Rachel as much as Aunt Emily did. Aunt Emily's way was extroverted and sentimental, but Aunt Bea was a practical woman. She was well aware of the gossip in town concerning the two of them, and she knew that one day it would reach Rachel. She wanted that day to be as late as possible in Rachel's life, which was why sending her away was a necessity. She also felt that Rachel did indeed need to experience a world outside the house. She and Aunt Emily had found their happiness together in this home set among the broom and the heather of the Devon valley. She knew she would leave money for Rachel when she died. But she never really contemplated marriage as a way of life for a woman; she wanted Rachel to receive an education that would enable her to earn her own living. All these thoughts she conveyed to Aunt Emily, who looked distracted and flustered. Finally, it came down to the argument in front of Rachel, and Aunt Emily's subsequent tears.

When Aunt Bea left the room, Rachel threw herself into her aunt's arms. 'Don't worry, Aunt Emily. It won't be for long.' Aunt Emily held her so tightly that Rachel felt she might smother. She pulled away and looked at her aunt. Aunt Emily had a strange, vulnerable expression on her face. Rachel had never seen her look so bereft and so weary. Aunt Emily knew that when Rachel left the house and made her way in the convent, she would lose her exclusive relationship with the child. For nine years, ever since the day Rachel had been brought to the house when she was just a few days old, she had become the most important thing in Emily's life.

Emily was a simple woman. Her love for Rachel was at once motherly and sensual. From babyhood on, there had never been any real boundaries between their bodies, and because of her aunt's frequent sensual displays of affection, Rachel had grown up to enjoy her life around her in a very erotic and tactile way. Emily realized that their morning and evening rituals would come to an end once Rachel met the other world, which would frown on such behaviour. Besides, unlike Aunt Bea, she always envisioned Rachel marrying and having children. Aunt Emily's idea of a suitor for Rachel was largely gleaned from the few Ethel M. Dell novels she had read: someone tall, dark and handsome, much given to bowing from the waist. Aunt Emily would have liked to have been married herself, but like so many women of that time the First World War had decimated possible suitors. Aunt Emily would always be immeasurably grateful to Aunt Bea, who came into her life at her father's vicarage in Charmouth and swept her away to this gentle house on the moor.

Aunt Emily's father, like most vicars, had rarely been at home. There were three girls in the family. Emily was the youngest. The vicarage in Charmouth was a white, square, Georgian house set in the middle of the High Street. Her mother worked hard at being a vicar's wife. In truth, both of them were so busy serving God and their parishioners that they had little time for their daughters. The advent of the First World War made their lives even harder, as many Dorset men were drafted, only to die smothered in the mud across the channel. Many of those that came home were to die coughing up their lungs from the mustard gas.

Emily's parents were busy caring for families whose men were away, and it was during a visit to a bedside that Emily's mother contracted scarlet fever and brought the disease home. She recovered, but Emily's two sisters died from it. Now Emily was totally on her own. She was a very lonely little girl. Her father was the youngest son of an impoverished middle-class family, and it was his duty to go into the Church like so many younger sons had done before him.

As the Church paid its vicars a pittance, there was never any question that its children should attend private schools. They went with the children from the village to the local school. It was difficult enough for Emily when the three girls attended together: at least they had each other. But after the sisters died, Emily had to face going to school on her own. There was an indisputable class barrier between herself and the other children, many of whom had received charity from the hands of her parents. They taunted her with chants of 'goody-goody two shoes'. They pushed her down on the playground, and she would feel her eyes fill with tears; but she never complained to her parents. Since the death of the two girls, both parents looked so worn that she felt obliged to be as little a nuisance as possible. She would attend school and then come home and eat her tea which was usually on a tray in the kitchen. Then she would listen to the wireless by the open fire until her mother and father returned from evensong.

They were too poor to employ a cook, but they had a daily who was the one person who spent time with Emily. She was a motherly Dorset woman. She smelled of Cardinal Cleaning Polish and sweat. She would give Emily a big hug every time she saw her and inquire into her day. There was not much to tell. In the summer Emily would play in the big garden with her dolls and her teaset, and in the winter she would move her make-believe world into the kitchen. There, in a warm, shadowy corner, she would recreate her huge extended family. In those days, all dolls were female, so Emily was obliged to dispatch the male members of the family to glorious deaths. They were much remembered in their absence by the cast of characters and occasionally grieved over, but it was a world untroubled by men.

Emily's world, although lonely, was also untroubled. The days stretched into months, and the months stretched into years. Finally, Emily was free of school and her parents had to face the fact that she had very little academic ability and therefore would probably stay at home until she married. Her mother occasionally and half-heartedly tried to introduce Emily to a young and eligible bachelor in the congregation. But to tell the truth, Emily was not very eligible. She was plump and shy. She had no prospects of a dowry to overcome her lack of physical charm, and she seemed to have no wish for a suitor anyway.

Gradually she moved into the role of mistress of the house. Her mother was glad of her help. Her father was getting older and needed more and more help in ministering to his far-flung parish. Emily enjoyed the role immensely. It was just like playing dolls but in a real house. She spent the days polishing and cleaning. When she could see her face in the walnut dining table, she would turn to polishing the family silver, lovingly fingering the heavy knives and forks with their complicated patterns, or she would prepare elaborate tea ceremonies for visiting clergy or the town clerk. She would spend several days making light-as-air lemon sponge cake. Her cucumber sandwiches were second to none, and the raspberry jam was thick and richly scented, made from the berries that she'd picked that week from the garden.

Sitting at tea, pink with exertion, she loved to light the small methylated spirit lamp under the shining silver teapot. Then she would pass the visitors the muffin tray. This ingenious contraption was set snug in its own pool of hot water. This way the muffins were kept warm and moist, and could soak up the jam and the thick clotted cream that spilled on to the tea plates and dripped down the visitors' chins.

Emily was fast becoming an old maid. Maybe some nights, as she sat at her window on the second floor overlooking the moonlit garden, she felt a longing for a strong pair of arms to hold her. Indeed, she was infected by a restlessness. But apart from moments of sadness when she watched a woman on the street pick up and cuddle her child, she was generally accepting of her lot in life. Until one day when Bea came to tea.

6

Bea was visiting the area with her widowed father, who was an historian, and a man with sufficient income to indulge himself in most of his whims. He was in Charmouth that day doing research for his new book which was devoted to the study of Dorset churches. His daughter accompanied her father on his trips, and indeed he would never have considered going anywhere without Bea at his side.

She was his only child. Her mother had died a few days after giving birth to her, and Lionel, her father, took it upon himself to bring up the baby. His family had not been at all pleased with the situation, particularly as Lionel, who had wanted a boy to share his passion for cricket, insisted on allowing Bea to behave in a rough-and-ready manner that was described by his mother in shocked tones as 'tomboyish'.

Lionel lived in a small village just outside Axminster. The house, which he had inherited from an uncle, was an old Elizabethan farmhouse. The farm land was tenanted, but he kept the stable block for his horses and a stretch on the River Yarte for fly fishing. Bea grew up in an idyllic fashion. Her first memories were of the fields by the river where she would play, and then of the day she would spend with her father, silently casting with her miniature rod for trout.

Lionel was a tall giant of a man. He was known in his youth for his temper, but by the time he was ready to marry he had firm control of himself. Only a tightening of the lips and a twitch of a muscle under his left eye would betray a rising irritation. Bea soon learned when to stop and when to obey.

Her mother had been a sweet, rather delicate English rose. Her family was not from Devon. Lionel met her on one of his infrequent business visits to London. Lionel's family had originally made money abroad. The rumour was that it was in slaves and gun-running. Whatever the truth of the matter, there was certainly sufficient money around for the various members of the family to live easily, and without the need for daily work. Just occasionally they were obliged to turn up for a board meeting in St James's Square off The Mall to listen to an incomprehensible report concerning the family fortune. The meeting would take up most of the morning, and when it was finished the family would retire to the Savoy to have lunch. Lionel had a permanent suite in the Savoy. He loved the luxury, and blessed D'Oyle Carte for his imagination and energy. No other hotel in London at that time was as sumptuous. The showers were a new idea from America. Lionel loved to stand under the twelve-inch rose and drench himself.

It was there that Lionel was introduced to Jennifer St Isle, who was the youngest daughter of the family solicitor. When the pair announced their engagement, both families were delighted. Lionel's mother had always worried over her favourite son, who seemed to need very little out of life except a fishing rod and a cricket bat. It was not that he was unintelligent, but he was a self-sufficient man, a product of an upper-middle-class background that consisted of nursery life, followed by prep school at seven, then boarding-school, with intermittent holidays when the parents were occasionally in evidence, if they were not otherwise engaged in Biarritz or taking the waters in Baden-Baden.

This was not the sort of childhood to encourage a small boy to grow up with any ability to form warm loving relationships. Indeed, Lionel found conversation a great trial, and as a youth he always swore to himself that he would have a pipe as soon as he became of age in order to be able to hide behind a dense cloud of smoke when in social company. He also knew that the cleaning, knocking, and sucking on a pipe would give him plenty of time to organize replies to the endlessly tiresome questions that well-meaning people would throw at him. He quickly learned at school that excellence in the field of sport brought not only respect from one's peers but also an immediate assumption from the masters at the school that somehow, because he had 'brawn', he did not have to convince anyone that he had 'brains'. That suited Lionel very nicely. He would far rather spend the long summer evenings practising his batting in the nets than sweating in the heat-laden library with several hundred wriggling restless boys struggling with their Latin declensions.

Lionel's mother did try to make some sort of relationship with her handsome but not very talkative son. She found it difficult. She was a matriarch, and even as she delivered orders to him she detected a sly hint of amusement in his eyes and a slightly insolent manner in his tone of reply. Little did she know that Lionel had very little opinion of women, starting with his nurse who had housed a lascivious soul under her white starched uniform.

The nurse would drink heavily, and on one never-to-be-forgotten occasion he remembered pulling her out of the nursery fireplace. She had bent over, drunk as usual, to poke the fire, lost her balance, and fallen in. Lionel, young as he was, heaved and shoved, and, with a bit of grumbling assistance from the nurse, pulled her free of the fire. She was not badly hurt, but for some singed hair. She wore her nanny's veil very low on her forehead for many weeks. Lionel did not tell anyone of this unfortunate incident because it was not done to sneak, and also because the nurse and her small charge shared an intimate secret.

Ever since she had moved into the nursery when Lionel was a few days old, she had put him to sleep by gently pulling his foreskin, while rocking him in the nursery rocking chair. As he grew older, their night-times became even more pleasurable as she would lie beside him in his bed and take his growing penis in her mouth. Lionel knew sexual pleasure from an early age, and thoroughly enjoyed watching his nurse dress and undress, particularly when she was half-drunk and would strip off her clothes and demand that he admire her body. Surprisingly, she had a good full-breasted body. Lionel was fascinated by the colour of her body hair, which was as red as the hair on her head. As he grew older and bolder, he used to ask her to spread her legs so that he could peer into that mysterious cavern covered by an enormous thatch. If she was in the mood to humour him, she would obligingly splay her legs, and he would gaze and eventually get up the courage to insert his fingers in between the lips and then further into the moist tunnel. It was not long before they both derived a great deal of pleasure from each other and, for a boy so emotionally deprived by his parents, it became a source of great emotional comfort as well as excitement. Her smell, which was peculiar to most red-headed women, led him to look for the same type of women in the many brothels he subsequently frequented.

His marriage to Jennifer did little to change his attitudes towards women. As with most men of his day, it was perfectly acceptable for him to have prostitutes in a brothel and a wife at home who was treated with great respect, and indeed love of a kind understood by men as 'romantic'. Lionel did love Jennifer. He saw her as part child, part saint, and a prized possession. All she had was his: her dowry, her body, and, above all, her virginity. Luckily for Jennifer, Lionel was a good lover. With all his experience with prostitutes, he knew how to be gentle and kind.

He stayed faithful to her until she was pregnant. Then, as her stomach grew, he returned to his favourite brothel where he had an almost permanent liaison with a prostitute called Regine, who looked uncannily like his nurse. Sometimes, with his head buried in between Regine's thighs, he would breathe in deeply the almost but not quite remembered smell of his childhood days, and a sweeping loneliness would roll over him. He would lie still and wait for it to go away. Regine knew these moments in so many men. She would lie still and stroke his head until he could lift up his face and smile at her.

When Jennifer died a few days after the baby was

born, Lionel was distraught. He felt somehow responsible for the death of something so fragile and delicate. His family gathered along with hers, and she was buried amongst banks of white lilies. Before they closed her coffin, Lionel looked at her beautiful, frozen face framed by her fair hair, and at her small white hands folded together with the gold of her wedding ring glinting in the candle-light. He swore to her then that he would never marry again, because nothing, not even death, would part them.

All during the demented days of her death and dying he had refused to see the child. A few moments after her birth he had been shown an ugly squealing purplish infant that looked more like one of the piglets produced by a sow than a human being. He made some obliging remark to the midwife and left. The future of the baby was under discussion by both families and it was almost decided that the baby should go to Jennifer's sister, who had two children already, when the nurse employed to look after the child came into the drawing-room and said timidly to Lionel, 'I'm sorry, sir – I've had bad news. My nan is ill and I must go to look after her. I'm sorry to be letting you down like this.' She was holding the baby in her arms. She looked down at the child. 'Poor little motherless scrap,' she said to herself more than to anyone else.

In spite of himself, Lionel looked at the child in her arms. The baby turned her head and tried to focus her eyes as the huge giant of a man bent over her. He looked deeply into her face, and to his absolute amazement, instead of the purple wrinkled screaming object he had last seen, he found himself looking at an exact replica of himself. He took the tiny wrapped bundle from the nurse and awkwardly held his child. The baby gazed contentedly at him and then curled her little fingers round his huge hand.

The nurse was shuffling with impatience, and the gathered members of the family were getting restive. Finally, Lionel raised his head and, looking around the room, he said, 'She will stay with me.' A babble of protest followed his remark. Jennifer's sister,

Elizabeth, was inwardly relieved, but outwardly she spoke for all the rest of the family when she said it was simply not done for a man to bring up a daughter alone unless he planned to re-marry.

'I'll never re-marry. I made that promise to Jennifer. But now I have our daughter . . .' He was silent for a moment. Then he said, 'I will call her Beatrice.'

That was the end of all discussion. The cook was called in and offered to care for the baby until a suitable nurse could be found. The present nurse left to look after the elderly ailing member of her family. The family took their various carriages back to their own homes. Many tittle-tattle letters passed between the women-folk, all of whom totally disapproved of Lionel's attitude, especially when they heard that Lionel had sacked each nanny after a few weeks on some pretext or another, and that the baby was virtually being brought up by the cook who kept her crib in the kitchen.

They were not to know that Lionel could hardly bear anyone to hold his Beatrice, and he found the nannies far too possessive. The cook, however, had had nine children of her own and by now had many grandchildren. There was absolutely no need for her to feel possessive about the baby. In fact, she treated Beatrice just like she did the kittens that lay tucked up in a box by the fire.

Mostly Beatrice would stare up at the huge copper pots and pans that hung from the rafters. Her first colour memories were of the fire in the kitchen range catching refracted spectrums in flawed window panes as the mist from the River Yarte gently pushed against the outside of the house. Then, when she was able to crawl, she was held by the waist by a length of cord, long enough for her to explore, but not long enough to reach the fireplace. In those Victorian days, there were plenty of kitchen objects to keep a small child amused. She cut her teeth on a wooden stirring spoon, and learned to walk using the edges of the big farm chairs.

Every day Lionel would come in after lunch and take her out. It never crossed his mind that she should have a pram. He carried her cradled in his arms when she was tiny, and later slung on his shoulders when she was old enough to hang on. This way they would walk for miles up and down the Devon hills. They were a strange sight, this huge man with his tiny charge.

People would stop and stare at him because he talked so earnestly to his daughter. He told her everything. Each evening, after his dinner had been served and the table cleared away, he would call for a bottle of whisky and send the cook to get his daughter. Then he would settle himself by the fireside in his study and, unwrapping her shawl, he would lie her across his knees and they would commune for at least an hour. 'Blaze fell at the races,' he would say. 'The trout are rising. Old Jack will have to be retired from the garden because his arthritis has been troubling him, but I've promised Jack his cottage for life plus a pension.' She would wave her legs and arms in agreement, and gurgle at him. The servants thought it was all a very funny business, but then those with all that money were always a little odd.

After the hour or so (depending on how much news he had to impart) was complete, he wrapped her up and took her back to her little room which was next to the cook's. He was perfectly capable of changing her nappy if he had to. This fact was another scandal in the house. Naturally, a lot of the time Lionel spent with Beatrice was not only because he loved her so, but also because he had virtually no one else to talk to. No one else except, of course, Regine. After the shock of Jennifer's death, it took many months before he felt like having intercourse with a woman. But gradually he began to feel human again, and the urge for sex became a source of impatient irritation. He went back to see Regine who was as warm and comfortable as ever. After they had made love, he lay in her arms and cried, probably the first time he had cried before another human being in his life. He cried for himself, for his dead wife, for his baby. Regine just held him. It was then that he resolved to make Regine his mistress. But no one was ever to know that he had a second household.

7

By now Regine was twenty-three. She had been a prostitute ever since she was thirteen. Like many young working-class girls of her day, the choices open to her were very limited. She had come from a very large family which lived in Honiton. Her father was a brutal man who drank too much and who beat his wife and children, when he could catch them. As each of the girls reached puberty, he believed it was his right to 'saddle and bridle' the child. The ritual bridling had taken place with Regine's two older sisters, and she remembered the screams and the pleading she could hear through the door. She resolved she would leave home before her time came. Her mother helped her pack. 'Go when he's sleep,' she whispered to her daughter. She would try her luck in the big city of Exeter. She had never been there, but she had always been an intelligent and lively girl who felt there had to be a better future than ending up like her mother. When it became obvious that her father was planning to rape her, she made ready to leave.

Thursday was market day in Exeter, and there was no shortage of carriages and wagons leaving Honiton. She had saved a very little money, but enough to stay the night at a cheap lodging-house, and then she hoped that the next day she would find employment. Things did not work out quite so easily. Work was hard to find even in as rich a city as Exeter. She was resting her sore feet (which were unused to city cobbles) when she was joined by a chatty girl just a little older than herself.

It was not a shock for Regine to learn that the girl

was a prostitute. Even in Regine's village there were women of known ill-repute whom none of the other women would talk to. In fact, Regine had noticed from an early age how much younger and less haggard they looked than the virtuous married women who were worn out with child-bearing and constant housework. After Caroline introduced herself and explained that she was no amateur who walked the streets, but was rather more grand than that, Regine decided it was definitely worth looking into. They both went back to the house which was in the middle of a very elegant Regency square, and Caroline introduced her to Madam.

Madam had a very good eye for quality in girls. She was rich and successful because of this very talent. She explained very explicitly to Regine that, if she decided to take up the profession ('and remember,' she said, 'it is, after all, one of the oldest and most honourable professions'), 'I expect you to see me as you would your mother.' Regine tried not to smile as she remembered the shrunken toothless figure of her mother in contrast to the large, imposing, richly-dressed woman sitting in front of her.

'First of all,' said Madam, 'I must see you without your clothes. It is your body that you are going to sell.' Oddly enough, Regine didn't feel that embarrassed. The woman looked at her very much as if she were taking stock of a horse, so obediently Regine took off her black dress and petticoat and then nervously removed her liberty bodice and her thick woollen underpants.

'Turn around slowly,' said Madam. Regine was lucky. Because of her red hair and white complexion, she would be a welcome addition to the house. Her figure was strong as one would expect from country stock, but her thighs were not too broad and her breasts, though bigger than usual, stood high and firm. The nipples were a curious shade of strawberry. As far as Madam could tell, she was clean and free from lice. It would of course take time to teach her gentle manners both socially and at the table. However, she seemed intelligent and willing.

'You'll do,' said Madam. Regine heaved a sigh of

relief. She had avoided any embarrassment while standing naked by looking around the magnificent drawing-room. Most of all she was entranced by the huge central chandelier lit with hundreds of candles. It was the richest and most beautiful thing she had ever seen. The rest of the room was lined with thick crimson and gold wallpaper. The carpet was from China and was a deep, deep blue. All the furniture was ornate ormolu, and the chairs were covered in brocades. To Regine it was heaven; she did not recognize true brothel style. That night she slept in the cleanest deepest bed, and as she closed her eyes she promised herself that if she was going to be a prostitute, then by God she'd be the best in the house.

It didn't take her long. She learned quickly. Most of the girls were friendly and only too willing to help. Madam was very pleased with her and she was told that she could have her first client very soon. Usually it took at least three months to groom a girl for the clientele of the brothel. Because it was well run and served a fine table with a noble wine list, it was patronized by the rich men of the town and surrounding countryside. The local judge was a frequent customer, and the Chief of Police also enjoyed the claret and the women, so Madam never had any trouble from the law. In all, it was a luxurious and contented family, apart from some girlish disputes.

Madam did not allow any dangerous or perverted pastimes in her house. In her own way she was very good to the girls and they respected her in return. If she saw any of her girls unduly bruised, the man concerned was politely asked to leave and never return. Also, she was meticulous in the matter of sexual hygiene. In the days when contraceptives were rudimentary in the extreme, she made her girls use sponges of vinegar after intercourse, believing vinegar to be effective as a spermicidal and also as a prophylactic. Every girl in the house was rigorously careful, because to catch any sexual infection meant time off work, and syphilis meant the end of her job at the brothel because it was incurable. However, there were very few cases of disease, thanks to the care of the doctor who inspected the girls weekly, and to the clientele, who tended to remain constant, using the place as a home from home.

Regine's first sexual experience was not as awful as she had imagined. After all, the alternative had been her smelly drunken father. So, when Madam told her that she was to receive her first client the next day in room 12 (which was to be her permanent room), she was very excited. It was all very well listening to stories from the other girls, but after a while it would be more fun to join in rather than just to listen. Caroline, who had remained her close friend, gave her plenty of good advice. As she was a virgin, she would be given extra money on this occasion, and if Madam was very pleased by the client's report she could even get a gold sovereign. The thought of all that wealth made her quite giddy. She resolved in a moment of virtue to send it to her mother, and then ran off to inspect the room.

There were twelve working rooms for the twelve girls employed by Madam. Each room was sumptuously furnished and had a small room off it which had a grate with a big jug of water. The water was always on the boil for washing. Because Regine was a virgin and the first few times were bound to bruise her, Madam made sure she had a pitcher of ice so that she could stem the swelling. It was not just concern, but also sound business sense, because she liked the girls to work at least three hours a night. Each client paid for an hour, and as they paid well the girls were able to give good service.

Caroline, who had been there for two years, told Regine that after a while there was nothing to it. If she got bored, and she frequently did, she counted sheep or did sums in her head. Occasionally, she even enjoyed it, but mostly it was just a routine, and she would dream her dreams about a lover who would come by one day and marry her. Regine looked at her incredulously. 'No one's ever going to marry us,' she said. 'We're whores, and whores aren't for marrying.' But Caroline just smiled and buried her head in her penny love story which she read day in and day out.

The actual moment of intercourse wasn't nearly as dreadful as Regine had been told by the other girls. The man who had paid the high price for her virginity was certainly not the one she would have chosen for the honour. But he was not a very large man, so the act of penetration wasn't as painful as she had anticipated. Regine was not particularly revolted by the grunting and the loud moans of pleasure that he gave while he thrust his way into her; she was more concerned that there should be a sufficient show of blood to reassure him that his money was well spent. To her relief she saw the sheet under her stain crimson, and he quickly dipped his white cambric handkerchief into the fresh blood.

'Why did you do that?' she asked.

'It is well known that the first blood of a virgin protects a man from disease and brings him good health.' He dressed and went his way.

Regine bathed herself in the hot water and gently applied the ice to her genitals. Could have been a lot worse, she thought, and went off to report to Madam who was well pleased with her and did indeed give her a gold sovereign.

That evening after the men had gone, the girls all gathered together in their parlour. The twelve of them lived in what had been the maids' quarters in the old attic of the house. The rooms were comfortable little cubbyholes, well furnished and kept warm by the small coal fires stoked daily by the scullery maids. The parlour was the only large room in the attic where all the girls could congregate to chatter and gossip about their clients, about Madam, and, above all, about their boyfriends. Madam was very strict, and no girl could see any of her customers out of the house. If she did it would mean instant dismissal

But many of the girls had their beaus and saw them on their days off. Mostly they were city lads who had no idea the girls they were courting were prostitutes. Indeed, many a girl had gone to her marriage from 'the

Big House', as the girls called it, without her suitor or his family having any idea other than that she had been a parlour maid. So the evening sessions, after the hours of entertaining men, were usually spent discussing love affairs or the men who frequented the house.

On the whole, the girls tended to treat their clients like small boys in need of a mixture of mothering and sexual experience unheard of by their respectable wives. Oral sex was a constant demand. There were many ways of fooling a highly aroused man into believing that his needs were being met, simply by using wet fingers covered by a fall of long hair. Different techniques were often discussed as to how to bring a particularly slow client to climax. It was generally agreed that men with huge penises were a nuisance because they were usually inordinately proud of them and tended to use them like a battering-ram, thereby causing pain and discomfort. Slow climaxers were definitely deemed very tedious. Most girls had their favourites who returned to them faithfully. But occasionally a man would feel like a change, so the previous and the current practitioners sat with their heads together exchanging notes about their clients quite amicably.

It was very much a house of women. The only resident man was Tom, who answered the door and took the hats and cloaks. He was huge, black, and evil looking. He was reputed to be the son of a slave who landed at Bristol. He was taken in by Madam when he was in his early twenties, and had worked for her ever since. He knew everything that happened, right down to the last sliver of gossip. He always told Madam everything. People often wondered if they had a closer relationship than at first appeared, but such suppositions were wrong. Tom saw Madam as his saviour, and she took comfort in his care and his strength. Madam herself had only loved once, and her fiancé had died just before the marriage. In the way of so many strong and powerful women, she knew that she was unlikely to find anyone to rekindle that first love, so she preferred to remain alone in her house of women.

When Lionel first broached to Regine that he might like to set up an establishment with her, she was like an excited child. 'Really?' she said, throwing her arms about him. 'Just you and me in a house?'

Lionel felt a deep warmth for this enthusiastic little life-force who was hugging him so fiercely, and for the woman who could also meet his needs so directly. 'You realize you won't ever be able to tell anyone who you are, or that we have any sort of liaison, and it will always have to be a secret?'

'I promise, I promise,' Regine said. It took several more years to fall deeply and sincerely in love with Lionel, although she was excited by him and she did find him an interesting and interested person to be with. When he put his proposition to her, she was still haunted by the possibility of losing her place in the Big House, either by ill health or by the pox. The grim image of life in Honiton often came to her in nightmares. Lionel's offer was a step up, and gave her more security, especially as he promised he would provide for her for the rest of her days. Indeed, the whole affair did remain secret until the day he died, when his will was read in the presence of Aunt Bea and Aunt Emily. It was the only time anyone had seen Bea completely out of control. She screamed and sobbed like a woman betrayed; which indeed she was.

Lionel was quite busy now. He saw Madam and explained his wishes to her. He paid her a handsome price for removing Regine from the Big House, and Regine left with Madam's blessing. They found a small cottage several miles from an obscure little village called Uplyme in Devon. It was within a few hours' riding distance from Axminster and far enough away to avoid gossip. The cottage sat at the end of a small cart track secluded from prying eyes by a wall of trees. Regine was immediately entranced by the whole place. Lionel allowed her a dog to guard her in his absence and a small pony and trap to get about her business. His allowance to her was very generous, and he was amused to see her redecorate the dingy little cottage into an almost exact replica of the Big House. As soon as she could, she took the pony and trap to Lyme Regis, and there she found little chandeliers, red embossed wallpaper, and imitation ormolu furniture.

'It's not every man that has his own private whore house,' Lionel joked when he saw the whole thing assembled.

'You'll never be sorry,' she said, kissing both his hands, and he never was.

Meanwhile his Beatrice flowered. She grew just like the dockweed that lined the banks of the river that ran by the house. She also grew wilder as she grew older. Her days were spent riding with her father, fishing in the long summer evenings, or if bored with that she would strip off and swim in the deep murky pools. One hot summer's day she dived into a particularly deep reeded pool, and as she rose to the surface she saw through the green mist of the water in her eyes the arched silver flash of a huge salmon leaping high into the air, only to return near her, and then disappear, on its way to the spawning ground.

That night she was full of it and told her father over dinner that she had decided she would like to be a game-keeper. Cook, who happened to be serving that day, as it was the butler's day off, gave a loud snort of disapproval. Lionel at first thought it all very funny, but he suddenly realized that his Beatrice had very little pretensions, nor any idea of how to act as a female. By now she was eleven years old, as skinny as a rail, and dressed usually in trousers which she had begged off the gardener's son. She was lively and intelligent, partly because of her father's huge library where she had spent most evenings reading his books. Also, as his constant companion, she had learned much from him. But he now realized that he would have to consider some sort of civilizing influence for her.

He consulted various members of his family, and it was his sister-in-law Elizabeth who said a good girls' academy would be just what she needed. 'The child is a wild thing,' she said, pursing her mouth. Lionel liked Beatrice that way, and indeed her manner was entirely his doing. He had taught her to ride astride instead of side saddle; he had also taught her to play cricket with as straight a bat as anyone in the county. She could ferret and shoot a pheasant as well as any lad of her age, but what she could not do was to sit still, in a lady-like manner, and make idle conversation. Her ability to fight with the local lads, however, was legendary.

He consulted Regine, who, without ever having met the child, knew the father well enough to point out that, if the girl was anything like he was, she would not last ten minutes at an academy for young ladies, but perhaps a very understanding governess would be a better solution. Because Lionel had a stable and loving relationship with Regine, he was not nearly as possessive of his daughter; rather, by now, it was the other way around.

It was quite by chance that Lionel found a tutor for Beatrice who regarded the child as a challenge. Helen was not an aggressive woman, nor was she particularly warm, which was a pity because Beatrice so needed some form of loving other than her passion for her father. But Helen did gently help Beatrice through the rudiments of good manners and teach her the art of genteel conversation. Helen, like so many women of her time, was from a poor but well-mannered family, and as she was not particularly attractive and had no dowry her only way out was either to teach or to tutor privately. She settled in quickly. Lionel was glad she was there in the evenings, because he had been in the habit of leaving Beatrice in the care of the cook while he was off to see Regine. He was always back before dawn. In all the time Beatrice was with him, he never spent a whole night with Regine. Regine never complained. That had always been their agreement: his daughter would come first all his life.

Then, quite by accident, Regine became pregnant when she was thirty-four. She begged Lionel to allow her to keep the baby: she so badly needed something of her own. She had so honestly kept her promise that their relationship would be a secret that she lived a very isolated life. Lionel knew that abortions were difficult and dangerous, and he was too fond of Regine to risk her life.

Although he was unhappy at bringing an illegitimate child into the world, he agreed she could keep the child, and was relieved when the baby turned out to be a little girl. Had the baby been a boy, he would have seriously considered legitimizing the union, as no son of his could be brought up a bastard. With girls, he told himself, it is different; after all, they can always get married.

Regine named the baby Caroline after her friend at the Big House. The child always called the man who visited her mother 'Uncle Lionel'. By the time that she was old enough to realize that her mother was having a clandestine union with her uncle, she had been so ostracized by the local community because of her mother's hermit-like life that she was a difficult and wayward child.

8

When Beatrice and Emily first met each other, they were both in their late thirties and were past a marriageable age. For Emily, being unmarried was a source of sadness because she had a warm and passionate nature. For Bea, as she now called herself, it was no loss at all. She had never considered men at all attractive. She had never met anyone who could hold a candle to the perfection that was her father. Every other man seemed callow and dull when placed beside him.

Things between Lionel and his daughter were not always sweetness and light. They both were bigheaded and stubborn. They could argue and raise the roof of the house when they were in a mood to, but the servants would just shake their heads and know that it would be all forgotten in a matter of hours. Bea always travelled on Lionel's historical research jaunts, and the visit to Charmouth had been uneventful until teatime at the vicarage.

Beatrice immediately recognized the untapped passion in Emily. She partly felt the mother/child in this grown woman. All that was soft and gentle and had been missing in Beatrice's life flowed across the tea table as they exchanged cups of tea. Emily sensed a woman of purpose in Beatrice; someone who strode through life not afraid of anyone or anything, sure and resolute, quite unlike the church people who had surrounded her. Emily looked across the table at this broad-shouldered woman with her flat boyish chest and her long muscular arms. She could almost be a man, Emily thought, but then she looked at the sensitive mouth and the deep expressive eyes. No, she couldn't, she decided, thinking of the spoiled patriarchal men who littered her life when she was forced to serve as the unmarried daughter of the house.

Beatrice and Lionel were staying in Charmouth at the local inn for a few days. Lionel loved the great white beaches, and he loved too pottering about in his car. He tended to think of cars as horses, and kept a full stable of all the new cars as rapidly as they were invented. Bea was one of the first women to drive in the county, and it was she who suggested to Emily that they might spend a day together driving in her Jaguar SS 100. Emily was thrilled with the idea. Lionel, finding himself much occupied with the local sexton who remembered much of the parish history, was quite pleased to see them off for the day, as Bea had a tendency to get restive when the two men, both in their seventies, got deep into their memories of the First World War.

It was a lovely summer's day. The sky was a washed blue with large white clouds, and the green hedgerows embraced the growing wheat fields. It was that perfect point of the year just before harvest time when the whole earth possesses a bursting ripeness. Soon the farmers would be out in the fields cutting down the crops, and the rabbits would be running for their lives. But for now, all was at peace, and Bea drove Emily just a little too fast along the winding roads towards Winterborne Abbas where she had an appointment to look at a bay mare.

They were quite nervous of each other for the first hour of the drive. Certainly Emily had good reason to be slightly nervous, as Bea raced the car round the corners, but they arrived in time for lunch with the breeder. Emily spent most of lunch mortified by the conversation. The talk was all about brood mares being covered by stallions; Bea proved to be an absolute expert on the best method of correctly mounting a mare so that the stallion should do the least damage. They were the only two women at the table, and the four men who sat with them seemed to treat Bea as one of themselves. Emily pushed her steak-and-kidney pie round her plate. But Bea sat bolt upright, her eyes shining and her big capable hands describing the shape of a head or the turn of a fetlock.

Upset as she was, Emily could not help but be impressed by her new friend's competence. After lunch Bea was invited to watch the new stallion mount a very valuable mare. The breeder turned to Emily and said, 'I think this is not for you - would you like to look at the young foals in the pasture? It's only a ten minute walk away.' Bea trooped off with the men, and Emily obediently and thankfully went the other way. But it was not far enough away to avoid the sounds of the urging of the men's voices or the loud echoes of the stallion roaring.

On the way home Bea was particularly happy. She had decided to buy the bay mare because the mare had a fine pelvis and a beautiful head. In time she would throw a beautiful foal. Bea was totally at home in the world of men, unlike Emily who had spent so much of her life in servicing them without any return except an expectation of more service; Bea had been brought up with all the rights to and natural feel of the superiority of the male world. She found Emily very vulnerable, and was even slightly amused by her timid approach to life.

Emily was sitting in the car looking out over the fields, thinking to herself, This is one of the happiest days of my life. There she was, sitting beside this capable woman who made her feel safe, and for the first time Emily really felt like a person, not just a mere appendage. When Bea dropped her off at the vicarage, Emily looked at her and very shyly, blushing furiously, said, 'Thank you, Bea. I really enjoyed myself.'

Bea immediately became gruff. 'Perfectly all right - enjoyed it myself. Must do it again sometime.' Bea found it very hard from all her male upbringing to be at all demonstrative, and she found herself quite moved by this shy little woman's honest pleasure in her presence.

They became friends, and over the next few years

they were often in each other's company. Emily could do none of the things that came naturally to Bea, but she was quite content to sit by her friend in the drowse of a summer evening watching the trout almost too lazy to jump for the fly lures, except for Bea's, who made her own so bewitchingly bejewelled that she was famous for her ability to catch fish. They were happy days together. Both women shared a common love of reading, though Emily tended to read romance.

Emily learned to ride, albeit a little precariously, to keep Bea company, but flatly refused to ride to hounds. Although she loved the pageant of the horses mounted by the assembled hunting fraternity in their pink coats, and the cries of the whips as they called their hounds out of a thicket, her thoughts were all in favour of the fox. Indeed, the one time she had attended a hunt, she had been following on foot. She was standing by a five-bar gate when the master of the hunt hurtled on his huge seventeen-hands gelding towards the gate, followed by a torrent of horses that poured over after him. It sounded like a thunderstorm with thousands of pounds of sheer horse power and muscle all on the move. Like a great wave they splashed into the next field with the hounds running at full cry ahead.

The fox broke cover too soon – he'd lost his nerve – and in a second he was surrounded. The last Emily saw of him was his head thrown back and his teeth bared in a deathly snarl. Then the dogs tore him apart. The whips moved in and beat the hounds off to rescue the brush, the paws, and the mask as trophies for the newcomers to the hunt. Emily was quietly sick behind the wall and never went again. She tried to argue with Bea, but Bea shrugged her shoulders and said, 'Much kinder this way. It dies immediately. Shooting is too risky. They move so fast you can end up just maiming them.'

Emily could never reconcile herself to Bea's attitude towards animals, which was firm and practical. Emily liked animals just as much as she liked human beings, and therefore had a tendency to spoil any animal that came her way. Bea definitely preferred animals to human beings, but they also had their place, and it was certainly not on her bed or on her lap. This was a bone of contention between the two of them all their lives. Emily usually won because she colluded with the animals and together they undermined Bea's authority.

Within two years of their meeting, the Second World War broke out, and their lives were to change dramatically.

When the whole country realized that war was inevitable, the people of England swung into action, and the fever of war infected everyone. Even Lionel in his eighties offered himself for homeguard duty. Regine, who had lived the life of a recluse, joined the local women's institute and knitted for soldiers. Her peace was punctuated with episodic problems with her difficult daughter who every so often would appear back into her life and stay for a while, demanding money and berating her mother for not providing her with a proper family. She made no attempt to work or to get married.

Regine bitterly regretted having the child. She realized now that it had been a very selfish act. She had used Caroline as a companion in her loneliness, and by choosing to remain with Lionel she had deprived the girl of a normal life. Unfortunately, as is often the case, the mother and daughter were temperamentally unsuited. Regine could see a lot of her own father in the girl, which made it difficult for her really to love her. Regine suffered a lot of guilt over the relationship, but she had given her life totally to Lionel and, although local tongues wagged furiously over the years, they still had a very warm, loving relationship.

Lionel took very little interest in Caroline except for giving Regine extra money for bailing Caroline out of one scrap or another. Then they were both quite cheered when they heard she had offered herself as a land-girl. 'Digging a few rows of potatoes might knock some sense into her silly head,' said Lionel one night as he sat comfortably by the little fire. 'I've been meaning to talk to you, Regine, for a while now . . . I'm over eighty, we've had four years of war, and I've been putting my affairs in order. I know some might think it odd, but recently I have been dreaming of Jennifer and I have a feeling I've not got long to go.'

Regine watched his beloved face and her eyes filled with tears. He was almost as hale and hearty as he'd been twenty years ago. They still made warm and gentle love from time to time. Indeed it was that which Lionel jokingly told her kept him so youthful. But she had noticed a certain weariness on his face.

She crossed the room to him and took his face in her hands. Gently they kissed each other. Each in their own way knew that this was good-bye. It could be weeks or months or even several years, but the good-bye had to be said because she would never be able to attend his death or dying. That night she held him close and felt the pain of the loss of this man who had rescued her and protected her so. Over the next few weeks, she watched him anxiously, but he seemed well.

When the end came a few months later, it was unexpected. He was thrown from his favourite horse one morning as he was riding round the estate. Usually he wore his riding hat, but this particular day he intended only to take a leisurely hack across the fields to see how the young pheasant were doing. The old horse was partially blind in one eye, and shied when frightened by a rabbit that leapt across the bridle path. Lionel, who had been lulled by the rambling gait of the old horse into fondly thinking of his early days of shooting game in exactly these woods, was thrown. He fell into a dense briar patch which hid a huge rock. He died in a few minutes, but not before he saw his Jennifer standing in front of him smiling at him with her arms outstretched. In spite of the head wound he was found with a beatific smile on his face.

The old horse went home after becoming impatient with his master, who lay so still in spite of the horse whinnying and nudging his protruding legs. As soon as he reached the stable, the head groom realized the old man must have been hurt. He called several of the stable lads and they followed the old horse back along the bridle path where they found Lionel. They unhinged a five-bar gate and carried their master home.

Bea was out with Emily attending first-aid courses. They had volunteered for ambulance duty. As soon as Bea got the phone message from the doctor, who had immediately been called, she froze. Often, during the last few years, she had imagined this moment, but when it came the pain was quite unexpected. She stood in the dingy green corridor for so long that Emily came out to find her. 'What's wrong, Bea? You look awful. What's happened?' She put her arms round her friend. 'You're freezing. Is it bad news?'

'My father . . . Lionel. He's dead.' Bea whispered the terrible words to Emily, almost in the hope that if they kept the news a secret between them it might not necessarily be true.

Then she drew herself up and squared her shoulders. 'Emily, will you come with me?' she said. They drove back to the manor without a word passing between them. There was no need for speech. They knew each other so well by now that their silent communication was sufficient for the moment. As the car drew up to the front door, the servants were waiting silently outside. As Bea walked through the little knot of people, she heard their subdued messages of sympathy. Lionel had always been popular with his servants. He had been fair and honourable, and they would all miss him. Emily followed Bea until they reached Lionel's bedroom. The doctor was waiting for her in the hall.

'There was nothing I could do, my dear. It was a blow to the head – he must have died instantly. It's the way he would have wanted to go.' He took Bea's hand in his. 'I've known you since you were a little girl, and your father's death will hit you hard. Come and see me if you find it unbearable. I have some sleeping pills here for you. They will help you get some rest.' He smiled at Emily and walked down the corridor. Thank goodness she has her friend, he thought as he left.

Bea took a deep breath and pushed the bedroom

door open. There he lay as though asleep, except for the bandage the doctor had wrapped around his head. His big strong hands were clasped as in prayer, and even in her grief Bea could see that he had died as though he had seen a miraculous vision.

She pulled a chair to the bedside and talked to him for many hours. All the love and all the passion she felt for him came pouring from her lips. She explained all the secret longings she had held inside herself for the need of his loving warm arms, which she had lost when she became an adolescent and their rough-and-tumble relationship had no longer seemed to him appropriate. She told him of her sorrow on the day when she was twelve years old and he pushed her off his knees and said she was too old for climbing on him like that. She reminded him of all their good times together, and she sorrowed as a daughter and a lover at losing her man.

Eventually Emily, who had waited patiently in the corridor, came into the room which by now was in darkness. She brought with her two candelabra which she put at the table beside Bea. Bea looked up at her friend in the moonlight that gently illuminated that corner of the room, and she smiled sadly. 'At least I have you,' she said.

'Always and forever,' said Emily. For the first time since they had met she bent over and gently kissed Bea on the forehead. The two women lit the candles, and then, after Bea had kissed her father on his stone-cold cheek, they left the room.

The next week went by in a daze for Bea. Emily moved into the house to help prepare for the funeral. Bea insisted it should be a quiet affair. But there were many in the county who loved Lionel, and there were also relatives as far afield as London who expected to attend.

When a local dignitary of the county died, the church bells were rung from one town to another to carry the news that something of note had occurred. Regine heard the bell-tolling from the small church in Uplyme – that particular slow mournful sound that meant a death within the community. She stopped stirring the soup and stood for a moment in silent prayer for the soul departed. Then the awful thought struck her that it could possibly be tolling for Lionel. 'Oh my God, I must find out,' she whispered to herself. She had never bothered with a telephone, so she had to get into her little Austin Seven which had replaced her pony and trap, and drive recklessly towards the vicarage. The vicar will know, she thought, but even as she drew up to the door she knew that Lionel was dead. She knocked at the door and the vicar saw a small, plump, grey-haired woman staring anxiously at him.

'Has someone died?' she asked him. She was wringing her hands and trying not to shake.

'Yes, my dear. Lionel Cavendish died falling from a horse. Did you know him?'

'Just slightly,' she said. 'Thank you.' She turned away and the tears came rolling down her cheeks. All the way back in the car she sobbed.

When she returned to the cottage she entered the little parlour and sat by the coal fire, gazing into the flames, feeling his absence, knowing that never again would he pull up outside the cottage in his latest car. She would never hear the squeak of the gate as he pushed it open, and she could never wait by the door for the moment when he opened it and she would fall into his arms and smell the warm male musky smell as he enveloped her in a great big hug.

She spent the night sitting in their favourite over-stuffed huge Victorian chair. In that chair they had shared their secrets, their fears, and often they had made love in it by the light of the fire. She would sit across his thighs, and she loved to watch the expression on his face in the firelight at the precise moment of his climax. He always expressed such primitive joy in his love-making that, when he finally stopped climaxing, his tenderness towards her was so touching that she felt treasured in his love. She remembered all those gold moments and sat half crying, half smiling till dawn. She then went to their bedroom and slept for a few hours.

* * *

The funeral was a dignified and formal event. Before they screwed the coffin lid down, Bea went into the room to see him for one last time. Death had cast a grey pallor on his skin, but he still looked peaceful. She saw the sudden flash of candle-light on his signet ring which he had always worn on his little finger. It seemed to her like an order from him to wear it always. She lifted his hand and slipped the ring off his little finger. Then she kissed him one last time and slipped the ring on to her wedding-ring finger.

The pall-bearers came in, and Bea joined Emily to take their places in the funeral cars. Bea insisted that Emily should sit with her in the chief mourners' car. The rest of the family bickered and quarrelled their way into all the other various allotted seats. The slow procession made its way to the Axminster Church which stood in the centre of the small country town. The church was full, and Bea felt numbed by the whole occasion. When they brought in the coffin and laid it on the trestle, she was amazed at how big the coffin looked. What a giant of a man he had really been. It was difficult for her to accept the solemnity of the occasion, and not to expect to hear his great booming laugh to come bellowing out of the wooden box.

There were so many mourners that no one really noticed a small, dumpy figure at the back of the church. When they laid the coffin to rest in the church-yard, sliding it gently down on long ropes until it finally settled on the dark warm earth, no one saw the same small figure standing a little way away absorbed in another grave stone. Once the earth covered the coffin, and the priest had said his usual ministering words, Emily gently pulled Bea away and they made their way back to the waiting cars and to the obligatory funeral feast with the family and friends.

Elizabeth was an invalid in a wheelchair by now. Her two children, a few years older than Bea, had done well for themselves. The boy was a stockbroker and Amelia married into a good family.

'She's "the Honorable" now,' Elizabeth said to Bea. Elizabeth gave a short self-conscious laugh and patted her hair. 'My goodness, Beatrice, whatever would have happened if Lionel had decided to let me take you on when you were a baby? You could have been married with children by now.'

Bea smiled at her aunt. 'It all worked out for the best, Aunt Elizabeth. My father would have been dreadfully lonely without my company and, as for marriage, it has never been a consideration of mine. I have yet to see a couple where I felt there was any equality between them. I do not have the nature to subject myself to the authority that the role of husband gives to a man. For the moment, we women have a great deal of freedom, because in times of war we are needed in public life. But as soon as the men are back, all provision for women in jobs are taken away and they are forced back into their homes.'

'But surely, Beatrice, you don't believe in all this new feminism nonsense,' said Elizabeth.

Other guests were getting impatient for Bea's time, so Bea just smiled and left Elizabeth in her wheelchair, and talked about her father with various people who had known him for so many years.

Most of the assembled company were quietly wondering what Bea would do now in this huge house all alone. Bea hadn't given the matter much thought. That night, as she stared out of the window of his bedroom still full of Lionel's things, Bea thought, I must consider my future. She opened the left-hand door of his big Edwardian cupboard and fingered his suits hanging in rows. Most of them were country tweed; only a few were for wearing to London on business. The shelves in the middle section held his shirts and underwear. He was an avid collector of socks. Bea smiled, remembering how every Christmas she would include a pair of socks in her pile of presents for him. His silver-backed brushes lay on the dressing table, and his stud-box, with his collection of shirt studs and cuff-links, stood beside them. She picked up the hair brush and smelled his familiar smell. In times to come, she would almost swear that she caught a glimpse of him as she turned a corner of a corridor, or walked into a room. It was never all of him, just a fleeting moment when she would see his back leaving a room or the back of his head.

Most of all she missed his nightly snoring. Lionel had always been a thunderous snorer and the noise had been her security on the nights he was home. Now all was silent, and the two women moved about the house putting things to right, after so many people had crowded in to give their condolences. Bea had decided to leave any plans for her future until the will was read, which was scheduled for the next week on a Wednesday.

Wednesday dawned bright and clear. The library of the house was arranged so that Bea and members of the family who had been notified that they had an inheritance were in the front row of chairs. Behind them sat the servants and various old retainers. Mr Rodgers, the family solicitor, arrived on time, and coffee was served with biscuits in the drawing-room.

It was not a particularly tense gathering because Lionel had always made it clear that mostly everything would go to his daughter. He had also notified all the old servants who might have feared his death that they would be given their cottages and that sufficient money would be invested on their behalf for a pension. So when the family and servants all sat together, the legacies, as they were read out, contained no surprises. Various nieces and nephews were left the odd hundred pounds, and the servants were relieved to hear it officially confirmed that their futures were secure.

Until the final codicil was read, Bea was really not listening. However, Mr Rodgers stopped reading for a few short moments and then he cleared his throat. It was enough to catch everyone's attention. He looked clearly embarrassed. ' "To my mistress, Regine, I leave the cottage at Number 1 Linden Grove near Uplyme in Devon, its contents, the car, and a sum of five thousand pounds a year for the rest of her natural life." '

There were little gasps and a shocked hum in the room. But it was Bea who terrified everyone by losing all control. Hysterically she rushed to the solicitor. 'It can't be true . . . it can't be true – he wouldn't do that to me.'

Mr Rodgers looked at her and said, 'I'm sorry you had to know about this distressing business at all, but you would have discovered the five thousand a year going to this certain woman when you examined the accounts. Yes, it is true. Your father has had a long liaison with a woman. I have seen her in order to advise her of the contents of the will. Please do not be too harsh with her. She has troubles of her own. Her daughter is pregnant and troublesome. I must also say that she is suffering very severely from the loss of your father. They did indeed love each other very much.'

For several days Bea was in shock. She lay in bed trying to rescue bits of fleeting memories that came and went. She had always accepted that his nights away from home were due to him visiting his cronies to play cards and to drink until the early hours of the morning. The feelings of betrayal were enormous – that he had deliberately misled her all her life, and had loved another woman while she had devoted her life to him – it was more than she could bear. At these moments she would be enveloped in a merciful swirling darkness. At times she raged against him and against the woman. Was the daughter his? Did she have an unknown sister? She cried bitterly for the loneliness of her childhood when all she had was the love of her father and her belief in their continued life together. She had always seen herself as his companion and had given her life to him, to save him (as she had believed) from a lonely bachelorhood.

All through these times Emily was there. She nursed Bea through bouts of anger and raging tantrums. She bore the pain of a woman losing a father and a lover, not only to death, but, worst of all, to another woman. It was many weeks before Bea returned to normal and before Emily was sure Bea would not go out of her mind.

'I must go and see this woman for myself,' she said to Emily. 'Will you come with me?'

'Do you think it's wise for me to be there? Of course I'll come, if it will make it easier for you, but why go and see her?'

'I want to know who my father loved – even as much as he loved me. I need to know if he had a child by her, if I have a half-sister. I just need to get everything sorted out in my head.'

'Well, we know the address. Let's send her a note and get one of the grooms to take it over, and ask to see her tomorrow at tea-time,' said Emily. 'We might as well get it over with.'

'You know, I think I'm going to sell the manor, Emily. Ever since I knew about this, I've felt as though the place has all been a lie.' Emily had the good sense not to argue, but to let her friend ramble on. 'I've spent too much of my life waiting in this house for him to come home. So much of it was very lonely. I feel I need to get away from under this shadow – to start life again as a person. You see, I don't really know who Bea is; I've always seen her as an extension of a man called "Lionel", my father.' Her eyes filled with tears.

Emily hugged her and said, 'Do what you think you must, Bea. Just wait a few weeks longer and you'll probably know what you really want. Bea, I realize that I've stayed with you for some time, but I must make my way back to my family. They need me, at their age.'

Bea looked at her, and said rather sharply, 'Emily, has it ever occurred to you that you have acted as chief cook and bottle-washer to them all your life, and if you dropped dead tomorrow they would hire a servant?'

Emily looked surprised for a moment. Then she said, 'I know the last few weeks have been awful for you, but for me it has been a revelation. I've only had you to look after, and all the rest of the work here has been done by servants. I've met lots of interesting people, and since we've been friends, I've even learned to drive a car. I have a lot to be grateful to you for, Bea.'

'I couldn't have managed without you,' said Bea. Linking arms they went down to dinner. The groom arrived back just as they had finished dinner with a note inviting them both to tea at Regine's cottage. Bea slept very badly that night and went into Emily's room, who stayed up until the early part of the morning talking to her.

All Wednesday morning, the two women busied themselves round the house. Promptly at three-fifteen they took the car over to Uplyme, and arrived at the door of the cottage at exactly four o'clock. Bea knocked, and Regine, who had been shaking with apprehension, opened the door. 'How good of you to come,' said Regine, and led them into her little parlour.

Bea was completely taken by surprise. She had expected some sort of exotic woman who would exude sexual charm. But here was a little plump woman in her late sixties, whose once Titian-red hair was now grey. She spoke with a soft Devon burr. 'Please sit down, and I'll get the teapot.'

Bea and Emily sat down by the fire. A small drop-leaf table had been laid with a traditional Devon cream tea. There were golden-brown muffins and a crystal bowl filled with clotted cream. By its side was a jar of home-made raspberry jam, and underneath the tea-trolley sat a magnificent lemon sponge cake. Regine came in carrying a large brown teapot. 'Your father loved this old pot,' she said to Bea. 'He never would let me throw it out – it came with this cottage.'

Regine spoke so normally of the man that Bea found herself relaxing. The woman could have been anyone from the village. It made the pain easier to bear to see that Regine did not treat her with any hostility. After Regine had poured the tea and they had made desultory conversation, Regine began to speak seriously to Bea. 'I'm sorry your father never told you about me. I feel I've known you all your life. In fact, I was all for telling you when you were older, but your father was a stubborn man and wouldn't change his mind.'

'But *why* didn't he tell me?' Bea interrupted.

'I honestly don't know,' Regine said. 'I often wonder if this way he kept both of us. He knew I would never leave him or do anything in my life but live for him. However, if you were told, you might well have gone off and made a life of your own. You must remember, dear, that most men are brought up to be very selfish.'

Bea nodded. 'It was selfish, but it's done now. Is your daughter his?'

'Yes,' said Regine. 'That's when I realized *I* was selfish. I had her for my insurance against loneliness, and both of us have paid the price. She is now thirty-four and pregnant. But she does not want to keep the child. I'm too old at sixty to cope with a new-born child, so I am thinking of having the baby adopted.'

'Where is your daughter now?' asked Emily.

'Caroline is a land girl. Look, that's her picture there.'

Bea got up and went over to the portrait on the writing-desk near the window. She took the frame in her hands and looked intently at the face that stared back at her. 'She doesn't look anything like him, does she?' she said to Regine.

'No, she takes after my side of the family.'

'Did he . . . I mean, did he love her?'

'No,' Regine shook her head. 'That was one of the problems for her. He paid very little attention to her at all.'

'Does she know about me?'

'No.' Again Regine shook her head. 'She had a hard time round here being a fatherless child. A bastard, she was called at school. No one knew anything about your father and myself. The few that guessed didn't gossip.'

'What will you do with your life now?' Bea asked.

The obvious loneliness of the older woman showed in her eyes. 'I'll see Caroline through her pregnancy and find a future for the child. No baby should have such a burden of selfishness and betrayal on its back. Then, I will see.' She had a faraway look in her eyes, and both women felt her pain which was almost unbearable to watch.

'We must go now,' Bea said. 'I want to thank you for being so honest. Please contact me if I can help you at all. I mean . . .' she looked a little embarrassed, '. . . if you need money or anything. Your legacy might take some time to clear. Just let me know.'

'Thank you,' said Regine. 'I'm glad to have met you. You are every bit as I imagined you to be.' They were moving towards the door when she took Bea's hand in hers. 'You always came first in his life, you know.'

'That's what was wrong,' said Bea. 'I can see that now. Thank you anyway.'

When she was outside the cottage, Bea took a deep breath and then looked round at the early autumn of the garden. Here her father had spent much of his life. The garden was suffused with sunshine. It was half-past five, and the shadows were beginning to lengthen on the lawn. At that time of the evening, the roses competed with the night-flowering stock to scent the air. The neat little garden seemed an oasis of peace and calm. There was a timelessness about the little secluded cottage that was very healing. 'I'm glad I've seen her,' she said to Emily.

Emily took her by the hand and led her to the car. 'Well, maybe it's settled you a bit, now that you've seen her in real life.'

'I'm surprised, you know. I'm not nearly as angry with her as I thought I would be. I suppose I had expected someone who was basically a manipulator. Actually, she looked more like a cook or a nanny – really, a comfortable sort of woman, not harmful or vicious.' Emily sighed. 'What are you thinking about?' asked Bea.

'Well, I was just wondering about the baby. It seems dreadful that a child will be born who is unwanted by anyone. At least you were wanted by your father, and Caroline was wanted by Regine. It must be awful to grow up and realize that no one wants you.' She stopped there, a bit afraid she had said too much. She looked sideways at Bea.

'I haven't really thought about the child as yet,' Bea said. 'I've been too taken up with his "other" life. But I will really have to come to some decision about whether or not I feel the child is my responsibility.'

They drove back to the manor, and as they turned the corner into the dirt road that led to the house Bea looked at the river running parallel to the road. She saw herself as a child playing happily in the reeds. She said to Emily, 'What ever happens, I don't think I can stay here. There are too many happy memories that have turned sour.'

Emily gave her hand a squeeze. 'I can understand that. Sleep on it – things have a way of resolving themselves by morning.'

By morning Bea knew she would take the child. She also knew she would be incapable of looking after the baby on her own. The most obvious solution occurred to Bea as she lay awake in the early hours of morning. 'Of course,' she said to herself. She closed her eyes and fell asleep. It was the first untroubled sleep she had had since her father's death.

She first broached the subject of the baby at breakfast. She and Emily sat in the rather gloomy dining-room at the large mahogany dining-table. Bea had just poured the tea when she looked at Emily and said, 'Emily, I thought about the baby all night. I've decided to keep it.'

'I knew you would. I couldn't see you letting anyone else having your niece or nephew. How do you propose to manage it?'

'Well,' said Bea, 'here's where you come in. I can't look after the baby myself. I've never been any good with small children. But you've always loved children . . . why don't I sell this place, and we find a house together and bring up the child?'

Emily's face was a picture of confusion and joy. 'You know, Bea, I've been waiting for you to ask me to live with you for weeks now. It's not just the baby. I feel as though we have always been together. It seems just natural to be in your company. I would love to bring up a child, and I would love to live with you.'

Both women looked at each other with affection. Bea, who usually found it so hard to show any emotion, said, 'At least something good has come out of all this rotten mess,' and she stretched out her hand and touched Emily's cheek gently.

The next few days were hectic. Emily's parents were partly relieved to hear of the arrangement, because they were free from the burden of supporting Emily, but they were also forced to look for a servant. It was not at all unusual for women to set up house together, as there were a large number of spinsters, thanks to two world wars. Bea made plans for the sale of the manor and decided to keep her present cook and a maid. The two women spent many happy hours looking round houses for sale, and when they saw the house on the moor they knew it would be their home.

Regine was very relieved that Bea had offered to take the baby. She promised Bea that she would never tell Caroline where the child was. If the child, at a later time, wanted to find her mother, Bea would tell the truth, but until that time she did not want to cope with Caroline coming in and out of the child's life. 'I'm afraid I feel the same about you,' Bea said to Regine.

'You don't have to worry about that,' Regine said. She was still in deep mourning. 'Caroline is expecting to give birth next week, and she plans to bring the baby here as soon as she is out of the hospital and then leave with some new man she has picked up. I will let you know immediately.'

'Thank you,' said Bea, and she and Emily went off to buy baby furniture for the child.

It never occurred to either of them that the baby would not be a girl. Fortunately, on a snowy February day, the news came that Caroline had given birth on the fourth of February to a baby girl weighing a healthy six pounds, eleven ounces. Regine asked Bea to be at the cottage to collect the baby at five o'clock on the evening of the nineteenth. Bea and Emily were thrilled. They spent hours thinking of names. Emily knitted like a demented spider, and Bea put finishing touches to the room. The cook bustled about, and the scullery maid smiled and clucked to herself. The house would soon be full with the sounds of a baby. The line outside would soon flap in the breeze with white nappies.

Of all of them, Emily knew Bea was the most apprehensive. Financially, the child would totally be Bea's commitment, because Emily would inherit only a small sum from her parents, but, emotionally, Bea had never had anything to do with babies. Without telling Bea, Emily had instructed the local kennels to find her an eight-week-old boxer bitch. 'In for a penny, in for a pound,' she said to herself a few days later when she went out to collect the dog.

That evening, amid barely stifled grins on the faces of the cook and the scullery maid, Emily put the carrying box with the puppy inside it under the dinner table. The puppy slept during the first course, but by the time they had finished their soup she woke up and whimpered. Bea looked around startled as the whimpering grew louder. She lifted up the lace tablecloth in alarm.

'Emily,' she said, 'what on earth is it?'

'Look and see,' said Emily, giggling with pleasure. She could see cook standing by the door.

Bea put the box on the table beside her and gently lifted out the tiny fat puppy. It was a large tummy on four little legs with a squashed-in black muzzle. Bea knew nothing of babies, but puppies she understood perfectly. She cuddled it under her chin, talking softly to it. The puppy yawned hugely in her face, and Bea laughed at the familiar indelicate smell of puppy breath. 'Emily, you shouldn't have,' she said. 'What shall we call her?'

'Well, you know, when I was going to get her, I thought about what a huge commitment we had made to the baby. I remembered the saying, "In for a penny, in for a pound" . . . what about calling her Penny?'

Bea laughed. 'That sounds fine.' So Penny it was. Like all puppies, within a few days she was waddling around the house chewing everything she could find. Having the puppy took away a lot of the tension leading up to the nineteenth, but finally the day came.

It was a bitterly cold day. The snow lay deep, and it was a hazardous drive to the little cottage. Bea had bought herself a shooting-break, and they brought extra heavy blankets to keep the little girl warm. When they pulled up at the cottage gate, the light was shining in the parlour. They knocked and entered at Regine's request. They were both a little taken aback at seeing how old Regine had become. She had lost an alarming amount of weight. She was sitting by the fire in the huge overstuffed Victorian chair, holding a little bundle wrapped in a rather grubby shawl. 'Caroline brought her a few hours ago.' Regine's eyes were swollen and red. 'She has Lionel's eyes. She looks so like him.'

Bea stood frozen in the middle of the room. Emily nudged her sharply. 'Pretend it's Penny. There's no difference, you know.'

Awkwardly Bea took the baby from Regine's arms. She unwrapped the shawl a little to see her face. The baby looked back at her with the same curiosity. She did indeed have Lionel's huge dark eyes, as well as his chin. Bea didn't know whether to laugh or to cry. To lose one beloved face and then to find the same features again caused a stirring of emotion in a woman who was not at all given to religious concepts of eternity. She looked at Emily. 'Look,' she said, uncovering the baby's legs. 'She has his huge feet.' She wrapped the baby again and handed her to Emily.

Regine's voice broke into their conversation. 'Please, Beatrice, could I ask you one last favour?'

'Of course you can.' Bea turned to look at her.

'Please call her Rachel. That was my mother's name. I would like to think of her with a bright future ahead of her.'

Bea and Emily looked at each other, and Bea said, 'What do you think, Emily? I really like that name.'

'By all means, let's call her Rachel.'

Regine smiled, and then she excused herself for not offering them a drink because, she said, she was very tired. Bea said they were anxious to get home anyway because of the snow. Both women said goodbye, and Regine took a last look at the now sleeping baby.

On the drive home Emily, who held the sleeping baby closely and warmly, said, 'You know, Bea, I'm worried about Regine.'

'I know, she looks awful. She doesn't seem to have anyone in the world to care for her. I'll ring the vicar in the morning and ask him to keep an eye on her.' But it was too late by morning.

Regine had long been planning to join Lionel. She had only put her original plan aside because she felt she must see to the future of the baby. With that assured, she took the bottle of pills that she had been saving for just this occasion. Without a fuss she made herself a cup of tea and went to their bedroom. She had a bath and put on the lace Victorian nightgown which he had given her one Christmas. They were very strong pills so she did not need many. She took the silver-framed picture of Lionel in his youth, and hugged it to her breast. That is how the vicar found her the next day. Regine looked perfectly happy and peaceful. She was where she wanted to be at last.

9

Charles hated the local primary school. It was a dingy little church school, and it stood in the middle of the town of Bridport. Most of the boys and girls were from the town, and they had all played in the streets together from their early days. They had gangs and alliances which excluded Charles because his mother had always considered the people of Bridport 'common'. Also, he was small for his age and very dark skinned, so he stood out as an object of curiosity among the blond, blue-eyed children from yeoman stock. He came home crying after the first day. His clothes were torn and his face scratched. His mother met him at the school-gate with Elizabeth in the Silver Cross pram.

'What ever happened to you?' she said angrily. 'Look at your clothes – torn to shreds. Stop snivelling. You're too old to cry like a baby.'

Charles, frightened of her, stopped crying and put away deep into his heart an urge to throw himself into her arms. There was little point because Julia now possessed a bony and unresponsive body. 'Jimmy O'Dwyer said I was a wog and they didn't want wogs at school so they beat me up. Him and three other boys.'

At this piece of news Julia's eyes snapped brown with temper. 'A wog? We'll see about this.' She pulled her hat down over her ears. 'Stay here and watch the pram,' she said, and she stalked through the children filing out of the school gates to find the headmaster. Mr Eccles was a very shy frightened little man. When Julia saw that she had someone in front of her whom she could bully, her manner changed instantly. 'Mr Eccles,

I have a matter to discuss with you concerning my son Charles. Charles Hunter.'

Mr Eccles looked even more nervous. 'I don't believe . . .' he began.

'No, no. You probably don't know him. He began school today. Well, I am very upset, Mr Eccles, because I know a man of your sensitivity and love of children would understand the pain that the poor little boy suffered when he was called . . .' here she dropped her head for even greater effect '. . . some of your boys called him a wog.'

At this Mr Eccles's eyes widened. 'Oh, how awful. I am sorry. What do you want to do about it?'

Julia thought, and then said she felt that the matter should be brought up at school assembly, where it should be made clear that Charles took after his mother's side of the family who were all Welsh, and that it was well known that the Welsh mountain people were all small and dark, and could sing like angels. 'As a matter of fact, Charles has an excellent voice,' she added.

Mr Eccles privately didn't think a lecture on Charles's ancestry would help at all in the playground. It sounded to him as if the boy had been brought up too soft and was now going to pay for it. But he smiled at Julia. 'I'll see that it is done, and I will ask his teacher to keep an eye on him.'

Julia returned to Charles and the pram well pleased with herself. She would invite Mr Eccles to tea, and in time he would become her ally in her bid to see that Charles would pass his eleven-plus and go on to grammar school.

Julia by now was in her late twenties, and William was just past thirty. He had been made an equal partner with Mr Fursey, who spent less and less of his time in the shop. This meant that William stayed later in the evening and worked all Saturday. This suited William, for as much as he felt he loved his family, he felt an outsider in the immaculate little house with the two quiet well-behaved children. He really saw very little of them except for a few hours at Sunday dinner when

Julia would carve the chicken and fill his plate first while he sat obediently at the end of the table. After the meal, he would help her wash up and then go off to his allotment. He would work there all hours, often coming in about eight or nine in the evening during the summer months.

Julia never minded. 'Marvellous cabbages this year,' said William. 'Here, look at those turnips.' He would show Julia whatever he had brought in for the kitchen with such pride that she would act enthusiastic over the vegetables to keep him happy.

Such a simple man – so easily pleased, she would think. Occasionally they would go out to the pictures, leaving the children in the charge of the old lady next door. Julia liked the American films full of dancing and romance, while William enjoyed Westerns. If a film bored William, he had a bad habit of laying his head back on the seat and snoring loudly.

During a particularly passionate film scene in their last outing to the cinema together, William had let out an unusually earth-shattering snore. 'Wake up!' Julia hissed at him, poking him in the ribs. 'Wake up, you fool!'

William, deeply asleep, felt the pain of her sharp elbow and jumped. 'What? What? What's the matter?' By this time the audience was hissing at them both. Julia fled in tears with William running along behind her.

'I'll never go to the cinema with you again,' she sobbed. 'How could you make such a fool of me?'

William was red-faced and embarrassed. For someone who so hates any form of romance at home, it seems crazy to me that we have to sit and watch it on a film, he thought. But he didn't say anything out loud, because he knew he was lucky to have Julia for a wife. She kept a perfect house and they had two beautiful children. It was just that there were days when the ache in his loins would become almost unbearable. Sometimes the sight of a full-breasted girl in his shop would excite him dreadfully, and he would feel disloyal. At home, even though they shared a bed, she very rarely allowed him to make love to her. When she did, he knew she disliked the whole event and he felt a brute for abusing her.

Many years later, he was to tell Charles on one of their embarrassing and infrequent talks together, 'You know, sex isn't all it's cracked up to be.' Charles just smiled a very superior smile. He knew all about sex by then.

'I expect you're right, Dad.' They walked home in silence, William feeling a bitter unfulfilled need to be able to talk to his son, and Charles thinking about Brenda Mason's warm wet vagina.

The bullying in the primary school playground continued unabated. Fortunately, Charles found a friend. He even looked foreign to Charles. 'Are you Welsh, too?' Charles asked him one day when he had sufficient courage to approach the boy.

'No, I'm a Jew.'

'What's that?' Charles was fascinated.

'It's a kind of religion. It's different to Protestant or Catholic . . . It's just different, that's all.'

Charles looked at him. 'What's your name?'

'Emmanuel. Most people call me Manny.'

'I'm Charles Hunter,' and he very formally (as he had been taught by his mother) shook hands with Manny. They soon became fast friends.

Julia was pleased to hear that Charles had made a friend, but was much less happy when she heard his name was 'Emmanuel Cohen'. 'What does his father do?' she asked Charles, looking for a loophole through which to declare the boy 'common' and unfit for Charles's company.

'I think he said he owns the men's outfitters called Bentley's in Bridport.'

'Well, maybe it's all right,' Julia said. 'Bring him for tea and we will see about it.'

Charles was relieved at the tea invitation, because it meant that there might be a chance he could have a friend of his own. At the moment, all he had was his sister who was two years younger and who was a proper little mother's girl. However, he had very little time to himself anyway. His mother made sure that when he came home from school he washed his hands and face, and then sat down to a cup of tea and cake. Once finished, he had to go up to his room and study. Even before he had attended the primary school, Julia had taught him to read and to write. In the early years, when there was little homework, she set him pages of sums and gave him subjects for essays. Her son, she was certain, was a genius, and one day the whole world would recognize that fact.

She was not nearly so bothered with Elizabeth. It was far more important that she learned to run the house, to cook, and to marry well. Mostly Elizabeth helped her mother. She was a cheerful sensible child. She recognized her mother's ambition and quick temper, and did little to explode it. She tried to have a relationship with her father but he was only comfortable while she was small enough to bounce on his knee. As soon as she left the toddler stage, he became remote and distant. She felt very hurt by his attitude, and would often ask Julia about this.

'Well, you see, Daddy came from a rather rough family. He doesn't really understand people like us. He's happiest in his garden. I know he's a very quiet man' (here, unmistakably, both children knew she meant dull and boring) 'but he's a good man. He loves his family, and he doesn't drink or go about with other women. Not like some men I know.' Here she would tighten her mouth and look sour. She was usually thinking about Uncle Max. By now they had a telephone, and the wires would hum almost daily concerning the goings on of Uncle Max.

Fortunately, when the day came for Manny and his mother to have tea, it all went very well. Mrs Cohen turned out to be very highly strung. She considered herself an intellectual. Julia was most impressed by her talk of the literature of the Dorset countryside. They got on famously. Ruth Cohen promised to give Julia a few books next time they met, and they both congratulated each other on their sons. The boys sat fairly silently together during the tea ritual.

'Milk first or after?' said Julia in her most social manner.

'Always after,' said Ruth.

Julia blushed furiously, but her admiration for Ruth knew no bounds. At last, here was someone she could learn from. After tea, the boys went upstairs to Charles's room. Manny sat on one of the twin beds, and looking round said, 'You keep a clean room.'

Charles laughed, 'Our house is always spotless. I bet my mum checks under the bed for dust every day of her life. Does yours do that?'

'No, but she goes on about art and literature all the time. She's always painting or repairing something. It bores Dad to death.'

Charles was faintly shocked that Manny would even appear to criticize his parents. But he felt a warm glow of affection for at least an honest discussion between friends. After that, they were almost inseparable.

They were both due to go to the local grammar school, and as they passed the age of nine the homework and the pressure grew enormous. The whole idea of the eleven-plus examination loomed like a huge cloud over the family. Manny was much brighter than Charles, so he did not feel the pressure so much. Charles's maths and Latin were poor, and Julia was in despair because it meant that he was fifth in the class instead of being first or even second at a pinch. She called on Mr Eccles who suggested a tutor. So, eventually, a huge gaunt man called Mr Fitch arrived.

He had grey Brylcreemed hair that clung to his pink scalp, and his long pink nose continuously dripped. He had a particularly disgusting habit of sniffing and then wiping his nose with the back of his hand in an upwards gesture that would expose his gaping clogged nostrils. Charles, who was fastidious to an extreme, found him revolting. When they shook hands on his first interview, Charles was upset by the moist soft lingering handshake, and he pulled his hand away sharply.

Julia, however, was delighted. Mr Fitch had actually been a teacher at *a public school*. 'Couldn't be bad,' she said later to a bemused William. William didn't mind the extra fees because they were now becoming quite well off.

In fact, William decided to buy a car the year that Charles was nine. He was glad he did, because at least father and son had an interest in common. It was a little black Morris Minor, and it was the joy of William's life. Now not only did he have the biggest and the most envied allotment in Bridport, but also he had a car upon which to lavish all his love and attention. He would spend hours polishing and waxing it. Then in the evening he would take Julia for a drive. Julia liked these occasions. Although they had little to discuss except the children and her family, she did enjoy driving through town and nodding to friends and acquaintances. The Hunters were going up in the world. She had her good friend Ruth who took her to small social coffee mornings, and Julia was slowly beginning to read the books she gave to her, most of which she privately considered incredibly tedious and long-winded, but it was necessary to keep up with the other ladies who seemed to have nothing else to do but lie around, read books, and discuss the cinema.

The tutoring sessions, which began a week after the first interview, were a source of constant alarm to Charles. Mr Fitch sat with Charles in the front parlour, which during those particular winter months had a fire especially laid by Julia. As soon as he arrived at four-thirty, Julia would give him tea and home-made cake. Fluttering round like an agitated sparrow, she would nervously flit from one subject to another in front of this great man who had taught at a famous public school and who could speak Latin. 'Is everything all right?' she would ask. 'Is the boy learning?'

'Everything is fine, Mrs Hunter. Just give me time. Together we'll get him through,' and he would give her a sly, conspiratorial, wolf-like grin.

Once Charles was settled in the parlour with Mr Fitch, she would shut the door firmly and retire to the kitchen with Elizabeth. Charles hated the whole business. As anxious as he was to get into the grammar school, the man made him feel so uncomfortable that he found it hard to concentrate. But he knew he had to get past that exam. He had often discussed it with Manny. They both hated Bridport. They were by now as ambitious for themselves as their mothers were for them. Manny wanted to make a lot of money. 'Probably on the stock market,' he said. 'I have an uncle who can help, but it means I have to go to university because I don't have the right connections to go straight into something like a family firm.'

'You're lucky you have anyone,' said Charles.

Both boys sounded more like little old men than like the ten-year-old children they really were. But their mothers gave them no time to play. If they failed to get to the grammar school, there was only the secondary modern – a school in theory designed to train unacademic children for a future on the shop floor in factories. In reality, however, these schools were dumping grounds. There were only a few places available at the grammar schools, and there were hundreds of children applying to get in. The thought of 'the secondary modern' was an absolute nightmare for Charles. It was with him every night for the three years preceding the exam.

What he did know was that Mr Fitch was a superb teacher, disgusting though he was. After half an hour sitting at the table by the fire, an unpleasant smell would begin to rise: the stench of Mr Fitch's unwashed body. He smoked incessantly, and the ash dripped down his pullover as the smoke blew around the room. For all these faults, though, he could get Charles to grasp the underlying concepts that lay behind maths and Latin. Charles had an excellent brain, but it was more retentive than creative, so that once shown an idea he could regurgitate information. Mr Fitch realized it would be a matter of twice-weekly drilling information into Charles's head. It was not difficult because Charles was anxious to learn. They had a whole year together before he was to take his eleven-plus.

'That is enough time,' said Mr Fitch. 'I've never had a pupil fail. Never.' He said this with such menace in his voice that Charles felt sure he was able to cause a boy to fail by merely laying a curse on him. He knew that Mr Fitch was his only hope.

It became obvious to Charles after the first four lessons that, from the beginning of the session, Mr Fitch's chair began imperceptibly to move closer and closer to Charles's chair. It was difficult at first to decide whether it was by design or accident. Mr Fitch was much given to rocking backwards and forwards in his chair, flinging his arms about when he was making a particularly pertinent point. So the chair took on a life of its own. Gradually, however, within the next half-hour, Charles would find Mr Fitch conversing volubly sitting thigh-to-thigh with Charles. This close physical contact made the boy very uncomfortable. Shuffling away was pointless; Mr Fitch just followed. Eventually Charles decided to put up with Mr Fitch's thigh pressed closely to his own.

What he was not prepared for, a few months before the exam, was to find Mr Fitch's large hand rubbing his knee. At first he thought Mr Fitch had just made a mistake and that his hand had strayed by accident from his own knee. Charles moved his knee away. Mr Fitch's hand shortly followed and continued to rub and knead his knee and upper thigh. Charles went bright red. Mr Fitch seemed not to have noticed his erring hand. He continued to read a passage from Virgil hunched over the text, sitting in a pool of light from a lamp over his shoulder.

Charles, after an initial panic, decided to ignore the hand. The lesson continued for the next twenty minutes with Mr Fitch calmly decoding Latin verse, and his hand gently and softly sliding up and down Charles's leg only to hesitate for a few seconds at the top of his thigh before moving down to the knee again. That night, after the lesson, he was particularly charming to Julia and very encouraging to Charles. 'I never fail my pupils, and they never fail me,' he said smiling at Charles. 'See you next week, my lad.'

Charles managed to smile back weakly. Julia saw Mr Fitch to the door. 'What a wonderful man,' she enthused. 'Mr Eccles tells me you moved up to second place. Wonderful! I'm so proud of you, Charles. One day, all our dreams will come true and we will have a big house . . .'

'Oh, Mother, not that again. You know you'll never get Dad away from his fruit and veg.'

'Well, if not for me, it will come true for you and Elizabeth.'

Charles was too distracted to want to indulge her in her dreams. He needed to think. He went upstairs to his bedroom and sat on his bed and stared at the wash-basin. He had very little knowledge of sex. He didn't actually know much of the details except for boys' talk in the lavatory, but he had always assumed that it occurred between boys and girls. However, Mr Fitch's hand had given him a certain sense of warmth in his groin. Much to his horror, he had to admit, after the first few minutes, he found it rather exciting. He did know about masturbation because he had discovered that joy for himself sometime ago. So, he now thought, that's what it's going to get to. He's going to do it to me.

He went downstairs to see if he could get his mother to understand and maybe have a word with Mr Fitch. Half-way down the stairs, he stopped. By now he knew his mother well enough to know that it was hopeless. In fact, he was so in tune with the way she thought that they often knew exactly what the other was thinking. She would merely refuse to believe him. Faced with a choice between her son failing to pass his eleven-plus or his being sexually abused by Mr Fitch for a matter of ten more lessons, Julia would choose the latter. She had an amoral quality that she passed on to her son. If something offended her, she merely rewrote the incident in her head and the new Julia-version became reality.

Charles sat in the dark of his room and thought exactly as his mother would think. If Mr Fitch was accused of sexually molesting him, Mr Fitch would leave and Charles would fail his exam. If it involved allowing Mr Fitch to play with him in order to get the exam, he would let him.

The next lesson was a maths lesson on a Tuesday. When Mr Fitch arrived, Charles was already waiting in the parlour. The man and the boy looked at each other. There was a silent agreement between the two of them that a deal had been struck. Mr Fitch sat down in the chair beside Charles. He made no attempt to sit at the other end of the table. Julia brought the tea in and put it down before him. If she noticed anything unusual about the tension in her son's face, she didn't care to register it.

'I'm off to see Ruth,' she said. 'Elizabeth will be late.'

They heard the door slam. Mr Fitch took his tea at a very leisurely pace. He drank noisily and spluttered cake into the text book. When he had finished, he wiped his mouth with the back of his hand, ignoring the napkin placed on the tray. 'Let's begin, Charles. Let me see ...' he rustled through several pages of Latin. 'Let's have a go at some declensions.'

A good half-hour went by and Charles began to relax. Apart from the feel of Mr Fitch's thigh close to his own, so far the hand had remained above the table. Charles began to feel that maybe nothing would happen. But he was shortly out of luck. In the middle of declining 'amo, amas, amat', he felt Mr Fitch's fingers on his knee, and he checked the table. There was indeed only one hand there and it was supporting Mr Fitch's head. Charles felt a peculiarly hypnotic rhythm as the hand sensuously rubbed his thigh, slowly getting as far as his fly buttons. This time, the fingers would rub his crotch and then return to the knee. All during this time, Mr Fitch recited Latin declensions, and Charles followed him. Their voices rose and fell in the quiet orderly room. They were watched only by the sombre gaze of a Victorian gentleman who hung in a frame over the tiled mantelpiece.

Charles felt a warm feeling of tension as an erection threatened to burst through his trousers. He found it more and more difficult to repeat after Mr Fitch. His voice rose and shook. Mr Fitch gave no indication that anything unusual was taking place.

Just at a point when Charles thought he would burst,

Mr Fitch removed his hand, closed the book, and said, 'We've worked hard enough for today. Let's stop and I'll see you next Thursday as usual.'

Charles had such a pain in his testicles that he was unable to stand up. 'I must just finish this,' he said. 'Do you mind seeing yourself to the door?'

'Not at all,' said Mr Fitch cheerfully, and he left.

As soon as Charles heard the gate squeak, he rushed up to the bathroom and masturbated furiously. It was his first significant climax of such intensity. He couldn't remember enjoying anything quite so much in his life. In fact, he realized he was quite looking forward to Thursday.

Thursday was slightly different, as it turned out. This time the lesson continued staidly until the last twenty minutes, by which time Charles was impatient and sexually aroused. When he felt the hand descend to his knee, he leaned back and prepared to enjoy himself. To his surprise, once the fingers had stirred him to bursting point, Mr Fitch said in a very business-like tone, 'Undo your trousers.'

Charles had been waiting for this moment, and took no time at all in undoing his buttons. Suddenly Mr Fitch's head disappeared under the lace table-cloth. Charles, with a sense of shock, realized that Mr Fitch was sucking his erection. He felt the man's lips and warm tongue pulling gently. The feeling was unimaginably pleasurable. He sat there in an ecstatic, coloured cloud of sensual pleasure until he exploded. His climax brought him quickly down to earth, and he was filled with an overwhelming sense of embarrassment. What on earth would Mr Fitch say? he wondered.

Mr Fitch said nothing. He removed his head from under the table, wiped his mouth with the back of his hand, adjusted his tie (which had moved round under his ear), and said as usual, 'We've worked hard enough today, Charles. Let's see . . . perhaps next time we will revise the Wars of the Gauls. See you next week. Don't worry – I can see myself out.'

Charles hurriedly did up his buttons and sat stunned on his chair. That was Charles's first sexual encounter with another human being.

During the weeks before the exam, he and Mr Fitch followed the same pattern at each lesson. Charles enjoyed it all very much indeed. He like his sexual needs to be met so immediately and without any effort on his part. In due course, he passed the eleven-plus much to Julia's delight.

At their last lesson, Mr Fitch shook Charles's hand, and said good-bye. Julia was wittering away as usual, but Charles looked at Mr Fitch with a new consciousness in his eyes. With it was a look of arrogance and power. Poor dirty old man, he thought. Off to find another young boy. He knew he would only have to suggest to lonely Mr Fitch that they meet again or that he should drop by for tea . . . but he didn't like the Mr Fitchs of this world. There were girls out there. Lots and lots of them. And he had some idea now of what to do.

10

It was a very different Charles who presented himself at the grammar school on the first day of the Christmas term. All summer long he had felt his freedom from study for the first time in years. He asked his father for a racing bike as a present for passing the exam. His father was glad to be of some use, and he bought his son a beautiful Raleigh racer. He told Manny, who promptly asked his mother for a bike. She was pleased that Manny also had passed, so she was willing to agree. The two boys took off on their bikes most days.

Julia found herself resenting her son's freedom. He was never there to talk to, and by now she found him rude and aggressive. 'Don't you think it would be nice if you had Sunday lunch with us occasionally instead of going off all day?' she asked him one morning.

'I really hate Sunday dinner, Mother. All you do is talk about the family. Elizabeth and Dad say nothing, and I get bored.' Charles looked at his mother through his lashes. Julia was cross. Usually he would back down when he saw her face freeze. This time, he thought, I'll try another tack. He put his arms around her and gave her a quick hug. 'Come on,' he said, giving her a peck on the cheek, 'let me go. I'll be in when I get to the grammar. It's just for this summer.'

Julia was so surprised and pleased with the hug and the kiss that she got all flustered and pink. 'Well, I don't know, Charles. I'll have to put it to your father. We do like to see something of you, but perhaps . . .' She looked at her son with a new respect. His intelligent brown eyes were laughing at her, and his smile was offering her a conscious collusion. It said: 'We both know it doesn't matter a damn what Dad thinks; it's all between you and me from now on.'

'Off you go,' she said. 'I've enough to do already.'

Charles walked slowly to the garage. That's the key to getting what I want, he thought. She's just like any other woman.

Julia went back to the kitchen sink with a tingling sense of a change in her life. Suddenly her young son was becoming a very attractive adolescent. She hummed to herself as she made lunch for William.

All summer long the two boys were like larks, wheeling and dipping their bikes through the Dorset countryside. They took hair-raising risks in the traffic. 'Look! No hands!' Charles would shout, diving down some precipitous lane. Manny, yelling and shrieking, would follow him. It seemed to Charles, free of Julia's clutches, that the whole world was bathed in a golden haze.

He and Manny would take their packed lunches to lie in the long green grass in the fields and talk incessantly. They mostly talked about sex. Charles never told Manny about Mr Fitch. Manny did tell him about the jerking-off circle in the boys' lavatory at school. It sounded such a good idea that they formed one of their own. 'Wow, Charles,' Manny said after the first time, 'you may be little, but you've sure got a big cock.'

'Do you think so?' said Charles looking down at it lying limply between his legs.

'Yeah,' said Manny. 'You know Danny Jones, Charles?'

'Yeah.'

'Well his measures nine inches, and he can shoot straight across the toilets.'

'No competition,' said Charles, stretching out in the grass. 'I bet I can outshoot anyone.'

'Remember Brenda Mason?'

'You mean the one with the big tits and lots of hair?'

'Yeah. Well she had it off with Danny.'

'Really?' Charles propped himself up on one elbow and looked at Manny. 'She's going to the grammar, isn't she?'

'Yes.'

'Well, she'll do for a start,' said Charles with a smirk.

The chemistry between mother and son changed that summer. She no longer treated him like a small boy to be scolded and nagged. Rather, she deferred to him, and when they were together there was a tension between them that they both silently acknowledged. 'What did you do today?' she would ask him as he came through the door.

'Nothing you'd approve of,' he'd say, winking at her. Julia would flush and look down at her hands.

When he was home, Charles, influenced by Ruth and encouraged by Manny who loved books, began to read. Julia began to talk to him about the books he was reading. They discovered a mutual love of poetry. One evening, two years after Charles had started the grammar school, they sat together at the kitchen table. Julia was peeling the potatoes for supper. Charles was reading *Romeo and Juliet*. He had recently become fascinated by Shakespeare's plays. He also found it very useful in chatting up girls, because, as he discovered, a sonnet or two whispered in the right tone of voice worked wonders at melting the female heart, to say nothing of covering the awkward moment between getting the jersey up and the bra undone.

'What are you reading?' Julia asked.

'Just some Shakespeare.' Charles was going out with Brenda the next day, and he was furiously committing relevant lines to his memory.

'Read some to me. I'm bored doing the potatoes.'

Charles began. ' "If I profane with my unworthiest hand this holy shrine, the gentle fine is this, – my lips, two blushing pilgrims, ready to stand to smooth that rough touch with a tender kiss." '

He looked up at Julia. She was gazing very steadily at him across the table. 'I'll play Juliet to your Romeo,' she said, and she stretched out her hand to take the book from him. ' "Good pilgrim, you do wrong your hand too much, which mannerly devotion shows in this; for saints have hands that pilgrims' hands do touch, and palm to palm is holy palmers' kiss." '

While she was reading, Charles looked at her face. It was young in the light of the late evening. She read that passage with such passion that Charles almost felt he knew the young Julia of many years ago who did dream of a lover.

She looked up again. 'Go on,' she said very intensely. 'Read some more.' She had stopped peeling the potatoes. There was a flush on her cheeks. She moved her chair round to his and they both bent over the book together.

Charles read on. ' "Have not saints lips, and holy palmers too?" '

' "Ay, pilgrim, lips that they must use in prayer," ' read Julia. There was a tremor in her voice. Charles, sitting next to her, smelled her warm, clean smell, and felt her sexual confusion in their relationship – half remembered, buried deeply, a memory of her warm breasts and giving nipples.

' "O, then, dear saint, let lips do what hands do," ' he said. His normally childish voice cracked to a lower register with the intensity of his demand.

Julia suddenly pulled herself together. 'Good heavens,' she said, 'You *are* growing up. Listen to you – your voice is about to break.'

'No it's not,' said Charles. 'Not for ages.' He suddenly felt confused, finding himself in the role of child again.

'What are you reading Shakespeare for? Is it for the new term?'

'No,' he said, feeling spiteful and sure of his power to hurt her. 'I'm seeing Brenda tomorrow, and I'm going to try it out on her.'

Now it was Julia's turn to look hurt. He watched her mouth become a thin line. 'That girl doesn't have a good reputation.'

'I know.' He looked down at her. 'That's why I'm taking her to the cinema.' He left the room before the guilt that always accompanied his hurting his mother arrived to sit heavily on his shoulder and ruin the rest of his evening.

Charles's grammar school years were hard and unrelenting. Julia would tolerate only Oxford or Cambridge as a university for her son. Charles's ambitions for himself surpassed even those of his mother, but either of those universities meant years dedicated to school work, for he knew two things were against him. The major problem was that he was not truly academically able to get there without a hideous struggle, and the second obstacle was that only a minute percentage of grammar-school boys would ever get into those bastions of privilege. The thought of failing himself was horrific, but the idea of failing his mother was unbearable. Julia helped him as much as she could. In fact, she virtually put herself through grammar school alongside her son.

William was left well in the background. Father and son had almost nothing to talk about except occasional conversations about cars. William resented his own position dreadfully, but he felt helpless. He believed he had so little to offer his wife. Charles with his books and long words could bring a smile to her face and a sparkle to her eye that he very rarely saw for himself. Fortunately, he was a man not much given to introspection.

He was too emotionally blunted by his early motherless upbringing even to notice quiet, shy Elizabeth who passed her eleven-plus without any fanfare or extra tutelage. 'Very good, dear,' was what Julia said when the letter arrived. Elizabeth didn't expect much more. She was enthralled by her glamorous, exciting older brother who was the pride of their family. She preferred his company to all other, and even if she did know the answer she would often ask him to help her with her maths just to gain a little of his time and attention.

If girls called for Charles, Julia very firmly told them that Charles had homework to do. She said it so fiercely that they didn't call again. 'I do think you should have a talk with Charles,' she said to William. 'I think you should tell him of the dangers . . . A lot of those girls that call here don't seem a nice sort at all.'

William looked very alarmed. 'Surely he'll pick it all up for himself at school,' he said. 'I did.'

'Yes, I know you did.' There was a bitter accusing note in her voice that William had not heard before.

'All right, all right,' he said hurriedly.

He found the subject impossible to broach, so he suggested to Charles that they attend a local football match together. Charles agreed to go, out of politeness, and also because he was hoping to broach the subject of a raise in pocket money. He hated the football match. He despised his father who shouted and roared with the crowd and sang *God Save the Queen* at the end, standing erect with tears in his eyes. 'Silly old fool,' Charles muttered to himself.

They walked home in silence. It was then that William told Charles that sex was not all that it was cracked up to be. Charles agreed, and asked for an extra ten shillings a week. William was so relieved to be able to report to Julia that his fatherly duty had been done, that he agreed without thinking about it. Charles wished he had asked for fifteen shillings. They both walked into the house well pleased with themselves that night.

The years while Charles was at the grammar school were the happiest of Julia's life. She had her son to herself, her daughter was no trouble to her, and William continued to prosper. When Charles was fifteen, they moved to a semi-detached house in a better neighbourhood. The house had three bedrooms, so Elizabeth had her own room as opposed to using the dining-room in the little bungalow. Julia's ambitions grew greater as she extended her circle to include parents she met through Charles's friends. She still saw Ruth to the exclusion of almost any other woman friend. They both enjoyed each other's company, while at the same time they were in fierce competition. Ruth's Manny was perfect, and was destined by his mother to run the World Bank. Julia had decided long ago that Charles would be a leading light in the London literary world. He would have a home where she could entertain for him. She always remembered the library at her old school with the sherry glasses. By now, William was such a respected member of the community and held such a good balance at the bank that they received a card from the bank manager signed by his own hand. It always took pride of place on the mantelpiece and she never failed to mention it to any passing visitor.

All holiday events meant Julia's family congregating in their various houses. They all bored Charles to death, especially Uncle Max. 'Had a girl yet?' he'd say raucously, thumping Charles on the back. 'Cheap and cheerful – that's what you want to look for.'

Charles would cringe looking at the man. As he grew older, Max grew fatter and louder. His wife looked sadder, and his children all twitched and failed their exams. It was just before Charles took his A-levels that he remarked to his mother, 'You know our lot, when they get together, look a lot like Manny's family when they all get together. In fact, Manny has an uncle who is just like Uncle Max – even down to all the gold jewellery. Have we any Jewish blood, Mother?'

Julia looked at him very angrily and said, 'Maybe way back, but *we* are Welsh.' That was the end of the subject for a long time.

11

It was six o'clock by the time Aunt Emily and Aunt Bea drove up to the school gates with Rachel. The sky was already dark, and the outline of the huge old Victorian building loomed over them in the night shadow. Rachel felt a mixture of fear and elation. She had prepared herself for boarding school by reading every available book on the subject. Her favourite was *The Naughtiest Girl in the School* which was full of midnight feasts and merry pranks. The girls all shared an intimate camaraderie quite unknown in Rachel's shut-off world.

Aunt Emily had spent hours talking over 'What it will be like'. It was all conjecture, as Aunt Emily had never been in a boarding-school in her life. Her only experience was when she and Aunt Bea had taken Rachel for her interview. 'The dormitories were nice, weren't they, dear?' she said to Rachel.

'I'll have lots of friends, won't I?'

'I expect so,' said Aunt Emily who was busy sewing Cash's name-tapes into Rachel's new clothes.

Rachel loved the piles of new clothes. She spent ages in front of the mirror adjusting her tie and gazing at the girl with the long, thick, shining hair, large serious brown eyes, and the rather wide mouth. The reflection stared solemnly back at her. She suddenly felt a lurch in the time-chart of her life. Everything was to change irrevocably forever. The warm cocoon that had surrounded her was broken, and she felt a shiver of apprehension. She ran to find Aunt Emily, and threw herself into her arms, bursting into tears. 'I don't want to leave you.'

Aunt Emily immediately started sobbing. 'It's only

for a short while. Half-term is only a few weeks away. I'll write to you every day.'

They were both hanging on to each other and sobbing on the front steps of St Anne's Convent when Bea finally decided to put an end to it all. 'Come along,' she said very firmly to Aunt Emily. 'Rachel, in you go – it's nearly suppertime. Don't be late.' Seeing how little and forlorn the child looked, she said, 'It'll be all right, Rachel. Believe me, once you settle down and make friends, you won't want to come home.'

'I want to go home now,' cried Rachel.

Aunt Bea gave her a big hug and said, 'We'll see how you feel after two weeks.'

They drove off down the drive and through the gates. They were silent on the way home. Rachel had been such an important part of both their lives that they knew it would be hard to fill the gap while she was away.

'I think we will have to tell her about how we got her,' said Emily. 'Most of the other children will all have families and fathers.'

'I've been thinking about that,' said Aunt Bea. 'Let's see if she asks during the holidays.'

After the first two weeks, Rachel was still in a state of shock. Apart from the noise of a hundred and twenty girls, there were seemingly endless rules to learn and to follow. 'Always curtsy to Reverend Mother' was the most sacred of all rules. Reverend Mother was a beautiful, serene-faced nun who glided down the corridors and was reputed to be so saintly that even the worst of the girls lowered their heads and bent their knees in veneration. 'No running in the corridors'; 'No talking in between classes' . . . the list was endless.

Rachel discovered that she was entitled to two baths a week, and also that she was allowed to change her white knickers twice a week, but the blue thick bloomers that went over them were to be changed only once a week. She mortified herself her first night in the dormitory by stripping off down to her vest and knickers. 'Rachel,' said Matron, who happened to be passing, 'don't be immodest.'

Rachel looked at her. The other girls, who were mostly unpacking their cupboards and side lockers, began to snigger.

'I'm sorry, Matron,' she said. 'I don't mean to be immodest; I'm just getting undressed.'

Matron, who turned out to be the only motherly woman in the school, softened. 'Get your dressing-gown, dear. Now, after you have removed your tunic, and before you remove your slip, you turn your back to the room and put the dressing-gown over your shoulders. You'll find it very easy if you just bend over a little. That way we preserve our modesty.'

'Thank you, Matron,' said Rachel, humiliated.

The dormitories were called after flowers. Rachel, being ten, was in a junior dormitory called 'Lilac' with a mixture of new girls and a few old-hands. At precisely eight o'clock each evening, Sister Vera, tall gaunt and unforgiving, stood by the light switch. 'Praise be Jesus Christ,' she called out. Snap, and the light went out. Rachel was almost too tired to cry until she heard rustled whispers: 'Rachel's immodest'; 'Rachel is immodest'; 'Rachel showed her bum'; followed by sniggers.

'Quiet, please,' ordered the dormitory prefect.

The room fell silent except for the sounds of the new girls stifling their sobs. Rachel cried and put a pillow over her face. 'Please, God. Let me go home,' she prayed.

Awful as it was, she did make a friend within the first few days. They were both in the same class, and the history teacher had been introducing the idea of a family tree. 'Now, here is Henry VIII. He had six wives. Let me see . . . we will put them down here.' She was busily drawing on the board. 'You see,' she said when she had finished. 'Now, at one glance you can see the whole panorama of this man's history. Let me see . . .' she said, looking round the classroom. 'Who shall we have to come up and draw their family tree for us?' She chose Rachel. Rachel found she was always being chosen out of groups because she was tall for her age. This time, it was definitely not to her advantage. She hung her head. 'Rachel, did you hear me?'

The history teacher was infamous for her bad temper. Rachel looked up and said, 'I don't have a family tree. I was given to my aunts when I was a baby.'

'Oh, I see, dear,' said the history teacher, and she immediately asked for a volunteer. A forest of arms shot up except for the girl sitting right in front of Rachel.

After class the girl in front turned round. 'My name,' she said, 'is Anna Compton, and I'm adopted.'

'Really?' said Rachel. 'Thank goodness I'm not the only one. Do you know who your mother and father were?'

'No. All I know is that the woman whom I call mother got me from the Catholic Adoption Agency in Knightsbridge. She said she felt I must have some good breeding because I came from a good address.'

Rachel looked at Anna. She looked more like a boy than a girl. Her hair was cropped; she had a thin face and a large nose. 'I have no idea even if I came from a place like that. I always felt I sort of happened . . .' said Rachel. 'How do you like this place?'

Anna shrugged. 'Well, it's a change from helping my mother run the stables. I'm here because I spent most of my time in the stables or out riding. She wants to make a girl out of me.' Anna looked suitably disgusted at the idea.

'Let's be friends,' said Rachel.

'Okay,' said Anna. For the first time in her life, Rachel had a friend.

The two of them were inseparable. Rachel was academically much more able than Anna, and she would help her with her homework. Anna was physically very strong and protected Rachel from the bullies in the school. Rachel, because of her isolated existence, had very little instinct for self-preservation. She had an innocent and trusting nature, whereas Anna, who grew up amongst the stable hands and the kennel maids, had very little faith in human nature.

Both girls settled into the severe routine school-life

that expected them to rise at 7.15 a.m., to strip their beds and fold their clothes, and to dress. They then went to mass for an hour, followed by a return to the dormitory where they made their beds and tidied their lockers. After breakfast they went to the gym for exercise, and then the morning classes began. Break at eleven. Lunch at one o'clock. Half an hour before afternoon classes, and then tea, followed by two and a half hours of study. Then a final recreation period, and then bed. Each event of the day was announced by the ringing of bells. Aside from when the bell rang and one hundred and twenty girls all moved in one direction or another, a silence lay over the whole school. Prison must be like this, Rachel thought as she moved silently up the corridor beside Anna. It seemed like a century passed before half-term. Rachel couldn't wait to see her aunts again.

Once home for the week of half-term, Rachel spent the first day lounging round the house loving the lack of restrictions, listening to Aunt Emily chattering about the vicar, the hydrangeas, and the problem getting a good replacement for Cook who was retiring. By the third day she lay in bed looking at the ceiling, and thought, I'm bored. She immediately felt guilty. She jumped out of bed and made for the kitchen. 'Here,' she said to Cook. 'Let me help you.'

Cook was happy enough to let her help make a pie for lunch. 'Like school, dear?'

'Yes and no,' said Rachel. 'I think the nicest thing about school is that I have a friend. Her name is Anna. Without her there, it would be horrible. Most of the girls are silly and giggle. Anna's not like that. We play horses most of the time . . .'

'Very good, dear,' interrupted Cook. 'Now go and call your aunts for lunch.'

Both young girls had promised each other that they would ask about their backgrounds when they were home. Wednesday lunch seemed an auspicious time. 'Aunt Bea,' Rachel asked, 'where did I come from?' Rachel had a disconcerting habit of getting straight to the point. She never lost it, however hard other people tried to teach her the niceties of manoeuvring a conversation.

Aunt Bea had been expecting the question. She put down her knife and fork, and said, 'Your mother was named Caroline. She couldn't keep you, and we wanted you, so she gave you to us.'

'Did she love me, Aunt Bea?'

There was a slight pause after which Aunt Bea said, 'Yes, dear. Very much indeed.' Then she picked up her knife and went on eating.

The thought of her real mother loving her made Rachel glow. It would have been nice to be a real family, she thought, but then she looked at the kind figures of her two aunts who so loved her, and said to herself, I'm lucky, really.

Aunt Emily smiled at her and said, 'It must be difficult for you with all those other girls at school who have mothers and fathers.'

'Not really. You see, I have Anna. She's my best friend . . .' And Rachel was off describing their make-believe horses. Both aunts were delighted. She was settled, and they quite understood her pleasure in returning to school with her tuck-box loaded with cakes and sweets.

Before Rachel returned to school, Aunt Bea took her aside and said, 'Rachel, do you know what menstruation is?'

'No, I don't.'

Aunt Bea explained without any fuss or bother. She was a country woman who had reared dogs all her life. 'Well, you see, when a bitch is in heat, she bleeds. You've seen our dogs bleed, haven't you?'

'Yes, all over the sofa,' said Rachel. 'I'm not going to do that, am I?'

'Of course not, darling. You just ask Matron for sanitary towels when you see some blood. Now,' she continued, 'when a bitch is in heat she bleeds – which means she can get pregnant – and then she can be mounted by a dog and have a litter of puppies. However, it's the other way round for humans. The female cannot conceive when she bleeds. But any time before or after that, she can.'

'Oh,' said Rachel. 'When is it going to happen?'

'Next year or so,' said Aunt Bea. 'I just thought I'd make it clear to you. I don't want you picking up a lot of rumours and nonsense.'

'Thank you, Aunt Bea,' Rachel said and thought, I must talk to Anna about this.

In fact, it was not until Rachel was twelve that she noticed a slight stain in her pants. 'I'd better tell Matron, I suppose,' she said to Anna.

'Oh God, I'll probably be next. I don't want periods, ever.'

'You can't have babies, you know, Anna, if you don't have periods,' said Rachel very seriously.

'I don't want babies.'

'Oh I do. I'd love to have lots and lots of children with a big house and dogs.'

'You'll have to have a man for all that,' said Anna.

'I hadn't really thought about a man. I mostly think about horses.'

'Well, you can't have babies without a man, and he has to make the money to keep you and all those children and dogs.'

'My aunts don't have a man – they manage all right.'

'I suppose my mother does too, but that's why we're the odd ones out, because our people don't have family.'

Rachel looked at her friend and said, 'I really don't mind any more. I've always felt odd, but now there is both of us I don't mind at all.'

12

It wasn't until the spring term when Rachel had her first period that she gave any serious thought to sex. Before then, she had shared discussions with Anna about sex, but mostly in the form of jokes. The nuns were savagely strict when it came to any information or discussion on the subject. The only mention in all the years Rachel was at the convent was when Arabella was caught in the school-grounds with a boy. The fact that she had encouraged a boy on to school property was sufficient grounds for her to be expelled.

'Sex, except for procreation,' lectured Reverend Mother, 'is a sin.'

The assembled girls lowered their heads in shame. Many of them thought of very little else in between attending confessions to relieve them of their guilt: 'Bless me, Father, for I have sinned.'

'How have you sinned, my child?'

'I had impure thoughts, Father.'

'Three "Hail Mary's" and an "Our Father".'

That's what Anna told Rachel (who was not a Catholic) she had to say. 'What sort of impure thoughts?' asked Rachel. Anna refused to elaborate.

By now the girls were in the senior school. They were mixing with much older girls, many of whom were taking A-levels. The senior school consisted of girls ranging from thirteen up to eighteen. Gradually, Rachel became aware of the senior girls around her. It was common practice to have a 'pash' on one of them. This usually meant that the younger girls wrote notes to their loved ones and slipped them under their pillows. Anna had a pash on Valerie who was a very attractive girl in the fifth form. Rachel found pashes all a bit odd. And Anna was getting very boring on her favourite subject, which was Valerie.

Every Wednesday night there was ballroom dancing. This regular event meant that all the girls changed from their uniforms and gathered together in the large ballroom, a room which must have once beheld grand dances and hunt balls. Now there was Mrs Malloy who pounded on the old Broadwood grand piano and shouted, 'Slow, quick, quick, slow . . . No, Virginia! Your right foot, use your right foot!'

There would be as many as fifty female couples swirling around the room at any one time, all muttering, 'Quick, quick, slow', for the quick-step, or 'One, two, three, hop', for the polka. But when it came time to waltz, a dreamy romantic mood would fall over the room. Arms about each other, breasts pressed together, the girls would move in languorous harmony. The air would be full of yearning.

Rachel found that Anna was more often partnering Valerie than herself. 'Why don't you dance with me any more?' she said one day to Anna.

'Well, uh, it's difficult.'

'What's difficult?' demanded Rachel. 'I don't see what's difficult about it.'

Rachel also had noticed that during break, and often at the weekend, Valerie would come into the dormitory and spend time with Anna. Looking round at other girls, Rachel saw many liaisons that were so close that they had no room for any outside relationships. It was not like the junior school, where 'best friends' met playing horses in the rhododendrons or challenging other make-believe horses to jumping events. Now here at the senior school girls walked with their arms round each other. Whispering secrets into each other's ears. Sly, knowing smiles. Giggles.

Rachel was much in demand for ballroom dancing because she was so tall that she could take the male lead. Occasionally she would feel her partner's disappointment that somehow she had failed to provide the proper amount of whatever it was that everyone else was feeling.

It continued to puzzle her until one day when she was awake very early in the morning. She had Blackie, the school cat, on her bed. She was lying on her back with the cat between her legs, and she was enjoying the sensation of the cat's loud purr vibrating against her thighs. The thought crossed her mind that it might feel even more pleasurable if she put the cat under the blankets and sheets, and she would be able to feel the cat's silky fur coat against her bare legs. The cat raised no objection to being moved, and within a few minutes she had settled down in the warm darkness.

Attracted by the slightly fishy smell of female sexuality, the cat began to lick Rachel's clitoris. For a moment Rachel had a flash of guilt, but as the cat continued to lick and to purr Rachel found she was unable to do anything except to lie there with her legs clenching and unclenching, until the rising tide of excitement let loose, and her whole body convulsed.

When it was over, she pushed the cat away. She took a surreptitious look around the room, and she could see that no one had seen what had happened. She sat up in bed to think about it all. 'So that,' she said to herself, 'is what it's all about.' Suddenly she was linked into the subterranean secret that bubbled away under the seemingly calm flow of convent life.

'Anna,' she said that morning, 'do you have impure thoughts about Valerie?'

Anna blushed furiously. 'Don't be silly, Rachel.'

But Rachel knew now. She watched the two girls pretend to wrestle. She watched them pause for breath, collapsed in each other's arms. She learned the game herself, and she flirted and teased. But most of all, she waited for the night-times when she would have a torch under her bedclothes, and with her fingers between her thighs she read books like *Gone with the Wind*, or historical novels full of panting women and domineering tyrannical men. The pages of these books were bent and torn. They were the staple diet of the whole school. Some of the girls saw themselves thrown across the saddle by some booted and spurred knight of the realm. Others saw themselves as the eternal temptress, like

Scarlett O'Hara. Rachel loved all those books, and the library was full of them. The librarian took each new romance into the library without giving it much thought. She never read them herself, and they all had nice, seemly jackets.

Time passed slowly. Anna came to stay with Rachel during a holiday, and was happy there. The two girls would go off and swim or walk for miles. By this time they were seriously considering their futures. Anna wanted to leave school and to go straight back to her mother's house where she would work with the dogs and the horses. Her mother was insisting she spend a year at a fashionable secretarial school.

Mrs Compton had even brought Anna over to see Aunt Bea and Aunt Emily to discuss the girls' future. All three women got on very well indeed. 'I'm worried, to be honest,' said Vera Compton. 'I've lived all my life alone. There were many of us without partners, and we had no choice because of the war. I consider myself fortunate to have been able to adopt Anna, but I would like to see her with a husband to look after her.'

Aunt Emily immediately agreed. 'I do think you're so right, dear. I had the good fortune to meet Bea, but if I hadn't, I hate to think what would have happened to me. I would probably have ended up a lady's companion like so many women of my age.'

Aunt Bea was not at all pleased by the turn of the conversation. 'Emily, we've brought Rachel up to consider herself an independent human being with a responsibility to her own future. I couldn't bear to think of her throwing it all away for some man. If she does want to get married, I hope she chooses somebody who will be at least mature enough to allow her an equal relationship. But unless she is economically independent, she cannot be anything other than in a begging position. At the moment she wants to go to university and then into teaching. I'm all for it.' Aunt Bea sat back. She was occasionally given to such outbursts. On matters of women's rights she held very strong views. She usually kept them to herself and just lectured Aunt Emily who would adjust her glasses and say, 'Yes, dear.'

Vera Compton looked at Aunt Bea and said, 'I don't think Anna can get into a university, but if she has a good secretarial college behind her, she can always get a job. It amazes me to think how things have changed over the years. I don't know about you, but the Second World War pushed so many women out into the world to take the place of absent men I feel that, unlike our mothers who meekly returned home after the First World War was all over, we stuck out our necks and said "No". So now our daughters have career opportunities that seemed unimaginable to us.'

Aunt Emily looked troubled. 'Don't you see any possibility of the future of family life as it is today? What about women who stay at home and want to have children?'

'I must admit, Emily,' said Aunt Bea, 'I've had a few qualms about Rachel's upbringing because she has had very little to do with men. Indeed, come to think of it, almost nothing at all. Going to university will be her first experience of a life that includes young men of her own age. I do hope she can cope with it.'

'Well,' said Emily, 'Rachel's such an honest soul, I think she'd tell us if she has problems.'

Rachel, honest as she was with her aunts, didn't feel she was able to tell them that she already had problems.

Every so often she would receive an invitation to a dance from one of the families in the area. She hated to go, but her aunts, fearful for her future if they made no effort at making her mix, made her. 'Only if Anna comes with me. I can't go on my own. I'd die.'

Emily would drive both the girls to the party. Anna would fidget and pull at her dress. 'Why can't girls wear trousers to parties?' she would demand in a belligerent voice.

'I have heard that they are beginning to in London,' said Aunt Emily placatingly.

'I can't see it ever happening in Devon,' complained Anna. 'I feel like a birthday cake. I'm only doing this to make my mother happy. If I go twice a year, she'll at least feel she's done her duty. God, this stuff itches.'

Rachel felt just as uncomfortable. She was horribly aware of her height and her big feet. Also, both of them had to use cotton-wool to pad out their bras. Rachel lived in fear that she might suddenly leak cotton-wool all over the dance floor.

This particular party made her especially nervous because Paul James would be there, and he had made a point of smiling at her at the last party. She felt excited by his interest, and intensely nervous of his glamorous image. Girls in the area all swooned over Paul, who was not only a handsome six-foot boy, but also the local doctor's son. Rachel couldn't think why he should find her at all interesting.

'Stop trying to lead,' he said when he first asked her to dance.

'I'm sorry,' she apologized humbly. It's all the other way round, she thought.

She had nothing to say to him because she was busy staying off his feet. 'I guess you don't dance much,' he said when he took her back to her chair.

She blushed furiously, feeling very humiliated. 'No, not really.'

He left her and she went to find Anna.

Anna always refused to dance with any of the boys. 'They're a really silly lot,' Anna said, looking over the assembled males all in dinner jackets and bow ties. 'Penguins. That's what they look like.'

'Oh, come on, Anna. They're not all dreadful,' said Rachel. They took up their position in the farthest corner of the room and began to compare notes.

'Look at Charlotte – she's falling out of her dress again,' said Anna. 'If I had a bust that size, I'd cut it off.'

Rachel was secretly envious of the girls who naturally filled out their dresses. She envied the way so many of them were able to joke and tease the boys. The girls looked very pretty in their long, off-the-shoulder dresses with matching stoles. The materials were taffeta and organdie with over-skirts made from layers and layers of net. Indeed, when the dance floor was full, the girls rotating slowly in the waltz looked like huge colourful poppies. The boys, awkward and perspiring in their black outfits, did their best to keep up with the exuberance of the girls.

Most of the boys carried hip-flasks in their pockets, and only really relaxed in the company of women when they had paid several visits to the lavatory to take a slug of brandy. 'Look at George. He's getting sloshed,' reported Anna, breaking into Rachel's reverie.

By now everyone was ready to dance the Highland reels. Rachel loved Scottish dancing. It always started with a 'Paul Jones'. Two rings formed with the girls on the inner ring, and boys on the outside. This way, everybody got a partner. Even Anna would join in. There would be much pushing and shoving on the outer ring as the boys tried to end up with the girl of their choice. Once the music stopped, whichever boy stood before Rachel danced all the reels with her.

'Just my luck,' Rachel muttered to herself. She saw Paul James a few feet away with a fluffy little girl who was gazing up at him with unhidden adoration. Rachel dutifully took her place next to her partner for the eightsome reel. He had fair, slicked-back hair. 'Brylcreem, I bet. And he'll smell of Old Spice.' She knew she was right on both counts when they linked arms.

However, she soon forgot her disappointment when the familiar sound of the bagpipes filled the room. Soon the boys were whooping and calling. Freed from the restraint of the more formal dances, somehow they were far more attractive. Finally, everyone came to an exhausted halt and went back to the sides of the room.

'It's this bloody dress,' said Anna. 'I've torn it again. I keep stepping on the ends of it.'

Rachel looked at her friend. 'Anna, don't you like boys, ever?'

'No. They're all stupid.'

Finally, the lights were dimmed and, to Rachel's surprise, Paul came across the room to her and said, 'Would you like to have the last waltz with me?'

'Uh, yes . . . Thank you,' she said shyly. No one had ever asked her for the last waltz. Usually she and Anna stole off to the cloakroom together. 'Do you mind awfully, Anna?'

'Of course not, you twit. Soppy music anyway.' And Anna stomped off to the ladies' cloakroom by herself. 'Bloody dance, bloody boys, bloody boring,' she muttered to herself to keep herself from crying. She was dreadfully hurt that Rachel should betray her and leave her to make the humiliating journey to the cloakroom alone. 'Just for bloody Paul,' she said.

'Are you all right, dear?' said Mrs Kinnard, the kindly hostess, as she saw Anna stomping up the hallway.

'No,' said Anna. 'I feel sick.'

'Oh dear. Here, let me help you.'

'I'm all right. I'm all right,' said Anna drawing away.

'I do hope it wasn't the food,' said Mrs Kinnard with awful visions of sixty cases of food-poisoning.

'No, it wasn't the food,' said Anna. 'It's just life.' She slammed the door to the cloakroom in the surprised woman's face. She threw herself down on a sofa piled high with coats. 'Why am I so different?' she muttered through clenched teeth. 'Even Rachel likes boys.' A dreadful pain formed in her heart. It was so painful she felt she would die. Lying there in the semi-dark she could just hear the strains of the waltz. 'I'll never, never go to a dance again,' she swore to herself.

Meanwhile, Rachel was thoroughly enjoying herself. Her feet seemed willing to cooperate, and her palms, for once, weren't sweaty. Paul pulled her close, and she was surprised to find that they fitted quite well together. 'Rachel,' he said, just as the music was about to stop.

She looked up at him. 'Yes?'

Paul very gently kissed her on her lips. 'Thank you,' he said.

Rachel was too surprised to say anything. It felt very nice indeed. She smiled at him. 'Thank you. I enjoyed it immensely . . . the dance, I mean,' she said suddenly flustered.

Paul laughed 'No doubt we'll dance again,' he said as he went off to join his friends.

'Had a good time, girls?' Aunt Emily said.

'Lovely,' said Rachel. Anna sat in a sullen silence all the way home.

She was staying the night with Rachel. As they both got ready for bed (still undressing in the same modest manner they had learned at the convent), Anna said, 'I'm never going to a dance again, you know, Rachel. I don't feel right in those places. I'm much happier at home among the horses. I'm going to tell Mother that she'll just have to forget a social life for me. I'm just not a sociable person.'

'Anna, you know I don't usually like those parties either, but I did enjoy dancing with Paul. He kissed me,' Rachel said with her eyes sparkling.

'I don't want to hear about it,' said Anna, and she got into bed and shut her eyes. I wish I were home with Mother, she thought sadly. I don't feel 'different' at home.

Rachel lay back in bed and thought about the kiss. It had felt gentle and warm and loving. The only kissing she'd ever read about had been in romantic books, and it all tended to be about passionate breathing and bruised lips. It never sounded very attractive to Rachel. But Paul's kiss had been totally different. She fell asleep reliving the last moments of the waltz and her first kiss.

Shortly after this party, the news came through that Rachel had passed her three A-levels, and with six O-levels already to her credit she was eligible to apply to various universities. Rather to her surprise, she found she'd taken to skulking around Gil's Café in Axminster hoping to see Paul. Gil's Café was a popular place for housewives, the retired, and young people to meet. There you could rest your feet after a day's shopping, or a boy could afford to buy a girl a cup of tea with cake or biscuits.

Rachel would sit by the window which looked out on to the street, and pretend to read a library book. Inwardly she scolded herself. 'You're a complete idiot. You're as silly as all those other girls.'

To her utter embarrassment, she found herself fantasizing about making love with Paul when she played with herself in bed at night. She still had a very hazy idea of how men and women made love, but as far as her fantasy of Paul went, it was usually fully clothed, lying in a soft bed, with their arms around each other. Just the moment of his mouth on hers sent her into transports of delight. Delicious tremors ran up and down her spine. Her feet tingled.

She was in the middle of yet another fantasy when she suddenly caught sight of Paul walking towards the café. She panicked and fled to the ladies' room. It was quite one thing to fantasize being in bed with Paul, but it seemed positively indecent to have borrowed him, so to speak, without his knowledge. She felt completely embarrassed. She washed her face and hands, and drew a deep breath. 'Don't be silly,' she told herself crossly, and she went back into the crowded café.

Paul was sitting with a girl at a table a few feet away from Rachel's. 'Hello,' he said as she passed by his table. 'What's happened to you? I haven't seen you for ages. Where have you been?'

'I've been filling in university applications and going for interviews.' Inwardly she was cursing the girl sitting at Paul's table. Stupid little idiot, she thought. Imagine looking like that. An awful pang went through her.

'This is Melissa,' said Paul. Melissa looked up at Rachel and smiled. Her teeth looked quite dingy against the white of her lipstick, and one of her false eyelashes was coming unstuck at the corner. However, her beehive hairdo stood piled high on her head, and she had the longest pair of winkle-pickers Rachel had ever seen. 'Melissa's from London,' Paul said.

'Oh,' said Rachel. 'How do you do?'

'Axminster is such a quiet town. What do you do here at night?' Melissa asked.

'Nothing,' said Rachel bitterly. 'Nothing at all. That's why we all leave.'

'I'm off to Oxford,' said Paul. 'Then I'll take over my father's practice.'

'I'd die if I had to live here,' said Melissa.

Rachel wasn't really listening to the girl chattering away about London. Obviously Rachel didn't expect to get into either Oxford or Cambridge. It was even harder for a girl to get into the few women's colleges than it was for men. So she wouldn't be going up to the university with Paul, and he looked very much attached to this Minnie Mouse. 'I must go now,' she said, collecting her books. 'See you some time.'

'Good luck,' said Paul.

Rachel caught the bus home and went to her room. She threw herself down on her bed, and she cried and cried. It was the first time she had ever cried over a boy.

A week later she heard she had been accepted by Exeter University. Both aunts were pleased. It was not too far away, and she would have other friends from school there as it was near St Anne's. She phoned Anna with the good news. 'Anna, I've got into Exeter.'

'Wonderful,' said Anna. 'I'm going to St James's Secretarial College in Bridport. I didn't want to go to the London one. I know I'll be much happier in the country. We won't be too far away from each other. I hate the idea of learning shorthand and typing, but Mother says I can always work for an animal organization – kennel maids don't get much money.'

'Paul's got a new girlfriend, Anna,' said Rachel, hoping to share some of her pain.

'Serves you right. I told you so.' Anna was delighted. 'Hope you're not still mooning about. Do you want to come over next weekend?'

'I'd love to,' said Rachel.

That night in bed she thought: Actually, it's really rather a relief not to have to stalk Axminster hoping against hope that I might bump into him. She had her own private revenge for his betrayal of her first kiss: she firmly crossed him off her list of lovers in her sexual fantasies, and returned to the trusted arms of Rhett Butler and the Arab sheikh who had a wonderful silken tent in the desert.

13

It was one of the bleakest moments of Charles's life when he had to face the fact that he had been rejected by both Oxford and Cambridge. He had never failed in his life before. His mother, as usual, refused to believe that her perfect son could possibly fail at anything. 'It has nothing to do with your academic ability, Charles. Everyone knows that rich people buy up all the places.' When Ruth 'phoned her with the news that Manny had been offered a place at Oxford, Julia had to sound thrilled. 'We decided,' she said, 'that we would prefer Charles to go to a local university. We feel he's a little young to be so far away.'

Charles felt very humiliated to hear his mother excusing his failure. 'You know, Charles,' she said when she had put the 'phone down, 'the Jews also always buy their way in.'

When Charles finally decided to go to Exeter, it was largely because of his mother's influence. She felt that, apart from Oxford or Cambridge, there was little difference between any of the other universities. She accompanied Charles for the interview. She liked Exeter. It was a rich city with a beautiful cathedral. She imagined herself having lunch with her son within the shadow of its walls. She immediately resolved to learn to drive.

Mother and son made plans all the way back in the train. Charles was planning the layout of his room. He had always wanted a bed on the floor and dark brown walls. His mother was planning his wardrobe. She saw him in check shirts, country tweeds, and V-neck sweaters. He saw himself in red silk pyjamas and, if he was lucky, underneath a variety of girls. He had heard they were a fast lot at Exeter. That's why he'd let his mother choose the place.

It took Charles about twenty minutes to realize that he was not going to be a large frog in a small puddle anymore. There were a few boys who looked as much out of place as he did: they were mostly farmers' sons. He walked through the long corridors of his college with his parents. The corridors were full of students rushing about greeting each other. The sound of hundreds of middle-class accents made Charles unbearably self-conscious. He was aware that his family spoke with a distinct Dorset accent, which had never been a problem before as he had grown up with the gently rolling sound all his life. Here suddenly was the sharp clipped sound of English spoken by machine-guns.

His Harris tweed jacket was a little too loud, coming as it did from Ruth's shop and not from a gentlemen's outfitter. Most of the students wore jeans with sweaters. William looked totally out of place. He wore his best suit which hung awkwardly from his huge frame. He hated cities at the best of times.

Only Julia was oblivious to it all. She had her very best grey coat on with its musquash collar. It was usually reserved for deaths in the family, but it seemed appropriate for this particular occasion. Eventually they found Charles's room. It was bare except for a single bed, a little desk, and a chair. Charles was thrilled with it. He had great plans for the room.

Julia looked at the bed and immediately the horrid thought crossed her mind that his bed would not be under her close supervision. 'I do hope you will work hard, Charles,' she said.

'Oh, I will.' He was anxious to get them off the university grounds and to get on with his life. He saw them into the car and waved as they drove off. He turned back to the building with a smile, eager to begin the plans he had for himself.

Driving home, Julia was very quiet. 'We'll miss the

boy,' said William, looking down at Julia.

'Yes,' she said. She kept her head down so he could not see the tears dripping on to her gloves.

William stared ahead of him. It was getting dark now. He felt a guilty sense of pleasure which he dared not admit. Now, surely, she would have more time for him.

When they got home, Julia made supper for her husband, her daughter, and herself.

'How did you leave him?' asked Elizabeth. 'Was he sad?'

William looked at his daughter. 'Charles never lets on. He looked to me as if he'll settle in all right.'

'Do you think I'll go there?' Elizabeth asked. 'My teacher says I'm clever enough.'

Julia looked up sharply. 'You'll not go to university. There's no need for a girl with your looks to do that.'

'But lots of girls are going to university now.'

'And they'll come to no good. Elizabeth, a man doesn't like a girl to be cleverer than he is. Mark my words. All those blue-stockings won't find a man to marry them. Then where will they be?'

Elizabeth was silent. She didn't have an answer to that. 'I would like to be a doctor,' she finally said.

'You can always marry one, dear,' was Julia's reply. She was a little sharp with Elizabeth because she had never considered that the girl, with her gentle nature and bland blue eyes, would want anything else out of life except a good marriage. Elizabeth dropped her head and didn't speak for the rest of the meal.

'William, tomorrow I want you to help me learn to drive.'

William looked startled. 'Learn to drive, Julia? You don't need to do that.'

'Yes, I do. The train's too inconvenient to Exeter, and you don't like going to the city. So I'll have to learn to drive if I'm to see anything at all of Charles.'

'He'll be home soon enough. Can't you let the boy be?' There was a note of irritation in William's voice. 'We've only been back a few hours, and you're already planning to go and see him. You'll have to let the boy go, you know, Julia. You can't keep him tied to your apron strings forever.'

Julia's mouth went into its usual thin line. 'A boy needs his mother 'til he has a good wife to look after him.' She got up and left the table. 'I don't feel well, William. I'm just going upstairs. Will you help Elizabeth with the washing up?' She made her way slowly up the stairs.

Once on the landing, she steeled herself to go into Charles's empty bedroom. Inside the room, she put on the little tablelamp she had given him as a Christmas present. The pain of losing him flooded over her. She gasped with the ache, and sat down on his bed. Then she swung her feet up and lay quite still. She closed her eyes and imagined him. She heard his laugh, his teasing voice: 'Oh, Mother . . .' But it was no good; he wasn't there. She opened her eyes and got to her feet. 'I'll change the sheets in the morning,' she said to herself. Later that night, with William snoring beside her, she lay with her back to him and cried silently into her pillow. She had never imagined it would hurt so much.

Charles spent his first night at Exeter talking to the boy from the room next to his. He was also new. 'What school did you go to?' he asked Charles.

Charles had been dreading this question. 'Don't think you'll have heard of it. It's a small private school in Dorset.'

'Oh. I'm from Sherborne.' He looked curiously at Charles. 'What are you reading?'

'English Literature.'

'Really? What do you want to do with it?'

Charles felt confused. He knew he was expected to do something glorious with his future. His mother's rambling dreams of his literary fame were not far from the truth. He was a secret, and melodramatic, scribbler. 'Well, I think I'll write.'

Michael looked impressed. 'I'm here because I was forced into it by my mother. She's as ambitious as hell for me. She wants me to be an architect so that I can design buildings and dedicate them to her. I don't want to be here at all. Three boring years cooped up in a dump like Exeter.'

Charles was astonished. Firstly that Michael should be so irreverent about his mother, and secondly, even though Exeter was no Oxford or Cambridge, Charles was still amazed to find himself at any university at all. He liked Michael. He realized quickly that he had a lot to learn from him. First and foremost, Charles resolved to lose his Dorset accent. 'Come on,' said Michael. 'Let's go down to the dining-room and get something to eat. Then we can check out the local pubs.'

A few hours later they were settled at a table in the Crown and Goat. Charles was feeling a little tipsy after a couple of pints of bitter. There had been no drinking in his house except on special occasions. 'What do you really want to do, Michael?' he asked.

Michael laughed. 'Chase pussy, I guess . . . there's plenty of talent here. I'll spend three years here getting an arts degree, then perhaps I'll go to the AA in London to study architecture or maybe I'll join the Foreign Office. By then I should inherit from my father's will. He didn't trust me, so when he popped off he left all my loot in trust until I'm twenty-five. Cunning old sod, but at least I got a car out of it now. Then, well I expect I'll marry some beautiful, ice-cold virgin who will bear me lots of brats, and I'll stay away from home as much as possible. And if I do have to see them, it will be in the library before dinner.'

'You're not very romantic,' said Charles.

'It isn't a very romantic business.' He grinned at Charles. 'Listen, you have to sort out what life is really like . . . Have your people got any money?'

'No,' said Charles in a sudden burst of honesty. 'I'm the first member of the family ever to go to university. My father's the local chemist in Bridport. My mother sounds a bit like yours. She expects me to be rich and famous, though how I'm supposed to do it without any family background or money, I really don't know.'

'You'll have to find a girl with money, and you can always invent a background. Don't worry about it.

Let's both agree to have a bloody good time for the next three years.'

They both drank to that, and to several other toasts, and staggered back to their rooms. Charles had a fleeting moment of home-sickness as he was kneeling on the cold tile floor vomiting up all the beer he'd drunk that evening. At least if he had been home, his mother would have been there to hold his head. Tears of self-pity filled his eyes.

Michael introduced Charles to several Sherborne boys who all seemed a cheerful Rabelaisian lot. They adopted Charles into the group, and within a few months Charles had transformed himself into an old Sherbernian. He was acutely aware that he lacked a lot of their social graces. He couldn't ride, shoot, or play tennis like the others. The Grammar had laid little emphasis on sports, and he had never been attracted to football, so he decided to investigate the university's newspaper and writing group. To his delight, he found he had quite a considerable talent. From then on, he represented himself as the artistic brooding type, and took to wearing brightly coloured shirts. The girls told him he was sensitive and 'different from all the rest'. He took to carrying around books on existentialism.

He opened an account at the local gentlemen's outfitters, and threw out most of his wardrobe. With Michael's help, he chose a more suitable collection of clothes. It cost an awful lot of money, but he felt sure Julia would understand. Very soon Charles was having the time of his life.

There were many parties, and he learned to dance almost overnight. Julia had always considered 'rock and roll' common, so it had never been allowed to be played at home. The grammar school had dances, but Julia had not encouraged Charles to attend. 'Plenty of time for that later,' she would say. Well, she was certainly proved to be right.

The first time Charles managed to smuggle a girl into his room, he had a little difficulty achieving an erection. He had always been forced to make love to girls either in a field or – if they had a car – in the back seat.

Sex, as far as he was concerned, was a gymnastic event which involved the minimum removal of clothes, and the maximum amount of effort to avoid the cold, stinging nettles or a watchful policeman.

Now that he had Pamela in bed with no clothes on, he felt almost virginal. 'You're not a virgin, are you?' he asked anxiously.

'Of course not, you twit,' she said.

'Have you done this a lot, then?'

'Enough,' she said. 'Get on with it, will you? I'm getting bored.' She lay back with her legs wide apart.

'I want to talk for a bit,' said Charles desperately. He could feel absolutely no sensation from the waist down. Somehow, Julia's presence was all around him. He could feel her disapproval. Charles tried to put his arms around Pamela's shoulders and pull her towards him, hoping that the embrace might excite him. But Pamela was petulant.

'I've got to be in by 11.30. What's the matter with you? Can't you get it up?' Charles, deeply ashamed, nodded. He couldn't bring himself to speak. 'Here,' she said, gripping his flaccid penis. 'This'll get you going.' She began a vigorous rubbing motion.

Much to his relief, it seemed to do the trick. He managed to pull a sheath on and plunge into her before he climaxed. But at the peak of his orgasm, he saw Julia's anguished face. 'Oh no,' he groaned. Pamela was well pleased with herself. She took the groan as a credit to her dexterity.

'You could be quite good,' she said generously to Charles. 'You just need a bit more practice.'

'Thank you,' said Charles humbly.

The next day Michael said, 'How'd she ride?'

'Nicely,' said Charles. 'Nicely.'

'You see, the thing is, most of these girls come across because they're afraid that as blue-stockings they're undesirable. They've all got pretty sisters at home waiting to snap up a man and get married. The girls who come here to get married don't sleep around.'

'What about Pamela, then? She doesn't seem particularly a blue-stocking *or* the marrying kind,' said

Charles, who had been laid so low by his experience of her that he could barely look her in the face.

Michael laughed. 'She's one of the man-eaters. They're women who have all sorts of ideas about being sexually free, like men. She even pays for her half of the meal. There are not too many of them around, fortunately.'

'They should wear labels round their necks,' said Charles bitterly. He tended to make sure he got into the girl's bed rather than his own after that experience.

14

Julia was over-awed by her son when she collected him at the station in Bridport. She had her L-plates on the little Morris Minor, and William was sitting beside her. He very gratefully gave up his front seat to his son. 'It's not right to be seen by people in town with the wife at the wheel,' he muttered to himself as he scrunched himself into the back. Neither Charles nor Julia was listening to him.

Charles was gabbling away to his mother about his new friends and the places he'd been. Julia kept looking at him surreptitiously as she drove him home. It's done wonders for him, she thought. He's got such confidence . . . it's made a gentleman of him. She felt very pleased with herself. The pain had been worth it, and she had him all to herself for the next few weeks of Christmas break.

There was quite a scene about the bill from the gentlemen's outfitters. Surprisingly enough, it was Julia who took umbrage.

'How could you spend so much money? Your father works day and night to keep you there.' She was furious.

'But you don't understand, Mother. I have to be like the others. They just don't wear clothes from a place like Bentley's. I stuck out like a sore thumb.'

'So you're saying my choice wasn't good enough for you then? Suddenly we're . . .'

'Leave him alone, Julia,' interrupted William. 'If he needed the clothes, he needed them. If you send him away to make a gentleman of him, then you must expect him to have to keep up with the others.'

Charles was surprised and pleased. His father very rarely took his side. Julia was not going to give up. 'How much did you pay for that jacket?' she demanded, pointing at his fleece-lined bomber jacket.

'It was on sale for ten pounds,' he said, lying with practised ease. He had always lied instinctively to Julia. Unlike Elizabeth, who told the truth and faced her mother's awful silent rages, Charles always managed to get away with everything by developing a scant regard for the truth.

'I think that's quite reasonable,' said his father. 'I remember those jackets during the war . . .' William began enthusiastically.

'A war you weren't part of' snapped Julia. William subsided, hurt.

Charles looked at Julia and then at his father. 'Let's go to the pub for a drink, Dad.'

William immediately brightened up. 'Good idea,' he said.

As they left the house, Julia was mounting the stairs, a pudding basin in one hand and a wet towel in the other. 'I'm going upstairs to lie down for a while,' she said to William.

'I'll stay if you're not well,' William said.

'Come on, Dad. She'll be all right. She'll be fine by the time we're back.'

The habit of a lifetime was too much for William. 'We'll go another time, son. I can't leave your mother when she's like this.'

'She's always like that when she doesn't get her own way. She wouldn't be like that if you'd stand up to her occasionally. I sometimes think you're not a man, you're a mouse.' All those years as a small boy rose up to haunt him. All the unfair and unjust times he had been a victim of his mother's totally unpredictable moods. His father was usually there, but always in the background, a silent presence who never came to his defence. Charles slammed out of the house.

William shook his head. Of course Julia was sometimes a little hasty, but she was usually right. He went up to see how she was. When she saw his face peer around the door, she kept her eyes shut, but she could not conceal a thin smile of triumph. 'All right, dear?' said William.

'A little better, thank you. I'll be down in a moment to make tea. I thought you might like a crab salad.' William was relieved. It was his favourite dish. She had obviously forgiven him.

Charles strode into the local pub, and he was soon joined by several ex-school mates who were working locally. There was a new and sultry-looking barmaid, he noticed. It was a little awkward for the first half an hour, as it became obvious to erstwhile friends that not only did he look different, but he had also acquired a 'posh' accent. Charles took the teasing gracefully. He had anticipated their reaction and didn't mind at all. At least I'm not trapped in a dump like Bridport, he thought.

At closing time he went up to the bar and offered to walk the barmaid home. 'Sure,' she said. 'But I only live around the corner.'

'Then maybe we'll have to walk a little farther,' he said smoothly. On the way out, he noticed she wore a wedding ring as he helped her on with her coat. 'Are you married, then?' he asked, surprised.

'He's away in the merchant,' she said unconcernedly. Charles felt a sense of excitement. He'd never had a married woman. He put his arm round her shoulder, and she snuggled into his side. 'Where shall we go?' she said. 'I've got kids at home.'

It suddenly dawned on Charles that she was a prostitute. Wait 'til I tell Michael, he thought. 'Where do you usually go?' he said, sounding as casual as possible.

'Either to the punter's place or behind the bus station. Your first time?' she asked curiously.

'Certainly not,' said Charles.

Later, when he had her up against the wall in the back of the bus station, he was fumbling for a French letter. 'You don't need one of those, silly. I'm a married woman. I've got a cap.' She was surprised at the savagery of his attack. She'd had some rough ones in her time. He's an angry boy, she thought. One day he'll do some woman a lot of damage.

When he was spent, Charles felt both elated and disgusted. Best ever, he thought, but as he looked around, he could see grubby evidence of other assignations. 'I'll take you home,' he said.

'That's nice of you.' She chatted to him all the way back to her little terrace house. As she put the key in the lock, Charles saw the curtain in the next-door window twitch. Oh God, he thought, I hope she doesn't know Mother.

It was when he woke up in the morning that he suddenly was seized by an absolute sense of panic. He had not used a sheath and he had been with a prostitute. He was probably diseased. When he had his first morning pee, he felt sure he could feel a slight tingle. He spent the rest of the day running to the bathroom to check. By evening, it definitely felt painful to pee, and the tip of his penis looked a different colour.

He lay awake all night in a state of shock. What was he going to say to his mother? He could tell his father, but William would just tell her anyway. He could go to the doctor, but he'd never been on his own; he had always been accompanied by Julia. By day-break he knew he would have to tell her at least a version of his problem.

She was furious.

'How could you, Charles? How disgusting . . . I'll ring Dr Evans right away. Meanwhile,' she said, 'don't sit on any of the chairs in this house without covering them with newspaper first.'

'Please, Mother. Just make the appointment. Don't come with me. I can go by myself . . . please.'

'Don't be silly, Charles. Of course I'm going with you. I obviously can't trust you out of my sight.' He heard her make the appointment. She then telephoned William at the chemist shop. 'Bring the car back, William. I need you to drive Charles to the doctor.'

When William arrived, Julia jammed her felt hat over her ear and frog-marched Charles to the car. She put a huge wad of newspaper on the back seat and pointed to it. 'You sit there,' she said. 'And mind you stand in the surgery until we are called in by the doctor.' All the way there, she regaled Charles with the hideousness of his behaviour. When it was Charles's turn to go into the surgery, his mother was right behind him. 'I want you to know, Dr Evans, that we're not that sort of people.' She was in a state of livid mortification. It had taken years before Dr Evans had deigned to return her Christmas cards.

Dr Evans looked at Charles, and he realized from the boy's miserable face that it was probably some sexual misdeed. 'Charles is perfectly able to consult with me alone,' he said. 'He's an adult now.' Poor boy, he thought. All his life she made his bowels her business, and now she's getting possessive about his penis. He got up and gave Julia a gentle shove in the back that propelled her out the door of the surgery. 'Now,' he said, turning to Charles, 'what's the problem?'

'I have . . . um . . . I have this pain. It sort of hurts when I . . .'

'Pee?' interjected the doctor helpfully. Charles looked down and nodded. 'Well, let's get down to business. What have you been doing with it?'

Charles hung his head even lower. 'I had intercourse with a woman.'

'Yes,' said the doctor encouragingly.

Charles got a bit braver. 'I . . . um . . . well, she had a cap. So I didn't use a sheath, so I might be infected.'

'Any reason why? Was it a local girl?'

'Well, not exactly. She works at the bar at my local. She's a prostitute.' Suddenly, the enormous consequence of oozing pus and possibly dying of syphilis was too much for Charles and he burst into tears.

'Come on, now. It's probably nothing. Let's have a look.' Charles couldn't wait to be reassured. In fact, he would have given the damn thing away at that moment. The doctor picked up Charles's penis with a pair of disinfected tongs.

Never again. Never, never again, Charles swore to himself as he saw his prize possession dangling limply from the tongs.

'Hmmm . . . looks a little red,' said the doctor. 'But there's no infection. I expect you went to it a little too hard. Too much youthful enthusiasm. Still, I'll take a swab to make sure, and you'll know the result in a few days. I don't think you've got much to worry about. Take my advice, lad. Always use a condom.'

'I will. Oh I will,' said Charles fervently.

'Well? What did he say?' probed Julia as soon as they were in the car.

'That's my business,' said Charles. 'It's between me and Dr Evans.'

Julia was furious all day. 'How dare he think he doesn't have to tell me,' she muttered to herself while she cooked lunch. During the meal, everyone was silent. Mercifully, Elizabeth was away at school.

'Charles, I want to know what the doctor said.' She glared at him across the table.

'You don't have a right to know about my private life. That's my business now. Even the doctor told you to get out. Don't you see. You don't own me.' Charles's voice rose.

'I'm your mother. I nearly died giving birth to you . . . I . . .'

'All right. All right. I'll tell you. There's nothing wrong with me. I just fucked her too hard. That's what's wrong.'

Julia's mouth dropped open. She was struggling for breath. William said, 'You don't speak to your mother like that. I won't have her upset like this.'

'I can see it will take a little time for you to regain your self-control, Mother, so I shall leave you for a while.' He got up and left the room. It was a nice day, so he thought he'd take a bike ride to Charmouth and let the sea blow away some of the tension. Riding along, he felt pleased with himself. He'd handled it all quite well. Next time, he'd try not to shout. It was more effective to be cold. He practised as he pedalled.

That night, when he was in bed reading, she knocked on the door. 'May I come in?' she said with a new-found humility. She sat down beside him. 'Charles,' she said, 'I'm sorry I was so angry. I do realize you have got to grow up and I am too possessive. Please believe me. I do it because I love you and I want what's best for you.'

Charles sat upright and put his arms around her. A familiar sense of warmth enveloped them both. He felt the usual confused mixture of guilt and love wash over him. He hugged her. 'I know, Mother. I'm sorry I shouted at you.' They kissed each other good-night.

On her way out, Julia picked up his dirty clothes from the floor. 'Do you want to read some more or shall I put out the light?'

'I'll read a bit,' he said.

Julia went to her room. 'He's becoming a fine young man,' she said to William.

'But I thought you said . . .' William looked bewildered.

'I know, I know. It's just growing pains, that's all,' said Julia. She fell asleep. Charles with a prostitute . . . I wonder who it was? was her last thought before she drifted off.

The result came the day before Charles was due to go back to university. 'Charles,' boomed Dr Evans's voice down the 'phone, 'good news for you. Just as I thought. The results are negative.'

'Thank you, Dr Evans. Thank you,' said a much-relieved Charles. Even though the doctor had reassured him that there was no infection, Charles had been aware that he felt absolutely no sexual urges at all. But as soon as he put the 'phone down, he felt a familiar tension in his testicles.

The next day he said good-bye to the family at the station. His mother gave him a long hug, which was unlike her. He returned the embrace a little embarrassed and resentful. His father slipped him an extra fiver without his mother seeing, because she held the purse-strings, and didn't like the children to have any more than the allowance she had set for them. Father and son grinned at each other. 'Have a good time, lad,' William said. The train pulled out of the station, and Charles waved to his mother who stood stock-still until he was out of sight.

The first and second years at the university passed very quickly. Charles went home several times with Michael and quickly took to the elegant Georgian house. He loved the luxurious old Axminster carpets and the shine of the parquet floors. Michael's mother Gloria seemed incredibly sophisticated to Charles. She was a tiny, delicate, blonde woman. She bubbled with laughter, and seemed abreast of the latest fashion. 'You could be Michael's sister instead of his mother,' Charles said to her one evening.

He was feeling very relaxed after a good dinner served by the maid. The three of them had retired to the library where they were having a brandy. Michael was lying on the sofa with his head in his mother's lap. Gloria giggled. She was playing with strands of Michael's hair. 'It's Michael that keeps me young,' she said. 'One day he'll go off with another girl and I'll be left all on my own.'

Michael lifted one hand and gently stroked her cheek. 'I'll never leave you, Mother. Never. Where else would I find a woman like you?' They lay there by the fire quite content.

Charles felt a little extraneous. 'I, ah, think I'll go and take a bath,' he said. Lying in the huge old Victorian bathtub, he felt totally at ease with life. Michael's a lucky sod, he thought. One day I'm going to live like this. Trouble is, Mother will never fit in. He immediately felt guilty. By now it was getting increasingly difficult for him to enjoy going home to Bridport and to the semi-detached house. He never invited anyone home, making the excuse that he had an invalid aunt who could not stand visitors.

By now, Julia would drive up to Exeter to see him. He would cringe with embarrassment at her appearance. She remained the same bony unfashionable little woman she had always been. 'Pleased to meet you, Michael,' she said, while Charles winced.

'Mother,' he said later, 'one doesn't say "Pleased to meet you." '

'And what else doesn't one say?' Her voice rose ominously.

'One doesn't say "toilet", or "lounge".'

'Yes, go on,' she said.

'Well, there's "couch' . . ." Charles suddenly

realized she was angry. 'I don't know what to do about you, Mother. You want me to be a success, to make lots of money, and to be famous. Then when I do try to get ahead, you resent me.'

'You're getting too big for your boots,' said Julia, and she marched out of the restaurant into the car, and drove off into the night. Charles went back to his room feeling miserable. Julia never paid a visit to the university again after that incident.

15

Charles was in his third year and living in a lodging house in Exeter when Rachel arrived. 'Let's go and take a look at what's new this year,' he said to Michael who was sharing lodgings with him a few days after the beginning of the new term.

'Okay.' They were not disappointed, because the new girls were a fairly spectacular crowd. Rachel was sitting on a bench with a girl she had made friends with. 'And what's your name?' said Michael to Claire.

'I'm Claire, and this is Rachel.' Claire had no problems with men at all. In no time, the four of them were in the pub. Michael and Claire got on famously. Rachel was left to talk to Charles. She was never a good conversationalist, and this was the first time she had been in a pub with two strange men. They hadn't much to say to each other, but because Michael invited Claire to a party the next evening in front of Rachel, Charles felt obliged to ask her.

'Quite a goer, that Claire,' said Michael on the way back in the car.

'Can't say I feel the same about Rachel,' said Charles.

'Still waters run deep, so they say.'

'Not with that one,' said Charles. 'She's the marrying sort.'

'Do you good to spend a chaste evening,' said Michael.

'Claire, do you really like Michael?' Rachel asked her that evening. They were sitting in Claire's room drinking coffee. The place looked as though a bomb had hit it. Claire had dumped everything from her many suitcases into the middle of the floor. 'Here,' said Rachel, 'let me help you tidy up.'

'I usually don't bother, because it just gets messy again.'

'Who cleans up after you at home then?'

'No one. My room at home always looks like this.'

'Oh. The nuns would kill us if we ever left a sock on the floor.'

'I didn't go to boarding school; I went to the local grammar. I always was clever. My father had money, but he drank it all away, so we lived from hand to mouth and from pickings from rich relatives. It's not too bad a life once you get used to the shouting when my father gets drunk. He spoils me. I'm his favourite.' A warm glow came over her face and she gazed at herself in the mirror. She was indeed beautiful, Rachel admitted to herself. She was about five feet tall with blonde hair. She had a finely boned face with light hazel eyes.

'What are you reading?' Rachel asked, to change the subject.

'Well, I decided to do a general arts degree. Mind you, if I had been better at science, I'd have done that because that's where all the men are.'

Rachel looked slightly scandalized. 'You're not here just for men?'

'Oh yes I am. I'm here to find myself a rich husband with a glittering future . . . who will pamper my every wish. Daddy wouldn't have it any other way. By the way, you asked me about Michael . . . there's money there, believe you me. I can smell it. And let me tell you about Charles: trade, not middle-class . . . grammar school . . . always shows.'

'Gosh,' said Rachel. 'You are sophisticated.'

'And I didn't know people still said "Gosh",' Claire laughed. 'Come on, let's have coffee.'

Claire was everything Rachel was not. Rachel had never met anyone as open in her life. 'Do your parents let you swear like that?' asked Rachel.

'Me? Swear? You should hear my father.' She was painting her toenails a particularly appealing shade of pink. 'Don't they look delightful?' she said stretching out her leg. 'You know, you should shave your legs, Rachel. You're very hairy. Men don't find hairy legs attractive.'

'I know. I've been thinking about it, and under my arms.'

'What are you wearing for the party?'

'Oh, our dressmaker made me a shirt-waist in taffeta.'

'You can't wear that, you idiot. It's a bottle party. You need a skirt and a jersey. That's what everyone else will be wearing. I must find a good hairdresser to dye my hair.'

'You mean it's not naturally that colour?'

'No. I have it dyed every six weeks or so. It's an awful nuisance, but "gentlemen prefer blondes", so they say. Besides, I have to dye my pubic hair to match. Otherwise, they'd guess.'

'Claire, you're impossible.'

'And you're a virgin, aren't you, Rachel?'

Rachel had often suspected various girls in the past of being less than virginal, but she had never met anyone who would talk about it. 'Yes, I am. But please tell me what it's like?'

'You get used to it. The secret is to make whoever you're doing it with think you've never done it before. Then they feel all male and responsible for you. And always pretend you're being driven wild with lust by their pale, hairless little bodies.'

'Is it always like that?' said Rachel, remembering her own orgasmic nights by herself. She had been hoping that one day she would find some man to share her pleasure.

'Yes, always. Men are like animals. Mind you, I'll have to play the field here for a while. I've got three years to hook a man to secure my future and, in a small community like this, you can't get it wrong or you'll be considered an easy lay, and no one will marry you. I'll just tease 'til I find the right man.'

'Well, I'll watch. You'll have to give me lessons,' said Rachel.

By this time, they had exchanged sufficient background information for Claire to realize why Rachel seemed so naive. She genuinely like Rachel's intelligent company. 'You wouldn't be bad looking if you'd do something with your hair, instead of winding it in plaits round your head, and if you wore some make-up. I don't suppose your aunts approve of make-up.'

'They don't approve or disapprove, really. They just never think about it. Certainly the nuns didn't allow it.'

'Do you have to wear knee-length socks?'

'No, not really. But I hate roll-ons, and if I wear nylons, they seem to run as soon as I get them out of the packet.'

'I'll make a woman out of you yet,' said Claire.

'Thanks, but what can an old fuddy-duddy like me do for you?'

'You can be my friend.' Claire suddenly looked very serious. 'I've never had a girlfriend in my life. Most girls want boyfriends so badly they'd kill you if you got in the way. I don't think you're like that. It would be really nice if we could be friends.'

'We already are,' said Rachel.

Claire threw her arms around Rachel and hugged her. 'That's great.'

Rachel was quite overcome with Claire's exuberance. Unwinding Claire's arms from round her neck, she blushed furiously. 'I must go now. It's late. See you tomorrow.'

'I'll supervise your make-up for the party tomorrow night,' said Claire.

'Great.' Rachel left the chaos of Claire's room and went into her own. I must get some posters and liven the place up, she said to herself. She walked over to her cupboard. Her dresses hung in a drab, neat row. 'Well-made, but uninspiring. Rather like me. Well. Claire can change all that.' She fell asleep in a cheerful frame of mind.

Claire maintained that they needed to start preparations for the party at seven o'clock. Michael and Charles would call for them at nine. Two hours seemed an extravagantly long time by Rachel's standards. 'Come to my room at seven exactly, and we'll prepare.'

Rachel knocked timidly on Claire's door at the appointed hour, and was shocked when Claire opened the door with only her knickers on. Seeing the surprise on Rachel's face, Claire laughed and said, 'Don't be silly. In our family we walk around with nothing on all the time. You'll get used to it. We're friends, aren't we?'

'Oh, yes. It's not that – it's just being in a convent and all that.'

Claire stood in front of her with her hands on her hips. 'Haven't you ever seen anyone naked before?'

'Actually, no.'

'Do you mind? Does it embarrass you?'

'Funnily enough, it doesn't.' Rachel realized that she was not at all embarrassed. Claire was neatly made. She had round breasts with pink pointed nipples. Her rounded, rather child-like shape made Rachel envious. 'I look like a bean-pole with no clothes on,' Rachel said.

'Don't moan. I have to diet almost all the time. Come on. Let's get going.' They managed to spend all of the two hours getting ready without any problem at all. Claire showed Rachel how to put rouge on her nipples. 'Men like that,' she said with great authority.

Rachel stared down at her exposed breasts. She had large, dark brown nipples. 'I think it looks silly on me. I don't have any breasts; just two sticking out nipples. I feel like Rudolph the Red-Nosed Reindeer. Besides, it'll take years before I undress in front of a man.'

'I think you look fabulous with your hair down like that.' Indeed, Claire had spent some time working on Rachel's face with pancake, rouge, and eye-liner. When she handed Rachel the mirror, Rachel was quite impressed. 'I've got an idea,' Claire suddenly said. She picked up a pair of nail scissors, and before Rachel realized what was happening, Claire had cut a fringe across her forehead. 'Look,' Claire said, delighted with herself. 'I've made you into Juliette Greco.'

Rachel was amazed. 'Actually, you're right, you know. I do look a bit like her.'

'Come on or we'll be late.' Claire led the way downstairs where Michael and Charles were waiting to meet them.

Charles looked at Rachel and was pleased that she looked less plain than when he had first met her. In fact, he thought, she's really quite striking to look at.

Rachel noticed that every time Claire laughed she had a way of sticking her little pink tongue through her teeth, and thought she must try that some time.

It was Rachel's first bottle party. The boys waved their bottles of chianti at the host who stood on the doorstep fending off uninvited guests. Once inside the flat, Rachel was struck by the grimy walls plastered with Lautrec posters. Old chianti bottles clogged with wax stood in the corners. A few held sputtering candles. Most of the light in the room was supplied by the orange bulbs in the light sockets. The room was packed with people. 'Let's try next door!' yelled Michael over the din.

They shoved their way through. All the girls seemed to be wearing the regulation black sweater, and many of them wore black sunglasses as well. Next door wasn't much better. The music was loudly belting out Buddy Holly, but there was no room to dance. Charles found a corkscrew and opened his bottle of wine. The four of them stood squashed together, swigging at the bottle. Rachel tried to avoid taking too much of the acid wine. The air was thick with smoke. 'Lovely party,' shouted Michael at a girl who passed by him.

People came and went. Michael and Charles had desultory conversations with many of the guests, and Rachel quietly said to Claire, 'If this is a bottle party, then it's my last.'

'Don't be such a spoil-sport,' said Claire. 'Come on, let's get them to dance.'

Blue Moon yodelled on the record player. Immediately the orange lights went off. There was just enough light to make out the silhouettes of various couples locked in impassioned embraces. Charles pulled Rachel into his arms. He usually made a point of choosing girls who were shorter than he was, but

Rachel stood five-foot-nine in her stocking feet. Thank goodness I wore my flat shoes, she thought. Cheek to cheek, they swayed around the smoke-filled room.

'Enjoying yourself?' Charles said.

'Lovely,' she mouthed back. It was hot, and Charles was preoccupied with trying to control an unwanted erection. With most of the girls he took out, it was no problem. They expected to be held so close to his body that they could feel the hardness of his excitement. Then she would rub and whisper in his ear until such time as she let him know either that she was in the teasing league, in which case he would disappear into the bathroom and relieve himself of the tension before taking her home, or that she was really interested in full intercourse, and they would make immediate plans as to where and when they would consummate. Charles quite liked the lavatory in the middle of a busy party with someone knocking on the door.

This time it was different. Rachel seemed to have almost no idea of how to smooch, let alone how to handle a man's erection. 'Sod Michael,' he said to himself, looking across at Claire who was wound around Michael's neck like a boa constrictor and nibbling away at his ear.

Rachel had never been held close enough to a man to feel his body, let alone anything else. She quite enjoyed being held close by Charles. Though it was hot and sweaty, he smelled nice and seemed so commanding and powerful in a room filled with such extraordinary people that she felt safe and protected.

However, she was soon aware of a large lump forming in his trousers and pushing against her groin. She was horrified. She knew all about erections in fact and fantasy. Various books had given explicit instructions and she had translated it all into her sexual fantasy-life. But somehow, in real life, it was all too intimate for Rachel. They both tried to avoid the growing problem. 'Let's go outside for some fresh air,' said Charles after vainly trying to control himself.

'What a good idea,' said Rachel with relief. 'I see there's a balcony through there.' She pulled Charles behind her until they reached the calm of the outside night. 'Whew, it was hot in there.'

They both stood in an embarrassed silence. 'Been to many parties?' Charles finally said.

'No. Only ones my aunts insisted I go to. I hate parties . . . not this one, I mean. I'm sorry. That sounded rude. No, I mean the ones where you dress up and everything.'

'Don't you have parents?'

'No, I was adopted by my two maiden aunts. I know I must seem very unsophisticated to you, but I went to a convent before coming here, so I've lived a very quiet life.'

Charles looked at her with a little more interest. She was quite attractive in an odd way. Her thick hair and her warm generous mouth gave a promise of great sensuous warmth. She was too thin, and her feet and hands were gauche, but she had an easy honesty and a lack of pretence which Charles was beginning to find charming. 'Let's go and find Michael, and see if we can all go back to the flat for a coffee.'

'Sounds like a good idea.' Anything, she thought, anything to get away from the party which by now was disintegrating into a drunken brawl. Charles dragged her through rooms of couples lying on the floor on top of each other or leaning up against the walls, writhing as though in agony. They passed the bathroom where some girl was vomiting into the basin, while another couple were busily investigating each other's attributes perched on the lavatory.

They found Michael and Claire, who were quite willing to go back to the boys' flat. 'It *is* only for coffee,' Rachel managed to whisper to Claire nervously.

'Of course, idiot. I told you I'm playing the field for a while. Don't worry – it'll just be necking.'

'Necking . . .'

It was too late to argue; they were in the car. Charles felt omnipotent. Sitting beside Rachel, he realized he had an old-fashioned, well brought up young girl at his beck and call. He decided there and then that he would make it his business to have her fall in love with him.

Also, he reflected, Mother would approve of her.

When they got to the flat, Charles went straight to the kitchen with Rachel and they made coffee for four. The flat in reality was a double bed-sit with a small kitchen and a bathroom. Rachel looked around the kitchen appreciatively. It was brightly painted, neat and clean. 'That's me,' said Charles. 'I can't bear dirt and disorder. Michael's such a pig.'

Rachel laughed. 'You should see Claire's room – they'd make quite a pair.'

They both fell into a companionable silence. Charles busied himself with the coffeepot. He prided himself on making 'real coffee' instead of the standard instant. He had first learned how to do it at Michael's house. 'Judging from the sounds next door, they don't seem to have time for coffee, and I don't think they'd welcome our company.'

'I think you're right.' Rachel felt an enormous surge of relief. 'Let's just sit here and talk.'

The warm smell of coffee beans hung in the air. They both surprised themselves at how much they really did have to say to each other.

'It's a bit different for me.' To his amazement, Charles felt himself confiding in her. 'I didn't go to a public school. I went to a grammar.'

'Does it make that much difference?'

'It does to me. It was like stepping into a foreign country coming here. The first year was awful, but I'm okay now. Michael's helped a lot.'

'I suppose it's different for me, too. I've never had a family, and round where I come from, if you've no family, you're sort of an outsider.'

'That makes two of us.' They grinned at each other. 'You know, you don't have to worry – I won't make a pass at you.' The look of relief on Rachel's face amused him. 'Most girls would be insulted if I didn't, and here you are practically passing out with pleasure at the idea of not being assaulted by me.'

'It's not that, Charles. It's just that I've had very little to do with men, and I've got a lot to learn. I can see that Claire is always laughing at me. I'm a slow learner, but

I do get there in time.' She smiled her big, warm, sensuous smile.

'The Claires of this world aren't nearly as expert as they sound. If she gets her teeth into Michael, she'll find she's bit off more than she can chew.'

Charles had no idea how accurate his prediction was. Next door Claire had discovered very quickly that Michael had no intention of fighting for her supposed virginity. Instead, he sat in a chair, unzipped his trousers, and said, 'At this time of night, I always feel like a little oral sex.' Claire was taken aback by his directness, but his commanding tone excited her, so she obediently fell to her knees and began to suck gently. Michael lay back with his legs splayed, and looked down at Claire working for his pleasure so diligently. Soon, he came into her mouth, and she swallowed the semen with practised ease. 'You've done this before,' he said.

'Oh, I love doing it,' she said. She smiled engagingly at him. 'It means I'm still a virgin, and there aren't any complications like pregnancy and all that.' Still crouched at his feet, Claire could have passed for a twelve-year-old child. She looked like a small puppy willing to please.

'We must meet more often,' said Michael. 'We obviously have a lot in common.' They were both laughing when they entered the kitchen.

'What were you doing with Michael while we were in the kitchen?' Rachel asked as soon as they were home.

Claire paused with her hand on her door. 'Sucking him off,' she said and smiled wickedly at Rachel who looked horrified. 'He's hooked. I can tell. What were *you* doing?'

'Drinking coffee, of course,' said Rachel. She went into her room feeling quite sick. 'Never in a million years,' she said to herself. 'Ugh.'

They became an inseparable foursome. Claire was infatuated with Michael, and – after a visit to the family home – decided that he was the man she had been waiting for. She also found herself less in control of the relationship than she usually was. Michael was never predictable. The only time she had him under control was when she was making love to him. He never tried to make love to her. He did occasionally return her favours orally, but she felt his lack of enthusiasm.

Not that Michael was undemonstrative. On the contrary, he was a great hugger and toucher of everyone. Sometimes she would complain, 'I wish you'd keep your hands to yourself. Some girls get the wrong idea and think you're after them.'

'How do you know I'm not?'

'Because,' she said sticking out her little pink tongue.

'Come here at once,' he'd say, hopelessly bewitched.

Rachel and Charles took it for granted that those two would behave like a couple of over-sized school children. Theirs, however, was the meeting of true minds. Charles found himself really enjoying Rachel's company. He could trust her with his social worries. She would never laugh, but would very seriously consider which way to spoon soup, and explain why the custom occurred. He was very happy to accept an invitation to Rachel's house for a long weekend.

'There's not much to do there, but we can catch up on our essays, and Aunt Bea has a good library.'

'I'd love to go,' said Charles, and they made their plans.

Claire was delighted for Rachel. 'He's really hooked on you, you know. Are you going to sleep with him?'

'At my house? Good heavens no. It wouldn't be fair to Aunt Emily or Aunt Bea. It's enough of a shock to have a man there for two whole days.'

16

Rachel was surprised to see how Aunt Bea had aged in the last few months. She was only in her sixties, but she looked tired and strained. 'Aunt Bea, you've been playing too much golf,' she said, hugging her.

'Not enough. I've been too tired lately – it's the weather. I need the spring to come, and then I'll be all right.'

Aunt Emily was quite smitten with Charles. She fussed over him almost continually. 'If I eat anymore, I'll burst,' he said, laughing at her. Emily had been piling his plate with food. 'Think of the starving in China,' she said, giggling like a schoolgirl.

After the first day, once the table was cleared and the two women were alone in the kitchen waiting for the kettle to boil for their nightly hot-water bottle, Emily said, 'I think he's a nice enough boy, Bea. Don't you?'

'Trade,' said Bea. 'Seems keen to get on. I just hope Rachel finds some other friends. You know how romantic she is. I do worry that she'll throw herself away on some man and not finish her education.'

'I don't think you've much to worry about, Bea. She has Lionel's stubborn streak, and when she sets out to do something, she usually finishes it. She's always been like that, ever since she was a child.'

'I hope so.'

'Dear, you do look tired. Go up to bed, and I'll bring your bottle up to you.'

Rachel found Aunt Emily in the kitchen a few minutes later. 'Do you like him, Aunt Emily?'

'Of course. We think he's charming – such nice manners.'

'Oh, I love you, Aunt Emi . . .' Rachel took her little fat aunt into her arms and kissed her. She felt the softness of her aunt's body against her own, and suddenly she longed for the security of the days when she was a child, and nothing was more complicated than the comfort of her aunt's warm body.

'I must take this bottle up to Aunt Bea. She's not well these days. I'm worried about her.'

'Really?' Rachel had always considered Aunt Bea imperishable. 'Has she seen the doctor?'

'He told her to rest. But you know Aunt Bea. She's never heard of the word.'

'I'll pop in and say good-night to her before I go to bed,' said Rachel. Indeed, when she saw her aunt in her grey dressing-gown sitting on the edge of her bed reading a passage from the Bible, she had a faint premonition that Aunt Bea was really ill. 'Promise you'll take it easy,' she said. 'Please.'

'I'm all right. But while you're here, I might as well lecture you. Sit down for a minute. Rachel, don't give your whole life over to a man. Keep part of yourself a free spirit. If you do get married – and the more I see of you these days, I realize that you probably will marry – keep part of yourself for yourself. If anything goes wrong, you'll need that bit of yourself to survive. If you've given your all and he leaves you, there will be nothing left.' The image of Regine with Lionel's picture in her dead arms rose before Bea's eyes. 'Promise me, whatever happens, you will finish your education.'

'I promise, Aunt Bea.' For once it was Aunt Bea who drew Rachel to her and brushed away the thick hair from her eyes.

So like *his* eyes, Aunt Bea thought. 'Good night, darling,' she said. 'Sleep well.'

'Good night, Aunt Bea.'

'You know,' she said to Charles who was waiting for her in the kitchen, 'I'm really worried.'

'You know, I've had such a lovely weekend,' said Charles. 'I envy you your lovely house and your two nice aunts. What a super way to grow up.'

'I'm so glad, Charles. I was afraid you'd be bored.'

He looked at her. 'I'll never be bored with you, Rachel' (. . . nor with this standard of living either, he thought). Later that night, he lay in one of the spare bedrooms with his hands behind his head. Maybe I really do love her, he thought. At least she's not a slag.

I really do love him, Rachel said to herself two rooms away. At least he doesn't spend his time pawing me.

They had just got back to the university on the Sunday evening, when Rachel received a 'phone call from Aunt Emily. 'Darling, I've got something awful to tell you.' Her voice was faint and shaky. 'I'm afraid Aunt Bea died an hour ago – just after you left.'

'Oh no . . .' Rachel stood in the hall.

Charles, who was putting her suitcase into her room, came running towards her. 'What's the matter? What is it, Rachel?'

'It's Aunt Bea. She's dead. I must go to Aunt Emily now.'

Charles was excellent in emergencies. 'Wait there. I'll borrow Michael's car. Tell Aunt Emily we'll be with her within three hours.'

'Thank . . . thank you, Charles . . . Aunt Emily? I'll be home soon. Oh, Aunt Emily.' They sobbed down the wires to each other. Life without Aunt Bea . . .

When the doctor left, he put his hand on Aunt Emily's shoulder. 'A merciful death,' he said, trying to comfort the grief-stricken little woman. 'You wouldn't have wanted her lying in bed like a vegetable for the rest of her life, would you?'

But it was useless. Aunt Emily was incoherent with grief. Cook took her down to the kitchen and made her a cup of tea. 'Plenty of sugar, love. It's good for shock,'

'I wasn't there . . . I wasn't there . . .'

Aunt Emily had been visiting in the village. She'd had a satisfying social gossip with Mrs Bridges who ran a small gift shop in Uplyme. With the pleasant taste of Earl Grey tea in her mouth, she'd driven home humming to herself. She'd called hello when she opened the front door, and was surprised to receive no answer.

She went into the library where Aunt Bea usually spent Sunday evenings at her Queen Anne writing desk doing the weekly accounts. Aunt Bea was there, slumped over the drop-leaf writing desk. She was already dead. Emily took her friend in her arms, but she was not strong enough to lift her. Instead, she put her gently on the floor. Cradling Bea's head in her arms, she said good-bye to her companion. 'I'll love you always, just as much now as I did before. Oh Bea, why wasn't it me first? You're so much better at life.' For the first and only time in her life, she kissed Bea on the lips, and held her beloved body for the last time.

Eventually, she pulled herself away and went to the kitchen. Cook was there. She saw from Aunt Emily's face that something awful had happened. 'Oh no, ma'am,' she said.

'Would you ring for the doctor?' said Aunt Emily.

'Of course, ma'am.'

The doctor could see that it was probably a massive heart attack. 'We'll have to have an autopsy, so I'll send for the undertaker.'

'Can't it wait until tomorrow?'

'Of course. I'll help you carry her upstairs to her room.'

Aunt Emily was sobbing hysterically when Charles drove Rachel up to the house. It was nearly midnight when Rachel stood by her aunt's bed. She looked down at her face, which looked even sterner in death. Aunt Bea was gone. It's like an envelope, Rachel thought. She put out her hand to touch her aunt's face. She pulled it back quickly once she felt the coldness.

Meanwhile, Charles was doing his best to comfort Aunt Emily. He gave Rachel a terrified look when she came into the room and took the distraught woman from his arms.

'I'm not very good at this sort of thing,' said Charles.

'Don't worry, Charles. I'll take care of her.'

'I think I'd better be getting back . . . we've finals in a few weeks. I've got to get Michael's car back.'

'Don't you want to wait 'til tomorrow? It's so late now.'

'No. It's all right. I'll be back in no time . . . tell you what: I'll ring tomorrow. If you need me, just say so, and I'll come back.'

'Oh, thank you, Charles. That's really good of you.'

Charles left. Imagine dying like that. No warning. Nothing. One day you're there, and the next day, you're gone. Charles drove back to Exeter very fast.

Rachel slept with Aunt Emily in her arms. Every so often, Emily would waken and realize that Bea was dead. Rachel would talk gently to her about their lives together. 'Remember, as soon as she died, she probably saw all the people she loved.' She spoke to Aunt Emily like a child. They were both comforted by their strong religious belief in the eternal.

Charles did telephone, and Rachel was tempted to ask him to come, but he did have his finals. 'I do miss you,' said Charles. 'You're my bad habit.'

'I miss you, too. Don't work too hard. I'm staying here until Aunt Emily is more settled.'

'That's a good idea. I'll ring every day.' And he did.

The funeral was held at Axminster Church. Aunt Bea had been a popular member of the community. Aunt Emily had to be helped up the aisle by Rachel and Cook. There were very few members of the Cavendish family from London, as they had all lost touch over the years. Mostly, the pews were full of local folk. The bell tolled for her as it had for her father. Finally, she took her place beside her father. Aunt Emily couldn't bear to watch the earth fall on the coffin. She was taken home by one of the villagers who sat with her while Rachel coped with the arduous job of listening to the many people eager to tell her of her aunt's goodness to them in their times of need or hardship.

'She was a grand woman,' said Ryan the town drunk.

'She was. That's what she really was,' said Rachel. 'She was a very grand woman.'

'You'll be like her some day. I can see the likeness meself . . . it's in the eyes . . .'

She didn't like to disillusion him. He was carried away on a rich vein of Irish whiskey and Irish sentiment. 'Thank you, Ryan,' and she moved on to the next pair of outstretched hands.

'Charles,' she said over the 'phone a few weeks later, 'I'll be back on Sunday. Aunt Emily is still very shaken, but Cook is moving into the house to be with her.' She sounded quite excited about something.

'You do sound better. It's not too much sherry, is it?'

'No. Guess what?'

'Don't be silly. I can't even hazard a guess. What?'

'I'm quite a rich woman.'

It didn't come as a surprise to Charles. He had worked out that when the old lady snuffed it, there would be only the two of them to inherit. Anyway, that was the impression Cook had given him. 'Nice little inheritance coming Rachel's way,' Cook had said to him. Cook was anxious that Rachel should find a good husband for herself. Although her own husband had been a drunken old sod, she still believed it was the natural order of things. She didn't like the thought of Rachel becoming an old spinster like her aunts.

'Well, what do you think? Will you still speak to me if I'm rich?' Rachel asked.

'Especially if you're rich,' said Charles.

'I'll see you as soon as I get back. I should be there about six.'

'Okay. I'll wait in your room for you.'

Suddenly Rachel wanted to see Charles very much indeed. I'm in love. This is what it must feel like – a part of me missing when I'm away from him.

'Michael,' said Charles back at Exeter, 'can I borrow the car to run over to see Rachel?'

Michael was reading. 'Okay.'

'Oh. If Carole calls, tell her it's all off.'

'What am I supposed to tell her if she asks why?'

'Tell her Rachel's back. She'll understand.'

'Are you serious about Rachel?'

'I think so . . . I'm not sure, but I think so.'

'Actually, I've been meaning to tell you.'

'What?' said Charles, impatient to be off.

'I'm going to be engaged to Claire before I leave for London.'

'Really? You want to get married?'

'No. I just want to keep her on ice. If the diamond is big enough, she'll remain faithful. I just can't bear the thought of anyone else getting their hands on her little round body.'

'You're such a pig, Michael.'

'I know. Mother's so distraught that she's doubled my allowance and wants me to spend Christmas in Kitzbul with her to see if she can distract me with a bevy of beautiful debutantes. I've agreed, of course.'

Charles went over to meet Rachel in a very pensive mood. An engagement sounded like a good idea. It was really a kind of holding operation. If everything worked out, they could marry and she would have both the money and the background he needed. If it didn't work out, he could always break it off. Either way, he couldn't lose.

Julia didn't take to the idea too kindly. 'You're far too young to think of getting engaged. You have nothing behind you yet.'

'But Mother, she'll be at university for the next two years. By then I'll be settled in London with a job. Anyway, if it doesn't work out, we can always break it off.'

'When are you going to bring her to see us? Are we going to be allowed to meet her, or is she too good for us?'

'I was going to ask her over next weekend. Elizabeth said her room will be free because she's away, so Rachel can stay there. You will be nice to her, won't you, Mother? Her people have been so nice to me.'

'Of course I'll be nice to her.' Julia smiled a razor-sharp smile. 'Why shouldn't I be nice to her.'

Rachel had wondered why Charles had taken so long to invite her to his home. Since Aunt Bea's death, they spent most weekends with Aunt Emily who was more than willing to lend them her car. 'I think I'll take driving lessons and then buy myself a small car,' Rachel said. 'What do you think, Charles?'

'I can teach you to drive. I learned in Michael's car.'

Within a week, Rachel had bought a small, soft-top MG. 'It has to be racing-green,' said Charles when they were discussing the colour.

'Don't you think it's a bit of a fast car for a beginner?'

'No. It's just right.' He bought himself a flat cap in honour of the occasion.

17

'You do drive it well,' said Rachel. Sometimes he wondered if there wasn't an edge on her voice. Maybe underneath that seemingly vulnerable and innocent girl, there lived a far more powerful being that was not yet awake. It made him a little uneasy.

'Shall we spend the weekend at my place?' he said.

'And meet your mother? You talk about her so much she must be a very special woman.'

'If it weren't for her, I'd be standing behind the counter of our chemist shop in Bridport working for my father. I owe her everything. Don't worry if she's a little sharp – it's just her way when she's nervous.'

'Sharp' didn't describe Julia's attitude to Rachel. 'Venomous' might be a more appropriate word, Rachel decided when she thought in retrospect about the weekend in Bridport.

Charles was very nervous on the drive there.

'Stop fussing, Charles. How much or how little your family has is unimportant. I couldn't care if you lived in a rabbit hutch.'

They were scheduled to arrive at teatime. Julia had invited Ruth to give her moral support. 'I do hope she's not some brazen hussy he's picked up,' she said to Ruth. 'He never tells me anything these days.'

'Manny's just the same,' Ruth's voice said down the telephone line. 'He never brings any of his girlfriends home. He just brings back these weird young men. All very clever, of course, but the world is changing, Julia. It's up to us to change with it. "Maybe it's the fashion for young men to wear hairnets," I say to myself. My Manny has come from a good home . . .'

'Ruth,' Julia interrupted.

'Yes, Julia? I do go on, but I miss the boy . . .'

'Can you come to tea and meet this girl? I could do with your opinion. If she's not suitable, we must nip it in the bud.'

'Of course. I'll be there, dear.'

Julia put the 'phone down with a sigh of relief.

When Rachel arrived at Charles's house, she realized that she'd never been in a semi-detached house before. She knew what the inside of the old Devon cottages looked like because she would visit old family retainers with her aunts. She had always loved the small square rooms with their thick walls. But this house was thin and mean. In order to fulfil the aspirations of a generation of working-class women who were determined to climb the social ladder through the control and manipulation of their offspring, it had a sitting-room, and a meagre dining-room with a pass-through hatch into the only really comfortable room – the kitchen.

Tea was served in the sitting-room. Ruth was already ensconced on the sofa when Charles arrived with Rachel. 'What's *she* doing here?' he hissed at his mother, taking her aside. Years ago he had grown tired of Ruth and her literary pretensions. Above all, he despised her for not recognizing that Manny had become queer as a nine-bob note. It was the joke of all Bridport.

'Just happened to be a day we always have tea together, dear.'

'It's not every day I bring a girl home.'

'I know, dear, but life goes on for the rest of the family, you know. We all have to get on with everyday things.'

Rachel was sitting on one of the armchairs of the Edwardian three-piece suite. She was relieved to hear the tea-trolley rumble towards the sitting-room door. This room gives me a head-ache, she decided. She stood up to open the door for Julia. Immediately she knocked over one of the many little nests of side-tables that dotted the room. In the ensuing mêlée, she shot Charles a desperate look. Hearing the noise, he had arrived in great haste and was nursing a finger that was burnt by the tea he was trying to pour when he heard the crash.

'Oh Rachel, I should have warned Mother about your big feet.'

Julia laughed loudly. 'Never mind, dear. Accidents will happen.' From then on, Julia felt much more in charge. 'I gather your people are from Axminster,' she said. 'What do they do?'

Rachel didn't expect an inquisition; she had imagined that Charles would have told his family all about her. 'Well, um, my Aunt Emily is the only one alive. I was brought up by two aunts: Aunt Bea and . . .'

'Do you mean you don't have family?'

'Not exactly. You see I don't know really, because I was adopted. So I have no idea where I came from.'

'Oh how tragic. I'm so sorry, dear. I shouldn't have asked. One doesn't like to talk about those sorts of things. Must have been the war. All those American soldiers, you know. Probably needed nylons – in those days.'

'Can't we talk about something else?' said Charles loudly.

'Of course, dear. I promise never to mention the subject again.' She bent over and took Rachel's hand in hers. 'I'm so sorry.' She gave the hand a little squeeze.

'How's Manny doing?' Charles said in desperation to Ruth.

'You wouldn't believe it, Charles. The boy is doing so well. He already has a firm in the city interested in him. He is brilliant, brilliant. He's home this weekend, by the way, and wants to see you both.'

The tea-trolley was groaning with food. Not only were there cucumber sandwiches, but Julia had done her best for her son, and there were salmon-paste sandwiches as well. The silver-plated teaset was shining, and the bottom of the trolley was loaded down with teacakes, a lemon sponge cake, and a magnificent chocolate loaf. 'My goodness,' said Rachel, 'what a wonderful spread.'

'I'm glad you like it, dear. The way to a man's heart is

always through his stomach.'

'Do you really think so?' Rachel asked anxiously. 'You see, I can't cook.'

'You can't cook? Not at all? How on earth do you manage at home?'

'Cook does it all. I often helped in the kitchen, but I couldn't do anything as wonderful as this. I don't even think Cook could. We just have biscuits at teatime. Poor Charles,' she said, laughing at him. 'You must have missed your mother's cooking.'

'It was always here waiting for him – he only had to ask,' said Julia evenly.

The four of them sat around the fire eating their way through the tea and cakes. Eventually, it was time for Ruth to go. 'I'll run you home,' said Charles. 'You help Mother with the tea things, and I'll be back in a minute,' he said to Rachel, and vanished.

Julia and Rachel heard the roar of the MG. 'Is that your car?' Julia asked.

'Yes. When Aunt Bea died she left me a little money, so Charles and I decided to get a car.'

'Can you drive?'

'Not yet, but I don't really like driving. Charles does it so much better.'

Julia felt a sudden growing respect for her son. The girl was soft as butter. So he's after her money, Julia thought. Well, if I have to tolerate a woman in his life, it might as well be one who needs a lot of teaching. Over the washing up, both women talked avidly about Charles. 'He was such a beautiful little boy. I'll show you pictures of him.' Drying her hands on her flowered pinny, she went off to sort out the old photographs. By the time Charles returned, they were both sitting on the sofa with their heads bent over the photographs. Charles was pleased that suddenly they got on so well together.

William joined them for supper. He greeted Rachel and gave her a rundown on the state of the allotment. 'She's not interested in that sort of thing, William – they have a cook.'

'No, no, you're quite wrong. When I was little I

practically lived with the gardener. I spent hours in the kitchen-garden planting vegetables. His specialities were leeks and onions.'

William warmed to the girl immediately. She seemed a simple homely type. Not at all brash as Julia had predicted. 'I'll show you the allotment tomorrow then.'

'Lovely,' said Rachel.

Julia surpassed herself at dinner. There was roast chicken, two kinds of vegetables, and three kinds of potatoes. To follow, there was the family joke. 'We call it "Mother's Secret Weapon",' Charles said. 'I've seen many a strong man fall in love with Mother for life at the mere sight of it.'

'Oh, Charles,' protested Julia with a laugh, 'be quiet. You'll embarrass me.'

I hope that some day, Charles and I will be so close, Rachel thought. It's so cosy being a family.

William sat at the bottom of the table. Julia took up her position at the head, and Charles and Rachel sat either side. Julia stood to carve the bird. 'Light or dark, dear?' she said to William, who was served first. Before Rachel had time to think about it, she found her plate piled high with food. Julia never seemed to sit still, nor would she allow anyone to help her.

'Do sit, Mother,' said Charles. 'You never have time to finish your food.'

'Only Elizabeth knows my ways,' she said very firmly, and continued to shuttle between the kitchen and the dining-room.

'Mother's Secret Weapon' turned out to be a sherry trifle. Inwardly Rachel heaved. Of all the things in the world she most disliked, the worst was trifle, with rice pudding and semolina coming in a close second. The trifle was brought in and examined by Charles and William. 'The custard is home-made, of course,' said Julia with great pride. It was useless for Rachel to protest.

The soggy, sherry-filled cake, covered with yellow custard and thickly poured double cream, stood waiting for the spoon. She looked at Charles for comfort, but he was bent over his plate, eating with an almost religious fervour. 'Come on, Rachel,' said Julia. 'I've never known anyone to hesitate over my sherry trifle.'

Well, here goes, thought Rachel. The first spoonful went down quite well. Rachel was just beginning to hope that her stomach would not betray her, when a wave of nausea hit her. She leaped to her feet and rushed to the cloakroom beside the kitchen. All her hosts could hear were the sounds of Rachel being very sick indeed.

'Poor child. Not used to good home cooking,' said Julia sympathetically. 'Charles, go and see to her. Father and I will wash up.'

'I'm so sorry, Charles,' said Rachel later. They were sitting on Elizabeth's bed. 'I'm afraid I really do feel that I'd be better off lying down. Would you mind awfully if I went to bed now?'

There was a discreet knock on the door. 'Cup of tea, anyone?' Julia said, poking her head around the door. 'Come along, Charles. Poor Rachel needs her sleep.'

'Coming, Mother,' and Charles followed her busy shape down the stairs.

Rachel felt an awful fool. What an energetic way to live, she thought. The rooms were small, but they were stuffed with furniture and bits and pieces. As she lay in Elizabeth's bed, she still felt sick. She longed for the peace and serenity of her own home. She couldn't even look out of Elizabeth's window. It was thickly draped with net-curtains. The multi-coloured stripes of the carpet confused themselves with the embroidered antimacassars on the backs of all the chairs. A painting called 'The Green Lady' over the dining-room mantelpiece whirled round in her head, and kaleidoscoped into oblivion.

'Charles? You're not, um . . . you know, I mean . . . she doesn't seem the type of girl who would . . .'

'Mother, we've had all this out before. It's none of your business.'

'I know, dear, but as your mother I do have to worry about your future.'

'Do you like her?' It was suddenly very important to Charles.

'She doesn't have family, Charles. That does worry me. She could be anyone's child.'

'Oh Mother, that's not important these days. People like us didn't used to go to university. It's all changing.'

'Some of us keep our standards,' said Julia, squaring her shoulders. 'If you can't look at a girl's mother, you won't know what you're marrying. Besides, Charles, she can't cook, run a house, or do any of the things that make for a good wife and mother. Have you thought of that?'

'That's all stuff she can learn from you. Any idiot can knock up meals and run a Hoover round the house.'

The kitchen Raeburn stove needed refuelling. Julia opened the doors. The red of the dying coals caught the tired lines on her face. She suddenly looked old, spent, and exhausted. She picked up the coal skuttle, and with a practised jerk poured the anthracite into the fire. She put down the skuttle, and looking at her son she smiled her familiar pained smile. She rubbed the small of her back with her hand. 'You're right, Charles. She can learn. There's not much to it.'

Charles went to his room feeling dreadfully guilty. How is it she can make me feel this way when I haven't done anything to deserve it? He spent a restless night waking up to hear his mother arguing with his father, her familiar rapid-fire delivery over-riding his mumbled, inaudible, muttered replies. Julia got up at least six times during the night to get a drink from the bathroom. She didn't quite trust Charles.

In fact, she need not have worried. 'If you're a virgin, then I respect that,' said Charles. 'I don't really feel I should take the responsibility of taking it away, and then if I left you I'd feel an absolute shit.'

'I honestly don't mind, you know. I love you, Charles. And if you want us to make love, I'll be quite happy.'

'No, I've given it a lot of thought, Rachel, and for both our sakes it's better if we enjoy what we have.'

They left it there. Most of their love-making consisted of heavy petting. Rachel found it very frustrating, but she was so aware that she had been lucky enough to find a man who respected women that she satisfied herself with her feeling of security. Charles was relieved because there were sufficient girls around who were guaranteed to be in need of a quick lay with no responsibility. The thought of a girl like Rachel getting pregnant, and the fact that he would be obliged to marry her, made him go quite limp anyway. He didn't bother to explain any of this to Julia. Why should he? If she wanted to imagine the worst, let her.

Rachel woke up in Elizabeth's room and wondered where she was. She could hear a loud clattering coming from downstairs. Of course. She was at Charles's house. I'd better offer to help with breakfast, she thought, and hurriedly put her clothes on. The little house was bone-chillingly cold. Julia had always believed that too much warmth lead to colds and to 'bad habits'. It was William's job when he got up in the morning to clean out the fire-place and set the fire in the sitting-room. The only warm room in the house was the kitchen.

It being Saturday, and because Rachel was company, breakfast was served in the dining-room. In honour of the occasion, Julia put on the electric fire to warm the room. Thank God, thought Rachel who had just managed to wash her hands and face in the bathroom. There was no possibility of taking a bath. Her teeth chattered as she tried to brush them.

Julia could see how cold she was when she came downstairs. 'Feeling a little better, dear?' she said kindly. 'You know, you could do with a little more weight on you. You wouldn't feel the cold then.'

Julia was cooking up breakfast. Fried bacon, fried bread, fried eggs, and grilled tomatoes. 'I don't eat much breakfast, Mrs Hunter. I really only have a cup of coffee and a piece of toast.'

'No breakfast? No breakfast? No wonder you're always ill.'

'I've never liked breakfast, even as a child.'

Julia sniffed. 'I wouldn't let any child of mine go without a good cooked breakfast. You're going to have to learn how to look after a man, you know. Women think nowadays that men marry them for their looks. But you mark my words. It's girls like my Elizabeth that men actually want to marry – a woman who knows how to take care of him and his house and family. All those little clever-boots will find themselves left on the shelves.'

'Life isn't all cleaning, cooking, and washing for men.' Rachel was beginning to feel a little irritated. 'What about companionship, sharing things together?'

Julia looked at the ceiling. 'It's like that for the rich, who have the time for it, or the lucky few who find it. But for most of us, dear, it does come down to looking after a good man like William. He's never had a day when he hasn't had two hot meals on the table in front of him, except when I was in the hospital having Elizabeth. Mind you, he's a good kind husband, but reading books or going to the pictures is not his line. He likes his vegetable garden and the television.'

'It must be awfully lonely for you with Charles away all the time. He's so full of life, isn't he?'

'He's wonderful company. Rachel, one day you'll understand how it is between a mother and her son.'

'I hope so,' said Rachel. The idea appealed to her enormously.

Charles came in full of good humour. 'Ah, I see my fan-club has convened.' He looked at the frying pan sizzling away on the stove. 'Not for me, Mother. Don't eat those sorts of breakfast anymore. Just coffee and toast.'

It took forever for William to work his way through his breakfast. Saturday was a savoured day for him. Now he had an assistant in the shop, so he could spend all day either on the allotment or watching football and racing on television. As soon as he was finished eating, Julia allowed Rachel to help her clear the table. 'I'll clean up the kitchen, and you can give the sitting-room a dust,' she said. 'You might as well begin somewhere.'

Rachel found herself standing in the stuffy sitting-room with a tin of polish in her hand and two yellow dusters. It took over an hour to actually dust and polish the multitude of objects in that room. The piano in the corner became a personal enemy as it refused to shine however hard she polished. But when she stood back to look at her handiwork, she was well pleased with herself. For a room that looked like an over-stuffed Edwardian nightmare, it at least smelled nice.

She reported back to Julia who came in and ran her finger along the window-sill. The smudge of dust sat accusingly on her index finger. 'Come along, dear. You'll have to do better than that. Just a little more effort.' She went out leaving a very disgruntled Rachel. Too much furniture . . . she thought. She was interrupted by Charles who stood in the doorway with a quizzical smile on his face. 'Never thought I'd see the day you'd clean a house. Mother got you at it, didn't she?'

'She says I'll never keep a man until I can cook, clean, and serve him vast meals at least twice a day.'

'Don't let that worry you, Rachel. All the women in my family have that idea tattooed on their behinds as babies. They all overfeed their men hugely, in order to compensate their guilt because they won't make love to them.'

'You're joking, Charles.'

'I'm not. I reckon my mother's only done it twice – once for me and once for Elizabeth.'

'What a waste.'

'Well, it makes for a spotlessly clean house, I'll tell you. Come on. Let's go and see Manny.' Charles was still chuckling to himself when they were in the car. 'She'll have you cooking brisket next.'

'I'd love to learn. Really,' said Rachel anxiously. The weekend was beginning to weigh heavily on her. There seemed so much in life that she was unable to do.

'I like you as you are. Don't change. My mother doesn't know anything about relationships. She married my father in order to get out of her family, and when you meet them you'll understand why.' Rachel was relieved to hear that Charles was planning a next time. Julia, she felt, would never accept a girl like herself who was unable to take care of her Charles. 'Anyway, we won't have all those problems. You have to remember that the house and two children are my mother's life. It'll be different of us.'

'What do you mean?' said Rachel, straining to hear Charles over the MG engine.

'If we ever decided to get married, with my job and your money, we could have help in the house. I don't ever want to see you work yourself to the bone like my mother, or make anyone else feel guilty like she does every time she rattles a dish.'

Rachel sat stunned with joy – Charles had actually considered the possibility of marrying her. She felt so grateful to him. She put her hand on his arm and said, 'I promise even if we don't have help I'll manage. And I won't make you feel guilty, ever.' Charles patted her hand just as they pulled up to Manny's house.

Rachel was much more comfortable with Ruth. It was obvious that she adored her son. She had lost twin girls shortly after their birth and was unable to have any more children. It was a source of real grief to her. She put much of her energy into helping her husband Bernie in his shop, but every available ounce of her energy was given to her first-born, her Manny, who was 'delicate' and only survived because of her chicken soup. Rachel found the house very relaxing.

Manny did indeed seem very effeminate, but then Rachel was always at home with the homosexual men at her university. She was no threat to them, nor did she demand any sexual attention, so usually she had several men-friends on her list who were just that: friends.

Manny smiled at her. 'You'd better watch out. Mom's going to come at you with cakes and coffee. I've never known her to allow anyone to leave the premises unfed. Even the Jehovah's Witnesses get cake and a lecture.'

Ruth was obviously on a sewing binge. Clothes were scattered everywhere. She came bustling in with a large tray of pastries and a small jug filled with very strong coffee. 'Come on, sit down. Just throw the clothes on the floor. They're for the temple jumble sale. Come on, Charles, help yourself. Rachel, some coffee?'

Then Bernie came by. He was a small affable man. He was as plump as his son was elf-like. Manny's face was translucent. Rachel could well believe he had been a delicate child.

'How's working in the city?' Charles asked Manny.

'I haven't started yet, but I've had second thoughts about it all. You know, you'll probably find this funny, Charles, but I think I'll probably study to be a rabbi.'

Charles nearly dropped his plate. 'A rabbi? *You*, Manny? I'd heard you'd changed.' He suddenly had a glimpse of the two of them on their bikes, wheeling round the summer countryside, swapping stories, bragging about sex.

'Don't you dissuade him, Charles,' said Ruth very firmly. 'Don't you know it's every Jewish mother's dream to have a rabbi for a son?'

Charles looked at Manny who dropped his gaze and stared at his long slender hands. Charles felt sorry he'd lost touch with him. Something was badly wrong. Ruth chattered away, and as she talked she patted her son's shoulder or she put more cake on his plate. Bernie sat very much in the background.

'Come,' said Ruth to Rachel. 'I'll show you Manny's room where I have all his trophies.' Obediently Rachel followed her. It took about half an hour for Ruth to go through a lifetime of Manny's successful accomplishments. Charles took that opportunity to get the truth out of his friend.

'Manny,' Charles looked up and checked the room – Bernie had slipped out. They were alone. 'Manny, what's up? You've lost so much weight – you don't look at all like yourself. What's this about being a rabbi?'

'Did you hear about our crowd up at Oxford?'

Charles shifted a little uncomfortably in his chair. 'Well, it was said, to be honest, here in Bridport that you'd gone as queer as a nine-bob note . . . not that I've anything against it.'

'No, no, don't say that. It's like saying "Some of my best friends are Jews." It's perfectly true. I am a homosexual. Many of our crowd went too far. Got themselves noticed. And one night a party was raided. We were all suspended. Those who were actually in bed together were sent down. I came back here and went to my rabbi. He told me there was only one way he could help me. So he contacted the dean and explained the necessity of me finishing at Oxford if I was to carry on with my future career in the temple. The dean agreed to let me back to take my finals. It's been a shock to realize how hostile people are to people like us, and maybe my life will be safer in a backwater. My mother doesn't know any of this. It would kill her.'

They could hear the two women coming back up the passage. 'I'm sorry,' said Charles. 'It's been rough on you.'

Ruth bustled into the room with Rachel following behind. 'There now. Rachel's had a tour of the house. Let me show you my latest drawings.'

After admiring the truly awful flower drawings, Charles made his excuses to get home. 'My father will be home for lunch soon. We promised to be back. I see little enough of them as it is.'

Ruth put her arm around her son. 'I can't tell you how happy I am to have my son back home.'

Lunch was roast pork chops, apple sauce, brussels sprouts, roast potatoes, and gravy, followed by chocolate pudding. Julia had been preparing the meal from the moment she had cleared the breakfast table. After lunch, Rachel said to Charles, 'I've got to go for a walk. I'll burst with all that food.'

'It's funny, you know,' said Charles. 'It's always been like that. I've never noticed how much food we eat because all my aunts are the same. But now I've eaten at your place and Michael's, I can't manage to put it all away like I used to.'

'Let's walk up to the allotment and see your father's vegetables.'

'Rachel, dear – come and give me a hand.' Rachel groaned as Julia's voice rang out from the kitchen. She remembered the state of the kitchen the night before.

Often, if Cook was busy or her family had had guests, Rachel would help out with the washing up. Cook always cleared as she went along. But Julia's kitchen looked as if carnage had occurred.

'I'll call Charles to give us a hand,' Rachel offered. 'This will take ages.'

'Washing up is women's work. I don't mind father helping me when we are on our own, or maybe after lunch on Sunday, but a woman should keep a man out of the kitchen as much as she can. Just as a man doesn't approve of his wife invading his office.' Julia sounded so impassioned that Rachel didn't dare argue.

After a very long time, she and Charles were able to go to the allotment. 'I've been waiting for you,' said William, his face alight with pleasure. 'Come and see my crop of carrots.' He pulled one from the ground and washed it off in the rain barrel nearby. He snapped the carrot in half. It gave a sharp satisfying crack, and he handed her a piece. 'When you go to buy carrots, always break one in half. If it doesn't snap like that, it means they're not fresh.' The carrot was sweet and crunchy.

'Your kitchen garden is amazing,' said Rachel. It was a real work of art. All the tenderness of the man could be seen in the beautiful display of autumn flowers. The roses stood elegantly amid a knee-high display of English wild flowers.

'I don't like rows and rows of beds. I like to imagine how they would live naturally. These are my babies,' he said as he showed her his winter cabbages.

'Would you like to have been able to garden all day?' Rachel asked.

'Yes. If it wasn't for Julia, I'd have given up the chemist shop. And what I would really like to do would be to take a job as a head-gardener at a big house. Then I'd have acres to plant.'

Charles was surprised. 'I didn't know you had ambition,' he joked.

'The trouble is, I don't.' William wasn't joking.

'Never mind. Mother's got enough for both of you,' Charles said with a laugh. They walked on. Eventually

Charles reminded William it was time for tea.

On the way home, Rachel said to Charles, 'I know it's not my business, but your father eats his way through so much food, I'd worry about his heart.'

Charles thought about it. 'It's all mother has to do. She only has Ruth for a friend, so she makes a hell of a hullabaloo about housework and cooking. Even I can't eat it all, but I shovel it down because I feel rotten if I don't. Poor Elizabeth is always trying to diet. She has a hell of a job with Mother.'

Elizabeth was home when they arrived for tea. Rachel was struck by how opposite she was to Charles. She was almost the same height as he was, but she was blonde and blue-eyed. 'Elizabeth, come and help me with the tea things,' shouted Julia from the kitchen. Tea was a repeat performance of the night before, except there were no salmon-paste sandwiches.

'How was God-bothering this weekend?' Charles teased his sister.

'Oh Charles, don't be such a beast. We had a wonderful time.'

'I can think of better ways to spend your time,' said Julia sharply. 'I really don't understand you, Elizabeth. None of us go in for any of this religious nonsense. I can't think what you get out of it. Besides, you should be doing other things like the other girls of your own age.'

'Most of my friends are away at university,' Elizabeth defended, 'and the rest of the girls in Bridport just wait to get married.'

'What's wrong with that?'

'Nothing, Mother. I just don't want to feel that all life has to offer me is a man and marriage.'

Julia was beginning to tighten her mouth. 'You've only had all these ideas since you've been mixing with those fanatics.'

'Leave her alone, Mother,' said Charles.

William smiled at Elizabeth. 'If it makes you happy. They seem a nice enough crowd.'

'We have a very strong group at our university . . . They don't drink or smoke,' Rachel said, hoping to divert some of the tension. 'Some of them are going to be missionaries and go to Africa when they graduate.'

Elizabeth's face went very red. 'That's what I'm going to do.' There was a dreadful silence. 'I've been meaning to tell you all, but I've had to wait 'til my turn came to join the missionary college.'

All eyes were on Julia. 'You are not going to be a missionary and go to some foreign country where you'll catch some awful disease. That's my final word on the subject.'

'I'm going to college, then I shall go wherever God calls me.' She's brave, thought Rachel.

'Can't we have this out another time?' Charles piped up. 'After all, Rachel is a guest here.'

'Elizabeth,' continued Julia, ignoring Charles, 'if you dare to join this college, you will not enter this house again.'

'Steady on here a minute . . .' William looked a bit alarmed at this turn of events. 'The girl only . . .'

'And you, you be quiet. You have nothing to say in this matter. I slaved and sweated to bring up these children. I've given my life for them.' She turned on Elizabeth. 'I kept you clean and decent, when other girls of your age were tramps on the streets. I kept the boys who were no-good louts away from you . . .' She paused, gasping for breath, and put her hand to her chest.

'What's the matter, love?' William was up out of his chair and by her side. 'What can I do for you? You look poorly . . .'

She sat there swaying with her eyes closed. Rachel was frightened. Was she going to have a heart attack? Rachel looked at Charles. His eyes were alight with amusement. She still fools the old man after all these years, he thought.

'Elizabeth, say sorry to your mother,' William said.

Elizabeth, defeated, said, 'I'm sorry. I didn't mean to upset you.'

'I'll just go upstairs for a moment and lie down,' said Julia.

'I'll take you up,' said William.

'It's all right, dear. I can manage. You finish your tea.' She slowly left the room, and they heard her struggle up the stairs.

'Well, Elizabeth, Mother always said no man was good enough for you except a Lord,' joked Charles. No one laughed.

'Do you think she will become a missonary?' Rachel asked Charles when they were alone together.

'I don't know. But the old lady'll blow a gasket. She fancied herself with a peer of the realm for a son-in-law.'

Julia was too ill to attend supper. Elizabeth cooked omelettes and they all ate in the kitchen. 'I'll be sorry to see you go, Rachel,' said William. 'I know you've got to go early tomorrow, so I probably won't see you. But we have enjoyed having you to stay. Do feel welcome to come any time.'

Rachel blushed furiously. 'Thank you – it's been lovely. We're off to see Aunt Emily early tomorrow, and then we go back to Exeter for the last few weeks before the Christmas break. I'll certainly be over to see you during the holidays.'

Rachel spent her last night there in Elizabeth's room with Elizabeth next to her on a roll-away bed. Rachel was nearly asleep in the darkness when Elizabeth said urgently, 'I'm serious, you know. I will be a missionary. I have to do more with my life than just be a housewife.'

Rachel propped herself up on her elbow and said, 'Funny, you know, here you are wanting your freedom, and here's me who has always wanted a proper home. I think you're so lucky to have a mother and a father. I always felt so left out . . . I've really enjoyed myself this weekend. Do you think your mother will change her mind about your plans?'

'Probably not. But she'll have to give in because in two years I'll be twenty-one, and I can leave anyway. By the way, you've improved Charles no end.'

'Really?' Rachel was surprised.

'Yes. He's much less arrogant. He used to think he knew everything. He was really bossy. Mother spoiled him rotten.'

'He won't get spoiled by me. I can't even cook.' They both laughed and were soon asleep.

Julia was up early the next morning. 'Rachel, dear, it's been such a pleasure to have you to stay. I'm sure Charles will bring you again.'

'I hope so,' said Rachel.

'No, Mother. I'll bring girlfriend number two next time, and then three and four.'

Julia laughed. 'Well, you both should have a wide circle of friends.'

'We *have* a wide circle of friends, thank you very much,' said Charles.

She stood at the door waving as they drove off. 'It must be lovely to have a mother,' said Rachel.

'Some of the time,' said Charles.

18

Claire was lying on the floor in front of her gas fire, staring at the ceiling when Rachel went in to see her. She was bursting to tell Claire about her weekend at Charles's house. 'You don't look too happy,' she said when she saw Claire's face.

'I'm not. Michael's mother is a clever old bitch. She's asked him to go skiing with her for Christmas.'

'Is he going?'

'Of course he is. "Darling, I need you to take me away from all these Christmas memories of life when Daddy was alive," ' Claire mimicked. 'She can really fool him, you know. He goes all soft and sentimental about her. Well,' she said, sitting up, 'there are certain things I can do for Michael that even she can't do. At least I hope not.' Her mood changed and she laughed. 'How did your weekend go with Charles?'

'Fantastic. I've never seen so much food in my life. I thought I'd burst.'

'Typical working-class. You're lucky. Most middle-class families starve themselves and feed the dogs and horses. How's his mother?'

'A bit frightening at first. She is, I suppose, a perfect wife and mother. I'll never be able to reach her standards, not in a million years. I suppose you need to have a mother to teach you how to run a house. Even the nuns couldn't teach me to sew or knit. His father's super. Very kind and gentle.'

'Sounds wonderful to me. All I learned from my mother was how to mix a drink. You know, I think I'm going to have awful trouble with Michael's mother. Michael says she's like that with any girl he brings home, but she makes me feel like a gooseberry. Then just when I feel really out of things, after a day of her pawing at Michael, she'll say, "Now you two . . . off to beddy-byes with my little love-birds." '

'She lets you sleep together?'

'The first night I was there, she had the big guest-room ready for us. It's like she gives Michael permission to have sex. She gives me the creeps. I feel she probably inspects the sheets.'

'Have you and Michael really made love properly yet?'

'No,' said Claire. 'We're going to wait 'til we get married.'

'So are we.' Rachel grinned at her friend. 'Charles talked about getting married for the first time this weekend.'

'How wonderful!' Claire leaped to her feet and threw her arms around Rachel. 'I'm so happy for you . . . Let's have a cup of coffee to celebrate. You know, just before you came in, I was wondering how I could get an engagement ring out of Michael before he goes away to Switzerland. I was thinking there's old James. He's followed me around like a little lamb who's lost his tail. He's been after me all year. Maybe if I gave him a little encouragement . . . it usually works. Nothing makes a man more jealous than the thought that he might be sharing his girl with anyone else. Particularly Michael. Sometimes I think he's insane, you know. If I so much as look at another man, he goes mad.'

Rachel shook her head. 'I sometimes wonder, Claire, how you manage to think up all your schemes.'

'Rachel, you need schemes to survive. I sometimes wonder how you'll survive. You're unbelievably naive. I suppose you didn't have to scheme. Your aunts protected you, really, from everything. Sometimes I wonder if they did you any favours.'

'You could be right. I don't really know how families behave. I mean, I find it difficult to know if what they're doing is right or wrong. Julia got upset because Elizabeth wanted to be a missionary. She refused to let her. Now, I find that strange. My aunts would let me do anything I wanted to do as long as I was happy and did it well.'

Rachel soon discovered that Julia's behaviour was mild compared with Claire's family life. Claire had reluctantly asked Rachel home. 'My mother insists that I invite someone over for Boxing Day. We don't have friends – you'll see why. My nightmare is having to introduce them to Michael.'

'If he loves you he'll understand.'

'Rachel,' said Claire, 'life isn't like that. You're so bloody romantic. Most men take one look at my family and I don't see them again.'

'It can't be as bad as that,' said Rachel. 'I'll come over for lunch on Boxing Day. You don't have to worry about me. It's you I like. I don't have to like your family.'

There were tears in Claire's eyes. 'Thanks, Rachel.' For a moment her hazel eyes lost their usual hardness. 'I hope Michael and I can make each other happy.'

'You will. I know you will.'

Rachel was wearing her engagement ring when Cook drove her over to see Claire on Boxing Day. During the journey by car, she held her hand to the window and watched the sunlight catch fire on the tiny diamond. 'It's not much,' said Charles when he gave it to her on Christmas Day, 'but one day I promise you I'll give you the biggest diamond in the world.'

'I don't want the biggest diamond in the world ever, you twit. I'd lose it.' Rachel hugged him. 'I'm so happy, Charles.' She smiled to herself as the car pulled up to Claire's house, remembering that magic moment. She had a tree which she kept in a part of her imagination. It was a huge old oak, so old that it had long ago lost the ability to bear leaves. Its branches were twisted and gnarled and black with age. Instead of leaves, Rachel hung her most treasured moments. It was a device she had learned during her bed-ridden years. By now, her tree had many magic moments adorning its branches. Her first doll, although torn to bits by Penny, hung on a lower branch. Her first Christmas stocking was nearby. She could see the bulges in that stocking and still remember the oranges and the coloured pencils on her counterpane.

As she left the car and thanked Cook for the ride, she was still in a happy dream. Cook was visiting friends in Shaftesbury. 'Telephone me, Rachel, when you are ready to go home.'

'I will.' Rachel rang the door bell. Claire met her at the door. She looked strained and tired. Rachel could feel the tension in her little shoulders as she stooped to hug her. 'Has it been bad?'

'Awful, just awful. They haven't stopped all Christmas. My brother left yesterday. He's had enough.' Claire took Rachel's coat. 'You didn't tell me Charles had given you an engagement ring.'

'It only happened yesterday. What about Michael? Any luck?'

Claire looked at the floor. 'He's got to get the ring from his mother. It's a family jewel.'

'You mean she has to take it from her own finger and give it to Michael for you? I don't think she'll do it – not the way she feels about Michael.'

'Well, he's got to do it.' Claire's face was set and hard. 'Either Michael gets it, or I'm getting out. I'm not going to spend my life struggling for money with a rich mother-in-law holding the purse-strings. I've been a poor relation in a rich family all my life, and I'll never be poor again.'

They were interrupted by a roar from the dining-room: 'Are you two going to go on chattering all day while we wait to eat? Come in here immediately!' Claire's father sat at the head of the table. He was a small man with a bullet-shaped head. The skin was tight over his cheek-bones. He had Claire's wide staring eyes, and she had inherited his innocent baby face. He smiled when he saw Rachel, and stood up to shake her hand. He was not wearing trousers and, as the bottom of his shirt was unbuttoned, she could see that he was also not wearing underpants.

'It's Father's protest because Mother tried to tell him which pair of trousers he should wear,' Claire explained.

'I see,' said Rachel. 'Aren't you cold?'

'It is a little chilly, now that you mention it,' said Jonathan Balfor-James. 'Cynthia, put some more wood on the fire.'

Rachel held her breath. Mrs Cynthia Balfor-James was skeletal and bore no resemblance to her daughter at all. She was sitting at the end of the long oak rectory table, holding on to the heavily carved arms of her chair. Her eyes were glassy. 'Certainly, Jon.' She rose steadily to her feet. Swaying dangerously, she went to the wood basket.

'I'll help you, Mummy, just a second . . . Do sit, Rachel . . . Here, Mummy. Put the logs there.'

Rachel breathed again.

'Drunken old bitch,' said Jonathan amiably. 'That's my wife you know,' he said, addressing himself to Rachel. 'Found her at Hammersmith Palais one night when I was slumming with a load of friends. There she was, kicking up her legs in the chorus-line, shaking her tits.'

'Please, Daddy, don't start.'

Rachel smiled at Claire. 'Don't worry, I'm interested. I didn't know you were in the theatre, Mrs Balfor-James.'

'It is something he never lets me forget . . .'

Cynthia Balfor-James had once been beautiful. But she had fallen in love with Jonathan, to her everlasting regret. 'Never fall in love with a punter,' she would tell Claire again and again. All her dreams of living like a lady of the manor crumbled away with the years of Jonathan's gambling and drinking. The family largely ignored them, and they lived on dribbles of income from old family trusts. Fortunately, just before they had to sell their family home, an old vicarage just outside Shaftesbury became empty. Jonathan's brother, a lawyer, made the property over to Jonathan on the condition that the little money that was left was to be handled by his firm, and Jonathan would receive an allowance. The uncle also paid the school fees for both Claire and her brother Robin.

It was a large, drafty, inconvenient house. There

was no money for servants, and as the years went by it fell into decay. Mrs Balfor-James attempted to cook and to keep the place vaguely clean, but it was a losing battle. The only happy members of the family were the many cats and dogs that roamed the house and grounds. Still, Jonathan liked to keep up appearances, and the neighbourhood families put up with his eccentricities because he was, after all, one of them. They did not extend the same welcome to his wife. Chorus girls were thought of rather on the same level as American women – fast, loud, and vulgar. Cynthia tried her best to prove them wrong, but gradually she took to nipping at the sherry bottle.

'When are we going to get something to eat in this bloody house?' bellowed Mr Balfor-James.

'I'll get it,' said Claire.

'I'll help you,' Rachel quickly offered. Once the two girls were out of the room, Rachel said, 'You weren't exaggerating, were you? It feels just like a play.'

'You should try living in it,' said Claire bitterly.

'I can see why you're so desperate to get out.'

They were now in the kitchen sorting out the cold turkey and ham. 'Don't bother with the potatoes in the oven,' said Claire. 'She burnt them. You take the meat, I'll bring the cheese and fruit.' On the way back to the dining-room through the long and dark freezing hall, she said slowly, 'You know, I've decided – actually I decided yesterday – if Michael does get that ring off his mother and we get engaged, I'll leave Exeter and live with him.'

'Without being married?'

'Without being married.'

They were already at the door of the dining-room, so their conversation was abruptly discontinued. Poor Claire, Rachel thought. And I had such a lovely day yesterday. She thought of Charles waiting for her. I'll ring him as soon as I get home, she promised herself.

Luckily Jonathan had taken a liking to Rachel. 'Good breeding there, Rachel, my girl,' he appraised. 'Fine hocks. Always tells, you know. Good blood. Who's the squire?'

'I don't know.'

'You don't know?' Jonathan looked amazed. 'You mean you're a bastard?'

'I suppose so,' Rachel laughed. 'You're the only person ever to call me that.'

'If that's the worst he calls you, you'll be lucky,' Cynthia smirked as she raised her glass to her lips. After emptying the glass, Cynthia vaguely attempted to get some turkey on to her plate.

'What about me, Claire? Don't I get anything to eat?' Jonathan banged the table with his spoon. 'Why'd you always fuss over that drunken whore of a mother of yours when I'm starving?'

The spoon continued to crash down on the table, punctuating his demand. The two dogs, who were lying by the fire, got up and sauntered out of the room. The cat left the windowsill and positioned herself under Cynthia's chair. She sat waiting and purring, her green eyes glowing. With any luck, the turkey would fall off Cynthia's fork and on to the floor.

This time, the cat miscalculated. Cynthia pushed back her chair, and clumsily attempted to throw her plate of food at Jonathan. She missed her mark, and the plate hit the wall behind him. The two dogs slipped back into the room and began pulling and snarling at the scattered food and at each other.

'I'll kill you!' Cynthia was yelling. 'No-good lousy sod.'

'Come on, Rachel. Let's leave them to it.'

'Won't they kill each other if they go on like that?'

'I don't expect so. I think if they were going to really kill each other, they'd have done it years ago. Sometimes I wish they would. Sometimes I feel like killing him myself.'

'Was your mother really a prostitute?'

'No. In those days, chorus girls were very strictly chaperoned. She could have been one if she'd wanted to, but I believe her when she says that her aim was to marry a rich man and get away from her miserable life at home.'

'She must have been very beautiful.'

'Yes, she was. But she was a fool. I know I can handle Michael because I've learned the hard way. I've had years of practice handling my father. He's not really drunk yet, but by tonight he'll be roaring. I'm the only one that can calm him.'

'How?' asked Rachel, thinking maybe a strait-jacket might be the answer.

'I treat him like a naughty boy. He likes to be whipped. I get a riding crop and lay into him until he screams, and then he's quiet as a lamb for several days.'

'Claire,' said Rachel, 'how awful.'

'No it isn't. You've no idea how many men like it.'

'Does Michael?'

'I don't know yet. It's too early to say.'

Their conversation was interrupted by the sound of more plates crashing and Cynthia screaming that Jonathan would be the death of her. Claire lowered her head and then said to Rachel, 'I think you'd better go now before it gets bad.'

'Okay, I'll phone Cook. I hate leaving you like this, Claire.' The yelling and screaming continued unabated.

'Don't worry. I've coped with it for years. Thanks for coming. Please go quickly before the war spreads. I'll go and find my riding crop.'

Rachel couldn't wait to get out. It's one thing to read books where the hero slaps his riding boot with a whip, impatient with his recalcitrant lover, and quite another to know it happens in real life . . . and to people you know. Thank goodness Charles isn't like that, she thought.

As soon as she returned to Aunt Emily's house, she eagerly rushed to the telephone.

Julia answered. 'Hello, Rachel. Happy Boxing Day. We did enjoy seeing you on Christmas Eve . . . Charles? Oh, he's out, dear. With an old schoolfriend. Brenda, I think that's her name . . . Yes, dear, I'll tell him you called.'

Rachel put the 'phone receiver down. 'Funny, I didn't know he knew anyone called Brenda. I must ask him about her.'

Julia hung up the telephone and smiled. Charles returned later that night, and his mother called to him from the kitchen. 'Rachel rang.'

'Oh yes? Did she leave a message?'

'No. Just asked me to say she'd called.'

'What time was that?'

'I should think it was about six o'clock.'

'Well, it's too late to ring now,' said Charles. 'I'll leave it 'til tomorrow.' He entered the kitchen to find a snack before going to bed. He bent over his mother to kiss her good-night.

'I see Brenda still uses the same cheap scent, dear.' Julia wrinkled her nose. They stood in the kitchen and looked at each other. 'Good-night, dear. Sleep well.' Julia smiled at her son.

Charles went to his room. He tried very hard to feel guilty. But then again, he reckoned, he had only been engaged for twenty-four hours. While they had been actually going out together he had never felt the need to be faithful to Rachel. What she doesn't know won't hurt her, he convinced himself. This principle had served him well enough in his relationship with his mother. Brenda Mason wouldn't tell. He was suddenly consumed with lust for her. He remembered the powerful odour of her unwashed body – the slightly sour smell of her sheets.

She lived in a rooming house in Bridport and worked at the local tea-shop. He remembered asking her to put on her black waitress uniform with the white pinafore and white cap. She looked particualarly young and innocent in that prim outfit. 'Bend over,' he had said. 'I want to take you from behind.'

'Bitch, you bitch,' he found himself yelling at the top of his voice. After he was finished, he flopped on the bed.

'Why were you cursing, Charles?' Brenda's voice whined.

'I don't know. I really don't know. I'm sorry.'

'I'll see you again, won't I Charles?'

'I'm engaged now, Brenda.'

'I won't tell. Honestly, I won't.'

Charles leaned over and patted her on the shoulder. 'I expect I'll see you again, Brenda. I can't say when because I've got to finish up my last two terms at university and then find a job. But here. Here's a fiver for the good time we had.'

Brenda giggled. 'I don't know where you get all those ideas from. Really, I don't. Look at the mess you've made of my dress.'

'It'll give you something to think about while you're serving tea to the old matrons of Bridport,' said Charles, and he let himself out of the room.

Lying now in his own bed, Charles reflected. Somehow he didn't see Rachel taking to sex like Brenda. Come to think of it, Charles found the idea of making love to Rachel very difficult indeed to imagine except in the most straightforward, unadventurous fashion. 'I've still got two years of freedom. Then I'll be faithful.' Charles fell quickly into a deep and contented sleep.

19

Michael had a miserable Boxing Day. He had promised himself that he would broach the subject of the engagement ring either on the day before Christmas or on Boxing Day, but he found it impossible even to begin to discuss his engagement to Claire with his mother. The day before Christmas Day, his mother had organized a non-stop stream of visitors through their chalet all day and all night until it was time to go to midnight mass. Christmas Day was out of the question, for Gloria always behaved as if every Christmas Day were her last. They had a tradition that they each filled a stocking, and then left it by the Christmas tree. The trick was to avoid being seen by the other person as they each placed their stockings. Gloria also insisted on leaving a plate of food for Santa Claus and a bucket of water for the reindeer.

Most years Michael looked forward to their private Christmas ceremonies, but this year he was anxious and preoccupied. He found himself missing Claire. She had such drive and energy. Her eyes sometimes held a particularly dangerous glint. They hinted at chasms and borderlines that they could explore together. Danger lurked in the curl of her mouth. He shivered just thinking about it. He had to have her.

His mother had done herself no favours bringing him to Switzerland. All the pretty young things tripping over their skis looked pale and uninteresting by comparison. He was polite enough, but apart from a very drunken episode on his first night at the resort – which ended up in a minor orgy in a lift in one of the hotels – he kept himself very much to himself.

* * *

'Oh darling!' Gloria squeaked, 'you shouldn't have. Naughty boy, Michael. You know I love it. I love it!' She had opened up her stocking and was holding out a particularly beautiful black evening gown.

'It's a Paris designer called Jean Claude. He promised me he'd make you something special.' Michael was pleased with his choice. Gloria took off her bathrobe and slipped on the dress.

'It needs a bra to create a bit more cleavage,' she said, 'but otherwise it's beautiful, Michael.' She twirled round the room laughing and tossing her hair. 'Look what I've got you this year.'

It was a Cartier watch. 'Oh thank you, Mother. I've been wanting one for ages.' He truly was pleased.

'Any *my* Paris surprise . . .' She handed him a small package.

'Black silk underpants,' said Michael. 'Mother, where on earth did you find them?'

'I also know a designer – you'll look marvellous in them. You have such a lovely tight little bottom.'

'You are so funny, Mother.' Michael collapsed laughing. 'I don't know anyone else's mother who would give them black silk underpants.'

'I don't see why not. No one else will ever love you the way I do.'

'I know that, Mother. Believe me, I do.' Michael looked at her very seriously. He put his arms around her, and pulled her very close to him. 'You do know that you're always first.'

'I know, my Michael.' She kissed him. 'Let's do *The Times* crossword,' she said.

'No, not now. I haven't cleaned my teeth. I'll go and shave, and you get the champagne and orange juice organized.'

Later, the drawing-room of the chalet filled with the Christmas Day guests. There were twelve for Christmas dinner. The catering was run very efficiently by a gaggle of marriageable debutantes. 'The table looks wonderful, Mother.'

'I know – it feels like such a happy day for us both, darling.'

During the meal, Michael, who sat at the head of the table, watched his mother at the other end. She was wearing the black dress he had given her. She was right about the bra; it did give a much better line to her breasts. She was laughing and joking with the two handsome men who sat either side of her. She was always at her best at parties, particularly her own.

It was time to pull the Christmas crackers. They had been flown in, along with the Stilton, from Harrods. Suddenly the room blossomed as the multi-coloured hats were crammed down on the heads of the slightly tipsy grinning guests.

'Christmas isn't Christmas without children, I always say.'

Michael turned, tracing the ring of these words to its source, and found himself looking at the lady on his left. 'Don't you think so, Michael?' Mrs Greenbaum was getting soggy with emotion and too much wine.

'No, I don't. I can't stand children.'

'You don't really mean that, do you?'

'I do, and if you ask most men, when there are no women around, they'll tell you the same thing. Most men don't want children. Children howl, they slobber, and they cost a lot of money. Besides, they age their mothers dreadfully.'

'Well I hope you change your mind, young man, because one day you're going to want to get married. How would your wife feel if she was to be denied children?'

'I'm about to get engaged, and it's already decided – no children.'

Mrs Greenbaum opened her eyes wide. 'I say, Gloria didn't tell me you were about to get engaged. How marvellous! Who to?'

Michael realized he had made a mistake, but it was too late to back down. Mrs Greenbaum was a very wealthy friend of his mother's. She, too, was a widow, and usually spent Christmas Day with them wherever they were. He usually managed to avoid her. 'Listen, everybody . . . Quiet, please.' She was up on her feet tapping her wine glass with a knife. The room fell silent. 'I give you a toast,' she said, raising her wine glass. Everyone looked at her in anticipation. It was usual to toast the Queen of England before any other toasts were called. But the news was too much for Mrs Greenbaum to contain. Let's see how old pussycat Gloria's going to take it, she thought. 'Let us drink to the wonderful news of the engagement between Michael Swann and . . . What did you say her name was, dear?'

'Claire Balfor-James,' Michael mumbled.

'Claire Balfor-James.'

Everyone rose to their feet and raised their glasses. 'To Michael and Claire,' the guests chorused.

Michael looked at his mother. She's amazing, he thought. She hasn't turned a hair. She looks as though it's the best news she's heard in years.

'Of course I knew,' he could hear her saying to the guests nearest her. 'Michael and I decided to keep it quiet until after the New Year.' She looked down the table at him. 'But you couldn't wait, could you, darling? Never mind. It all adds to the festivities.'

After the guests had gone, it was late. The last to leave was Mrs Greenbaum. 'I must be on my way. Michael, do see me to the car.' The snow was thick and hard. Michael had to hold Mrs Greenbaum up. He resisted an urge to throw her face-down into the snow and stamp her head in. 'I'm so happy for you, my boy. You'll change your mind about children . . . what will your mother do without you?' She kissed him a flowery powdery kiss.

As the car drove away, Michael looked up at the moon: it was huge and full, casting elaborate shadows around the chalet. He stood gaining time before dealing with his mother. I wonder which tack she's going to take, he thought. By the time he re-entered the chalet, she had gone to her room. He could hear her crying. Soon, if she ran true to form, it would be the full hysterics. For the first time in his life, Michael left her to cry herself to sleep. It took her a long time to realize that he wasn't coming in to comfort her. Michael fell asleep with a pillow pressed against each ear.

Boxing Day morning dawned bright and clear. Gloria was huddled over the fire in the sitting-room when Michael went out to the kitchen to get a cup of coffee. He could tell she was angry. He was used to that particular posture of hers. It reminded him of a bow bent ready to fire an arrow. 'How dare you?' She leaped to her feet when she saw him. 'How dare you make a fool of me like that!'

'I meant to discuss it with you, but when have we had time?'

'Since when do you get yourself engaged without telling me, and to that little nobody . . . scheming little bitch. What does she do that you're so anxious for marriage, huh?'

'I don't want to lose her.'

'What about me? Don't you love me? Don't I always come first? I'm not even first enough to be told about your engagement.'

'Mother,' Michael tried to reason with her, 'I *was* going to tell you, but Mrs Greenbaum caught me on the hop. You know I would have told you. I tell you everything.'

'Right, then. If you tell me everything, tell me why you *have* to marry her. A little nobody – why can't you just screw her, like you did all the others? I've never stopped you – you had girls in your bed since you were fourteen. How many mothers would allow that? You tell me.' She was beginning to work herself up. 'What's wrong with the love *I* give you? With the life we have together? What's this Claire have that I don't have?'

She was screaming at him. 'Look, Michael.' She tore off her bathrobe. 'Look at me. I'm still beautiful. There's not a mark on my body.' She stood naked in front of the fire. She crossed her arms behind her head. 'Aren't I beautiful?' She slowly turned, watching him from under her eyelashes. Her skin was as pale as marble. Her pubic hair was thick and blond.

'Yes, Mother,' said Michael obediently. It always ends like this, he thought. Ten more minutes and it'll be over.

'Kneel down and adore me,' she said. He slid to his knees, and then bent to kiss her extended foot. 'You're mine, Michael. No one else's. If you have to have that puny little cow, you'll have to have her. But she'll never own you. Will she, Michael?'

'No, Mother.' He crouched at her feet.

She smiled. 'Well, that's that, then. I'll go and have a bath, and we must decide where to have the engagement party.'

'Mother?'

Gloria was walking off in the direction of the bathroom, trailing her bathrobe. 'Yes, darling?'

'Can I have the family engagement ring?'

'Of course, Michael. I'll get it out of the bank vault as soon as we get home.'

'Thank you, darling.' Michael sank into a chair filled with love. It had been easier than he had expected.

Rachel was reading the *Daily Mail* at breakfast. 'Look, Aunt Emily,' she said. 'Look at William Hickey's column. There's a piece about Michael getting engaged to Claire.' While Aunt Emily was fumbling with her glasses, Rachel ran to the telephone. 'Claire? Have you seen the *Mail* this morning?'

'No. We don't have newspapers in this house. Why?'

'There's a bit here about you and Michael.'

'What? I don't know anything about this. Read it to me.'

' "The engagement of Michael Swann, son of Major and Mrs Swann of the Manor House, Axminster, to Claire Balfor-James, was announced at a Christmas dinner in fashionable Kitzbul. 'I'm absolutely thrilled,' said Mrs Swann. Michael Swann has always been one of the most eligible young bachelors in the West Country. There was no comment from the Balfor-James family." '

'Oh, that must have been who Daddy was roaring at on the 'phone just after you left yesterday. Thank God they didn't print what he said. He was too drunk to remember what it was all about.'

'Have you heard from Michael?'

'Yes I did. He 'phoned last night. It's all on. He got the ring.'

'Claire, you're supposed to think about loving him, not about rings, at a time like this.'

'I can't afford to think of anything except getting away from here. Rachel, Michael and I have agreed that we will live with each other in London after he finishes his finals.'

'So you'll give up university?'

'Yes. It's Michael I want when it comes down to it, and if I don't stay with him, I could lose him. He feels the same about me.'

'I'll miss you dreadfully,' said Rachel. 'Still, we have until May. Then I'll get up to London to see you both.'

'And I'll be back often. Don't worry. Gloria will want to see as much of Michael as she can, so I'll be staying in Axminster. We won't lose touch. With any luck we can have a double wedding.'

'I don't think so. Michael's family are far too posh for us. But it's a nice idea anyway.'

'It'll all work out, you'll see. Michael already has an offer for a job in the Foreign Office. Bye-bye, Rachel, and do send Aunt Emily my love.'

Rachel went back to the breakfast table. 'Aunt Emily, Claire is going to live in sin with Michael.'

Aunt Emily's glasses rose. 'Oh really? How will her parents take it?'

'I don't think they'll notice. They're mostly pretty drunk.'

'Poor child. Mind you, I hear that it's not unusual now for young people to live together before marriage. Do you want to live with Charles?'

'Sometimes I do, but I promised Aunt Bea I'd finish my degree. And I would like to be married in a church in white. I'd feel awful if I'd been living with Charles and then had a white wedding. I suppose it would have been nice to have had a father to give me away,' she said as she looked at her aunt with great affection, 'yet when I look at all the families I know, even Charles's, I've had a much happier time than any of them.'

Aunt Emily blinked emotionally. 'A loving home is a happy home, Rachel.'

'I hope I'll make one for Charles.'

'You will, darling.'

Rachel was suddenly overwhelmed by a feeling of contentment and gratitude. I'm so lucky, she thought. Somehow I've already found a future that will be secure and happy. Charles is so good to me, I really will try to be a good wife to him. Imagine finding such a kind man when so many people go through their lives all alone. She thought about Anna. She had been meaning to telephone her, but she had been so caught up in Charles, university, and her happiness, that contact with Anna had been pushed aside. She promptly dialled Anna's number to apologize.

It turned out that Anna had managed to complete the secretarial course in nine months instead of the usual year. 'Don't apologize, Rachel. Honestly. It's my fault as well. I've been up to my ears in double-entry book-keeping – it's a swine to do. I've got the diploma and a job in London with the RSPCA. Just what I wanted. I'll be working for an inspector and rescuing animals from bad homes.'

'Well done. That's marvellous. Did you hear that I'm engaged to Charles Hunter?'

'Yes.'

'Is that all you have to say on the subject?' Rachel laughed. 'Come on, Anna, don't be such a sour-puss. I'm really happy, honestly. Be happy for me.'

'Oh well, if it makes you happy . . . I think you're an idiot, getting tied down to a man.'

'I want a family.'

'Which do you want most, Rachel, Charles or a family?

'I don't know. I've never really thought of it like that.'

'Just remember, Rachel. You often romanticize what you want. You've no idea of what a married life is like.'

'That's true. But it'll be all right. I know it will, because we'll make it work. You'll see.'

'What's Charles going to do?'

'He hopes to get an Upper II in Literature and History.

He says he wants to be a journalist, so he's applying for a job on a local paper. You have to do that before you can get onto the big papers. I'm staying on at Exeter to finish my degree, then we'll get married.'

'You must come and stay with me in London before the dreadful event.'

Rachel laughed. 'You're incorrigible, Anna.'

'I know. That's what all the girls tell me here. All they do is talk about men. It's like some awful catching disease.'

'You're so funny, Anna. Your turn will come.'

'Never. I'd rather live with a horse.'

'Okay, okay. I'll see you soon.' Rachel hung up. I'll miss Claire and Anna, she thought, but it does give me two years to really concentrate on getting a good degree.

Book Two
Charles and Rachel

20

London, 1970

Rachel was lying in the bath looking at the crease on her stomach. Absolutely disgusting, she thought. Her second child, a girl, was now eight weeks old, and Rachel was still struggling to breastfeed her. Her breasts leaked milk into the hot bath. Charles was the only person in the family who had no trouble with her breastfeeding. After both births, he relished regressing to an infantile need to suck at her nipples. It made her faintly embarrassed, but he assured her it was perfectly normal. She tried a taste of the milk that flowed so freely for him and not for the babies. Surprisingly enough, it was very sweet, rather like condensed milk from a tin. I think I'll give up breastfeeding, she thought, heaving herself out of the bath. She stood on the bathmat looking out the window at the row of houses facing their house. '11 Ashley Road, Hammersmith, London, West 6.' She was talking out loud. 'Imagine living at 11 Ashley Road, Hammersmith.'

It was January, the suicide month, she thought. She could hear the baby crying next door. 'Coming . . . coming . . . hang on, Sarah . . . I'm here.' She picked up the wet little bundle and hugged her to her chest. 'You're not going to live in Ashley Road, Hammersmith all your life, my baby girl. You're going to grow up and live away from London. Away from these mean streets and shut-off people.' She looked at the perfect pink ear and smelled the special baby smell. She carried the child downstairs into the kitchen. It always took a large gin-and-tonic to calm her down enough to let the baby feed. Unfortunately, it also took several cigarettes to keep her relaxed enough to stay in the chair for the long and boring business of feeding, burping, and then feeding again.

She imagined the look of horror on the midwife's face if she could see Rachel now. Sterile old bitch, thought Rachel. She took a large swig of gin and a deep drag at the cigarette. 'I've really got to give this up – what's the point of me struggling to prove I'm a good mother and please a midwife when I'm going to end up an alcoholic or dead from lung cancer?'

'I did feed Dominic for six months,' she explained to the cat who listened politely. 'He looks all right.' She felt an enormous sense of relief once she had made the decision. She remembered the last time they had visited Julia and William. She was pregnant with Sarah and not in the mood to be bullied by Julia. 'I fed Charles until he was two, dear.'

'Mother,' said Charles, 'we'll engrave that on your tombstone.'

Later in the kitchen, Julia turned to Rachel who was sitting at the table, tired after a long day. Dominic was finally in bed in Elizabeth's room. 'You know, I don't know about you, but breastfeeding Charles was a sexual experience for me.'

Rachel looked startled. She blushed. 'Really, Julia? I find it anything but that. I really don't want to feed the next one.'

'You should, dear. A baby needs its mother's milk. I expect you have problems because you weren't mothered. You must remember that two maiden aunts are not any substitute for a good mother.' A little martyred smile played on her lips. 'We have to pay a price for our babies. They come, we love them, and then they leave us. That's how it is and how it should be.'

'You mean Elizabeth, don't you?' Rachel looked at Julia. She lost that battle, Rachel thought. 'Any news?'

Julia shook her head. 'No. We did have a letter saying she was in Nairobi and expecting to go out into the bush to teach. Of course, the girl must do as she pleases. I'm not one to influence my children one way or the other. As long as she's happy, Father and I are proud of her.'

It had been hard for Julia. Charles moved to London after Rachel graduated. He was offered a job on a local paper in Hammersmith, the *Hammersmith Evening Argus*, which was a huge step forward from the *Bridport Gazette*. Elizabeth, as soon as she reached twenty-one, left home and joined the missionaries in Africa and hadn't really been seen since.

Pity, Rachel thought, I liked Elizabeth. She rocked Sarah in the rocking chair. 'I've got to have more in my life than just children.'

Rachel was dimly aware that she needed more out of Charles than she was getting. On the surface they appeared a very happy, sociable young couple. Charles took to London like a duck to water. Rachel hated the city, but she knew she must make the best of it for his sake. Fortunately, Anna was living in Kensington and occasionally Claire would sweep through with Michael on leave from his Foreign Office station in some exotic country or other.

'I don't know what it is,' Rachel complained to Anna. 'I just don't seem to be able to communicate with Charles any more.'

Anna was not sympathetic. 'Charles doesn't bother to communicate with anyone, love. He's usually too busy staring at himself in a mirror.'

'Anna, don't be beastly about him.'

'I'm not. I'm just bored with coming round here and seeing you looking like a human vegetable. Lately you smell of sick every time I've been here.'

'I know. It's awful. Sarah just spits up all the time. All over me, the furniture, the carpet. I do scrub myself and everything else, but it's an awful smell. I'm sorry.'

Anna looked at her. 'You're not really happy, are you, honestly?'

'I don't know. If I'm not, it's my own fault. I don't understand why I feel so different from the other women in the street. I just can't go endlessly to tupperware parties. I have tried. I sit round the table and we all admire the boxes and the mixing bowls, and then we have coffee. There's nothing wrong with that – it's just that no one says anything real to each other.'

'They wouldn't dare – if they ever admitted how miserable they were, their whole world would come crashing down around their ears.'

'It's easy for you, Anna. You never wanted a relationship with a man, so you don't have to compromise.'

'It's very hard for me, Rachel. That's part of why I get impatient with you – you've been five years locked away in your little house in a suburban street. I don't suppose you've even looked at newspapers.'

'Well, to tell the truth, I'm too tired most times. I do watch the Nine O'clock News, and Charles tells me what's going on.'

'There's a big world out there and it's changing very fast. I have to make decisions about myself that never would have occurred to me before I came to London.' Anna lit a cigarette. 'You see, Rachel, I'm a lesbian – it wasn't a shock to me. I always knew there was something different about me, right from the early days at St Anne's. But whereas my mother's generation kept their private life very private, there is a move for people like myself to get together and insist that we should be able to live like anyone else. It scares me . . . all the time. How do I tell my mother? What would the nuns think? What do you think? Now you know.' She looked quizzically at Rachel. 'Do you still want me to be Sarah's godmother?'

'Of course, you idiot. You know, Charles has always said you were gay. When he's in one of his foul moods, he's often suggested that we've slept together. In fact sometimes he says he's sure I'm gay. That doesn't hurt so much. It's when he goes on about my aunts. Actually, living with women is something that feels natural to me. It's living like this with a man that seems so wrong. Charles says it's because . . .'

'Don't go on about Charles,' Anna interrupted. 'Charles talks a lot of shit. I do think you have to make an effort to get out of the house – like you never come over to my place. I always have to come here. There's no reason why you shouldn't tell Charles to babysit, and we could have dinner together.'

'That would be lovely, Anna – it really would. I'll ask Charles this evening and give you a ring.' As they stood at the front door Rachel gave Anna a big hug. 'Don't think I'm upset about you being a lesbian. At least you know what you are, I'm the one that's confused. I keep feeling that if we went back to Devon, it'd all get simple again.'

'Rachel the romantic, again. You can never go back. You have everything you've always wished for. You know, you remind me of the girl who always gets the last biscuit on the plate.'

Rachel laughed. 'You mean the last biscuit – a handsome husband and £10,000 a year? Well, we certainly don't get £10,000, but the rest is true.'

'I must go now. Take care, Rachel. Ring me.'

'Okay. By the end of the week.'

Charles was late for dinner. Rachel heard his key in the lock, and she looked up and smiled as he came into the kitchen. 'Can't you do those nappies during the day?' he asked abruptly.

She felt a surge of anger. 'You bloody well stay home and try and run a house and look after two kids and a husband who is hardly ever home,' she snapped.

Charles looked surprised. 'What's got into you? You're not usually so ratty.'

'I'm not ratty, Charles. I'm desperate. I have to do more than just bring up two children . . .'

'Oh not that again. Let's talk about it later. After supper.'

Rachel shrugged her shoulders. She knew there would be no 'after supper'. The television would be on, and Charles would sit glued to it until it was time for bed. Later that night, as he ground away on top of her, she thought, I will go out to dinner with Anna. The thought cheered her up so much that she put her heart into the whole performance.

'That was nice,' said Charles, flopping on to his side of the bed.

'Wasn't it,' said Rachel. 'Will you babysit? I want to go over to Anna's place next week for dinner.'

Charles raised himself on one elbow. 'But, Rachel.

You've never been out without me in five years.'

'Exactly. That's why I've got to do it. You remember that party we went to at Christmas at your office?'

'Yes I do. You got drunk,' Charles said disapprovingly.

'Do you know why I got drunk?'

'If you remember, you cried all the way back in the car, and then you were sick on the front step. All you kept saying was "Measles".'

'That's right. Absolutely. It was then that I realized I had to do something about myself. Do you know, no one would talk to me at that party? It was like all the other occasions. "What do you do?" "I'm a housewife." "Oh really. I must get another drink, if you'll excuse me." And there I was standing alone again until I found this other woman cowering in a corner. She was "just a housewife", so we talked about whether or not Sarah should have an injection for measles.'

'Riveting.' Charles fell back on the bed. 'Okay, I'll babysit, but don't let that bull-dyke give you any ideas.'

'Thank you, Charles.' Rachel leaned over and gave him a warm kiss. I'm such a cow, she thought. I'm so lucky to have a man who works hard for us and loves us. I'll try and be less angry tomorrow.

'Try valium,' said Mary who lived two doors away. 'It keeps me sane. One in the morning, one at lunchtime, and one just before I go to bed.'

Rachel was sitting in Mary's kitchen, which had exactly the same 'Habitat-ery' as all the kitchens down the road, except for Mrs Molsky's. Mrs Molsky had eight children and was on the Dole. She chose to spend her ill-gotten gains on drink and parties. 'At least she gets paid for it.'

Mary looked shocked. 'Really, Rachel. You do say the oddest things sometimes.'

'Can you honestly say you've never thought that it would help if you got paid? Not the times you enjoy it, but all the times you feel you *have* to do it?'

Mary was about the only woman in the neighbourhood whom Rachel could really talk to. There were several houses up and down the street where Dominic played and where she was able to spend a little time talking between the shopping and the cleaning. But Mary had been a convent girl, and they had immediately recognized a common bond between them. Mary's husband was a successful insurance broker. He was driven to work as if by demons. Rachel would look at his nails bitten down to the quick and at the yellow nicotine stains on his fingers. 'He'll kill himself if he goes on like that, Mary.'

Mary would shrug her shoulders. 'No, Robert won't. He likes living that way. Even when he's home he's always on the telephone. I don't mind. I married him because I knew he'd do well. He was always full of ideas and surprises. For a boy from a small Irish town, he has done well. I can't imagine what I'd do without him. It's like living with a bolt of lightning.'

'Don't you ever feel fed up? Look, I'm twenty-seven, and I have two children. Every day, from Monday to Friday, I get up at seven. I get breakfast ready for Charles and Dominic. I then get the baby dressed and fed. Charles leaves at exactly eight-thirty. Then I clear up the breakfast things and argue with Dominic about which coat he's going to wear. Next, I get the baby in the pram and we go to Dominic's school. Dominic runs in and I push the pram back. Twenty minutes later I'm at my own front door. I let myself in. With any luck, the baby's asleep, and I sit down and have a cup of coffee and a cigarette. Usually there is a major disaster area to deal with. Sometimes I pretend the kitchen is China, the living room is Russia, and our bedroom is America. I'm Henry Kissinger, and I sort them all out by lunchtime. I celebrate my victory by eating the baby's leftover lunch. I turn on some music and let her lie on the floor and wave her legs while I iron whatever happens to need it. Though why Charles needs me to iron a handkerchief so that he can pull it out of his pocket and blow his nose on it, I shall never understand. His mother even irons underpants and tea towels.

'Anyway, it's time to collect Dominic, so Sarah gets put back into her pram. We wait outside the school gate. Rows of mothers with little children attached to their hands or in prams or running around screaming. It doesn't matter how cold it is; none of us dare ask the headmaster if we could wait inside the hall. And then the children run out. Twenty minutes later, we are back home. I get supper organized for Dominic while he watches Children's Hour. The baby cries most of the time because she wants to be picked up, but I haven't the time. After Dominic has had his bath, I read him a story with Sarah on my knee. Usually Charles arrives home about then, just in time to kiss his son good-night, and then I get the dinner organized for both of us.

'Charles plays with Sarah while I cook. I put her to bed while he lays the table. We eat dinner. I listen to his day and try to make mine sound equally interesting. He helps me wash up. We watch television and then we go up to bed. Most nights Charles has an erection he wants to do something with. Unless I have a period, and then he won't come near me. Most nights I try to avoid it because I don't feel at all interested. However, if it is inevitable, I make the best of it. That means if, for some reason, he does turn me on, I can come. If I simply can't agree with myself that I'm going to make the best of it, I do shopping lists or grit my teeth and say silently to him, "Get on with it." That's when I think Mrs Molsky is a lucky woman. It's those moments that a fiver would at least mean I could alter tomorrow in some way. I could take the kids out and buy toys.'

Mary said, 'Really, Rachel. You should be an actress. What's so tragic about a life like that? You're so dramatic. It's like that for all women – unless they're really rich. You chose Charles, after all.'

'I didn't think it would be like this. If I read that last speech of mine in a book, I would recommend that the woman should take a dose of cyanide while watching The Magic Roundabout washed down with gripe water. Anyway, you haven't answered my question: Do you ever feel like that?'

'Yes, but I keep it to myself. And I *don't* go down the street making other mothers feel uneasy. All of us have chosen to have children, and we have to compromise

. . . Oh dear, look at the time. Come on, Rachel, it's school time. We'll be late and get notes from the headmaster.'

The two women went flying down the road. It's come to this, thought Rachel. I'm frightened of a headmaster. My God.

21

Rachel's visit to Anna was a great success. Anna introduced Rachel to her 'partner' Alice. Alice looked just like Valerie from St Anne's. The three women ate spaghetti, drank lots of red wine, and laughed. Rachel felt as though she were a young student again. Alice was a very blunt, straightforward Yorkshire girl. She wore jeans and a roll-neck sweater with a red bandana round her throat. She had shoulder-length hair with a fringe. Rachel was surprised. She had been a little nervous at the thought of meeting the woman who was making love to her friend Anna, but once inside the door she relaxed. The flat was warm and cheerful. 'I'm the cook,' said Alice by way of introduction. 'Here. Give me your coat.'

Anna or Alice occasionally gave each other a hug during the evening, but they did not embarrass Rachel at all. In fact she was very pleased to see Anna looking so happy and relaxed. Just before she caught the last bus home, she said to Anna in the hall, 'I really enjoyed myself. Thanks a lot. I think Alice is lovely. I'll give you a ring.'

When she arrived home, Charles was sitting in front of the television. 'It's lonely,' he said, 'all by yourself in the house . . . You look radiant, Rachel. What have you been doing? Attending an orgy?'

'Don't be silly, darling. Alice is a really nice woman.' In bed that night, she felt so grateful to Charles for her wonderful time that she genuinely enjoyed making love. 'I wish it was always like this,' she said, lying in his arms.

'It mostly is, isn't it? Charles sounded anxious.

'Mostly,' she said, and they fell asleep.

Those were years that went by in a haze of exhaustion. Her only break was staying with Aunt Emily. 'Why don't you persuade Aunt Emily to sell that big old house and move into something smaller? She could let you have some of the money then.'

'I couldn't, Charles. That house is her life. As long as she is living there, she feels Aunt Bea is near. She did talk about moving once, but I couldn't do that to her.'

'You're so bloody sentimental, Rachel. Here we are, struggling to survive, when we don't have to. She doesn't need a cook and a maid just to look after her.'

'She does. She can't cook now. Her arthritis is awful, also she needs the company. It's her money, Charles, not mine.'

Charles and Rachel did live very frugally. Any money left over went on clothes for Charles. His job demanded it, he explained. Privately Rachel couldn't think why he needed quite so many suits. 'But I've seen all those baggy little aldermen you go and interview. They all wear grey wrinkled suits. I don't see why you have to take so long to get dressed just to impress them.'

'It's the job, darling. It won't be long before I get onto one of the big papers, and then I can really get into news-reporting.'

When Charles did get an offer from a major London newspaper, his salary tripled overnight. The job involved a lot of overseas work. He would cover any news story that required a reporter from England. They were both thrilled.

'I don't know,' said Julia. 'You'll be away from home a lot. Mind you, if a man strays, it's usually a woman's fault.'

'Don't be silly, Mother,' said Charles.

Rachel laughed. 'Honestly, that's one thing that has never bothered me. Charles isn't the unfaithful type.'

He gave her a reassuring hug. 'Of course I'm not.' Suddenly he felt stifled. The little Bridport sitting-room closed in on him. 'Come on, Rachel, let's go and see Ruth. She'll be pleased and she may have news from Manny.'

Ruth was thrilled for them both. She clucked and fussed and plied them with cakes and biscuits. 'Manny will be home soon. He's leaving New York on Saturday, and will be here for a few weeks before going to Israel for a while.'

'I'd love to see him,' said Charles. 'Ask him to visit us while he's here.'

They had left the two children with Julia. Recently, Rachel had become uncomfortable with Dominic. He was now eight and Julia adored him. 'Grandma lets me stay up late,' he would argue.

'That's because it was the holidays and you didn't have to get up for school.'

'She cooks better than you do.'

'I know, dear. She's been doing it for much longer.'

'I heard her say to Mrs Cohen that you didn't know how to bring up children.'

Enough, Rachel said to herself.

Her son looked at her with his grey calm eyes. 'I'd like to live with Grandma.'

'Actually, Dominic, you're too old to hang about your grandmother and get thoroughly spoiled. I'm your mother, and you're stuck with me. Besides, Daddy's going to be away a lot and I'll need you.'

Sarah was so uncomplicated compared to Dominic. She knew what she wanted even at the age of four. Julia wasn't particularly interested in her.

Why is child-rearing such a ghastly business? Rachel was given to asking herself on numerous occasions. As Dominic grew older and made even more friends, she was obliged to invite an ever-growing band of boys and occasionally girls to the house after school and during the holidays. The truth was, she discovered, that, although she liked her own children well enough, she didn't care for other people's.

She was the first mother in the street who rebelled against the birthday party syndrome. The year Sarah was born, she went out and bought the cake for Dominic's birthday which made her feel guilty. 'Don't be silly, darling. You know you can't make cakes anyway,' said Charles when she wept in his arms that night. 'Some women are naturally maternal like Mother, and some aren't.'

'Don't you think I'm maternal, Charles?'

'Look, darling. You know you're a bit sloppy in the house, and you don't remember dentist appointments for the children do you?'

'No, I suppose not. I do hope Sarah doesn't grow up like that.'

'She's got Mother's example, so she'll be all right. Look how well Dominic's done.'

'Actually, Charles, I was going to talk to you about that. You know. Julia isn't exactly loyal to me in front of Dominic. I sometimes feel Dominic believes I'm a real failure of a mother because Julia does everything so much better than I do, and she does criticize me in front of him – it's not very fair.'

'She's getting on, darling. She won't change. She's always had a sharp tongue. By the way, she's coming up to town next week to see Max and his family. Shall we have them over for dinner?'

'I suppose so. I wish she didn't make me feel so inadequate.'

'She doesn't really mean it. I think you're over-sensitive.'

This was one of the times when Rachel let Charles get on with making love, while she devised a passable menu that would not attract a lecture from Julia. Charles was going through a heavy stage of enjoying oral sex. When Charles did it to her, it felt like being in the clutches of a thoroughly enthusiastic Hoover. When she did it to him, usually at his request, it felt like their old garden hose that unpredictably erupted while she struggled to water the garden. 'How was it, darling?' said Charles, coming up for air.

She could just see his eyes over the fringe of her pubic hair. 'Lovely, Charles,' she replied. 'I think I'll make coq-au-vin, with chocolate mousse for pudding.'

'That sounds interesting,' mumbled Charles.

'Good night, darling,' said Rachel, shutting her eyes quickly. She didn't feel like grappling with Charles's erection tonight. How can any mother spend a day with a toddler like Sarah – wee-wee, poo-poo, and bums – and feel randy? she thought, waiting for Charles to settle.

Charles loomed over her. 'You tired, darling?'

'Um.' She pretended to be half asleep.

'All right then.' He leaned over her and kissed her. She tried not to grimace. She never did like the smell of her own vagina on his lips.

He rolled over to his side of the bed. By next year, the field will be a lot bigger, he thought. Anthea's getting a little too pushy, and she's too local. Away from home, games are a lot safer. Even if I have to use French letters with Rachel for the rest of our lives, at least I'll protect her from any infections. The damn women's movement, with all that yelling and screaming about contraception, has made it impossible for a man to protect himself from infection. Not like the old days, when you slipped it on and had it off. Girls like Anthea take the pill, and God knows where she's been most of her life.

Charles had already picked up several doses of the clap. The family doctor was very good about it. 'Tell Rachel to come and see me,' the doctor had said to Charles.

'But Dr Burns, you can't tell her she has to go to the VD clinic – she'll guess.' There was real panic in his voice.

'No, no. I won't do that. I'll tell her it's time for her routine cancer smear, and I'll slip a swab in and send it off to the clinic myself.'

'That's very good of you, Dr Burns.'

'Don't like to see a good marriage in trouble. Rachel's a splendid girl – and wonderful children.' The two men shook hands.

Rachel was mulling over Julia's visit. She drew up several lists of things to be done before her arrival. 'I must get the sitting-room curtains cleaned.' Julia had long ago lost the battle over the net curtains.

'The neighbours will see,' said Julia.

'There's nothing for them to see, Julia. I don't care if

they get pink-eye staring into my windows. I can't bear net curtains.'

'Not good enough for you, I suppose.'

This phrase usually made Rachel feel guilty. Years ago she would have humbly apologized. But since the day Julia reduced her to tears when Rachel refused to put Dominic out in his pram in the bitter cold for 'an airing', as Julia called it, Rachel vowed to herself that she would refuse to be intimidated by Julia. She would no longer call her Mrs Hunter, and she was beginning to realize that it wasn't a matter of her own unworthiness as a woman who lacked a family background, but more a matter of class. Julia, she decided, is not going to rule our lives.

'Grandma's coming,' Rachel said to Dominic and Sarah at Sunday supper.

Dominic looked pleased. 'Oh good. She's making me a suit – a real one – with an inside pocket in the jacket.'

'Is she, darling? That's very clever of her. A suit is very difficult to make. What colour is it?'

'Brown. Grandma and Grandpa said it's a good colour for a suit.'

Damn, thought Rachel. Everything is always brown or green. They'd got wardrobes full of Julia's brown and green clothes. 'How lovely, Dominic,' she said, smiling at him. 'Would you like to stay up for dinner when they come?'

'When is it?'

'Next Wednesday.'

'No, I can't. I'm staying with Sam that night.'

'All right, darling. I'll tell her.' Inwardly Rachel was relieved. It would be hard enough to see Charles regress to behaving like a small schoolboy waiting to have his head patted, without coping with Dominic who sat by his grandmother and practised an oozing charm that had Julia pink with pleasure and made Rachel want to batter the child.

'Where's Daddy?'

Rachel looked at Sarah. For a four-year-old, she was remarkably astute at picking up on Rachel's moods.

'He's working, darling.'

'But it's Sunday, Mummy.'

'I know, but he has to work. And when he gets the new job, he'll be working even harder.'

'Nobody wants us to visit them at weekends without him, do they?' Dominic asked.

'I suppose not.' Rachel felt sorry for the children. Dominic was right. Usually, she made great efforts to take them out if Charles was busy, even if it was only to dog-encrusted parks, but this weekend she had been preparing for Julia's visit, and they were bored and miserable.

'Other families only want other whole families to visit at weekends,' said Dominic. 'You know my friend Sam?'

'Yes, of course.'

'Well he doesn't have a daddy. He says his mother has a lover called Patrick who gives him sweets and presents.'

'Really, Dominic?'

'Yes, and she doesn't get asked out at weekends. Sam says it's because he doesn't have a father.'

'Well, let's just think we're lucky to have a good Daddy who loves us and works hard for us.' Rachel knew this sounded a little pious, but she was busy worrying about Dominic staying the night on Wednesday.

'Don't you think it's a bit risky, Charles?' she asked the next time she saw him 'She's a nice enough woman, but we don't know anything about this lover of hers.'

'Oh Rachel. Don't be so hopelessly old-fashioned. People are getting divorced and having affairs all over the place.'

'Not down Ashley Road, they're not. No one has time to have affairs. Imagine me trying to have an affair under the eagle-eye of Dominic and Sarah.'

'I can't imagine it,' said Charles seriously. 'You're not the sort to have affairs.'

'Neither are you, darling. Thank goodness. I'd hate to be the sort of wife who felt she had to check her husband's pockets.'

He put his arms around her. 'I do love you, Rachel.'

'Is anything wrong, Charles?'

He looked at her. 'No, not really. I'm quite nervous about the new job, I suppose. It's such a cut-throat business.'

'You always have us behind you.'

'I know – that's what makes it all bearable.'

Funny, she thought as she went into the kitchen to make him a cup of coffee. It's not like Charles to be so affectionate. That night she was happy to make love to him. 'I know we feel far apart at times, darling, but a lot of the problem is having two children and being stuck in the house. You know, I was thinking, as you're going to be away so much and we will have more money, I think I'll get a little car with my allowance from Aunt Bea's trust.'

'Rachel, you'll never be able to drive. Remember your little green MG we had? The one we sold for the honeymoon. You never did learn to drive that. You just don't concentrate enough. You'll daydream and crash.'

'I suppose so. Anyway, I'm thinking about it.'

Anna telephoned on Wednesday morning. 'How about coming to a meeting with us at the Women's Centre?'

'Oh Anna. What's it about this time?'

'Contraception and abortion.'

'That does sound interesting. I'm getting very bored with Charles's French letters. They smell like old rubber tyres – puts me off making love. There must be some form of contraception that isn't terminal.'

'There isn't, said Anna. 'If it were men who had to use contraceptives, there'd be a solution overnight.'

'I suppose so,' Rachel laughed. 'But Charles is very noble about it really. You're really getting into the Women's Movement, aren't you, Anna?'

'Yes, I suppose I am. But I do wish I could get you to come to some of the meetings.'

'I've got Julia coming tonight, so I must get on.'

'Oh God, you poor thing.'

'I know, but I *am* getting tougher with her. I tell you what, I'll ask Charles if I can come to a meeting another time.'

'Rachel, you don't have to ask Charles if you can go to a meeting. He doesn't ask you if he can go out.'

'But that's work, Anna. It's for us, the family. You don't understand family-life or marriage.'

'Neither do you, Rachel,' said Anna. 'I'll call you when the old war-horse has paid her visit, and maybe I'll get you to come with us.'

'Okay. Look after yourself, and love to Alice.'

'Good luck with Julia, and if she gets difficult, just tell her to fuck off.'

Rachel laughed and put the 'phone down. She wouldn't know what that means, she thought. She spent all day in the kitchen making coq-au-vin and the chocolate mousse.

Everything was bubbling smoothly when Charles arrived home with a bottle of sherry for his mother. 'Smells wonderful,' he said, sticking his nose in the casserole. Rachel was really pleased with herself. The house was spotless. The drawing-room curtains were hanging brightly in the front windows, and the brass door-knocker gleamed. Charles looked at the kitchen floor. 'I can see you've been working hard, darling. I can see my face in the lino. You know, I should get Mother to visit us regularly – it would turn you into a first-class housewife.'

'I suppose it would, but I'd be dead in a few years or completely mad like Mrs Bridges. They took her away, you know. She's number twenty-four down the road. No one ever saw her except through the window. She was always dusting and polishing, and her children were immaculate. Awful, really. Imagine being driven mad by housework.'

'It's not going to be a problem you're going to have to worry about, darling.' Charles laughed good-naturedly. 'I'll get the sherry glasses out.' He went over to the Regency corner cupboard in the dining-room which was divided from the kitchen by an arch.

'Charles,' Rachel said, raising her voice. 'Anna 'phoned. She wants me to go to one of her Women's Lib meetings. What do you think?'

'I think it's load of nonsense, Rachel.' He was back in

the kitchen. 'All this rubbish about men oppressing women. I don't oppress you, do I?'

'Of course not, Charles.' She looked at him seriously. 'I thought a meeting about contraception and abortion might be interesting. There needs to be more research into both. I do think that women should be allowed to have abortions if they want them.'

'So do I, but really, Rachel, those women are all into politics. That's not you at all. I bet you don't know how many men are in the Prime Minister's cabinet. Do you?'

Rachel blushed. 'No, I don't. I'm dreadfully behind in that sort of way. I expect you're right. I'd be out of place anyway because I'm not into politics, so I probably wouldn't understand it all.'

'Sensible girl,' he said. 'Come on. Let's have a drink.'

'Hitting the bottle, I see,' Julia said to Charles as he opened the door.

Charles kissed his mother on her cheek and shook hands with his father who stood awkwardly in the bright little hall with its orange and brown geometrical wallpaper. It always made William acutely uncomfortable. It was not natural to have a house with different wallpaper in each room, he thought. And it was always too hot.

'Come on in,' said Rachel. 'I'll get Sarah to come and say good-night.'

Sarah reluctantly left her doll's house to say good-night to her grandparents. She was fond of William who smelled of clean air, not sour like so many men smelled who came to the house. She ran to him and sat on his lap. 'How's my little sugarplum?' he asked, bouncing her on his knee.

'She's getting to look like one,' remarked Julia. 'Really, Rachel. You should watch her diet. Remember Elizabeth had a problem with her weight.'

'How is Elizabeth?' asked Rachel. 'Have you heard from her?'

Julia's face tightened. 'We haven't,' William interrupted. 'We're thinking of writing to the mission in Nairobi. Last time we heard was when a party of them were going into the interior – didn't we, Mother?'

Julia smiled. 'There's nothing to worry about. I expect she's found some nice young man and is too busy to write.'

'Funny if it's a big black African with a bone through his nose.' Charles snorted with laughter. 'Imagine . . .' He stopped when he saw his mother's face. 'I'm sorry, Mother. It was only a joke.'

'I don't see why Elizabeth couldn't marry a black man,' said Rachel. 'There can't be that many white men around. Anyway, I've always said you could have been a Jew. Look at your nose.' The temperature in the room seemed to have dropped to freezing point. 'Well, I must get Sarah off to bed. Kiss Grandpa goodnight, Sarah.'

Sarah saved the situation by hugging her grandfather noisily and then her grandmother. Rachel was carrying her upstairs when she heard Julia say, 'I don't know when that girl is going to learn any manners, Charles. I told you from the beginning. She'll hold you back in your job. People are not going to put up with silly remarks. You'll need a proper wife at your side if you're ever going to get anywhere. Jewish indeed. We're Welsh.'

'I'm sorry, Mother. She doesn't mean it.'

Damn him, thought Rachel, climbing the rest of the stairs. Why can't he ever stand up to her?

She put Sarah into her cot. 'Don't be sad, Mummy.' Sarah put her little arms round her mother's neck.

Rachel hugged her fiercely. 'Don't worry. Mummy's a bit tired. That's all. You go to sleep.'

'How's Aunt Mary?' Charles asked as they sat down to dinner. Rachel ran her eye over the table. Everything was in order. Charles and his mother were talking about various members of the family.

'Joseph died,' said Julia. 'I told you that, didn't I?'

'Yes, poor Aunt Mary. I haven't seen her in years. She was a wonderful aunt when I was little. Actually, she's the only one of the family I can stand.'

'Don't be so rude, Charles. Blood is thicker than

water, and if you end up with nothing, living in the gutter, your family will always take you in.'

Rachel was watching Julia who surreptitiously wiped her knife and fork with the end of the tablecloth. 'William,' said Rachel, 'I have beer for you. It's in the kitchen. I'll go and get it.' Rachel walked off through the alcove and stood behind the kitchen counter. As she poured the beer she could see Charles and his mother deep in an energetic conversation. Suddenly she felt very much alone. We never talk like that any more, she thought. Not really since we were married. She returned to the table with the beer.

'Thank you, love,' said William.

'You look tired,' Rachel said to him.

'It's the city and the folks, Julia's family always argue and I'm not an arguing man.'

'I envy you living in Dorset. I wish we could live down there. I always feel our children looked stunted compared to the country children.'

'It's a matter of diet,' Julia interrupted, breaking off her own conversation with Charles. 'If you give them all this fancy foreign food of course they won't grow. Just look at the Chinese.' Julia was off on her favourite subject.

'Any more chicken, anyone? Charles.' No one wanted any. Charles and Rachel cleared away the first course and carried the plates to the kitchen.

'She looked in the 'fridge and saw yesterday's left-over Chinese food, didn't she?'

Charles laughed. 'She's on form tonight.'

Rachel served the chocolate mousse. 'You know, William,' Rachel said while Charles and Julia resumed their private conversation, 'I've decided to buy a car and take driving lessons. What do you suggest I buy?' Rachel looked at William who visibly brightened up. Cars were one of his favourite subjects.

'I think the new Ford Escorts are a good buy.'

'You're probably right, but I rather fancied a Renault.'

'You've got me when it comes to fancy foreign cars . . . You'll have to think about the repairs, love.'

'Is Rachel going to drive, Charles?' Julia asked, overhearing their discussion.

'She says so at the moment. It's all tied up with a friend of hers from the Women's Movement. She gives her all sorts of ideas. I don't expect it to come to much – you know Rachel.'

'Brenda Mason got married again this summer.'

'Oh really? How many times is that?'

'I don't know,' said Julia. 'I've lost count. When do you start your new job, Charles?'

'First of January ... I've been thinking, Mother, maybe we should look for a bigger house.'

'A better area would be a good idea.' Julia hated coming to Hammersmith. 'I also think Dominic should go to a private school. He has an awful cockney accent.'

Charles frowned. 'I know, it's trendy now for middle-class kids to be part of the proletariat, but I can't bear to hear him speak at times, never mind understand what he says.'

'I'm so glad you've come to your senses, Charles. I never did understand why you didn't buy one of those nice little private houses on a good estate instead of moving to an area like this – full of Irish.'

'It was me,' Rachel butted in. 'I couldn't live on an estate. It would have killed me.'

'It's good enough for most young couples, Rachel,' said Julia.

'I know, but we're not most young couples.'

Julia's face froze. Too bad, thought Rachel. She went off to make the coffee. A new house? Charles hadn't discussed that with her yet. Maybe we can move a little way out of London. The thought made her very happy. She took the coffee into the sitting-room.

'Your curtains do look nice, dear. I've never noticed the pattern before.'

'I had them cleaned for the first time in ages.'

'They're cotton, aren't they? They must be washable.'

'Yes, but I shrink everything, I'm afraid.'

They all settled down in front of the sitting-room fire

with the coffee. 'This is nice, Charles,' Julia said, slipping off her right shoe to relieve the pressure on her bunion.

Charles glowed. 'Yes it is. I like this room.'

Rachel smiled. 'I'm sorry Aunt Bea never saw all her furniture here. She would have been happy to know that we've given it a good home. She was particularly fond of that writing desk. I remember her doing the bills when I was a child, and I used to play with the secret drawers.' Rachel's face was alive with memories.

'That's nice, dear,' said Julia. She was rummaging through her voluminous handbag.

'What're you looking for, Mother?'

'It's just my indigestion tablets, Charles. One for you, William, or you'll be up all night.' She smiled at Rachel. 'At our age we can't be eating all this rich food without paying for it.'

'I am sorry,' said Charles.

Rachel looked at him. 'Why are you sorry, Charles?'

Charles looked shocked. 'That's very rude, Rachel.' Rachel left the room. 'I don't know what gets into her, Mother. She's been a bit strange lately.'

'I did warn you. There's bad blood there. We have no idea who her mother was. Maybe she came from an insane asylum. They used to put the babies up for adoption, you know.'

'Really, Mother, you're not suggesting Rachel might be mad?'

'No, dear. But blood will out.'

Later that night Charles and Rachel had the first of their titanic rows. 'I don't understand why you had to make me look a fool in front of my mother.'

'I am sick and tired of watching you behave like a small boy in front of her. You're thirty-one, and you're still frightened of her.'

'I'm not.' Charles was shouting. 'And you'd better pull yourself together, Rachel, and realize that there are millions of women just like my mother who loved their husbands, ran beautiful homes, and gave their lives for their families. You do nothing but complain. My mother's quite right. Why didn't we live on an estate like everyone else? What's wrong with you that you've always got to be different? You'd better be careful that you don't get so different from normal people that *you* end up getting carted away like Mrs Bridges down the road.'

'That's not fair, Charles. I can't help what I am.' She was crying by now.

'Well you must think about it.' He marched off to spend the night in Dominic's room. Rachel sobbed herself to sleep.

22

'Am I anybody, Aunt Emily? Do you know anything about me except that my mother's name was Caroline?'

Aunt Emily looked very embarrassed. 'I promised Aunt Bea I wouldn't tell you, dear.'

'You must, you have to. Please, Aunt Emily. Julia says I've bad blood in me. She told Charles that I'd probably been adopted from the local mental hospital.'

Aunt Emily's face was stern. 'What a wicked thing to say. I must confess, Rachel, I've never liked the woman. She reminds me of a cook we once had – always making nasty remarks. Very bad form. I must admit you have looked strained, and you've lost weight, darling.'

Rachel and the children were staying with Aunt Emily for a few days during the Christmas holidays. Rachel deliberately chose the middle of the week so that Charles would not be able to come with her.

'The train tickets are so much cheaper than at the weekend. I'll telephone you every night to see you're all right and not too lonely,' Rachel had explained to Charles.

'Don't worry, darling. I'll telephone you in case I decide to go up the road to Mary's house for a meal or a chat.'

'Okay.'

Charles was relieved. That'll give me a couple of days to say good-bye to Anthea, he thought.

Aunt Emily was very pleased to see Rachel with both the children. She was shocked at the sight of Rachel's strained face. They were now in the library after dinner, sitting by the log fire. 'What's so awful is that now, every time we have an argument, Charles says I'm mad.'

'Oh dear, Rachel. Are you unhappy with Charles?'

'It's me, Aunt Emily. I'm different. The only other person I know who is adopted is Anna. Do you remember when I asked Aunt Bea who I was? Well, Anna promised she'd ask her mother too. I never did find out who Anna's real mother was. I think she lost her nerve when it came time to ask, but at least I went back to St Anne's with a name to say in my prayers at night. But now I really feel I must know, even if my mother was insane and I was born in the Axminster loony bin. If I know then it's not so frightening.'

Aunt Emily got up and went to a chest of drawers which stood where the writing desk had once been. She rummaged around for a while, and then she came back to her seat. She held two faded yellow photographs and a letter. She gave them to Rachel. 'The younger woman is Caroline, your mother. And the older one is your grandmother, Regine.'

Rachel looked at the picture of Caroline and then at the photograph of her grandmother. 'I look more like my grandmother, don't I?'

'Yes, you do. Very like her. You can't see it in the photograph, but she had bright red hair. That's where you get the red tinge in your dark hair.'

'Do you know where my mother is?'

'She died, darling. Quite a few years ago.'

'Not in a mental hospital . . .'

'Oh no, Rachel. No, dear. Don't worry yourself. She died of a cancer.'

'Why did she give me away, Aunt Emily?'

'The answer is in the letter. Aunt Bea said that she would prefer to tell you herself if you ever wanted to know. I'll go upstairs and see if the children are asleep, and then I'll make you a cup of coffee.'

Rachel looked at the envelope. She recognized Aunt Bea's dear familiar handwriting. She opened the envelope and began to read.

*   *   *

'Dear Rachel,

'I find this a difficult letter to write to you. I realize that there must be some strain in your life for you to have asked Aunt Emily for your background and for Aunt Emily to have deemed it wise to tell you.

'Briefly, you are my niece. My father, Lionel Cavendish, had (unknown to me until his death) a relationship with a woman who had been a prostitute. He vowed when my mother died that he would never marry again. However, men have their needs, I suppose, and he took Regine, your grandmother, from the brothel and set her up in a house in Uplyme. Much to their surprise, I do believe, Regine became pregnant and gave birth to your mother Caroline. Subsequently, Caroline became pregnant by an American pilot who deserted her, and you were born. Caroline was unable to take care of you herself, and Regine was too devastated by the death of my father. Aunt Emily and I both felt that your home was here with us.

'Much as it pains me to reveal the past and some of its sordid details, I do want you to know that your grandmother Regine was a fine woman. She loved my father all her life. Indeed, she ended her life shortly after she had made provision for you. I know Emily and I have not given you the family life that could have been yours had you been put up for adoption, but I want you to know that our love for you could not have been matched anywhere else. Also, you are a Cavendish, and your place is with your family.

'All my love,
'Aunt Bea'

Tears were running down Rachel's face as she finished the letter. I must ring Charles, she thought. She looked at her watch. It was eleven o'clock. It's not too late. He had telephoned her at seven and said he was going round to see their neighbours Mary and Robert. He should be back by now. She stood in the hall, waiting for Charles to answer the 'phone. 'I am family. I'm a

Cavendish. I have a grandfather and a grandmother . . . Oh, do pick up the 'phone, Charles . . . Thank God that nightmare's over. I'm not mad. I *am* different. My grandmother was a prostitute.' She was crying and laughing hysterically.

Aunt Emily came out of the kitchen. 'I don't think he's there, darling. Come into the kitchen and have your coffee.' She took the telephone receiver from Rachel's hand and put it back on the hook. She put her arms around Rachel and led her to the kitchen.

'Did you know my grandmother?'

'No, darling. I only saw her twice. Once to arrange to pick you up, and the second time we went to get you.'

Gently and kindly Aunt Emily listened while Rachel poured her heart out in the comfort of the old kitchen with the big Aga breathing warmth and sympathy. Eventually exhausted, Rachel went to bed. As Aunt Emily tucked her in, Rachel put her arms around her aunt and buried her head in her warm breasts. 'I'm so glad you chose to keep me. I know I've had a much better life than I could have ever had anywhere else.' She was nearly asleep before Aunt Emily unwound her arms and put them under the sheet.

Emily walked down the corridor to Bea's room. It remained unchanged. She sat in the armchair by the window for her nightly chat with Bea. 'I must say, Bea, I do think Rachel took it very well. I do hope you felt I was right in telling her at this point. I can't say I feel that she is very happy with Charles. She doesn't look herself at all. Maybe it will blow over. I do hope so. I must get to bed now. It's so late, and the children are up early in the morning. I want Rachel to have a lie-in. Good night, Bea.' She stood up, and went over and patted the bed. Then slowly she moved across the room, opened the door, and went back to her room.

Having said good-night to Rachel on the 'phone at seven. Charles was free to spend the night with Anthea. After a particularly exhausting bout of sex, they were lying on Anthea's floor, talking about anal sex. 'Do you really like it, Anthea?' Charles was surprised. 'Most women complain that it hurts too much.'

'Most women aren't into pain,' said Anthea.

'Are you?'

'A little. Not too much. Enough to enjoy sex that way.'

Shit, thought Charles, just when I have to dump her, she tells me. He began unsteadily, 'Actually, Anthea, I've been meaning to tell you. We're going to have to give it a break.'

'Why?' Anthea sat up.

Charles rolled over onto his stomach. 'It's Rachel. She's getting suspicious about my absences. Tonight I had to tell her that I was covering an all-night election party at the Town Hall to be able to spend this time with you. I hate having to lie to her like that, but I do so enjoy being with you.' He put his arms round her and pulled her close to him.

'Would you ever leave her, Charles?'

'Anthea, you know I couldn't. We've had this out before. She couldn't manage without me.'

'Plenty of women do,' said Anthea bitterly. 'What's so different about Rachel?'

'She's not that steady. She couldn't cope with the children, for a start. She can't even run the house properly. You know she was adopted by those two dykes, and they brought her up like a princess in a castle. She was a virgin when I married her, you know.'

'Oh Charles, I couldn't bear not to see you.'

'It's only for a while. Let's give it six months. By then she'll have calmed down again. We'll see if we feel the same about each other by then. If we do, then I will have to think seriously about my marriage to Rachel.'

'I know my feelings won't change.' She hugged him passionately.

The look of naked longing in her eyes made him immediately erect.

'I hope so, darling,' he said as he pushed her to the floor, expertly parted her legs, and lunged deep inside her.

'It hurts. It hurts,' she moaned.

He thrust harder. 'But you said you liked it,' he panted.

She looked at his face. The veins were bulging in his forehead, and his eyes glistened in the light from the gas fire. 'Not this hard,' she said to herself. She was groaning with pain when he came.

He was immediately contrite. 'Are you all right, darling?' He cradled her in his arms. 'I didn't really mean to hurt you.'

'You didn't really, Charles. Honestly. I enjoyed it. You're such a good lover.'

'Best ever, darling?'

'Best ever,' she said. She could feel the warm blood trickling down her legs from where he had lacerated her. Damn, it's going to stain my white carpet, she thought. Oh well. I've got six months to get it out.

'Good-bye, darling,' said Charles the next morning.

Anthea had decided she would take the day off work, so she was sitting up late in bed. 'I can't bear to think of six months without you.'

'I know, it will be hard,' said Charles, 'but keep busy like I will. Go out with lots of people. I'll give you a ring some time in June – how about the fifteenth? We'll have dinner and see how we both feel. We owe it to Rachel and the children.'

'You're right, Charles. We do really.' The door slammed and he was gone. Anthea threw herself into her pillows and cried. Then, being a practical girl, she got up, tidied the flat, washed up the dinner plates from the night before, and then, grimacing with pain, she crouched down on the sitting-room floor with a bowl of detergent and began to rub gently at the edges of the red stain on her carpet. Six months will go by really fast if I organize some evening classes. I'll give some of my old friends a ring . . . She planned the months.

Six months will give me time to sell the house and move away, Charles thought. It usually takes six months to shake them off. Funny how women always believe you'll eventually marry them. Even if you make it clear from the start that you've no intention of leaving your wife. Eventually, it always comes down to the nitty-gritty. Time to move on. Charles began to hum to himself. Rachel would be back in two days. He opened the front door of his house. The house was unusually clean and quiet. He quite missed the disorder, he realized. I'm a family man at heart, he thought.

Rachel was sitting up in bed with a breakfast-tray across her knees. She was lying back on her heaped pillows, trying to grasp the significance of the change in her life. It's not an outside change at all, she thought. It's inside. The old Rachel doesn't exist anymore. I'm not a poor adopted child from some orphanage. I'm Rachel Cavendish. I have an aunt and a grandmother, a mother and a father, and I'm half American. That new thought struck her as very funny.

'What are you laughing about, dear?' asked Aunt Emily who had come to check on Rachel.

'I'm half American, Aunt Emily. Do you know where my father came from?'

'New York, I think . . . I'm not sure. How do you feel? I must say, you do look an awful lot better than you did.'

'I feel great. Actually I feel like a new person. I must have other Cavendish relations, haven't I?'

'Oh yes. Most of the family are in London. I'll look them up for you, dear.'

'Don't bother, Aunt Emily. I just wanted to know. I don't see myself socializing. I'm not a very social person at the best of times.'

When Charles telephoned that evening, Rachel said at the end of the conversation, 'I know who I am, Charles. I'm a Cavendish. I wasn't born in a mental hospital. You can tell Julia it was much worse than that . . .' she laughed.

'What do you mean?' said Charles. 'How could it be worse than that?'

'I'll tell you when I see you.'

'I miss you, you know, Rachel.'

'I miss you too, Charles.' She put the telephone down and thought, Huh. That's not true. I haven't missed him at all.

* * *

'When are we going to see Grandma?' Dominic asked on the train journey home.

'Soon, I suppose.' Rachel was actually looking forward to seeing Julia's face when she told her the news. Especially the bit about her grandmother. She sat back in the train. I wonder if that's why I've always enjoyed sex so much. She remembered how surprised Charles had been on their wedding night when she immediately climaxed when they were making love.

'Hey! Wait for me . . .' Charles had protested. 'Are you sure you're a virgin?'

'Sure,' said Rachel. After he had puffed and panted himself into a climax and then had slid into a deep sleep, she remembered lying beside him with a feeling of disappointment. I can do better myself, she thought. Maybe it'll get better.

The rhythm of the train on the tracks always made her feel sexually aroused. 'I want to pee,' said Dominic.

I suppose it didn't get better because we had Dominic almost immediately, she thought as she struggled with the children to the lavatory at the end of the swaying corridor.

'You look quite different,' said Charles when he opened the front door on the Friday evening.

'I am quite different.'

'Am I going to like the new you?' said Charles suspiciously.

'Probably not. But it's too late. There's no going back.' She talked all through the evening. Charles hardly got a word in edgeways. She finished up by saying, '. . . so you see why I said it was much worse, don't you? Julia will die when I tell her my grandmother was a prostitute.'

'Do you have to tell her?'

'Yes, Charles, I do. I have had years of her patronizing me and I've finally had enough.'

'All right, but don't expect her to be nice about it.'

'I don't care anymore. I know she's your mother, but she is a raging snob and socially she gets almost everything wrong. I don't care what she thinks any more. I'm off tomorrow to the house agents. We can sell the house and get out of London.'

'I'm not moving out of London.' There was a sharp edge in Charles's voice.

'Okay, we'll compromise.'

'No further than Twickenham.'

'All right. Richmond has some beautiful houses,' said Rachel.

'That seems reasonable to me.'

'I take my driving test next week. If I pass I want to buy a Volvo. Aunt Emily has offered to pay.'

Charles was delighted. He was thinking of buying a car for himself. 'Great,' he said. 'That's good of the old bird. Now I can have a Bentley.' Charles had avoided owning a car until the time came when he could afford the best. He remembered with shame his father's Morris Minor.

'We should be settled within six months,' said Rachel. 'These houses have rocketed in value. We bought this for £5,5000, what, twelve years ago? Mary says they have theirs on the market for thirty thousand. I'll pop in and ask her for the list of estate agents.'

Rachel was up and dressed early on the Saturday morning. There was the last of the Christmas shopping to do. She wanted to buy Charles a sweater, but he hated to have his clothes bought for him, so she would try and get him a first edition for his collection of rare books, although he never read any of them. She left the children with Charles and went to see Mary. 'Thanks awfully for giving Charles dinner the other night.'

'What other night?' said Mary, looking mystified.

'Oh, I was at my aunt's for a few days, and Charles telephoned to say good-night and just mentioned he was going to pop over and have dinner with you. I expect he got waylaid by his boss. It's always happening – a sudden fire or a panic, and Charles is gone for the evening, or sometimes all night.'

'I couldn't bear that,' said Mary. 'At least Robert is home every night, even if he does spend all his time on the 'phone.'

'I'm used to it. It's going to be much worse when he

starts working for the *Daily Reporter*. He'll be abroad a lot. That's why I'm glad we're getting a new house. I'll throw myself into that. It'll keep me busy while he's away. I'll miss you, Mary.'

'I know. *I* don't much look forward to life in Plymouth. All my roots are here, but Robert's got the chance to manage a big district office, so I'll make the best of it.'

'I hope you'll be happy, Mary.'

'And you, Rachel.' They hugged each other.

'I must get on with the last of the bits and pieces before the shops get too full and you can't move.'

On Christmas Eve, Rachel was lying on the sofa by the little coal fire in the sitting-room. Everything is happening so quickly, she thought. The 'For Sale' sign was outside the house, and they had already had an offer for £34,500. Rachel had spent the week before Christmas scouring Richmond and had found a beautiful old vicarage on a quarter of an acre. The main part of the house was Georgian with a Victorian addition which was a rabbit warren of wine cellars and marbled pantries. The Church Commissioners were only too willing to sell. The house had been on the market for a long time.

'Oh look, Charles. You can see the graveyard. I love graveyards.'

They were standing in the big master bedroom. 'It needs a lot of work,' said Charles.

'I've got plenty of time to do it all. You'll be away most of the time. The children and I can camp out 'til it's done. It's a real bargain.'

'You're right about that,' Charles agreed.

23

'It's our house, darling.' Charles put his arm around Rachel's waist. 'This is the happiest moment of my life.' He looked at her. 'I have everything we've always wanted: a fabulous job, a fabulous house, and we'll be rich and famous.'

'I don't want to be rich and famous. Speak for yourself,' said Rachel.

They were standing at the front door of the house. 'I should really carry you over the threshold like a new bride,' Charles said. He swept her into his arms and walked over the threshold into the square and dingy hall. As he opened the door, there was a soft brushing flap of wings. Rachel screamed. Charles let her slide awkwardly to the floor. 'Bats,' he said. 'Of course, we've disturbed them.'

Rachel got up shaken. 'I'm sorry. Silly of me. I'm not usually such a wet, but it took me by surprise. The removal van should be here in an hour or two. Let's get on with sorting out the rooms.'

They walked around the house planning their future together. 'That'll be a good room for my study,' Charles said, choosing a corner room with French doors opening out on to the garden.

'I will need some extra help in the house, Charles. There's no way I can cope with all the extra work.'

'I've been thinking about that. I think we ought to have an au pair, like the Davidsons.'

'You mean that sulky French girl?'

The Davidsons were the proprietors of the local newspaper, the *Hammersmith Evening Argus*, which Charles had worked for. For his leaving party, they had kindly gathered all the staff together in their home. It was the first time they had ever invited Charles to their house. He knew it was not merely a friendly gesture, but also a tacit recognition that he was a bright young man going places who could turn out to be a useful connection in later years.

The Davidson family had originally made its money in wool in the North of England. As the succeeding sons attended private schools, the family set out to gain social acceptance. They had bought the *Argus* some fifty years ago, and by dint of much charitable work and political manoeuvring, the present owner received a knighthood. Charles was entranced by their lifestyle. He stood in the drawing-room, with a snifter of brandy in his hands, looking at the au pair who was handing round the coffee. Splendid tits, he silently remarked. I'd soon take the sour look off her face.

Sir John Davidson came over to him. 'Miss you, my boy. Don't often get lads of your calibre. You'll do well. You're ruthless enough.'

Charles was a little taken aback. Ruthless? He felt quite hurt. However, he decided to take it as a compliment. 'Thank you, sir.'

'Don't forget the old firm, will you . . . Any bits of information you can pass our way, we'll always be grateful. Of course, we'll do the same for you, not that anything that happens in West London is news for an international paper like the *Reporter*.'

'You never know,' said Charles amiably. Inwardly he was making a mental list of exactly how his house would reflect this lush, rich, exotic style which seemed to him the height of luxury.

'You see,' he told Rachel as they drove home in the newly acquired Volvo, 'we will have to do a lot of entertaining. It's not *what* you know in this business; it's who you know.'

'I hate entertaining. You know that, Charles. That's why you've always taken people out to restaurants.'

'It's big league now, darling. You're going to have to try. Wasn't that house fabulous? That's what I want ours to look like.'

'We don't have that kind of money, Charles. Anyway, we have much better furniture than they have.'

'Darling, I know you love Aunt Bea's old stuff, but I must be honest and tell you that I prefer more modern furniture. It goes with my image.'

Rachel fell silent while Charles rambled on. She was hurt. She couldn't see how anyone could not love the old soft, glowing mahogany dining-table with matching Regency chairs, or the elegant writing-desk. The whole house looked disgustingly tacky, she said to herself. Maybe Charles is right, though. Probably people in his business make their homes as modern as possible to reflect their exciting jobs.

'We could put Aunt Bea's furniture in the spare bedrooms,' she offered.

'I was thinking of selling it. We could get a lot of money for the dining-table and chairs. The chap at Sotheby's reckoned a couple of thousand if they were in good condition.'

'I don't really want to sell the furniture, Charles.'

'But we do need the money to do up the house. It'll take several months before we feel the benefit of my new salary, and I need to start inviting people and to get into the swing of things right away. It's for all of us and our future. Remember, the children are starting private schools. Look at it this way: it's for their education.'

'I suppose so.' Rachel looked at Charles. 'But I won't sell the writing-desk.'

Damn, thought Charles, there's more money in that heap of wood than in all the other stuff put together. 'Of course not, darling. I suppose I can always borrow the money from the bank.'

'Thank you, Charles.' She squeezed his hand.

The next six months flashed past. The children were settled in a local private school in Richmond, and Charles seemed to come and go at all hours of the day and night. He was in his element. He left lists of instructions for Rachel and the builders. He telephoned his orders to Rachel from all over the world. 'Darling, has the carpet arrived?' he said during his usual nightly telephone conversation with her.

'No. Where are you?'

'I'm in Ceylon.'

'What's it like?' She imagined the hot starry night and the smells of the Orient.

'Deadly dull. You'd hate it. It smells awful. What about the kitchen cabinets, are they in yet?'

'Mr Barstow says he'll be in to fit them tomorrow.'

'Good. How about the 'phones? Have they put the plugs in all the rooms? Have you checked the colour? They're ivory, not white?'

'Yes I have. They'll be here next week.'

'I must go now. It's time for dinner and you have to wear a suit even in this god-awful heat.'

'I miss you, Charles. It's so lonely at night.'

'I miss you too, darling. It's just as lonely for me, you know.'

'I know. It must be awful – you don't even have the children.'

'Good-bye, darling. I'll ring you tomorrow.' Charles put down the 'phone.

He waited for the knock on the door. Suma was reputed to be the best lay in the whole city. Poor old Rachel. It must be a bit lonely, now she has no neighbours to gossip with. He felt a familiar surge of guilt tinged with lust. With his hands on Suma's splayed buttocks, he looked at the back of her head, her face buried in the pillow. An au pair should sort out the problem. He had a sudden vision of a golden-haired, big-breasted au pair lying under him in the spare room. He came quickly.

Rachel was expecting Anna for lunch. When she put the 'phone down, she busied herself in the kitchen. She had been camping in the house for so long now that she had become quite proficient at producing fast meals for herself and the children. 'My God. It looks as though a bomb has hit the place,' said Anna as she marched in through the front door and looked around. 'What's the matter with you, Rachel? Have you been taking *House and Garden*? It looks like an architect's showplace.'

Rachel laughed self-consciously. 'I know. It's Charles. I really don't have any taste at all. So he makes all the decisions. I just carry out the orders, though I don't know how I'm going to keep this wall-to-wall pale blue carpet clean with the children and their friends.'

Anna stared at the white walls. All the woodwork was covered in shiny white gloss. It made the rooms look much bigger. 'Well, I suppose it *is* all a matter of taste, but it's not going to be the sort of place where you can open a tin of beans.'

'I can't open a tin of beans anyway. Charles goes potty about the children's nutrition if I get anything in tins. He starts quoting his mother who, as far as he knows, never even owned a tin-opener.' They were in the kitchen by now. 'But,' said Rachel, 'I must admit – while he's away I cheat. So here you are – baked beans on toast. The trouble is, Dominic tells on me.'

'That boy always was a rat. You shouldn't have left him with Julia for so long.'

'I didn't have much alternative. I was so sure I was a rotten mother and she was so perfect, I reckoned he'd be safer spending his holidays with her rather than me. He *is* difficult, you know, Anna. I don't even think he likes me very much. Anyway, I'm not going to go on about children to you. We haven't seen each other for ages. What happened to Alice?'

Anna slumped into a chair. 'I don't know. She left me for a woman called Lou. She says it was because I was too possessive. She said that she didn't leave the world of domineering men only to be possessed by a jealous woman.'

'Are you jealous, Anna?'

'I don't think so. I just happened to believe that people should be faithful to one another in a relationship. It wasn't that she wanted to leave me, it was more that she insisted that she had the right to make love to anyone she fancied. She said it made no difference to our central relationship. In fact, it got so bad that one night at a party, when I found her in bed with our hostess, I attacked her. She knew I'd find her, and the awful thing was that she seemed to enjoy being hit. I realized that night that I had to get out. She always had me on the knife-edge of exploding. I hated myself for staying, and I hated her for making me hate myself. She only had to look at another woman and I'd go mad with rage.'

'Oh Anna.' Rachel put her hand on her friend's arm. 'Darling Anna. That's not at all like you. You're not violent. I always thought it would be so much easier for two women living together without all the problems of coping with a man.'

'Are you actually admitting Charles has a fault in his otherwise flawless making up?'

'Don't change the subject, Anna.'

'I think you have a romantic image of what it's like to be a Lesbian because you lived with your aunts.'

'They weren't Lesbians, though, were they?'

'That's the point, Rachel, they weren't. Even if they had wanted a relationship with each other they would never have allowed it to happen. Thousands of women during two world wars were resigned to being spinsters and sexually unfulfilled. I don't think my mother ever had a relationship with a man.'

'Did she ever tell you who you were, Anna?'

Anna looked bitter. Her nails were bitten to the quick. Her short hair, usually quite sleek, looked unbrushed. 'She said my real mother was one of the kennel maids and the groom, my father, wouldn't marry her. He ran off, the bastard, and left her. So my mother, who was really fond of the kennel girl, took me in. So for seven years of my life, the senior kennel maid, who was so good to me, who I called Bridget, was really my mother. My adopted mother always told me stories about me coming from Knightsbridge just to make it all seem respectable. Apparently, Bridget met an Irish jockey and went back to Ireland where her people came from. She came from Mayo, I think.'

'Do you want to look for her?'

'No. She won't want me turning up on her in an Irish Catholic community. Anyway, my other mother has been so good to me, I would feel disloyal.'

'What is it you hate about men?'

'Personally, I can't stand the idea of a prick. They're so ugly, with their huge throbbing veins and awful reds and purples.'

'I didn't know you had any experience with pricks.'

'Not first-hand. The stable boys would toss each other off when I was at home during the holidays.'

'No wonder you don't like men.'

'That's pop-psychology, Rachel. The truth is, I don't like men personally or politically. I don't see why they should dictate my life financially, biologically, or emotionally.'

'Anna, you sound like your political pamphlets. What are you going to do if you want a child, assuming that you do want a child?'

'You must be psychic, Rachel. Actually that's why I've come to see you. It's really strange. I reached thirty absolutely convinced I'd never want a child. After the fracas with Alice and all the relationships I've made in the past, I do realize that a lot of the time I've been running around mothering so-called helpless little girls until they kick my teeth in. Now, at thirty-four, I'm financially secure. I can always go home if things don't work out in London. I know I do actually want a child.'

Rachel looked startled. 'How would you do it though, if you can't bear the idea of a prick inside you?'

'Some women I know pick a man, chat him up for a few months, then grin and bear the sex, and get pregnant. But Jo, a friend of mine, said you've really got to be able to tolerate the whole disgusting business.'

'Hey, hang on. It's not that bad.' Rachel was laughing. 'I quite enjoy it sometimes.'

Anna looked at her seriously. 'You won't know anything about sex until you make love to a woman who understands another woman's needs.'

Rachel changed the subject quickly. She found it difficult when Anna discussed sex with other women in those direct terms. 'Anyway, back to your dilemma, Anna.'

'Jo said she finally got it together to get into bed with

this fellow from her technical college. He looked like a good stud. She'd timed it all okay with her ovulating week, or whatever you do. She got into bed with him, but as soon as he tried to get into her, she freaked. He lost his temper and called her a prick-tease, and they had a dreadful fight.'

'No, oh how horrible.' Rachel shuddered.

'Anyway, she decided she had to find another way. She found an American idea: self-insemination. Apparently, what I have to do is to get a gay friend. I've already lined that up, because a gay man is so much more likely to be sympathetic than a straight. Julian, my friend, waits for me to call him, and for the days I'm fertile, he brings me a jar of fresh semen, leaves it with me, and I get a turkey baster and blast away at myself at my own convenience.'

'Sounds a bit lonely,' said Rachel.

'It's better than putting up with pricks. In about ten years' time, it will be possible to take a cell from a woman's body and do a process called "cloning". The cell makes more cells 'til finally you have a person. This way, women can reproduce an exact replica of themselves – only girls. Then men will slowly become redundant.'

'Not if women like me are still around. Are you serious about all this, Anna? What happens if the baby is a boy?'

'In most cases, where women honestly feel they couldn't handle a male child, they put them up for adoption. Soon we will be able to know the sex of our unborn children, and that won't be necessary.'

'Anna, you make the future for men so bleak.'

'Believe you me, it is.'

'I honestly think you overestimate the effect that kind of attitude has on most women. Not everyone's going to think it's such a wonderful idea. Remember, I'm "most women". I have a husband, and I have two children and a lovely home.'

'Then why aren't you happy, Rachel?' Anna said, looking at her. 'What happened to the rather dreamy laughing Rachel? Every time I see you, you're thinner, more harassed looking, and you hardly ever laugh.'

'I am happy, honestly, Anna. It's been a strain getting this house together, and Charles being away so much. I did go through a bad stage when I was in the little house on Ashley Road with not enough to do, but I'm okay now – really.'

'You can only do up so many houses, and caretake your husband and your children for so long, and then the day comes when you have to deal with yourself. The gay movement is full of married women who baled out.'

'I can never cope with the idea of large political groups. I can only deal with things in personal terms, Anna, and I don't see that any of your relationships have been any more or less successful than relationships I've seen between men and women. Giving up on men just seems an easy way out.'

'I don't think you can call finally responding to thousands of years of men dominating women "giving up on men". Since when have men made any attempt to make room for women, either personally or financially, or emotionally? It's a stronghold, whether it's in the family – like Charles is an absolute patriarch in this house, everything revolves around him – or in the business world where a few women have clawed their way to the top. And certainly men have offered women nothing emotionally. The old school-tie still props up the stiff British upper lip, largely because there's no chin to get in the way.'

'Anna, you do get carried away.' Rachel looked at her watch. 'I must get the kids. It's been lovely having you here. I do need you to help me keep in touch with the outside world, but I've made a resolution that once this house is together, I'm going to get out and do something for myself – even if it's just filing in an office in the mornings.'

'There are lots of Women's Centres that could do with your help,' Anna said eagerly.

'No thanks, Anna. You and your girlfriends are all I need to know what's going on in the movement, but I *will* attend some abortion and contraception meetings. That does interest me. Anna, are you really serious about a baby?'

'Yes. Serious enough to telephone Julian next week.'

'I just can't imagine you with a turkey baster,' Rachel giggled.

'They're not easy to find in this country. I had to go to Selfridges.'

24

Rachel arrived at the school feeling unusually happy. Housebound is a sort of mental constipation, she thought. Just a few hours talking about something other than my children, my husband, and my house, and I feel whole again. She parked the Volvo down the side-road and walked slowly around the corner to the front entrance of the school. So far, she found all the mothers horribly intimidating. ARTS (Alternative Routes for Teaching Students) on Richmond Hill was the most famous progressive school in the area. It was famous not for its academic standards, but for the wealth and social position of the parents that supported the school's varied liberal policies. ARTS, known affectionately as FARTS by its students, offered a totally non-directive education that was designed not only to equip children with any knowledge that the children might wish to acquire, but also to allow the children to develop a sense of self-esteem that would enable them to grow into whole, well-rounded adults. The ideal appealed to Rachel enormously. She had felt thoroughly depressed by the other schools in the area, and grateful that she had avoided school for so many years during the time she was in bed as a child with rheumatic fever.

As far as Dominic was concerned, he already disliked reading because of the tyrannical teaching system in his state primary school. He was also a dreadful bully, because the playground at his former school was a nightmare of mostly unsupervised children, many of whom were violent. Even going into the school lavatories, where the older boys boasted of their sexual prowess or roughed up the smaller boys, was an ordeal. 'I hope ARTS will calm him down,' Rachel had said to Charles as they drove back to the vicarage after the interview with the headmaster, Mr Bacon.

'He's got to learn to stand up for himself. I had to.' In fact, Charles had fond memories of jerking off with his classmates. 'Dominic's very like me – he can look after himself.'

'You do like the school . . .?'

'I think it's marvellous. Did you see John Ravensborne, the actor, on the list of parents? I counted two film directors I've actually heard of. There were nine famous actors, and several television stars.'

Rachel remembered that conversation now as she stood in the front courtyard, waiting for the school day to end. Usually she stood by herself in a corner watching the fashionably dressed mothers, chattering like starlings, form small knots: 'Did you go to Priscilla's, darling? It was *such* fun. Henry says we must give a dinner party this year that reflects the economy. "Riches to Rags" I thought I'd call it. All of us can go in rags. It's too awful – we can't go skiing this year. Giles is going away to boarding school, and the fees are enormous.'

Rachel found most of the women unbelievable. Privately she had nicknamed this particular woman 'Piranha teeth', and she was far from pleased to discover that Dominic had taken to Giles and that the two boys were bosom pals. Piranha teeth, alias 'Mrs Jameson', upon seeing Rachel, descended on her with much flapping of her Jap coat. 'Rachel, Giles tells me your husband works for the *Reporter*. Excellent paper, excellent. Henry says we must get together. Let's set a date.' Rachel mumbled that Charles was away. 'Never mind, just as soon as he's back.' Piranha teeth swirled off to gossip to another group of friends.

Rachel heaved a sigh of relief. It was so audible that a dark, intense woman standing by her laughed. Rachel looked at her, surprised by the warmth of her gaze. 'I guess I'll have to introduce myself. I'm Jane Houseman.

I'm new to England, and I've been watching you – I feel like a Cape Cod flounder with all these women, but you look as if you feel out of place too.'

'I'm Rachel Hunter. Yes, I do really. I suppose it's because I've lived most of my life in the country, and we've just moved into a new area, really a new way of life. My husband has just changed jobs, so . . .'

'Same for me,' Jane interrupted. 'We're New Yorkers, but Jerry's been transferred to the American Bank here in London. We don't know a soul in Britain except for the bank people, and they are all American.' There was a terrible desperation in Jane's voice that touched Rachel. She knew how she felt. Days with only the children for company often meant that the first adult she talked to would find themselves deluged by a torrent of words. 'I'm so goddamned lonely here. Richmond is out in the sticks, as far as I'm concerned. I'm used to the high of New York. I didn't realize that English was a foreign language until I came here.'

'How many children do you have?' Rachel asked her. She felt both sorry for Jane and also comforted that at least they shared a feeling of isolation from the rest of the mothers who seemed so sure of themselves and their rich pampered worlds.

'I have three kids. Liza who is twelve – I know she's in the same class as your Dominic – Suzanne who is seven, and Jake who is five.'

Rachel smiled at Jane. 'Let's get together sometime.'

'I'd really like that. The kids came home the other day and asked me for "pudding". I had no idea what that was.'

'I'll have to teach you English . . .' Rachel laughed. 'I'll give you a ring and we'll have a cup of coffee together. I'm afraid the house is a mess, but at least the kitchen cabinets are in so that's a reasonable area to sit in now.'

Jane's eyes filled with tears. 'You don't know how good that sounds.'

'Oh yes I do,' said Rachel. She patted Jane's arm. 'I really do. London's a very lonely place.'

'I guess so. At least in New York everyone talks to you.'

'That's not British. You see, an Englishman's home is his castle . . .'

'And the wives are prisoners,' said Jane. 'I've been here three months and not one of my neighbours has been near me.'

'You're supposed to invite them in for a drink first.'

'Oh – it's totally different where I grew up. I'm small-town American. All your neighbours visited within the first few days with chocolate brownies or cookies of some kind or another.'

'It's the other way 'round here. English people would think they were intruding on your privacy if they came over uninvited.'

'I guess you've made my day, Rachel. I thought it was *us* they didn't like.'

Just then the door opened, and a flood of children streamed into the courtyard. They do all look happy, Rachel thought.

'Can I go to tea with Giles?' Dominic said.

'Not today, darling. I can't drive over to collect you, because I have the plumber working at the house, and I must be there.'

Dominic's face fell. 'You never let me go to tea.'

'I do, Dominic, but I can't be everywhere at once, and I'm not your private chauffeur.' Driving the children home, Rachel realized just how much their lives had changed. Not only did ARTS parents have a hectic social life, but so did their children. 'Dominic, how on earth do all the mothers manage?'

'They have au pairs, or if you're really rich, you have a Norland nanny. Those are the ones you see in the stripy dresses. Giles's parents have a yacht. They keep it in the south of France. He says he wants me to go with them this summer. They all go swimming with nothing on, even the grown ups.'

'Do they?' Rachel was shocked. 'Are you sure?'

'Well, they walk about the house with nothing on. Remember when I stayed the night two weeks ago? When I was in the bath, Mrs Jameson came in and had a pee right next to me.'

'Weren't you embarrassed?'

'Yes, I was. But she made it feel so ordinary . . . She smelled awful.'

'Why didn't you tell me, Dominic?'

'I told Dad.'

'Oh, I see.' (I suppose it's natural for a boy to confide in his father, she comforted herself. He's twelve, and mothers seem rather boring and incomprehensible to him. All I do is nag him to get up, wash up, clean up . . . I must seem like some old harridan). 'I'm sorry I couldn't let you go to tea today, Dom. I'll ring Mrs Jameson when we get home and arrange for Giles to spend the night.'

'Only if Dad's home. Otherwise Giles would be bored.'

Rachel laughed. 'I suppose so,' she said.

Later that night she looked in the mirror. I really must do something about myself. She took off her clothes and stood gazing at her reflection. At least I don't have awful stretchmarks like some women. Her breasts, though small, were firm. I wish I could carry just an extra ten pounds.

'Charles,' she said, when he 'phoned from Ceylon, 'I feel awfully ugly compared to all those women who are outside the school.'

'Don't be silly,' he said reassuringly. 'You're not that kind of woman.'

'What kind of woman do you think I am?'

'Ah, let me see. I think you're mildly eccentric.'

She could hear the amused tone in his voice. 'But do you want a mildly eccentric woman for a wife?'

'For better or for worse, darling.'

'Charles, be serious.'

'Okay, I'll be back by Saturday. Have the kitchen cabinets been fitted?'

'Yes. They look lovely. It's amazing how the kitchen has really taken shape.'

'Have Peter Jones delivered the dining-table and chairs?'

'Yes, they've arrived and I've unpacked it all and put it up in the dining-room.'

'What do you think of it?'

'I don't know yet. It takes a bit of getting used to. It's odd seeing your knees while you're eating. But I'll get used to it. It certainly looks very elegant. The smoked glass matches the curtains exactly, and the steel-framed chairs are more comfortable than I expected.'

'Good. I can't wait to get back to see it all.'

By Saturday evening a tired but contented Charles was home surveying his domain. 'It's going to look fabulous. As soon as we've finished we must have a dinner party.'

'Oh must we, Charles? Couldn't we just have people to supper?'

'Rachel, we've been through this before. Claire and Michael can come. They're back now, and should be settled and in circulation. Give her a ring and make a date for about a month ahead. I have a colleague named Bill – he's a bachelor – I'd like to invite, and there's a girl called Sally who works in the office. She covers women's stuff. She's a bit militant, but maybe she'll hit it off with Bill.'

'I'd like to invite an American couple that I know from the school.'

'You mean Jane, the woman you've been chinwagging with instead of getting on with the housework?'

'Oh Charles, don't be beastly. You know I find it difficult to make friends, and she is a friend. At least her idea of a super day out is not like so many of the other's – having coffee then trailing up to Harrod's.'

'But Rachel, that's why you're different. Most women like shopping for clothes. They love make-up. That's also why you don't make friends easily. If you don't do those things, what on earth is there to talk about?'

'Nothing much, I suppose. But Jane tells me a lot about America, and I help her with her problems settling in England. I really like her, Charles. She's very clever. She has a degree in sociology . . . a PhD in fact.'

'Really? What's their name?'

'She's Jane Houseman, and his name is Jerry. He's

one of the directors or something of the American Bank.'

'That means they must have lots of money.'

'They do, but they live very differently from us. I notice the 'fridge is always full of fresh fruitjuice and she keeps the bread in there as well. She's never heard of a breadbin.'

'Rachel,' Charles suddenly became very serious, 'I really have been thinking about you an awful lot, especially on this last trip. I feel we must get an au pair, and you must get out of the house and back into the real world. You see, it's when you spend your time noticing where she keeps her bread that I wonder if one day I'm going to come home and find you imagining that you're a Hoover.'

'It would be wonderful if I could have an extra pair of hands. I thought, with money, life would be easier, but it's actually much more complicated. I now spend a lot of my time driving the children to different tea-parties. They don't play out like they did in Ashley Road. Instead, I have to take them and collect them. So if I had an au pair who could drive, it would take a huge weight off my shoulders. I could even get a little job.'

'We don't need the money, Rachel. It would just boost my income tax to where whatever you earned I'd lose in tax. So you'd be working for nothing. No, I want you to socialize. Go out and meet people.'

'Oh dear.' Rachel shook her head. 'Honestly, you'd better trade me in for a new model.'

'There you go again, totally negative. Besides, there's no divorce in our family.'

Rachel laughed. 'You're so right. As far as Julia is concerned, a divorced woman is worse than a whore. She reckons that any woman who gets a divorce for any reason – doesn't matter if the man is a mass killer – might as well be dead. Do you remember when your Uncle Max was infatuated with that lean and hungry hyena called Lydia? I remember Julia screaming at him down the 'phone: "The disgrace . . . a shonda . . ." That was the only time the Welsh story slipped up on her.' Charles's laughter was a little forced, but he was really only half-listening anyway. He was busy thinking about his date the next day with Anthea.

'But, my sweet, you must realize that I am at a point in my career when it just isn't appropriate to get divorced.' Charles and Anthea were sitting in the Gay Hussar at lunchtime. Charles enjoyed the other newspaper men, who frequented the place, seeing him with a beautiful woman. Such a tasty arse, he thought. So sad to have to give it up. 'Besides,' he continued, 'I'm really not good enough for you. You know me, and I can't be faithful. You wouldn't want me to go into marriage with you, and then a few months later you'd be searching my pockets and checking out where I was. That's not what marriage is about.'

'It's what your marriage to Rachel has been about.'

'Rachel is totally different. She lives on another planet from the rest of us. She wouldn't suspect me in a million years.'

'She might if someone told her.'

'You wouldn't do that, though, would you, darling?'

Anthea stared at him. 'I just might if I get lonely enough. The poor bitch at least has the right to know what you're up to. You must have to tell a stack of lies. But of course, it does come so very naturally to you, doesn't it?'

'Anthea, please don't be so hard on me. I couldn't wait for this moment. I've been dreaming about you and I've missed you. You're the best ever, darling.'

Anthea suddenly softened up. 'So are you. Best ever.' She raised her wine glass.

Charles gazed tenderly into her eyes. 'I've got a lovely fun present for you from Ceylon.' He smiled. 'I can't give it to you here – you'd blush. When we go back to your flat I'll show it to you.'

'Oh Charles, you're so kind.'

The manager of the Gay Hussar saw them to the door. 'Nice to see you again, Mr Hunter.'

'Wonderful meal,' said Charles.

The waiter was clearing their table. 'I don't know how he gets the women . . . Such a tightwad – look at his tip.'

The manager, who was one of the wisest men in London, said, 'Those sort of men usually are. They feed their women and charge it to their expense account. She'll probably go down as the Archbishop of Canterbury. But he's going to have trouble with that one, I can tell.'

Oh God. She's going to be difficult to shake off, Charles thought as they sat in the back of a taxi on the way to her flat. Never mind. At least I'll get a leg-over this afternoon, and then I'll try the 'unavailable' strategy.

When they got there, Anthea ran on ahead. Charles paid off the taxi and walked up the familiar flight of stairs. He was already feeling sexually aroused. He walked into the flat to see posters all over the walls saying 'WELCOME HOME CHARLES'.

'I spent ages designing them all. Do you like them, darling?'

'I'll tell you when we've made love. I'm going to burst, and my balls hurt.'

'That's not very romantic, Charles.'

'Get undressed and I'll show you your present. It's very romantic.'

'Ughh . . . what is it, Charles?'

'It's a Ceylonese ring with goat's hair stuck to the outside. It's supposed to give you an absolutely amazing sensation. See?' he said, slipping the ring over his penis, 'I was thinking of you even when I was far away. "What would please my Anthea?" '

Goat's hair, she thought as he pushed his way into her. I wonder where the bloody goat's been. She obligingly moaned and screamed and scratched him a little, just to let him know how much she was enjoying herself.

'Wow! That felt great. Could you feel the goat's hair?'

'Mmm . . . wonderful. Must be a lot of bald goats in Ceylon.'

'Anthea, it's so nice to be with a woman who enjoys sex as much as you do.'

He remembered Rachel's look of absolute disgust

when he'd tried to persuade her to let him use one on her. 'Don't be so bloody childish, Charles,' Rachel had said. 'I don't need goat's hair to enjoy making love.'

'Sometimes I wonder if you need me at all,' Charles replied.

'I'm beginning to wonder myself,' said Rachel very crossly. 'Especially when you bring home something like that.'

'It's only a joke.'

'I don't think it's funny.'

'Rachel, you're such a prude. It's like the time I gave you that book *A Gourmet's Guide to Sex* for Christmas . . .'

'I don't think I'm at all prudish. I just thought it had a totally unnecessary amount of fairly perverted information. That might turn some men on, but it does very little for women, if they were ever honest enough to admit it.'

'You're wrong, Rachel. It's your problem with reality again. That book sold by the millions, and it does turn everyone on, everyone except Rachel Hunter who thinks she's an expert on the subject.'

'I don't think I'm an expert, Charles, I just don't need to spend my life looking for new or better ways to come. If I'm randy, I come. It's never been a problem for me. I enjoy making love with you sometimes. Sometimes I don't. But I do it for you because it gives me pleasure to see your pleasure. I never have understood why there's such a fuss made out of it all. Sex is only part of my life, not an endless pursuit. Tell me, are you bored with me, Charles? Because if you are, you must say so.'

'Don't be silly, darling. Of course I'm not bored with you. I just wish you were a little more adventurous and a little less inhibited. Look how upset you were because Dominic knows a family who walk about naked.'

'It's not the naked bit I mind; it's the family. They're not naked because they're just comfortable . . . You should see Mrs Jameson. She exudes an odd kind of sex. It feels slimy.'

'Sounds interesting,' Charles laughed. Lying in bed

with Anthea now, he remembered the look on Rachel's face. 'That is the difference between us, Charles. I don't find it funny at all, or exciting. I think we are both changing.'

'I haven't changed, Rachel. It's you. You're just finding out that there's a whole big world out there that doesn't think like you do. Your narrow, rather bigoted, ideas aren't shared by everybody . . . it's you. Not me.'

She looked at him very seriously. 'I don't want to be part of that world.'

Now he remembered that look. He felt an icy finger touch his heart. He pulled Anthea to him. 'Darling, I can't hold on to you this way. Honestly. I'm thinking of your future. You're twenty-nine now. I can't offer you anything in the foreseeable future. It's morally wrong for me to hold on to you like this. You should be looking for a man who is free to marry you – if that's what you want.'

Anthea got out of bed and went over to the fireplace to get a cigarette. 'You're just too frightened to tell Rachel, aren't you?'

'I honestly don't think it would make any difference. She wouldn't divorce me anyway. She's not that type. She needs me too much. She can't even run a cheque-book without getting into a mess. I do feel very responsible for her, I suppose. Then there's the children. Dominic is at a very vulnerable age. We're very close. He doesn't really get on with Rachel, you know. She doesn't know how to bring up children. I mean, she's warm and loving, but she has no idea about running a house.'

'Well, your new house is going to take a lot of cleaning.'

'Anthea, you've been spying on me.'

She smiled at him. 'For a man who has shared my love and my bed for two years, "spying" seems a bit of a harsh word.' She was standing by the fireplace, smoking nervously.

Charles lay in her bed, his mind racing. 'Anthea, why are you doing this to me?'

'Because I know I'd be a much better wife to you than

Rachel is. You complain about her all the time. I'm better in bed, I'm a better housewife, I'm a better cook, and I love entertaining. You're just too weak to tell her.'

'It's not just that . . .'

Anthea was getting impatient. 'I know it's "not just that". Charles, all your married life you've had your safe, unquestioning, dumb wife at home and a woman on the side like me. I'm not prepared to be like my friend Rose Johnson – half mad because her lover Stephen booted her out. Anyway, if I go, it would only be a few months before you replaced me with another woman. Always with the unsaid promise that you'll leave Rachel, and the woman, poor fool, will believe you. This time you chose the wrong woman. I've had six months to cry, six months to suck valium, and six months to realize that I want you. She's had you for nearly . . . is it twelve years?'

'Thirteen,' said Charles. He wanted to scream, to jump out of the bed and run away. He knew his only chance was to stay calm.

'Well, thirteen years, then. Now it's my turn.'

'Come back to bed, Anthea, and let's be practical.'

'I am being totally practical. You see, I know you better than she ever will. I don't expect very much from you. I know you'll have affairs. We can have an open marriage. I'll tell you and you tell me.'

Charles could bear the tension no longer. He pulled her into his arms and began desperately to kiss her. Anything to shut her up, he thought. To his horror, he was unable to arouse even a flicker of sexual interest.

'Don't worry, Charles. I know why you can't get it up – you feel trapped. I won't trap you, ever. You can have as many affairs as you like.'

'That's wonderful, darling.' He hugged her closely. 'You'll have to give me a little time.'

'I'll give you exactly a year.'

'You really have thought it all out, haven't you?'

'Yes, thanks to you. For six months I sat alone every night and thought about you, and then I realized the only way I'd get you is to fight for you. I want you enough for that, so you're stuck with me.' She smiled at him. 'I know what you're thinking. You think I'm an absolute bitch. Don't worry, darling. We'll suit each other.'

Charles wasn't even thinking about her. I should have chosen Rose Johnson instead. Oh God, what will Mother say? he asked himself.

25

That evening Charles listened to Rachel chattering on about Claire. 'I'm off to see her next Monday. She's delighted to come for dinner, and I've made the date. Jane and Jerry are coming too. Have you done anything about your two?'

'Huh? . . . un, no. I've been very busy today.'

'You do look tired. Why don't we go to bed early. I'm exhausted myself, just thinking about au pairs, dinner parties – and by the way, the Jamesons have invited us to a buffet. We have to go in rags.'

'In rags?'

'Yes. They lost a lot of money on the stock exchange, and her husband says it's something to do with creeping socialism . . . I really don't understand it all. Anyway, it's in two weeks' time. Will you be home?'

'I don't know, Rachel. You know I can't predict my movements.'

Rags, he thought lying in the hot bath, sounds interesting. I'll tell Fiona to rearrange my schedule. A good party will cheer me up. He began to think about Anthea. If only you could exterminate women like her. It would make life a lot easier. What right does she have to try and wreck a perfectly good marriage? He thought back to a conversation he'd had with her when they had been together for a short while.

'I'm not into marriage, nor are my friends. We're the first generation of women who want to take responsibility for ourselves. I have too much to lose if I marry a man.'

'You're quite right,' said Charles. 'I really do admire women like you. I've always believed it possible to find women who have the same sexual needs as men, but don't try and trap them.'

'I would never trap you, Charles. How could I? Love you like I do, and then trap you? Anyway, I don't need to be married. I have a lovely flat, a great job with the advertising agency, and a wonderful lover. What more could I want?'

Scheming bitch, he now thought in the bath.

'Darling?' said Rachel as he got into bed. 'Let's make love.'

'I'm too tired tonight. Do you mind?'

'Poor Charles. You're working far too hard. Maybe we could have a holiday abroad this summer. Most of the women at school go to France or Spain. Wouldn't that be wonderful? I've never been abroad. What do you think, Charles?' But he was asleep. 'Oh well.' She rolled over onto her side, and slid her fingers between her legs, moving her body quietly so as not to awaken him. When she came, she found herself crying into her pillow. There must be more to marriage than this. She suddenly recognized that she was dreadfully lonely. She had always thought of herself as lonely because Charles was away, but now this lonely feeling was to do with Charles being at home. She fell asleep confused.

Anthea was not asleep. She was talking to her friend Rose Johnson. 'I did it, Rose.'

'How did it go?'

'Too early to tell. He's in a state of shock at the moment, but he'll see I mean business.' Anthea had asked Rose over for dinner. During her six months in exile from Charles's arms, she had really only confided in Rose, partly because they had been friends from the early days of the Women's Movement, and partly because Rose was going through the same depression as Anthea.

'You're lucky that Rachel is no competition. Stephen's sodding wife doesn't care how many affairs he has as long as he pays the bills. This new woman he's got on the side is Eurasian. I've seen them together in our favourite restaurant. Can you believe it? They were sitting in our favourite place.'

'Yes I can.' Anthea laughed. 'Men are creatures of habit.'

'He even uses the same hotels.'

'How do you know?'

Rose looked at Anthea. Her eyes filled with tears. 'He does. I checked with the Swan in Bath. We always loved Bath. He's been there with her . . . I could kill him.'

'Could you really, Rose?'

'Yes, I could. At least that way no one else would have him. I can't go on like this. I can't eat, I can't sleep, I keep having these fantasies of them in bed together.'

'Poor Rose. You spent five years with him?'

'Yes, and I feel I've wasted those years. I'm thirty now, and it's not as if I'm unattractive to men. There are plenty around, but they're all such monsters. They don't even bother to make any sort of relationship with me. It's "Wham, bam, thank you ma'am", and if I don't come across, there's plenty more who will. Five years ago, it was okay by me. Do you remember those long talks we used to have about how we'd never get married? Well, to be absolutely honest with you, Anthea, I feel as if I'm up against some sort of time-clock in my body. I do want children.'

'Really?' Anthea, who hadn't really been listening, suddenly sat up. 'My God, Rose, that's a change. We both swore to each other we'd never marry or have kids. You even lived with Shirley for a while, the most rampant anti-male woman I've ever met.'

'I know, and then I fell in love with Stephen. In the last year I was with him, I stopped taking the pill.'

'Did he know?'

'Not at first, but then one night I got drunk and maudlin. I told him I loved him and wanted to have a baby by him. Stupid of me, because that's when he started to get out. Anthea, I'm frightened of myself.'

Anthea looked at her, startled by the intensity of her voice. 'Why, Rose?'

'I find myself following Stephen and that woman

around, and the other day I stood outside his house and watched him over the garden wall having dinner with his wife.'

Anthea dropped her eyes for a moment. 'It's not that unnatural to be curious about how he lives.'

'I don't want him to live without me. I don't want to have a baby, even his, out of marriage. I need a good warm loving man.'

'Stephen's not any of those things, Rose. You know it.'

'I could change him. He has all those good qualities in him, he just needs someone like me to bring them out.'

'Rose, Stephen won't change any more than Charles will. That's why I decided to take Charles for what he is – a spoilt mother's boy. Do you know that he often calls his wife "Julia" by accident when he is talking about Rachel? Mind you, he spends more time talking about his mother than anyone else. To him she's perfect. But I'm more than a match for her. I know those suburban women who look as though butter wouldn't melt in their mouth. They're lethal. They devour their sons and then leave them wrecked for other women to carry around. I've grown very cynical lately. I don't think there are any men around who aren't mother-damaged, so I'll marry Charles and cut my losses.'

'Do you still love him like you did?'

'No, it's become a matter of survival for me. I really did love him those first two years. I believed he loved me, and gradually I found myself pretending that he would leave his wife for me, until I had the six months to honestly look back and suddenly see that his pattern was no different from any other man's I know. A wife at home and women like me on the side. He changes them every few years like a car. But always the promise that if you're good enough in bed, and behave yourself, and keep the relationship a secret, one day he will divorce his dreadful shrew of a wife. I really thought I would become a respectable married woman. Now I know it will take a fight.

'In a way, I wish I'd spent my time sorting out some

sort of a good relationship with a man. I left all that 'til last. I have the other things I fought for. I'm a director of my agency, I have my own place, and a Porsche, but I'm alone.'

'Don't. I can't bear it.' Rose was sobbing.

'It's awful, Rose. But don't worry. I will have Charles.'

'But what about me?'

'I think the best thing you can do is to leave London for a while and try to get Stephen out of your system.'

'I suppose you're right. Thanks, Anthea. You're always good for me.' She laughed. 'If only I *were* gay . . . I wouldn't have all these problems.'

'That's probably true.' Anthea kissed Rose on the cheek. 'I must get to bed. It's three o'clock. I've got to get up and get going early.'

Anthea later lay in bed looking at the ceiling. At least I'm better off than poor old Rose, she thought.

26

Standing on the doorstep of the Jamesons' house, Rachel felt for a moment a dreadful sense of panic. Charles looked marvellous in his torn shirt and patched jeans. She just felt silly in one of her old dresses. She had taken quite some time fraying the ends of the skirt, and she'd taken out a sleeve. Now she felt self-conscious when she realized that the top of her arm looked awfully bare and skinny. The door was opened by old Piranha teeth. 'Rachel! and you must be Charles.' She pulled them into the hall. She kissed Rachel on one cheek and Charles on both. 'Come. Let me take you in and introduce you to people.'

The vast drawing-room was packed with people who all seemed to know each other. The noise was deafening. 'It looks like the parrot house at the zoo,' Rachel whispered to Charles.

'Now you're not going to ruin a perfectly good party with your snide remarks, Rachel.'

Belinda Jameson was already introducing them to a small group of people who were earnestly discussing a painting on the wall. 'I think,' said a tall man with a shock of red hair, 'I think the lighting used by LeMaitre is unusually subdued.'

'I quite agree.' A very beautiful woman stood by him. 'Remember when we saw his last exhibit in the Museum of Fine Arts in Boston? I loved his nudes.'

'Rachel and Charles Hunter, meet Alison and Mervin Gould,' introduced the hostess.

Charles leaped into the conversation feet first. 'LeMaitre? I saw some of his work in Russia last month.'

'You go to Russia?' Alison looked at Charles.

'Yes. I'm a journalist. I write for the *Reporter*.'

Rachel was quite amused. Magic words, she thought. Charles only has to say them and he's suddenly everyone's best friend. It wasn't like that on the *Hammersmith Evening Argus*. She felt a sudden pang of homesickness for Ashley Road, but she mentally shook herself, and smiled at Alison.

There was a break in the conversation, so she said, 'Do your children go to ARTS?'

'Yes,' said Alison.

'How funny. I don't think I've ever seen you there.'

'I have a Norland nanny. She does the collecting. Charles,' Alison said, turning her back on Rachel, 'Charles, do tell me. Is life as awful as they say it is in Russia? One does read, of course, but it's so nice to get it from the horse's mouth.' Her gaze rested for several seconds on his lips.

Charles looked at her left nipple which peeked at him out of a strategically located hole in her costume. I could have her pussy in a minute, he thought. He sighed. He had always made it a rule for himself – it was Michael who first taught him – 'Remember, Charles: a gentleman *never* shits on his own doorstep.'

He smiled at Alison. 'It's absolutely ghastly, but I'm always all right because I can get all the caviare I want, and foreign visitors to the Soviet Union are encouraged to buy opera seats.'

Rachel was rather desperately looking around the room to see if she knew anyone. She saw Jane in the distance. They made faces at each other. Alison and Charles were walking towards the dining-room leaving Rachel to partner Mervin. He had mean close-set eyes, and very white skin with lots of sprouting red hair on the backs of his hands. His eyes looked cruel.

'What do you do, Rachel?'

'Uhhh . . . nothing much. I'm afraid I'm just a housewife.' She realized he was a bit drunk.

He swayed as he walked beside her. 'Your husband and my wife seem to hit it off together.'

'Charles is very gregarious, not like me,' she laughed nervously.

'Alison's very greg . . . gregarious,' he slurred. 'You should see her when she's had a skinful. D'you know what her favourite party trick is?' Rachel shook her head. 'No? She's the only woman I know who can smoke a fag through her cunt.' Mervin leered.

'Oh,' said Rachel, completely lost for words. Fortunately they had caught up with Alison and Charles. Rachel slipped her hands into Charles's for comfort. She could hardly look at Alison. They were at the end of the huge buffet table, which was piled high with lobsters, salads, and several huge fresh and smoked salmon. I've never seen anything like that in my life,' Rachel said to Charles.

'Ssshhh . . . Rachel. Not in front of other people.' She fell silent.

She saw an amused gleam in Alison's eyes. I hope she gets smoker's cough, Rachel said to herself. Finally, after much manoeuvring, she managed to get close enough to Jane to say, 'I'll come out tomorrow. I need to talk to you. You're the only other housewife in the room. We're a dying species.'

'I'll get out the valium and the coffee,' Jane laughed. 'Don't go into the pool area.'

'Why?' but Jane was tugged away by Jerry who was making friends furiously.

Charles was having a wonderful time. 'Come on, Rachel. Let's go and look round the house. It's fabulous, isn't it?'

'Yes, it is.' Rachel trailed along beside him. They followed a throng of people who were making their way to the back of the huge house. They passed through a magnificent study into a carpeted hall. She could see through the open door a barman standing by the pool with a trolley of drinks. Various people were sitting or lying on the numerous deckchairs and patio furniture that lay round the pool. Some people were swimming. 'Charles,' Rachel said, squeezing his arm very hard, 'they've got nothing on.'

'So?' said Charles amiably. 'So what if they want to

have a swim? I wouldn't mind one myself.'

'You don't mean that, do you?'

'Of course not.' He patted her hand. 'Let's get a drink.'

Rachel sat bolt upright on her deckchair, sipping a glass of champagne. I've always wondered what an orgy would look like, she thought. She saw Mervin swim past them. The lights from under the water illuminated his white form. Men's pricks look so silly dangling like that, she thought. Suddenly she saw Belinda Jameson standing stark naked at the end of the pool. Poor Dominic, thought Rachel. Belinda looked like a scrawny plucked chicken. Her breasts resembled cricket balls dangling on the end of thin stalks of tissue precariously connected to her chest. She raised her hands above her head and did a belly-flop into the water. A cheer went up, and various other people threw off their clothes and dived in. 'I think we should go, Charles.'

'Oh all right.' There was no point in staying if Rachel was going to be a spoil-sport, and if Alison took her clothes off, there was no knowing what he might do. Charles followed Rachel through to the library. Then they got lost. They finally found their way back to the drawing-room, but not before they saw an ugly fight erupt in the passage between a man and his wife.

'You dirty old whore!' The man was beside himself. 'You cunt! I can't let you out of my sight for one minute, can I?'

The woman was cowering against the wall. 'Don't hit me . . . please don't . . .'

'Charles, do something.'

'It's none of my business, Rachel. Come on.' He dragged Rachel past, but as she was pulled by Rachel recognized the woman. She often saw her outside the school. She never talked to anyone.

'For God's sake, Charles. Why don't you do something? He's hurting her.'

'Listen, Rachel, those sort of women ask for it. Even if I did wade in, she'd probably tell me to piss off and mind my own business. Then what would I do? Believe me, I know those women.'

'I suppose so, but she didn't look as if she was enjoying

it to me. I really want to get out of here. I hate this place.' Rachel was in tears.

Charles suddenly turned on her. 'I'm sick and tired of you and your sanctimonious way of life. Can't you see *I* like it here? These are my sort of people. If you want to go home, go home. I'm staying.' He held out the car keys to her.

'Okay. I'll go home.' She snatched the keys out of his hand and went to find her coat. As she left the house, she saw Charles chatting away to a group of people. She drove home with the tears running down her face.

Charles soon found Alison. 'Where's Rachel?' she asked.

'She's gone home. Headache, I think.'

'Oh poor thing.'

Later, on the floor of the master bedroom, Alison looked up at him and said, 'Your wife's a bit of a country-mouse, you know.'

'I like her that way,' said Charles loyally.

'But you like other women . . . all sorts of other ways.' She had her index finger up his rectum and was giving him a prostate massage.

'That feels marvellous. Where did you learn that?'

Alison laughed. 'I used to be a nurse. That's how we got semen specimens in the fertility clinics.'

Charles's orgasm was interrupted by Belinda Jameson. 'Oops. Sorry, my loves.' She stepped over them to get to her bed.

'Ohhh . . .' Charles groaned as he ejaculated all over the thick pile carpet.

A small neatly dressed woman joined Belinda on the bed. They frantically removed their clothes and fell on top of each other. 'Come on,' said Alison. 'I can't bear watching Belinda ball her little bitches.'

She was pulling Charles up off the floor when the door opened. Rear Admiral Hugo Jameson was standing with a drink in his hand, swaying. 'I'd recognize that arse anywhere,' he said to no one in particular. The light from the corridor fell on his wife's bare behind which was rising and falling at an ever-increasing rate. 'Good evening,' he boomed as his eyes focused on Charles and Alison. 'Don't believe we've met.'

'Shut up, Hugo,' said Alison. 'Come on, Charles. Let's go downstairs.'

'Won't your husband suspect if we walk into the drawing-room together?'

'He won't just suspect, darling. He'll be waiting for every last juicy little detail. It's the only way he can get his rocks off. Unless I can persuade you to join both of us in bed. He likes a threesome. Closet queen, that's his problem.'

'Oh.' Charles didn't much like the idea of a discussion over his sexual prowess. 'I'm not into that sort of sex, Alison. I'm sorry.'

'You soon will be if you hang about this house.'

Suddenly Charles very much wanted Rachel. He took a taxi home.

Rachel had sobbed herself to sleep. She was lying with her face to the window. Dear Rachel. She's been crying for me, Charles thought. I'll make it up to her. I'll book tickets tomorrow for a holiday abroad. He fell asleep dreaming of hot sunshine and a little whitewashed villa.

Rachel was up early the next morning. 'I'm off now, Charles.' She had been very quite during breakfast. Charles didn't say much either.

I'll surprise her with the tickets tonight, he promised himself.

After Rachel dropped the children at school, she went off to see Jane. 'I had a dreadful time last night.' Jane looked at her. She had seen Charles without Rachel later on in the evening. 'I just couldn't mix with those people.'

Jane looked at her sympathetically. 'Well, either you learn to, or you won't keep your husband for very long.'

'Charles isn't like that, Jane. We've always been faithful to each other. He'd tell me if he had anyone else.'

Jane laughed. 'You're lucky, Rachel. Most men aren't faithful, you know.'

'What about Jerry?'

'Jerry's no problem. He's so boring, no one else would

have him. All he ever talks about is money. He gets his kicks out of the bank rate.'

'He's a good father to your children, Jane.'

'Yes he is. And I thank my lucky stars that he's such a good husband in so many ways. But honestly, Rachel, he's too good. He doesn't drink or swear or smoke. Our sex life is like banking hours – utterly dependable. He doesn't really like making love. He keeps a kleenex beside the pillow, and as soon as we finish he mops me up and rushes off to wash himself.'

'Oh Jane. That must be awful.'

'It is sometimes, but I'm going to get some extra interests. Take some classes maybe. But then he hates me being out in the evening. He doesn't say anything, he just fidgets around the house until I come home. On the other hand, the three kids take up all my time. There are the ballet lessons for Liza, violin for Jake, and the oboe for Suzanne. On Saturday they go horseback riding, and then there are the remedial classes. I have to take Liza to Twickenham for those. There's not much time left for myself.'

'What would you have done if you hadn't married?'

'I don't know. As far as my family's concerned, it doesn't matter what happens. The most important thing in life is to marry a good Jewish boychik.'

'It's not very different here, but it is changing. Almost all the women at school are doing something with their lives, even if it's a question of just taking dance classes.'

Jane looked suddenly haggard. 'How do I get time to do any classes? I'm just the hired help round here. We have to entertain at least three times a week. I'm expected to throw magnificent dinner parties for eight people. Your country's so backwards that this rented house doesn't even have a dishwasher.'

Rachel laughed. 'Anna's always going on about the oppressed working classes, but I think lots of us live in gilded cages. Life was a lot easier back in Ashley Road days, even when I had to dry nappies all over the sitting-room because we couldn't afford the driers in the launderette.'

'Here,' Jane said as she reached into a drawer by the refrigerator. 'Look. I have notebooks filled with recipes that I've used over the years. You might like to look at it for your dinner party.'

'Jane, you're marvellous. I don't know how you do it. Your house is always immaculate, there are flowers everywhere, beautiful plants. Charles says I have black thumbs. Everything dies in my house.'

Jane looked at Rachel, sitting on the kitchen stool with her knees tucked up under her chin. 'Rachel, don't let him put you down like that. Why do you always accept that he's some sort of God in your life, that he knows all the answers?'

'I don't know. Maybe it's because he knows a lot more about life than I do. Maybe I'm just lazy, and it's easier for me to let him run my life. But last night was a turning point for me. Do you know, he actually gave me the car keys and told me to go home? He said, "These are my kind of people." I decided that those might well be his kind of people, but they are certainly not mine. And if he wants to go to places like that, he can. But without me. We did go to the swimming pool, by the way. There were people swimming up and down in the nude. And Belinda Jameson did a belly-flop. God, she looked awful.'

Jane laughed. 'There were a few in when we were there. Jerry didn't even notice they were naked. He was too busy computing the cost of the pool.'

Rachel picked up the bottle that was sitting by the coffeepot. 'You weren't joking about the valium.'

Jane made a face. 'No. I've taken them for years.'

Rachel nodded. 'I remember going through a very bad patch in Ashley Road. I was sitting in Dr Burns's waiting-room, and I looked round, and three of my friends were waiting with their children. I didn't ask, but I bet they were waiting for tranquillizers as well. I took them for ages. I remember lying in bed thinking only a sane person would take tranquillizers, because you'd have to be insane to be able to get up every day and clean a house you'd cleaned the day before without being sedated.'

'I'm a bit worried about myself.' Jane's face tightened. 'You see, I'm taking three a day. I find if I don't dope myself, I get so angry with the kids. I can't get angry with Jerry. He just shrugs his shoulders and says I'm due for a period.'

'I know what you mean. Charles has a wonderful way of reasoning with me so that everything always ends up my fault.' They both laughed. 'I must get back, Jane. Keep sucking the tablets. It's better than going ape with a meat cleaver. Can I borrow those recipes? I'll give them back to you tomorrow.'

'Sure. Take care.'

Rachel was in the hall when she turned and gave Jane a big hug. 'It must be difficult being so far from your family.'

Jane rested her head for a moment on Rachel's shoulder. 'It is. I came from a large, loving, screaming, touching Jewish family. I find most English people so cold – uptight, really.'

'They are,' Rachel laughed. 'You know, I was collecting Dom from school with Sarah and Charles. We were waiting outside, and Dom came running out. Charles hardly ever collects him, so Dom threw himself into his arms, and Charles pushed him back and said, "You're seven now, Dominic. You're far too old for kissing and hugging. Men shake hands." And he shook him by the hand. Dom hasn't hugged or kissed either of us since that day.'

'Jesus. That's awful.'

'That's how Charles was brought up. Apple of his mother's eye, but they don't touch each other.'

'Wow. I can see why English men are so blocked off. Then again, ever since the Women's Movement, American men touch all the time, but most of it is just to prove they're "sensitive". It's a new tyranny. "What's the matter? You don't like me now I'm sensitive?" as a guy sticks his hands on your boob. You know, I don't think men like women very much.'

'I'm not surprised really. It's not that I think men *don't* like women,' Rachel thought aloud, 'it's more that they're afraid of us. Anyway, I must get on with the shopping. See you at school.'

'Bye,' said Jane, and Rachel was gone.

Jane went back into the kitchen and lit a cigarette. One more cup of coffee, and I'll clean the floor, she promised herself. When I die I'll probably be clutching a cup of coffee and a packet of Marlboro on a clean kitchen floor. The thought cheered her up. She put the kettle on. At least I've got Rachel . . . And the kids are settling down well.

Charles telephoned just after five o'clock that evening. 'I'm sorry about last night, Rachel. I had a bit too much to drink. I've got a really nice surprise for you.' It was so unlike Charles to apologize for anything that Rachel was surprised and touched. 'It's all right, darling. It's partly my fault. I just can't cope with those sort of occasions. I'll cook something nice for you. By the way, have you been trying to get through to me on the 'phone?'

'No,' said Charles.

'It's odd. The 'phone rang just before you telephoned, and there was no one there. It's happened quite a few times in the last two days. Must be a heavy breather,' she laughed. 'It's quite scary though.'

'I shouldn't worry about it, darling. It's probably just our antiquated English 'phone system.'

'I expect you're right. Bye, love.' Rachel put the 'phone down and went to see if they had any steaks in the 'fridge.

'That's better.' Charles swallowed his mouthful. 'Last time you put so much pepper on your steak au poivre that we had to throw them out.' Charles was sitting at the dining-table with the tickets in his pocket. 'That's very good, darling. You've got it nearly right.'

Rachel was delighted. 'Next time I'll get it perfect.'

'Here.' Charles passed the wallet from the travel agent across the table.

Rachel opened it and let out a squeal of pleasure. 'Two weeks in the Camargue in a villa. How wonderful!' She left her chair and threw her arms around Charles.

He suddenly felt an urge to make love to her. 'I feel

really randy. It must be all that hot pepper,' he joked. 'Come on. The kids are asleep. Let's make love now.'

'Here on the floor? Honestly, Charles. I told you before I don't see the point of making love on the floor when we've got a perfectly comfortable bed upstairs. Anyway, I had to spend hours hoovering up crumbs. I certainly won't get turned on lying on the bloody thing.'

'Let's go upstairs then.'

'I'm sorry, Charles. I really don't feel like it. I want to look at the photographs of the villa. Do you mind?'

'No. Not really. But I do think you could show a little appreciation.' He did mind dreadfully. If he'd bought Anthea tickets, she'd have been all over him. Rachel just didn't know how to treat a man. She had been saying 'No' a lot lately.

'I'm sorry, darling, but if we did get into bed, I'd just have a vision of that hairy red-headed man's prick in the pool . . . Oh look, Charles,' Rachel said, turning her attention to the travel brochure, 'that's where they have the white horses.'

'We must have an au pair by then. I don't want to be stuck in a villa with the kids every night,' said Charles.

'Actually, I telephoned an agency today, and they'll be sending us details of the girls they have on their books. They're mostly European.'

'A French girl would be good for the children.'

Rachel laughed. 'Funnily enough, that's what Dom's ordered.'

'I don't mind who you get as long as she's efficient and doesn't drink all the brandy.'

Later that night, Charles looked at himself in the bathroom mirror and thought, So Dominic's going to be a chip off the old block. I'd better see he has a packet of French letters on him at all times. He might need a little fatherly advice at his age. He went to sleep with a happy smile on his face. We'll have fun when he's a bit older.

'Anthea, have you been 'phoning my house?'

From the slight hesitation in her voice, he knew she had. 'No, darling. Why should I do that?'

'I don't know, unless you're sick in the head.' Charles was furious.

'I didn't. Honestly. I wouldn't do a thing like that.'

Oh yes you would, you bitch, he thought. He kept his voice very calm. 'I'll be over to see you in a couple of days. Friday night actually.'

'Wonderful. I'll have a surprise supper for you.'

'See you about seven-thirty then.' Charles put down the receiver. Keeping Anthea under control was going to be more difficult than he had thought.

Anthea bent back in her chair in her office and stretched like a cat. She was amused. He's really wired up. It's fun to see him do the jumping for a change. Oysters and chilled white wine in bed. She could see it now. He would find her lying naked on the bed with half a dozen oysters neatly arranged on her stomach. He could take it from there. Charles would love it. I must remember to take the 'phone off the hook. She didn't want to be disturbed by a call from Rose.

Rose's drunk, incoherent, rambling conversations were getting boring. The last one had been all about her father's double-barrelled shotgun, and how she could blow a pheasant out of the sky. 'There aren't many pheasant in London, Rose. Anyway, they're out of season – you'll have to wait.' She remembered Rose's high-pitched snicker. It was creepy.

Sarah was helping Rachel in the kitchen when Charles telephoned on Friday evening. 'Dreadfully sorry, darling. Just heard that I've got to go out of London for the night. I've got to interview a man early tomorrow morning. I'll be back for lunch.'

'Oh dear. I'm just trying out one of Jane's recipes, and Sarah's helping me. We were looking forward to watching you eat it. Oh well, it can't be helped.'

'I'll ring you later to say good-night.'

'Thank you, Charles. I love you.'

'Love you too,' said Charles. He smiled affectionately. She really was trying to improve her cooking. 'Get two bunches of mixed summer flowers,' he said to his secretary. 'Bring one back with you, and send the other to my wife.' His secretary raised her eyebrows. 'Go on, you sharp little baggage.'

She wiggled across to his desk. 'First sign these letters.' She bent over the desk. He could see her breasts like two soft puppies.

Shit, he thought. She does it on purpose. When he had finished signing, he looked up at her and said, 'I really do think you should wear something a little more suitable for the office. This is not a night-club.'

'Yes, Mr Hunter.' Dirty old sod, she thought as she left the room; can't keep his eyes off them.

27

Charles was asleep in Anthea's arms when Julia telephoned his home at two o'clock in the morning. Rachel, alone in her bed, answered the 'phone. 'William is in hospital. He's had a heart-attack.' Her voice was cold. 'Where's Charles?'

'I'm so sorry, Julia. I don't actually know where Charles is. He telephoned at about eight o'clock to say good-night. I know he's out of London. How serious is it?'

'He's not expected to last the night.'

'Oh my God. I'll ring the paper right away. They'll know where he is. Do you want me to bundle the kids into the car and come down right away?'

'No, thank you, Rachel. I just want Charles. Don't bring the children down, it will just upset them. If he dies they'll have to come to the funeral anyway, so come down then.' Her voice quivered a little.

'Have you contacted Elizabeth?'

'Yes. The college is calling the mission.'

'Have you anyone with you?'

'Yes, Ruth is here, and she'll stay until Charles comes.'

'All right.' Rachel was relieved she was not by herself. 'I'll find Charles.'

She telephoned the night editor at the *Reporter*. 'No,' he said, looking at his sheet of assignments, 'he's not on here.'

'It must be an unscheduled assignment,' she said.

'Could be, or maybe he's moonlighting.'

'I suppose so.' She knew that Charles often took reporting jobs on the side using another name. Lots of reporters did it, Charles had explained. 'Thank you. If he calls in, will you tell him his father is dying in hospital?'

'I will. I'm sorry to hear that.'

'Thank you,' said Rachel, and she hung up. She suddenly found herself crying. He was such a good man. She sat by the window in the bedroom and looked out over the lawn. Poor Julia. What on earth will she do without him? Charles will be broken-hearted. They never had much to say to each other, but William always admired Charles. 'My son in London,' he would say to the neighbours. She smiled and got up to go to bed. What a wonderful man Charles is. How many women still get bunches of flowers after fourteen years of marriage?

The night editor looked at his secretary. 'Charles Hunter is out tom-catting again, and his poor bitch of a wife still doesn't know. I don't know how he gets away with it.'

Charles didn't get back until lunchtime. Rachel was distraught. She threw herself into his arms. 'Oh, darling. Your father died at ten o'clock this morning. I've been trying to get you, but the night editor said you weren't on the list. I asked the police to see if they could check all the chain hotels, but you weren't in any of them.'

'No, I know.' He held her close to him. Shit, what am I going to say? Think fast. 'No. I forgot to tell you, darling. I was doing a bit of moonlighting, and I stayed with a friend so I could make a bit extra on the hotel bill for our holiday.'

'I'm so sorry, Charles. Ring your mother right away. She's waiting for you.' Charles telephoned Julia and arranged to catch the train to Bridport.

The funeral took place four days later. Charles spent the days with his mother who was unusually quiet. She seemed resigned to William's death and quite calm. 'It's better he goes before me. He could never have coped on his own. I'll miss him, of course. It's been a long time.'

'Did you ever think of leaving him when you were younger?'

Julia looked up at Charles. 'Leaving him? You can't *leave* your husband. You make your bed and you lie in it. He was a good man, a good husband, and a good father.'

'But Mother, you did say he was boring.'

'Charles, this is no time to talk like that. You can't have everything in a marriage, and I'm grateful for what I've had.'

'It's such a shame Rachel doesn't get on with you, Mother. You could live with us.'

Julia sniffed. 'It's not that I don't like the girl, but since she's moved into that new house of yours, it's gone to her head. Did she tell you about the curtains?'

'No.' Actually Charles had heard all about the curtains and the tablecloth ad nauseum.

'Last time your father and I visited, we packed the car with all sorts of good second-hand curtains. I made the tablecloth and she refused both. All of it.'

'She didn't refuse, Mother. She just told you that we were having blinds made for the windows, and the table is made of glass. A tablecloth would have been useless.'

'There you go, defending her as usual. I must say, I was very hurt. Anyway, there's no question of my living in your house. Her sloppy ways would drive me mad.'

'We do have an au pair coming next week.'

'An au pair? You mean one of those fancy foreign girls?'

'She's not a fancy foreign girl. She's French, and her name is Marie-Claire. We all liked her immediately.' He saw a look in her eye that made him laugh. 'You've got a dirty mind, Mother. Of course I wouldn't.'

Well, at least I hope I don't, he thought that night as he lay in his little single bed. He had given up making promises to himself a long time ago. Thank God Elizabeth's going to be here tomorrow. I haven't seen her since she left home.

Elizabeth arrived unannounced with her husband.

'You didn't tell us you were getting married.' Julia fired the opening shot.

'There would have been no point, Mother. You would have objected. I'm not here for you anyway. I'm here for my father. I loved him.'

'Well, you broke his heart.' Julia was flushed with anger.

'Mrs Hunter, please don't upset yourself. I quite understand the shock,' said the husband. 'My people were certainly not happy when they heard I was going to marry a white girl. In my country it is a matter of shame to marry out of the tribe.'

Julia could hardly bear to look at him. He put out his hand. Gingerly she took it, and then as soon as she could she washed her hands very carefully. He was everything she had always feared. He was huge with fuzzy hair, a flat nose, and thick lips. How could she? Julia thought. How could her own daughter do that to her? A wog. Her first instinct was to forbid them to leave the house. All the neighbours would know that her daughter was married to a black man.

'I'm going to take Elizabeth and Tom out for a drink while you get over the shock of it all, Mother.' Charles put his head around the kitchen door. 'He's really a nice fellow, so pull yourself together. They'd better have my room, and I'll sleep in Liz's bed, or . . .' he grinned, 'you could always vacate your double bed for them as a gesture of good will.'

'I don't feel well, Charles.'

'I thought you wouldn't. Get your bowl and lie down. We'll be back at ten.' The door slammed.

It was then that Julia really cried for William. They have their own lives now. They don't really want me. Even Dominic doesn't want to stay here anymore. Dear William, gentle, dependable, loving William. His side of the bed was empty. Julia wept into her pillow.

Charles had told Rachel that Elizabeth had arrived with her husband. 'Frightened the life out of Mother. You should have seen her face.'

'Poor Julia,' said Rachel down the telephone. 'Don't

you think it would have been kinder if Elizabeth had at least warned her?'

'No, I don't. I think it was a sort of revenge. Not the marriage . . . I mean, they seem very happy, but just turning up like that. I don't think she's ever forgiven Mother for refusing to let her be a missionary.'

'Oh well, I suppose it'll just add to the sheer hell of the whole thing. I hate funerals. I'll be down tomorrow. The kids are very upset, but they're old enough to go now. Where are we going to sleep?'

'Mother's arranged with Ruth that Elizabeth and Tom go there. She's got Manny home, but they have the spare room. Sarah can sleep with us in the other bed, and Dominic can have Elizabeth's room.'

'Okay. See you tomorrow. Good-night, darling.'

Charles put the 'phone down and went into the kitchen to see Elizabeth. 'Where's Tom?'

'He's gone to bed. The flight took ages, and it caught up with him.'

'Has Mother upset him?'

'Not really. He's used to prejudice. Both of us are, but Mother's such an old cow.'

'Really, Elizabeth, that's not very religious.'

'I don't have to be saintly, and I do feel very angry with her. It took me many years to realize what a rotten mother she was.'

'Do you really think that?' Charles was surprised.

'Yes, I do. She spoiled you and she took over my life. I hate being near her because I feel as though I'm getting sucked into her awful narrow bigoted world again. That's why I've stayed away.'

'Lots of people are like her though.'

'No, Charles. Lots of people aren't like her. Only some people, and they are the sort of mother she is: domineering, possessive, and dangerous. They cripple their children, not physically but emotionally, so that they're incapable of forming a good warm trusting relationship with anyone else.' She looked at Charles. 'Tell me, Charles. Are you happy with Rachel?'

'Absolutely. She is as honest and trusting as she always was. We have two splendid children and a lovely house. We're going to the Camargue for two weeks in August. It'll be Rachel's first trip abroad. Here, look at these photos. See, Dominic looks like me? And Sarah's more like Rachel's side of the family. Are you going to have kids?'

Elizabeth shook her head. 'No. We have to work way out in the bush. It's too dangerous for children. Maybe if we decide to work in a mission in a town I might have a late baby, but I don't think so. We're very happy as we are. It's strange that I have to go across the world to Africa to find a man who shares my belief in God and who gives me such happiness.' She stretched her arms above her head. 'Just when I'd totally given up on men.'

'That's great, Elizabeth. I wish I could share your optimistic sense of eternity. For me, once you die, that's all there is.'

'I'll pray for you, love.' Elizabeth put her arms around his neck and kissed him.

'Do I need it?'

That night he dreamed of Anthea with an oyster in its shell nesting in her pubic hair. The oyster suddenly gave Charles an obscene all-knowing wink. He woke up in a sweat. I'll never eat oysters again, he swore to himself.

The funeral took place in the local Protestant churchyard. Rachel watched the coffin go into the ground. She remembered Aunt Bea's funeral, and she held Sarah's hand very tightly. She had already explained the ceremony very carefully to Sarah who fully accepted that her beloved grandfather had gone to be with God. 'We should have buried him in his allotment,' Rachel remarked when they were all driving back to the house in the black limousine. Julia's face tightened.

'She was only joking, Mother.' Charles put his arm around Julia's shoulders and scowled at Rachel.

'No she wasn't,' said Sarah. 'We talked about it on the way down. Grandpa never went to that church. I think he would have preferred the cabbage patch.'

'You are so like your mother, miss.' Julia's voice was acid.

'I know. Lots of people tell me that,' said Sarah, smiling at Rachel. 'Aunt Emily says I have the same eyes as Aunt Bea and Great Grandfather Lionel.'

'Your mother wasn't married, was she?' Dominic asked Rachel.

'No, she wasn't. Somewhere in America I have a father who doesn't even know about me.'

'Does that mean that you were a bastard?'

'Dominic!' Julia's voice rose. 'Don't you dare speak like that.'

'Don't fuss, Grandma. It's not a rude word when properly used,' Dominic reassured.

'Is that what they teach you in that newfangled school of yours?'

Rachel looked across at Dominic and said, 'Grandma's right. I prefer the word "illegitimate". I was a war-baby. I was much luckier than most other illegitimate babies. Their mothers either had to give them away or suffer dreadfully from everyone's disapproval. It was an awful thing in those days to have a baby and not to be married.'

'And so it should be. Surely, Rachel, you don't approve of all these girls running around pregnant calling themselves "single parents" and taking money from those who work hard and lead decent lives, do you?' Julia accused.

'I don't think I can make sweeping moral statements like that. All I know is that Anna is having a baby, and I feel she has that right because she'll be a good mother, and she has sensible plans for the child.'

Julia shook her head. 'I don't know what the world is coming to these days.'

'Don't let it bother you, Mother – it's not your problem. I'll make you a nice cup of tea when we get in.' Charles turned to Rachel. 'I really do think you should try not to argue with Mother, Rachel, especially on a day like this.'

Rachel looked at her lap. There was a faint smile on Julia's face. 'Thank you, Charles,' said Julia.

Sarah slipped her hand into Rachel's. 'When are we going home, Mummy?'

'Tomorrow, darling.' They drew up outside the house. How I hate this house, Rachel thought. It's so claustrophobic. Thank God we're leaving.

People were filling up the rooms. William had been well liked by the people of Bridport. Julia was delighted to see the bank manager, who had called in to pay his respects. 'Do have a cup of tea, Mr Brinton. Or would you like something a little stronger? A sherry perhaps?'

'Never touch a drop 'til the sun's over the yardarm.'

Julia looked confused. Charles came to the rescue. 'He wants a cup of tea, Mother. Off you go. I'll look after him . . . Poor Mother,' he said to Mr Brinton. 'She doesn't drink at all,' he laughed.

'Good man, your father.'

'Yes, he was.'

'He'll be sadly missed you know.'

Charles looked around the room. 'I must say, I had no idea that he was so well known.' The local doctor was there. He was retired now. Charles had never quite forgotten the feel of those cold tongs below his waist. He flinched. I hope he's forgotten it by now, he thought.

In a corner of the kitchen, William's cronies were discussing rooting geraniums. Julia was coldly polite to them all. I'll never know why he needed to mix with such common men, she thought. Their huge boots were staining her clean floor. Tom and Elizabeth were handing round the food. 'Tom, you pour the tea for me,' Julia said, taking away the plate of sandwiches he was carrying. Can't have him touching other people's food . . . Tom looked at her. Why, he's laughing at me, she thought, and flushed furiously.

After the last guests had gone, Manny (who had come to the funeral), Charles, Rachel, Tom, and Elizabeth went out for a drink at the pub. Charles was pleased to see Manny. 'You haven't changed a bit, you know.'

'Well you have. You look rich and successful. Rachel hasn't changed at all.'

'How's New York?'

'Wonderful. I'm the rabbi of a temple in a mixed

area of town. The people are hardworking and very religious. I started at a temple in a much richer area, but most of the Jews there only went to temple on the High Holidays and for Bar Mitzvahs, so I quit. I'm much happier now.'

'That's great,' Charles said. 'I feel like getting blind drunk.'

'You'll have to do it on your own,' said Rachel. 'Elizabeth and I promised to go back and finish the clearing up, so we won't be able to stay much longer.'

'I've got to pack tonight,' said Elizabeth. 'We're catching the three o'clock plane tomorrow from Heathrow.'

'Just have another one for the road.' Charles went up to the bar.

'You must come to New York some time. You'll love it, Rachel.' Manny leaned forward and put his hand on hers. 'Take it easy, won't you? You look very strained to me.'

'Oh, no. I'm fine. It's just the high life – it doesn't suit me.'

'I could have told you that years ago.'

'I'll get used to it.'

Rachel and Elizabeth walked back to the house. The streets were empty and there was a light drizzle. 'It's odd being back here again.' Elizabeth looked at Rachel. 'I don't know how you put up with her.'

'Habit, I suppose,' Rachel laughed. 'Charles is so fond of her, there's no point in making it difficult for him. I do wish he wouldn't turn into a small boy when she's around. He hardly ever argues with her.'

'He's always been afraid of her, even when he was little. I remember I'd be the one to catch the back of her hand because he'd always lie his way out. The fact is mother both terrorized and spoiled him.' Elizabeth's tone was bitter. 'She didn't really notice me except when I was old enough to work around the house. Charles was never asked to lift a finger.'

'He doesn't now. Thank God Marie-Claire starts next week. He expects me to be like Julia, a demon housewife. I'm an absolute failure.'

'No, you're not. I think Sarah is a great credit to you, and Dominic . . . well, he's going to be just like his father.'

'Yes, he is. Julia had him a lot when he was little. He doesn't really feel like my child at all. He's sort of Julia's and Charles's, and I'm the nanny. Does that make sense?'

'Yes it does, really. Possessive old bitch that she is.'

'I must pee,' Charles said back in the pub, as he stood up unsteadily. The bell sounded and the pub-owner called for the last bar orders.

'I'll come too. My bladder isn't used to all this English beer.' Tom followed Charles to the lavatory. Standing side by side, they chatted about the day.

'I'm glad it's all over. I hate these events,' Charles said.

'It wouldn't be over in my family. In Africa, a funeral is a momentous occasion. The entire tribe gathers and it lasts at least three days.' Tom was finished.

'I'm grateful for all your help, Tom. It's not the easiest way to get to know your new family.'

'No, but we won't be back again. Elizabeth doesn't have much time for your mother, and I feel it's better for her to be with my family who have all accepted her and love her. Julia could never do that for me. She barely tolerates Rachel.'

'I know, she is difficult. But she's too old to change, so I don't try.'

'You could stop her being quite so rude to Rachel, you know. It must really hurt her.'

'I can't do anything about that. Rachel will open her mouth and say things that upset Mother without ever thinking of the consequences. I've tried with Rachel again and again. I've even taken to visiting with Dominic and leaving Rachel and Sarah behind.'

Tom stared at Charles. 'You don't know Rachel very well, do you, Charles?'

'Women,' Charles laughed, 'who knows any of them anyway? Come on. Let's go home. I'm tired.'

They collected Manny from the bar. 'You two go

ahead,' Charles said. 'I've just got to have a word with an old friend of my father's in the corner over there.' He pushed his way purposefully across the crowded room.

'All right. I'll see you before you leave tomorrow,' Manny said and waved good-bye. Manny and Tom disappeared into the night.

'Anthea?' Charles spoke in the 'phone-box.

'How's it been, darling?'

'Absolutely awful.'

'You poor thing. I wish I was there to hold you.'

'I'd rather be where you are than in this one-horse town. I'm back tomorrow so I'll be round on Wednesday.'

'All right, darling. Give me a ring about the time you're back. Good night, love.'

Charles put the telephone down. That should keep her quiet. Walking home he looked up at the sky. Suddenly he was aware that he felt enormously angry. He shook his fist at the sky. 'You bastard,' he shouted. 'You never cared enough.' He felt a hand on his arm. He looked up.

'Can I help you?' The man was a complete stranger.

'No, no. It's all right.' He was sobbing. 'It's my father. We buried him today. I'm just a bit upset. I'll work it off.'

By the time he got in, he had calmed down completely. I don't think I've done that before. Too much beer, he thought as he got into bed. Funny, all that stuff about black men's cocks. Mine's bigger than Tom's. I must tell Anthea.

28

'I want to bring round a letter for you to keep for me, Anthea.' Anthea sighed. It was Rose on the telephone.

'Are you calmer now, Rose?'

'Never felt better in my life.'

'Okay. Come over now, and we can have a cup of coffee.'

Charles was giving Anthea a lot of trouble. He kept making excuses and breaking appointments. Tonight he was having his first dinner party. He was very pleased with himself and it hurt Anthea to think that she would not be at his side. She needed company, and if Rose had straightened out, she might even open a bottle of whisky that she had bought for Charles.

Rose arrived shortly. 'Can you keep the letter for me, and only open it if you hear some news?'

'What are you talking about, Rose? Is this a game?'

'No, it isn't. I'm just asking you as a friend. Please, Anthea. Don't even think about it. Just put it away.'

Anthea looked at her. 'Well, okay. I must say, you do look better.' Rose had become very thin, almost emaciated. But instead of that wild insane glitter in her eyes she now looked resigned, even calm. 'Is it all over?'

'Yes, it is.'

'Come on then. Let's open the whisky and celebrate.'

'What have you been doing?'

'I've been at my parents' house. I haven't been doing much. Riding helped.'

'What's happening with Charles?'

Anthea frowned. 'He's being difficult. I have to threaten a lot to bring him to heel. I think I'll have to tell that horse-faced wife of his a few home truths. He says she won't ditch him, but he's a lousy judge of character anyway. I've seen her a few times. She looks to me like someone who could bail out if she was really upset. If you watch her walk, she's got a sort of assurance that surprises me. Charles always makes her out to be so helpless.'

'Have you been following her around?'

Anthea blushed. 'Doesn't everyone?' She laughed.

'Everyone I know,' said Rose. 'Here's to us and our uxorious futures.'

Anthea felt uneasy. She didn't know why. Rose was throwing back the whisky, and even though she was talking quite normally she had a slight smile on her face. It was almost as though she had a secret. She was waiting for something.

Rachel had put an enormous effort into getting the evening right. 'Start with yourself first,' Jane had advised very firmly. 'I'll take you to the hairdresser, and they have a make-up artist there.'

'Thanks, Jane. I hate going to the hairdresser. I don't think I've been to one in years. I'll have to get a new dress. All my stuff is dreadfully old-fashioned.'

'Buy a long black dress. You can't go wrong in that.' Jane was in full swing. 'Don't serve a hot first course. Get a good pâté from Harrods. Or, this would be a good idea, serve bagels and lox. They're hard to find in England.'

'What's that?'

'It's a very famous Jewish dish. Lox is smoked salmon, and bagels are round hard bread – they look like doughnuts. You spread cream cheese on them, and then you put the lox on top. I'm going over to Bloom's anyway to get some fresh knishes, so I could pick them up for you there.'

'Sounds wonderful. Charles will be delighted to have something so exotic.'

'Bagels? Exotic?'

'They may not be in New York, but they are here. Anyway, Charles loves to be different. Have you noticed how he's changed the way he dresses?'

'He looks more like a male model than a newsman. I thought newsmen were supposed to look rumpled with a pencil behind their ear.'

'Not Charles. I'm lucky if I can get into the bathroom these days. He spends hours in there. If he's not in there, he's staring at himself in the bedroom mirror. Still, I can't complain. He's doing awfully well. His boss has already told him that next year he will become a senior reporter. I don't suppose I'll see him at all them.'

Jane reached out for her mid-morning valium. 'At least you do have something to talk about when he comes home. Jerry's day at the bank is very rarely worth discussing. Never mind. At least they don't cheat on us.'

'That's one way of looking at it, I suppose.'

'Do you know that Liza is hoping to take eight O-levels? She's working very hard, and I'm pleased with her.' Jane proceeded with her usual half-hour speech listing the accomplishments of all three children. At the end of it, Rachel said, 'Don't you think you're pushing them a bit too hard?'

'Too hard?' Jane snorted. 'You should see kids in New York. England's laid back by comparison. How's Dominic getting on?'

'Sarah is really the academic one, but Dom is good at games. Fortunately you can get into university if you're a really good athlete, and Dom already plays county cricket, so we hope with that, and some tutoring nearer the time, we might get him into Oxford or Cambridge. Charles never really got over the fact that he didn't get in. I hate the whole business. It has nothing to do with our kids as people.'

'I know. I'm a bit of a slave-driver myself.' Jane inhaled some smoke. 'But I don't see how my kids are going to get ahead without some pushing. It's not easy for Jews anywhere, particularly in England.' She let the smoke out slowly.

'I think you're a really good mother, Jane. I've never seen anyone put as much effort into their children as you do.' She patted Jane's hand. 'Let's go shopping for my new dress together. What about tomorrow? I'd love to come with you to Bloom's, and then we can go to Oxford Street.

'Sure. That would be great.'

The next evening, Rachel smiled at her reflection in the mirror, remembering the hairdresser's mirror. Her hair was coiled into a soft roll on the top of her head. 'I know it will make you taller, but it will be elegant this way,' the French hairdresser had said, drawing his fingers through the length of her hair. 'You have beautiful hair, Madame.' Rachel wished he would stop pressing his crotch against her shoulder. He looked at her face in the mirror. Lovely eyes, he said to himself. She could be a real beauty. 'Oh, Madame 'as not been taking care of 'erself, 'as she?' He had a soft French accent.

'No, I suppose not. I'm too busy being a housewife.'

'A French woman takes care of 'erself first, and then the 'ouse second. Otherwise, she will lose 'er 'usband. Come. I take you for the make-up, and then we do your 'air.' He led her to a booth across the room.

Women were sitting in long rows down the centre of the salon. Jane was already having her hair washed. 'Don't worry. I won't desert you. I'll wait,' Jane said, looking at Rachel's stricken face. 'No one's going to hurt you. Don't be such a baby.' Rachel felt horribly awkward and out of place as she lumbered along behind her hairdresser.

'When you are finished, ask for me – Jean Paul – and they will bring you back.'

'Hello, Mrs Hunter. My name is Tina. What would you like done?'

'I've no idea. I've never been made up before. You do whatever you think I need. It's for a dinner party tonight, and I've bought a black dress.'

Tina studied her for a moment. 'Good,' she said. 'You have excellent skin, and good colouring. Lie back.' Rachel lay back in the chair and gradually relaxed. 'Look up.' Tina ran the mascara brush through Rachel's long eyelashes. The only painful part was when Tina plucked her thick bushy eyebrows. 'I'll give them a shape, and you just keep them tidy. Sit up now and have a look.'

Rachel couldn't believe her eyes. 'I look quite different.'

'You do. You see? You have a wonderful face for make-up. You have very wide cheekbones. I've shaded your nose down a bit, and put blusher in the hollow of your cheeks to fill them out. I don't think even your husband will recognise you.'

'He won't. I hope he's going to like me like this. It's really a surprise for him.'

'Come on now. I'll take you back to Jean Paul.'

As Rachel stepped out of the cubicle, she saw rows of eyes looking at her from under the hairdriers. A rustling whisper followed her progress back to the other end of the salon. Suddenly the women started to clap their hands. She turned to see Tina smiling at her. She felt immediately ridiculous. What on earth am I doing here with all this junk on my face? She asked herself. She felt a powerful impulse to keep straight on walking to the front door, but Jane was still having her hair set.

'Ahhh . . . Merveilleuse! A masterpiece!' Jean Paul caught her hand. 'Come. You feel sad, no?' Rachel settled into the chair. Jean Paul said, 'I wash your 'air first before I cut the ends a little.' He swung her round and eased her head down into the washbasin. 'I wanted to see what she do with your face before I decide the style.' His hands were gently rubbing the shampoo into a rich lather.

She thought, I've never had a man wash my hair before. The last time was when I was expecting Sarah, and Charles had to do it because I couldn't bend over the sink. She closed her eyes so that she didn't have to look at him. His touch was light and soothing. I could get used to this very easily, she thought. Jean Paul chatted away to her. Gradually he felt her body relaxing.

Poor woman, he thought. She has not been made love to by a man yet. Englishmen . . . they only love each other. When her hair was washed he swung her back. For a moment their eyes met in the mirror. The circle of lights framed their faces. Those eyes, they could have such fire, he thought. Jean Paul was an expert on women. The walls of his cubicle could tell many stories of his sexual exploits with his clients. Not this one, he decided regretfully. As he dried her hair, he softly rubbed the nape of her neck. He could see the flush rising in her cheeks and a tell-tale redness at her throat. Such passion, he thought.

Rachel wondered if all women felt like she did at this moment. She was quite shocked with herself, but really didn't want it to stop. No wonder hairdressers are packed with women, she thought. At one point she panicked. What happens if I come right in this seat? The thought was enough to scare away her erotic feelings.

'Madame, the 'air is dry now. I must make the design.' Jean Paul became very professional. 'A beautiful woman like you needs a simple style for formal occasions. Look. I will show you 'ow to do this. Are you watching?'

'Yes,' Rachel said obediently.

Jean Paul had been right. It did make her look taller, and it did make the black dress look twice as expensive as it actually was. Rachel now put the finishing touches to her make-up, and then moved back into her bedroom. She was still glowing from Jean Paul's appreciative hands. She looked at her watch. It was seven-thirty. Half an hour to go. She went downstairs to join Marie-Claire in the kitchen.

Not very far away, on the other side of Richmond Hill, Rose was parking her car. Although she had drunk an unusual amount of whisky, she felt absolutely calm. As she took her father's double-barrelled shotgun from the boot of the car, she could feel the blood running through her veins. It feels like iced fire, she thought. Now, I must walk up the road with the gun under my cape. She counted the steps to the front gate. She looked around. The affluent street was deserted. It was dark. She slipped like a shadow into the garden. I must stay on the grass so there are no sounds of footsteps. She circled the house until she reached the dining-room window. She crouched under the ledge of the sill. They were not there yet.

Suddenly the lights through the window lit up the lawn. 'Don't use the main lights, Stephen. I have a slight headache. Shall we use the candles?'

'Of course, darling.' Stephen reached into his jacket for matches.

Rose saw the lights go out, and she raised her head. Perfect. Stephen's head and shoulders were softly outlined by the candlelight. 'All I have to say now is "goodbye",' she whispered. 'I'll be with you soon. I love you so much, I can't bear to live without you. If you must die, then I will too.' She raised the gun and took aim. Stephen and his wife were deep in conversation.

There was a flash and a roar. Rose unleashed both barrels into the back of Stephen's head. His body crumpled immediately over the table. The damask walls were splattered with his blood and his brains. The cook rushed into the room, followed by the chauffeur. Stephen's wife was screaming at the top of her lungs. It was the cook's day off; he had been watching television in his room. He saw Rose outside the shattered window, struggling to reload the gun. Fearing for his life, he leaped feet first through the window and landed on Rose in a shower of glass. Rose didn't struggle. She clung to him. 'I want to die. Please, please let me die.' She cried like a child.

The cook was a sympathetic man. He knew that Stephen screwed around like a rabbit. Bloody fool, he thought. Old sod picked the wrong woman this time. 'Come on in out of the cold.' He had to carry her. She couldn't move.

29

Jane arrived promptly at eight as she had promised. 'Come first,' Rachel had said. 'I can't bear making polite conversation.' Rachel had just given Jane and Jerry a drink when Charles arrived.

'I say, Rachel, you do look stunning.' Charles was very pleased with her. 'Good for you, old girl.' He gave her a pat on the bottom. 'I'm sorry I'm late. Had some papers to sign.' Thank God for Listerine, he thought. It was a necessary lie. He had been at a farewell drink for a departing colleague, and anyway, Rachel had Marie-Claire to help her.

Michael and Claire arrived at eight-fifteen. Rachel took Claire upstairs to leave her coat, and Charles took Michael into the drawing-room. 'I know it's not polite to leave your guests for long,' Claire said, 'but let's nip upstairs just for a few minutes. Charles can hold the fort for a while.'

'Oh Claire. You have no idea how thrilled I am to see you.' Claire threw off her coat. 'My, you're thin, Claire. Are you always like this?'

Claire laughed. 'Still the same direct Rachel. You haven't changed.'

'You have. You look like something out of *Vogue*.'

Claire smiled. 'I suppose I do try to look like that. Michael likes me to be as thin as a rake, but it does age one so.'

'We must stay in touch, Claire. I know we've been writing while you've been abroad, but now that I actually have time on my hands we can meet each other for lunch and things like that.'

Claire looked at her friend. 'I really would like that.

You're the only person who knows the real me. To everyone else, I'm the elegant Mrs Swann. The perfect foil for Michael.' Her face grew hard. 'I play the part well.'

Rachel hugged her. 'I've been dying to hug you. It's like having those happy days at Exeter back again. Do you still love Michael as much as you did?'

'Rachel, *still* such direct questions . . .! In a way, I do. I'll tell you about it some other time.' There was hurt in her eyes. 'Let's go downstairs. The other guests should have arrived.'

'Rachel,' said Charles when the two women had come down the stairs, 'I'd like you to meet Sally from the office, and this is Bill.'

Sally was thin and intense. She was in her early forties. 'I've heard so much about you, Rachel. I'm delighted to meet you.' Her grip was unusually strong for a woman.

'I didn't know Charles even thought about me during office hours.'

'Oh yes he does, and the children. You're a model family.' There was a sour note in her voice.

'Do you have any children, Sally?'

'No. I have the newspaper. My articles are my babies. I was married once to a drunken psychopath who beat me for his thrills. I got out, but not before he kicked me so hard in the stomach that he ruptured my uterus. I was in intensive care for two weeks. The damage was so extensive they had to remove most of my insides. So,' she gave a bitter laugh, 'that was the end of motherhood for me.'

'I'm so sorry,' said Rachel. 'You read about these things, but you never really think they happen to people you know.' She was shocked, not only by Sally's story but that she should confide in her at their first meeting.

'The joke was I was taken to the local hospital, and he was one of the senior gynaecological consultants. So he visited me every night bearing flowers and boxes of chocolates. No one ever suspected. Even my surgeon believed that I had been mugged by a stranger.'

'Has he married again?'

'Yes, the bastard. Three times. You can take away a man's licence for ill-treating a dog, but it's okay if you're only the wife.'

They were interrupted by Charles who took Rachel's elbow. 'Rachel, don't let Sally put you off men for life. Meet Bill. He's a sensitive, caring, liberated man, not like me.'

Sally glared at him. 'Charles, you're so boring when you play the Greatest Male Chauvinist of all time.'

'And you're so boring when you do your militant female bit.'

Rachel intervened. 'Actually, Charles, we weren't talking about men in general.'

'Oh yes we were.' Sally looked at Bill. Her face softened.

She really looks quite pretty when she smiles, Rachel thought. She took Bill's hand and said, 'I gather you're one of the night editors.'

'Yes. That's why I've seen Sally around occasionally, but we've never met formally. *Hello*, Sally,' Bill said.

Michael and Claire were busy talking to the Housemans, Sally and Bill were exchanging office gossip, Charles was pouring drinks, and Marie-Claire was taking small trays of canapés around to the guests. Rachel breathed a sigh of relief. It does look like something out of *House and Garden*, she thought. She watched Sally and Bill. For a woman who hates men, she certainly wears a very low-cut dress. Bill was slight with a thick mop of curly yellow hair. He had intense blue eyes, and he gestured a lot with his hands.

Rachel went into the dining-room for a last-minute check. The table looked beautiful. She had a lovely central floral piece which she had created with the autumnal berries and leaves from her garden. The Georgian candelabras stood at both ends of the table. Aunt Emily had given her Aunt Bea's Limoge dinner service for a housewarming present. 'You'll be needing this,' she said with a smile. 'Now you're going to be the lady of the manor.'

I wish Aunt Emily could see it now, Rachel thought. Aunt Emily had become too frail to make the journey to London. I'll take a picture of it laid out like this so she can enjoy it, Rachel promised herself. She lit the candles. I do miss my dining-table. Somehow glass just can't do those plates justice.

'Marie-Claire?' she called.

'Yes, Madame?'

'Could you put the toast in the oven for me?'

'Yes, Madame.' What a nice girl she was. Rachel watched her glide into the kitchen.

'Right. I'll call them all into dinner. It's rather like conducting an orchestra.'

It's very like conducting an orchestra, Rachel repeated to herself as she sat at the end of the table watching her guests tucking into the boeuf bourgignon. The overture of bagels and lox had been well received. She could hear Charles booming away at the other end of the room. Michael was punctuating Charles's bass with his high-pitched tenor. Jane was arguing with Sally, and Bill was making soothing noises in the middle. Glasses clinked, plates rattled. A symphony, Rachel thought. 'Lovely,' she said.

'What did you say?'

'I'm sorry, Jerry. I do have a bad habit of talking to myself. Are you enjoying yourself?'

'It's the best boeuf bourgignon I've had in years, Rachel.'

'It was one of Jane's recipes actually.'

Jerry beamed. 'I should have known. That girl's a marvellous cook.'

He was interrupted by Jane who yelled down the table at Rachel. 'Aw come on, Rache. Help me out. Sally says men are incapable of being faithful. I don't think that's true. What do you say?'

Rachel thought about it. There was an uncomfortable silence as everyone waited for her answer. 'I think there are many couples who trust each other like we do.'

'What about women?' Charles asked, looking at Sally. 'How many women double-cross their husbands?'

'Not that many. The numbers are growing though. On the whole, women tend to get divorced if they're involved with another man.'

Jerry looked at Jane. 'I'd kill myself if Jane had an affair.'

'Isn't that a bit extreme?' Charles said.

'Not for Jerry, it isn't.' Jane laughed raucously. 'Anyway, Jerry, when would I have the time or the energy to have an affair? I suppose I could trap the milkman in between taking Liza for a horseback riding lesson and collecting the other two from the swimming pool.'

There was a gust of laughter. Then Claire said, 'I think all men are totally faithful. That's the real problem.'

'What on earth do you mean?' Jane leaned forward.

'Most men are totally faithful to their mothers, you see. Don't you think so, Michael?'

Charles broke the moment of tension and rescued Michael. 'How *is* your beautiful mother, Michael? I always lusted after her as a boy. My God, she was something. Do you remember all the undergraduates at Exeter on our floor turning out just to look at her? Is she still as stunning?'

Michael laughed. 'She's just the same as ever. In fact, people think she's Claire's older sister. She's taken to the antiques business. She has a shop in Sloane Street. We both do a bit of buying and selling. I really enjoy the shop. It's such a contrast to the Foreign Office.'

Claire made a face. 'I find all that junk in there very boring.'

'Well, you don't have to come, darling.'

'I know, and I won't in the future. Instead, Rachel and I are going to have lascivious luncheons at the Savoy, and meet rich Arabs who will hang diamonds from our nipples and bury emeralds in our pubic hair.'

'Hey, hang on, Claire!' Charles looked at Rachel. He was half laughing and half serious. 'You wouldn't be interested in that kind of thing, would you?'

'Oh Claire, you haven't changed a bit.' Rachel was laughing. 'Well, Charles, I'll go as far as the diamonds the first time.'

Claire grinned at her. 'We'll have fun, Rachel. I intend to be very bad indeed for you.'

'That sounds wonderful.'

The rest of the evening passed off remarkably smoothly. Bill offered to drive Sally home. They both stood at the door saying an effusive farewell. 'It's been the nicest evening I've spent in ages.' Sally gave Rachel a hug. 'He's nice, isn't he?' she whispered into Rachel's ear.

'Um, I think so.'

Jane said, 'Come on, Jerry. You'll have to carry me home. The wine's gone to my knees.' They left loudly, and Jane got into the car with as much grace as she could muster.

Michael and Claire stayed for one last brandy. The four of them sat by the open fire in the drawing-room. 'That was an excellent meal, Rachel.' Michael looked at her. 'You've come a long way from the country mouse that you were when I last saw you.'

Rachel slipped off her shoes and tucked her feet up under her on the sofa. 'I've been bogged down with children for so many years that it was all a matter of survival. But now I am beginning to have time for myself. I don't normally look like this,' she laughed.

'Well done,' Claire smiled. 'Thank God I have lots of servants. I haven't the patience to do all the nitty-gritty – shopping, cooking, laying the table, and then the cleaning up.'

'I wouldn't want to do it too often. Tonight was a fluke, and I knew everyone except Sally and Bill. I must say, Charles, it was nice to see Sally and Bill get on so well. She's had such a rough time.'

'If she thinks Bill is going to be any better than the other men she's shacked up with, she's in for yet another shock,' said Charles. 'At the office we call him "Wee Willie Winkie". You remember that song? "Upstairs and downstairs . . ." '

'Oh no. Poor Sally.'

'Bill loves liberated women. They never say no, and they can't hang on because it's against their religion. He says it's like taking candy from a baby.' Charles and

Michael roared with laugher.

'Stop it, both of you.' Claire got up. 'Rachel, we must go. We're leaving for the country early tomorrow morning. Michael has some business with the estate manager. Let's have lunch in the next week or two. I'll telephone.'

'Lovely. I'll come up and get your coat with you.' Once Rachel was in her bedroom, she looked at Claire. 'Is his mother still around that much?'

'Yes.' Claire nodded. 'I gave up years ago. I can't compete in that relationship. They do everything together except screw. He can't even screw me.' Her face was set and hard. 'I could cope if I came home and found him in bed with other women, but I can't cope with the men.'

'Do you mean he's gay?'

'I would hardly describe his relationships as gay. They're usually sordid little Italian waiters with big bums.'

'I'm sorry, I mean "homosexual".'

'Don't apologize, Rachel, I know what you meant, but Michael isn't homosexual either. He's just hopelessly mother-damaged. She owns his prick and she doesn't mind if he puts it up boys. That way he's not being unfaithful to her. Another woman would be an act of betrayal. She's done her job well.'

'Did you know before you got married?' Rachel took Claire's hand.

'No, but to be honest with you, I'd have married him anyway. Anything was better than my family. Anyway,' she laughed a tight bitter laugh, 'I do enjoy spending her money. I'm not joking about having fun. London *is* fun if you've got lots of money.'

Rachel looked into Claire's eyes. 'Wouldn't you prefer just to be loved?'

'No. I thought about it, but then I realized I'd be bored to death.'

'Claire, you're incorrigible.'

'Don't tell anyone, Rachel. About Michael, I mean. Will you? Not even Charles.'

'No, I won't,' Rachel promised.

'Come on, Claire. Stop gossiping.' Michael was at the bedroom door. 'We've got to go.' He stood alert and suspicious. 'What's all the gossip about anyway?'

'Just catching up,' said Claire pleasantly, picking up her coat.

His face has changed, Rachel thought, smiling at him. He's much more feminine than he used to be. Claire seems to have taken over the male role.

'Come on, Michael. Let's get going. I'll drive. You've had too much to drink as usual.'

'All right.' He followed Claire obediently out of the house.

Rachel was in bed half asleep when Charles went into the bathroom to brush his teeth. 'I think I'll have a bath,' he called.

'Okay. I'm exhausted. I'll be asleep by the time you get into bed.'

'All right. Good-night, darling,' Charles shouted to make his voice heard over the gushing water. Should be able to hear the late news, he thought as he was drying himself in the dressing-room.

He switched on the radio. '. . . A shooting incident occurred in Richmond Hill earlier this evening. The police are holding a woman for questioning. The man who died was Stephen Akerson the well-known industrialist. More news later.'

'Poor sod,' said Charles. 'You never can tell with women.'

The radio news continued. 'Here is a late-night news flash: Rose Johnson has just been formally charged with the murder of Stephen Akerson. She shot him in the back of the head while he was dining with his wife at their home in Richmond Hill. The motive is thought to be revenge.'

Charles stood rooted to the spot. That name rang a bell. Rose? Stephen? Anthea? Of course. Anthea had once mentioned a Rose. Christ, he'd even thought Rose would have been a better bet than Anthea. My God, I hope Anthea wouldn't do a thing like that. He went down to the drawing-room and poured himself a whisky. He sat by the dying embers of the fire. Rachel put on a good show tonight. Didn't think she had it in her. He was beginning to recognize that, for all her slovenly ways, she had a natural aristocratic manner that carried her through almost any occasion. She's never had to struggle for anything – not like Mother, he thought. He remembered Aunt Bea's tweed skirts and her lisle stockings. Somehow she always made Julia in her neat little suits look like a servant. Anthea hasn't got Rachel's class, he mused. I suppose I will have to tell Anthea it's over. Still, I've got nine months before Anthea expects an answer or blows the whistle on me, so I might as well enjoy it. He went up to bed. He didn't sleep well.

Rachel brought up the morning papers. 'Look at this.' She pointed to the front page of the *Daily Mail*. 'It happened right near here, only a few roads away.'

'I know. I heard it on the radio last night.'

Rachel got back into bed. 'Charles, she crept up to the dining-room window and shot her lover in the back of the head. My God, poor woman, she must have been desperate.'

'Poor woman? What do you mean "poor woman"? He's dead, isn't he?'

'Yes, but it says here that he had a string of mistresses. She was kicked aside for the present one. Look at the photograph of the new woman. She's beautiful.' There were two pictures. Charles was looking at the second transfixed. 'No, that's not her,' said Rachel, 'that's her best friend Anthea Walters. She was the last one to speak to her before she went off and did it. She's very pretty too. But it's the other picture.'

Charles buried his face in his pillow. It's too much, he thought. Rachel was rabbiting next to him. 'Don't, darling,' he said. 'I've got an awful headache. Don't talk about such a gruesome subject first thing in the morning.'

'Poor you. I'll get some coffee and aspirin.'

Charles groaned.

Later that day, Sarah came in. 'Mummy, they're filming at the big house two streets away. Can you come with me? I've never seen a film being made.'

'I don't think it's a film, Sarah. There was a murder there last night.'

'Really? How exciting! Come on, Mum, let's go.'

Rachel laughed. 'All right, you horrible little ghoul. I'll get my coat.'

They arrived just as Anthea finished her interview for the ITV news report. '. . . I knew she was upset, but of course I had no idea how upset.'

'That's Anthea Walters, the last friend who saw her before she shot her lover.'

Anthea looked at Rachel. She missed the next question. 'I'm sorry. Can you ask that again?' Anthea smiled at the interviewer.

'I know. I'm sorry. You must be dreadfully upset. Take your time. Was she drinking when she was with you?'

'Just a few glasses of wine. Nothing serious. No, I feel Rose couldn't live without Stephen. He had promised her that he would never leave her, and he broke his promise. Maybe,' she glared into the camera, 'maybe that is what happens to men who break their promises.'

'Thank you very much, Miss Walters. That about wraps it up. Take Miss Walters to the car.' He flagged down a passing research assistant. 'Beth, can you look after Miss Walters?'

Beth walked Anthea to the car. 'Awful business,' Beth said. 'Still, it serves the bastard right. Some of the women at Thames want to start a defence fund. Would you let us use your name?'

Anthea thought for a moment. 'Why not?' She had enjoyed the publicity so far. She walked right past Rachel and Sarah.

'I say, wait 'til Daddy hears. I saw a murderer's best friend – he *will* be impressed.'

He wasn't impressed at all. 'I think it's disgusting of you, Rachel, to take a child to see such a scene. Typical, if I might say so. Normal mothers do not take their small daughters to houses where murders have been committed.'

'We didn't go because there was a murder. We went because Sarah had never seen a film unit in action.'

'I didn't see any blood. Honest. No brains either.'

'Sarah, I'm eating lunch. Please don't discuss it again,' said Charles.

Rachel had just poured Charles a gin when the six o'clock news flashed on to the screen. He winced as Anthea glared at him. '. . . That's what happens to men . . .' He got up and snapped off the television. 'They've done that story to death all day. Anyone would think it's never happened before.' He stomped out of the room.

'Daddy's really upset about it all, isn't he, Mummy?'

'Yes, I suppose he doesn't like to think of that sort of thing happening in his neighbourhood or near his children. It does give you goose-bumps. Have you done your homework, darling?' Rachel nagged.

'Yes, I have. I'm going over to see Suzanne. Jane invited me for tea.'

'All right, darling. Take care on the roads.'

'I will, Mum.' She gave Rachel a big hug. 'You're a super mother. Don't listen to Daddy. He sounds just like Grandma.'

Rachel laughed. 'Don't worry. I'm used to it. Off you go.' I'm so lucky with Sarah, she thought. Maybe I'll get closer to Dom when he's older.

30

'I'm getting a social life of my own together at last.' Rachel was sitting by Richmond Swimming Pool with Jane. 'It's great really, because I'm home when Charles is around, but I go out now when he's away.'

'How does it feel to have friends instead of pills?' Jane's voice was bitter.

'Oh Jane. I do know how difficult it is for you. Your time will come. After all, Liza and Jake are fairly self-sufficient. Why don't you come over for dinner one night, without Jerry?'

Jane looked at her. 'Are you kidding? If I left Jerry at home with the kids, he'd set the house on fire or lose one of the children. He wouldn't say anything, but I know he'd be dreadfully hurt if I even suggested that I spend an evening without him.'

'Don't you find that a little claustrophobic?'

'A little? Jesus, it kills me sometimes. I look at his kind warm face, and I get an irresistible urge to smash it in. I don't though. I take another valium . . . Jake!' she shrieked at the top of her voice, 'Jake, quit fighting Sarah! . . . That feels better. One of the advantages of being a New York Jew is that you don't need a megaphone, and you learn to scream young.'

Rachel lay back on her towel in the sun. 'I'm so looking forward to going to the Camargue. What are you doing this summer?'

'We're off to Italy. I've got every book ever written on the Pope and stuff like that, and we'll join millions of other Americans all doing the same thing. But for me, Europe has always been a goal. My people came from Poland. We even have a kiddush cup from the old country that is hundreds of years old. My grandmother never learned to speak English. You have no idea how just the history of England affects us. America is such a new country, only a couple of hundred years old.'

'I think I take it for granted, I suppose. The house my grandfather owned was Elizabethan, and one of the walls was even from before then. It was supposed to be at least a thousand years old.'

'Wow,' Jane laughed. 'No wonder you have such trouble with your English men. Their traditions are entrenched in all those years of history. At least in America, the pioneer women played a very active role in settling the new territories. That's why we're so aggressive.'

'I honestly don't think you're more aggressive, Jane. I think you're just a lot more truthful than most women I know. Women in England are always taught that the hand that rocks the cradle rules the world. "Lead from behind" was Reverend Mother's advice.'

'It's not that different in America. A good Jewish mother rules the house, but never raises her voice in public. God, it's enough to give you cancer, all that manipulating.'

'Anna is coming round to lunch. She's one of the collecting agents for Rose Johnson's trial. You know, the woman who shot her lover in a house near ours. I'm giving five pounds.'

'I'd have shot him for her if I'd known her.' Jane took out her cheque-book. 'I do hope the more useless end of the movement won't scream and shout and make her a political issue.'

'I expect they will,' said Rachel, 'but there are always sensible women like Anna who has been through a lot in the movement, and is really very interesting to talk to, apart from being my oldest friend. It was Anna who kept me sane with news from the outside world when I was bouncing off the walls with baked beans sticking to my hair.'

'I suppose you're right. I'll give five pounds. Who's defending her, anyway, Rachel?'

'I don't know. As she's confessed, it's a matter for the jury. I just hope they get a lot of sympathetic women. It's the judge you've got to worry about, Jane. Anna says if he belonged to the same club or even if he moved in the same social circle as Stephen Akerson, Rose has had it.'

'I know. We have the same problem in America. Would you shoot Charles if you unearthed a string of women?'

'No. I asked myself that, and I don't think I'd do anything. I couldn't imagine it, anyway.'

'You know, I think I'd be delighted.'

'You're joking, Jane.'

'I'm not. It would at least make Jerry more interesting.' They both laughed.

'Come on. Let's go. Tomorrow is one of my dinner parties.' Rachel began to collect the towels.

'Oh God. I just threw one for Jerry last night.'

'Claire's been marvellous. She lends me her butler and a maid when it's for business people. I have to do two a week. Thank God Claire introduced me to Harrod's delivery vans. Charles was outraged at first, but lately he's let me spend pretty much what I want.'

'I have noticed your new clothes, Rachel.' Jane bit her lip. 'I just can't get into spending on myself. Now, for the children, that's different. I love buying their clothes and Jerry's, but on me I just end up feeling guilty. I've discovered the good old English jumble sale. I get more of a kick out of buying a 40p dress than I do out of anything I get in Regent Street.'

'Actually, most of those dresses were chosen by Claire. She has a marvellous eye for what suits people, and all the time in the world to indulge herself.'

'Lucky her.'

'No, Jane. She's not lucky. I'd rather be me.'

'I don't have a choice.'

'Oh . . . Jane, there's lots of women worse off than you. Anyway, I'll see you in the next few days.'

'I've sent Dominic an invitation for Liza's birthday party. Liza tells me she's been offered pot in school.' Jane looked worried.

'I know. Some of the other mothers have been getting paranoid. It's always the mothers who are popping the most pills who create a stir about their children smoking pot and sniffing glue. Don't add that scare to your list of problems, Jane. Liza's far too stable a child to get hooked.'

'Are you sure?'

'I'm sure.'

'That's a relief. I saw a lot of my friends burn their brains out on acid. I'd hate it to happen to my kids.'

Poor Jane, Rachel thought as she walked back to the car with Sarah. Trapped like that, she's going to have worries. It's all she's got to talk about. I know how she feels. Thank God I've got Claire and time for myself.

Anna marched through the front door. 'I'm pregnant, Rachel. It's just been confirmed.'

'Congratulations!'

Anna swung Rachel round the kitchen. 'I feel marvellous.'

'What did your mother say?'

'I went to stay with her and I told her that I was planning to get pregnant. She was a little upset at first, because she wanted me to get married. That's natural, I suppose. And then,' Anna's rather severe face glowed, 'she came up to my room that night, and she sat on my bed and she asked me if I was a homosexual. I nearly died. I didn't know she even knew the word. I told her about my life in London and my girlfriends, and she listened. Then she put her arms round me and said she loved me and she'd do anything she could to help me. If I want to go home when the baby arrives, I can. Isn't that marvellous?'

'Yes it is. And will you go home, Anna?'

'For a while, anyway. I want to have her in the hospital, and Mother says she'll stay with me for the birth. When all is said and done, you know, apart from you, my mother is my best friend. I know it's not fashionable to get on with your parents, or if you do everybody starts quoting Freud, but we have always had a very loving relationship. She has a huge horsey world of her own, so she's always given me plenty of space, and I'm going to live with a baby. It'll be good for us both to have a grandmother in the house. I'll need her help anyway.'

'You certainly will. All I had was that monster Julia who made life hell for me. Just imagine, Anna with a baby. Here, let's toast the baby.' Rachel raised a glass of white wine. 'Have you any names?'

'I think I'll call her Vanessa.'

'Anna, you can't order the sex. It's not all under your control, you know.'

'I know, but I do hope it's a girl. I don't feel I could cope with a boy.'

'You'll be surprised, Anna. Once you have your baby in your arms, you won't mind which sex it is, as long as it's safe and in one piece.'

Anna sipped her wine. 'I've retired the turkey baster with honours. I didn't really think it would work. But Julian says he will always acknowledge that he was the father of the baby, just so that the child will know who her father was. I think that's important.'

'So do I.' Rachel sighed. 'It was such a wonderful day in my life when I knew I belonged to Aunt Bea. It's funny, it was Aunt Emily who mothered me, and Aunt Bea who did the fathering . . .'

'About the Rose Johnson Fund . . .' Anna began.

'Oh yes. How's that going?'

'Well, the trial comes up next year. She's in prison 'til then, and I expect that time will be sufficient. They may transfer her to a mental hospital for a while, but I don't expect the judge will do much more than agree that a year in prison, and maybe eighteen months under psychiatric supervision, should be enough. After all, she has no other record. She was obsessed by only this one man.'

'I still don't think she should have shot him.' Rachel frowned. 'I don't think anybody should be obsessed by anyone else to where they want to kill them rather than live without them.'

'How do you know about any of these things, Rachel?

You've never even had to feel rage or despair or jealousy. I know how Rose felt. I could have killed some of my lovers many times.'

'You're right, I suppose. I'm lucky really. Anyway, here's five pounds for the fund in appreciation of my life with Charles. I've also got another five pounds from a friend of mine who's not quite so lucky.' She laughed. 'Let's finish the bottle with lunch.'

'Why can't you come, Charles? You're making me sore.' Anthea pushed him off and sat up. She lit a cigarette. 'What's the matter with you? You used to live with a permanent erection. Now you don't even want to experiment.'

Charles stared at the ceiling. 'I don't know. Business pressures, really. I suppose I'm tired.' His voice became petulant. 'I can't keep up with my home life, an office life, and you always pestering for attention. Anyway, ever since you volunteered your services to your maniac friend, your face has been all over the newspapers.'

'I know. Isn't it fun? There's a little nobody like me suddenly becoming a star overnight. We've collected a lot of money.'

'You haven't been propositioned by any other men, have you?' said Charles hopefully.

'No way. It's you I want, Charles. Rose and I shared a single-minded obsessional nature.'

He sighed. 'We can't even go out to dinner or lunch any more in case you're recognized. Rachel contributed five pounds to your fund. She follows you on television. She would, the daft idiot.'

'Why don't you get it over with now?'

'You promised me a year, so I've got until after June. I'll tell her then, but you'll see. I know her better than you do. She won't leave me.'

'Well, it's a gamble I'm prepared to take. Do you want me to suck you off?'

'No thanks, Anthea. I just want to go to sleep.' He rolled over on his side. What a mess now, he thought. She had trapped him. She bored him to death.

Weedkiller, he thought. They say it's undetectable. He fell into a troubled sleep.

She'll go, Anthea thought as she lay beside Charles. She smiled. I must get curtains for those big windows. Blinds don't do them justice.

31

'Do you always lunch at the Savoy?' Rachel asked Claire.

'Yes.' Claire smiled at the waiter. 'No, Rachel. Let him put your napkin on your lap.' Rachel blushed. 'Don't worry. You'll get used to it. I keep a suite here.'

'Good heavens, Claire. That must cost a fortune.'

Claire looked very seriously at Rachel. 'It saves my sanity.'

'Is it that bad?'

'Sometimes.' Claire then laughed. 'Come on, Rachel. Order something. I didn't ask you to lunch to give you the sad story of my life.'

'You don't have to be so defensive, Claire. After all, I am probably the only person you can talk to.'

'That's true. I used to talk to my father when he was sober, but now that he's dead I don't have anyone except you.' She smiled at Rachel. 'The lobster salad is the best in London. Do you want white wine?'

'What are you having?'

'My usual.' Claire looked at the wine list. 'I only have half a dozen oysters for lunch. I can't eat huge meals, and we're usually out to dinner in the evening, or entertaining. After a while, everything begins to taste the same. Oysters seem to be the only things I can eat that always taste purely and simply of the sea. What about a bottle of Pouilly Fuissé?'

'That sounds nice.' Rachel took the wine list from Claire. 'I always let Charles deal with wine.'

'You've let Charles deal with everything for far too long.' Claire looked very serious. 'You know, I feel you've spent the last fifteen years in a time-warp.'

'Oh Claire, that's not true. It's having children. It does that to everyone.'

'Now who's being defensive?' Claire reached out and patted Rachel's hand. 'I'm not being mean, Rachel. I just know that there's lots more to life than a husband and two kids.'

'Would you still say that if Michael wasn't homosexual and you had children of your own?'

'Yes, I would. Anyway, I never wanted children if you remember. Just as well, as things turned out.' She frowned. 'But I've seen too many women throw their lives away over a man only to end up as wrecks with the kids gone and the husband off with some other woman. At least that's never going to be my worry.'

'Do you think Michael would ever leave you?'

'No. Why should he? He has everything he wants in life.'

Claire remembered the first time she'd caught Michael in bed with a man, her hairdresser. She had returned unexpectedly from her mother's house in Dorset. Her mother had totally gone to pieces once her father died. 'For God's sake, Mother, you did nothing but scream and shout at each other when he was alive. What on earth are you doing sobbing and crying all these months later?'

'You'll never understand, Claire. We loved each other.'

'You can't call that terrible relationship "love".'

'What do you know about love?' Cynthia's face grew red. She was clutching her sherry bottle, her only companion. The house was even dirtier than Claire remembered. 'What do you know, you and your faggot husband? Tell me, Claire,' she said as she lurched unsteadily towards her, 'has he ever got it up?'

'You're drunk. You don't know what you're saying. Don't ever speak to me like that again.' Claire's voice was ice cold.

Her mother pushed her face into Claire's. 'What's the matter, high and mighty, haven't you guessed by now?'

Claire drew back her hand and slapped her mother's face. 'Shut up, you drunken old bitch. Don't you say that about Michael. I don't know why I bothered to come and see you. I'm leaving right now.' She was sobbing.

Her mother was clutching her cheek with one hand and swigging from the sherry bottle with the other. 'I don't need you. I didn't invite you here. It was your father you always came to see anyway.' She was muttering to herself. 'Never loved me . . .'

Claire drove herself back to the Savoy. She arrived in the middle of the night. The doorman took her keys. She felt safe once she was inside the door. The night porter lifted his head and smiled at her. 'Good evening, or should say "good morning", Madam.'

'Oh it's so good to be back,' she said to him. She walked across the hall and up some stairs to the lift. The place was deserted except for the night staff who went about their work quietly and efficiently. It was like a huge luxury liner, safely afloat in a world full of turmoil and horror. Michael will be surprised to see me, she thought. She let herself into the suite. Very quietly she went to the bathroom and changed out of her clothes into the white towelling robe provided by the Savoy. Softly she crossed the sitting-room and pushed open the bedroom door. She stood for a moment, waiting for her eyes to get used to the dark. Vaguely she could see what looked like another figure in the bed. Don't be stupid, she scolded herself. It's only the pillows. She felt her way around in the dark. She put her hand out and she touched the body that was sleeping soundly on her side of the bed. 'Michael!' Claire's voice was hysterical. 'You've got another woman in my bed!'

He was up instantly. She ran back to the door and put on the main light. 'Paul!' She was stunned. 'Paul, what are you doing here?' Paul huddled under the blankets.

'I'm so sorry, Claire,' said Michael. 'Really I am. I'm sorry you had to find out this way.' Michael's eyes were like sheets of ice. 'Don't make a scene, Claire.

Leave the room. Paul will get dressed and go. I will come out in a minute and talk to you.'

Claire did as she was told. She walked back into the sitting-room of the suite and sat down on the sofa. What do I feel? she asked herself. Why aren't I more upset than I am? I suppose it does answer a lot of things. Claire had never really understood why Michael had never attempted to make love to her. He assured her in the first few years that it was just a temporary problem and that he was undergoing various tests. Every time they came back to London on leave from the Foreign Office, he went to see his doctor.

Even the psychiatrist had eventually called Claire into his office and said, 'It's really a matter of time, my dear. Michael has been devoted to his mother. You must be patient and not ask for too much.'

'Is it too much to ask for your husband to make love to you at least once?'

The psychiatrist took her hand. 'As I said, it will take time. Find yourself a good lover.'

Claire sat in the sitting-room as Paul hastily let himself out of the door of the suite. Sitting in the armchair, Claire found herself smiling, waiting for Michael to come out of the bedroom. Oh well, no more blow jobs. At least that's a relief.

'Well,' Michael was standing in front of her. 'What do you want to do?'

Claire looked at him. 'Why, Michael? Why?'

He was so taken aback by the gentleness of her voice that his defences crumbled. He knelt at her feet and put his head in her lap. She stroked his thick brown hair. 'I've never been able to make love to any woman. You see, as soon as I get an erection, I see my mother's face. When I was younger, I tried all sorts of women. I even tried taking them from behind. But it was no good.'

'Funnily enough, Michael, I can understand some of that. Remember how I used to beat my father with the riding crop?' Michael looked up at her. 'Apart from you, he's the only man I've ever wanted. That's why I've never had affairs.'

Michael looked at her. 'You don't want to leave me?'

'No.' Claire shook her head. 'Why should I? We get on well enough. It's almost a relief now I know it's not me that turns you off – it's all women. Does your mother know?'

'Yes. I told her after we were married.'

'Did she mind?'

'It was odd, she took it very well.'

Michael could see his mother now, standing by the window of her elegant house in Hampstead. She was gazing out over the Heath. 'I always knew you'd never be unfaithful, Michael,' Gloria had said. The memory made him shiver.

'What's the matter, darling?' Claire asked.

'Nothing. A goose just stepped on my grave. I don't want to lose you, Claire. Maybe a couple of sexual misfits should stick together.'

Claire looked at him. 'I do want separate bedrooms. Even separate suites when we stay here.'

Michael's face relaxed. 'I think that's wise.'

'And,' Claire's voice tightened, 'you're to get rid of Paul. He's a good hairdresser but an awful gossip.'

'All right,' Michael promised.

'Also, I don't expect you to introduce me to your little boys.'

'I won't. We might as well go back to bed and get some sleep.'

'I'll stay here for a while,' Claire said. 'you go back to bed.'

'All right. Call me if you need anything.' Michael strolled across the room to the bedroom. He climbed into bed. Fortunately, he thought, Gloria likes my lovers. I'll have to take them round there in the future. Still, I'm glad it's all over. He felt an odd pang of regret. He realized that, now Claire knew, half the fun had gone out of his life.

'So you see, Rachel, we are both very much the same type of people. We're survivors.'

'What do you do for sex, Claire?'

'I don't.'

'Never?' Rachel looked surprised.

'No. I realize,' Claire hesitated for a moment. 'I realize that I could be like Michael. He picks up deviant little boys with tight bottoms from the sewers of London, screws them, and then throws them out. I could do the same thing. Only I'd probably pick a violent man like my father. I decided long ago that it's a road I'm not going down.'

'It must be awfully lonely.'

'It is, but mind you,' Claire grinned at Rachel, 'the money goes a long way to keep me company.' She poured Rachel another glass of wine. 'Let's go shopping. I hear Zandra Rhodes is back in town. Her fabrics are exquisite.'

Rachel looked at Claire. 'I feel so out of place, even here. My clothes are so anonymous.'

'You'll never be out of place, Rachel. You have a natural style that goes anywhere. You mustn't let Charles dictate to you like he does. Remember, all his values and ideas are imported from Julia. Dreadfully bourgeois.'

Charles, bourgeois? Rachel was amazed at the idea. 'Are you sure, Claire?'

'Sure,' said Claire firmly. 'Come. Let's go upstairs while I change.'

'Do you still have a suite here?'

'Yes. It's one of the stipulations that I made with Michael. I need my own refuge. You can use it if you ever want to get away from Charles. It has two bedrooms.'

'I can't ever see that happening. We don't get that much time together anyway.'

'Spend a weekend here with me. Do you good to get away from the children. Come on, Rachel. Say yes. Charles can take care of the house.'

'What a stupid idea.' Charles was furious. 'What am I supposed to do with the children?'

'Well, look after them, of course. Come on, Charles. You're always away. I never get a break. It's only two days. I'll stock the 'fridge.'

'Oh no you won't. I'm not coming home to cook my

own food. Marie-Claire can't cook. I'll have to call my mother and ask her to help out.' His lip quivered. 'Claire has far too much time and money. She's putting ridiculous ideas into your head. You're not the sort of person who fits in at the Savoy.'

'Oh yes I am. Claire says I have a natural style, and I feel very much at home there now.'

'A natural style . . . more like dowdy.'

'Charles,' Rachel's voice became serious, 'I really don't like you saying things like that about me.'

Charles's eyebrows shot up. 'Since when did you decide that I can't criticize you?'

'Since just now.' Rachel looked very determined. 'I don't need to hear it.'

'Hoity toity,' Charles said, as he went to 'phone Julia. 'Can you come for a weekend to look after me, Mother? . . . When is it, Rachel?'

'The weekend before the holiday,' Rachel shouted from the kitchen.

'Oh please, Mother. I know you don't like coming up, but it is important. Rachel's deserting me and going away for the weekend.'

Rachel made a face. Bourgeois, that's what he is. She immediately felt guilty. 'It's all right, Charles. If you really want me to stay, I won't go.'

Charles put his arms round her. 'I'm sorry I was so awful. It's perfectly all right. I'll manage. If I'm called away, Julia can cope. You go. It'll do you good.' He kissed her on the forehead. 'Let's go to bed and make love.' He patted her affectionately on the bottom. 'You go on ahead. I'll just check the doors are locked.'

Rachel climbed the stairs. I *am* lucky, she thought.

Every cloud has a silver lining, Charles thought as he checked the back door. At least I can promise Anthea two days. That should please her. He was whistling as he went up the stairs.

'Do you know Charles is going to babysit while I stay with Claire at the Savoy?'

'Really?' Jane looked impressed. 'Gawd, Jerry would shoot himself if I did that. Anyway, I couldn't leave the kids. Jake would get an asthma attack.'

'Oh Jane, don't you ever see yourself free from the kids?'

Jane looked at the ceiling. 'I do sometimes think about it. But what would I do? The thought terrifies me. I mostly think about having a wild affair, but my boobs are so awful, I wouldn't dream of getting in bed with anyone else but Jerry. So I just fantasize.'

'Do you?' Rachel was really pleased. 'I thought it was only me.'

'Yup. It makes it all much more interesting. I lie back and dream I'm getting laid by Robert Redford, and I have just finished having an orgiastic climax, and then Jerry scuttles across the room to the bathroom to wash his prick.'

Rachel giggled. 'Do you suppose Jerry and Charles fantasize?

'I'm sure Jerry does. Probably about the Dow Jones Industrial Average.'

'I'll ask Charles.'

Later that evening, Rachel said, 'Charles, do you ever fantasize about other women when you make love to me?'

'Of course not, Rachel. You do say the most awful things.'

'Oh, I just wondered.'

'I'm ringing to see how you are and to say good-bye. I'm having two days with Claire, and then Charles, the kids and I leave for the Camargue.'

'Really?' Anna sounded surprised. 'That's wonderful. It's time you did something other than service the family.'

'Don't nag me, Anna. How are you anyway?'

'I'm fine. Really happy. I felt a flutter today. I suppose it was probably wind, but Rachel, I felt as if I owned the world. I'm quite busy really. It's lovely to be away from London, and I'm showing a few dogs locally.'

'How's it going, sharing with your mother?'

'Fine. We have a lot to talk about. She's breeding

hunters. It's actually very interesting. I didn't realize how complicated it all was. Listen, Rachel, if you can get it together to leave Charles for two days this time, maybe you can visit us some time after the holiday.'

'I'd love to, Anna. I must go down and see Aunt Emily anyway. Charles is being marvellous about looking after the children. Julia will be here for the time I'm away. I suppose I'll just have to put up with her snooping about and checking the linen cupboard.'

Anna laughed. 'I didn't think Charles would look after them on his own.'

'It's not that, Anna. Don't be so mean. We have Marie-Claire, but if he *is* suddenly called away, the children still need an adult.'

'Come on, Rachel. Charles never lifts a finger in the house.'

'Why should he? He works all hours of the day and night to bring in the money.'

'Oh, Rachel, you're hopeless.'

'Well, I *am* going away for two days.'

'That's true,' said Anna. 'It's a beginning.'

32

'Huh,' said Anthea. 'Imagine Rachel spending two days at the Savoy. What a waste.'

'Claire's loaded,' said Charles. 'Anyway, I can't take you anywhere like that. You're too well known.'

'I want to be the well-known Mrs Hunter.' Anthea's voice was petulant. 'Why can't you tell her on holiday?'

'I'll tell her in my own good time.'

'Charles, I'm tired of waiting. I'm afraid your own good time isn't good enough.'

'What do you mean?' Charles asked nervously.

'I've decided that waiting 'til next summer is simply too long. I want you to tell her by the new year. You can make it your New Year's Resolution.'

'But Anthea, you promised you'd give me a full year.'

'I know. But I've changed my mind. A woman's prerogative, darling.'

'But Anthea . . .'

'But Anthea nothing. I'm serious, Charles. Either you make it your resolution or I'll make it mine.'

'You don't give me much choice.' Charles was cornered.

'That's right. Well?'

'Well, all right. I'll tell her after Christmas when we're back from France.'

'Ah, there's a good Charles. Now, *what* are you actually going to tell her?' Anthea looked at him. 'I mean, have you ever begun to think it out?'

Charles looked uneasy. He had avoided thinking about the actual scene. 'Anthea, what's the point of getting all worked up now? She might have a lover by

Christmas, and then everything would be okay.'

'She won't do that and you know it,' Anthea said. 'You're a coward. You're weak. You're banking on the fact that she won't leave you.'

'She certainly won't divorce me.' Charles was smug. 'Just remember, before you go making too many plans – she might agree to an open marriage.'

'Rachel? Agree to that? You must be out of your mind, Charles. Is that what you really want? Your wife to give you permission to screw around?'

Charles shifted uncomfortably in his chair. 'Shut up, Anthea. I don't want to talk about it any more.' He finished his wine and looked around for some more.

'Well I do. I'm going to talk about Rachel all evening.'

'Then I'll go.' Charles stood up.

'Fine. I'll phone the Savoy.'

'You cunt.'

'Takes two.' Anthea pushed back her chair. She advanced slowly towards him. 'You see, I've told you before. I understand you very well.'

Charles glared at her. 'Stop it, Anthea.'

'Mummy's boy,' she laughed. 'I'll bet Mumsey-wumsey's at your house right now, cooking all sorts of wonderful things for little Charlie-warlie.'

'Anthea, I'm warning you.' Charles's fists were clenched. 'For the last time, shut up!'

'Maybe,' Anthea was circling him now, 'maybe she's ironing your silk underpants. Does Charlie fancy his mummy?'

Charles never really remembered what happened next. His rage grew and covered him like an enormous black pall. He could dimly see glasses flying, and he heard the dining-table crash to the floor. He heard Anthea screaming in the distance. He came to his senses with his hands around her neck. 'You disgusting bitch! I hate you!' he heard himself say.

She looked up at him. One eye was beginning to close. There was blood rushing from her nose. She wiped it on the sleeve of her jersey. 'How long have you been waiting to beat up a woman?'

'All my life.' Charles shook his head in astonishment. 'Did I say that?'

'Yes, you did.' Anthea pulled away from him.

'Come here.' Charles pulled her into his arms. He fumbled under her skirt.

'So who's randy now?' Anthea unzipped his fly. 'Come on then, big boy.' He burst into her. She lay with her legs wrapped around his body, waiting for him to finish. Broken glass and plates littered the floor beside her. She smiled to herself. Well, at least that got him going again. Now I know what to do. Next time I'll make sure we're somewhere he can't do too much damage. Damn. Those were my Baccarat glasses. She was just adding up the damage for a bill for Charles when he came. For Charles, it was the most complete orgasm he had ever had in his life. He lay on top of Anthea totally spent.

'Who did that?' Charles sat up in bed the next morning.

'You did, darling.' Anthea's eye was swollen and purple.

'Oh, I didn't. Are you sure?' He flopped back onto the pillow and groaned. 'I must have had too much to drink. Funny, I don't have a hangover.' He sat up again. 'I'm so sorry, Anthea. I feel awful. Does it hurt?'

'A little. You made a dreadful mess of the place. You broke all my plates.'

'I'll pay for them. Honestly. I can't tell you how awful I feel. I'll never do it again. I promise.' Anthea smiled sweetly at him. It hurt to smile. Both her lips were swollen. Charles got out of bed. 'I'll get some coffee.' He went into the dining-room. 'God all-mighty,' Charles muttered. 'What was I doing?' He began to clear it up. Anthea joined him. They carried the broken china to the kitchen. 'Here, I'll get a black bag. It'll be quicker this way. Anthea, as soon as it's all cleared up, I'll go out and get new plates and glasses.'

'All right. I think I'll spend the day in bed.'

'You do that, darling.'

Mooching round Harrod's, Charles thought longingly of the Savoy. I can't believe I'd do that to a woman, he thought. He did remember the climax. I'd better get her a bottle of champagne. I slept like a baby . . . Maybe she'll give me up now. The thought cheered him up. Ah, there's the smoked salmon. 'A quarter of a pound, please.'

'Look at that trolley.' Rachel had never seen a whole side of salmon like that before. 'Claire, it looks delicious.'

'Well, it's the best. It comes from a special place in Scotland.'

'I love smoked salmon.' The waiter was carving paper-thin pieces onto Rachel's plate. 'I can't wait to taste it . . . Mmmm. It's marvellous.' She sank her teeth into the brown bread piled high with the salmon. She shut her eyes in ecstasy. It was indeed the best smoked salmon she had ever had. 'I love that slightly waxy fishy taste it has.'

Claire raised her glass. 'To our weekend.'

'So far it's been wonderful, Claire. Imagine having a little chocolate in a gold box on your pillow every night. It's like a fairy story. I think this was the first morning of my married life that I've actually done nothing other than float around in the bath and get dressed.'

'We talked until at least four o'clock last night.'

'It's a shame Charles was called away. I did hope it would do him good to spend some time with Dominic and Sarah.'

Claire didn't say anything. She resolved to speak to Charles herself. There were plenty of rumours about Charles flying about in certain circles. She remembered Bill's face. Claire had met him first at Rachel's dinner party. They met again at a dinner party in Kentish Town. 'I see you have a new lady?' Claire's eyes were teasing.

'I wear them out,' Bill laughed. 'What about you?'

'I'm not in the meat market.'

'One of those, are you? I must say, I wondered.'

Claire smiled and shrugged her shoulders. 'Dear Bill. It must be wonderful never to have to think above your waist.'

Bill made a face of mock offence, but his face quickly became serious. 'Listen, you'd better tell your friend Rachel that her perfect husband's been screwing around for years, and he's shacked up with a particularly virulent lady at the moment.'

'Really?' Claire looked at him. 'How do you know so much?'

'I've been on that particular flight deck several times myself. She'll get him in the end. Rachel's no match for her.'

Claire wasn't particularly surprised. Charles had always seemed a bit too uxorious. But she was now concerned for Rachel.

'Darling, what would you like to do this afternoon?'

Rachel leaned back in her chair. 'I think I'd like to buy a swimsuit for the Camargue. I can't believe I'm actually going abroad.' She looked out of the dining-room window. The Thames slid smoothly along. 'It's so beautiful here. Look at the water, Claire . . .'

'I always think of this place as a huge ocean liner, keeping me safe from the world.'

Rachel laughed. 'I could get very accustomed to living here.'

Claire drew a deep breath. 'I've got a present for you. Here.' She handed Rachel a key. 'I had a second cut for my suite. Even if I'm out of town, I'd like you to feel able to use it.'

Rachel took the key. 'That's wonderful. Thank you, Claire.'

'But,' said Claire, 'I want it to be "our" place.'

'You mean I can't bring Charles?' Rachel was immediately disappointed.

Claire put her hand on Rachel's arm. 'Darling,' she said, 'think of it as an escape from reality.' She laughed. 'You may never need to use it, but you know it's there.'

'Okay. I can see after what happened with Michael you need to feel secure here.'

Claire smiled. 'Let's get going. We've got tickets for the ballet tonight.'

* * *

Charles arrived at Anthea's flat exhausted. He parked his Bentley and unloaded the shopping. Anthea was lying in bed plotting when she heard the key in the door. She closed her eyes and lay quite still. Charles came over to the bed. He looked down at her bruised face. It was curiously exciting. He put his hand on her shoulder. She jumped. 'Oh Charles! I was asleep.'

He sat down beside her. 'I'm sorry to wake you, darling. I'm exhausted.' He went back into the kitchen. 'Look what I've bought for you.' He had a bottle of Möet Chandon. 'And,' he said triumphantly, 'there.' He showed her the smoked salmon.

'Darling, how lovely. Come here.' She held out her arms.

Later that night, after they had made love, Charles said, 'I would have expected you to throw me out.'

'My dear Charles. Nothing you could do to me would make me throw you out – nothing. It's a "'til death do us part" relationship.'

'Oh.' Charles had a sudden flash of Stephen with most of his head missing. 'You're joking, aren't you?'

'Try me.'

'No, no. I believe you,' said Charles hastily. He took some time getting to sleep.

'I bought a bikini, Jane.' Sarah and Suzanne were playing electronic battleships in the playroom. Jane's kitchen was as spotless as ever. 'I don't know how you do it. Even with Marie-Claire around, I can't keep anything clean for long. She's in love at the moment.'

Jane was pouring coffee. 'Who with?'

'Charles, of course. I gather from other women it's a perfectly natural puppy love. Charles is thrilled.'

'I hope he doesn't get too thrilled.'

'Jane, you've got a dirty mind.'

'And you've got a very bedable French girl.'

'She'll find a boy somewhere round here. It's just a stage. Here, I brought the bikini to show you. Do you like it?'

'Like it? I could eat it. It's marvellous.'

'Claire took me to this shop in Bond Street.' Dangling

the suit from her fingers, Rachel said, 'That snip of material costs as much as a dress.'

'I'll say.' Jane frowned. 'I've got stretch marks like train tracks all over my stomach. I can't ever wear a bikini.'

'I just hope I don't look too thin. I'll look a bit better when I'm brown.' She finished her coffee. 'I'll see you when we get back.' She was walking to the door when she noticed Jane's shoulders were shaking. 'Jane,' she came back and put her arm around her, 'what's the matter?'

'It's nothing.' Jane sniffed. 'I guess it's just I'm due for a period. Don't worry, Rachel. I get blue like this. I'll snap out of it.'

'I do know how you feel, Jane. Maybe when I get back we could go out to lunch together.'

Jane smiled through her tears. 'That would be lovely.'

Rachel drove home. The memory of Jane's lined and desperate face stayed with her for a long time.

33

'I wish I looked like Marie-Claire.' Rachel was lying on her stomach on the beach at Les Saintes Maries de la Mér, looking at the grey-blue sea washing the sand away from Sarah's sandcastle. They had been in their villa for nearly a week now. For Rachel, it was pure enchantment. If she wasn't lolling in the sea or sunbathing on the beach, she would take the hired car and drive out to the marshes. The famous white horses of the Camargue moved in groups of five or six mares with foals and a stallion. Rachel thought she was in heaven.

'I feel a different person now, you know, Charles.'

'Well I don't.' Charles was staring out of the villa window at the sea.

'I suppose you're much more used to travelling abroad than I am, but it's all so beautiful. Come on,' she took his hand, 'let's go for a drive by ourselves and see if you can find a flock of flamingoes.'

'No, I don't think so. I've seen too many bloody flamingoes.'

'Are you bored, Charles?'

'No, of course not. It'll pass. I'm just finding it difficult to do nothing all day when I'm used to London. Let's get drunk and go to bed.'

'Charles, it's only eleven o'clock in the morning. I don't want to go back to bed.'

'Why not? After all, it's a holiday.'

Rachel looked at him. 'Exactly, and I want a holiday too.'

'What do you mean by that?' Charles's tone was nasty.

'It means I don't want to feel I have to spend it screwing with you to keep you occupied.'

'I knew it – it's that bitch Claire. You would never normally speak to me like that.'

'I will from now on. This is only the beginning of our second week here, and you've done nothing but sulk. If you don't feel that you can have a good time, you're not going to ruin my holiday. Marie-Claire's having a wonderful time with Sarah and Dominic. I just don't see why you can't enjoy yourself.'

'Enjoy myself? With a frigid wife who can't even bear to make love because it's eleven in the morning? You haven't changed, Rachel. You're still the same little convent girl. God, I wish I was home.'

Rachel shrugged her shoulders. 'Why don't you make the best of it. It's only one more week.'

'Okay, come to bed, then.'

'No, Charles. I won't. I'm going down to the beach to join the children.'

'All right. Go then.' Charles threw himself into a chair.

'Good-bye,' Rachel waved to him and walked off to the beach. She was wearing her bikini and she carried a red towel over her arm. The holiday had relaxed her. She was lithe and brown. She moved gracefully down the path.

Sod the ungrateful woman, Charles thought. He could feel the tension of his erection in his swimming trunks. It would only have taken her a few minutes. Anthea seemed infinitely attractive at such a distance.

He stood up and went over to the 'phone. 'Darling, it's me.' Anthea sounded as though she had been asleep. 'I'm missing you.' Charles's voice was strained.

'What's the matter, Charles?' Anthea was amused. 'Not getting your leg over enough?'

'I wish you were here.'

'Well, it was your decision to leave me in London and take your uptight little wifey.'

'Are you thinking of me?' Charles felt abandoned in the middle of a little white-washed concrete villa on the edge of nowhere.

'All the time. Guess what I'm doing.' Her voice took on a liquid sensuous tone. 'Imagine where my fingers are?'

'Oh don't, Anthea. I can't bear it.' A shadow fell on the floor by his feet. He looked up. It was Marie-Claire. She gazed coolly at him. He knew she could see that he was aroused. She smiled a dimpled smile, showing perfect white teeth. 'Excuse me a moment,' he said into the 'phone. 'What do you want, Marie-Claire?'

Marie-Claire grinned. Her little pink tongue flickered at him 'A towel, Monsieur. Just a towel.' She strolled past him humming to herself.

'I must go now. I have to join the family on the beach,' he said to Anthea.

'You lying old sod,' Anthea said. 'You're just off to see if you can lay the au pair.'

'I wouldn't do a thing like that,' Charles said primly. 'She's far too young.'

'Charles, you know perfectly well that you'd screw anything as long as it had a hole somewhere.'

Marie-Claire came back into the room. She carried two towels. 'One for Monsieur,' she said demurely, and walked out of the villa.

'Must go, Anthea. I miss you.' But Anthea had slammed down the 'phone. Ungrateful bitch . . . Women. He wrapped the thick towel firmly around his waist. Must go and join Rachel. He suddenly felt a lot better about life.

Rachel was lying in her usual place on the beach reading a book. Charles flopped himself down beside her. 'I'm sorry, darling. I didn't mean to be so beastly. I was just in a foul mood.' He kissed her cheek. 'Forgive me?'

'Yes, but I do mean what I said.'

'That's all right. I do understand. It does all become a bit of a routine.'

'It's not just that, Charles. I just feel recently that you never touch me unless you're randy.'

'But that's perfectly normal for a man.'

'Are you sure? Does it mean that men only feel affectionate if they have an erection?'

'The two things do tend to go together.' Charles was laughing.

'Well, I'd like to feel that just occasionally you could hold me in your arms and love me with your heart without a barometer between your legs taking over.'

'Where do you get all this crap from, Rachel? Is this the sort of thing you talk about with your girlfriends?'

'Sometimes.'

'I hope you don't discuss me?' Charles sounded very shocked.

'No I don't actually. Not much, anyway.'

Dominic came up. 'Come, on Dad. Let's play catch in the water.'

Charles was soon having an amazingly good time grappling with Marie-Claire who was kicking and struggling. Rachel looked at them all shouting in the water. I am a beast, she thought. Just because Charles is more highly sexed than I am, I don't have the right to say 'No' really. I'll have to make it up to him. He is trying.

They all trooped up the beach towards her.

'I tell you what – let's all go out for lunch,' Charles said magnanimously.

Later that afternoon, Rachel lay across the bed while Charles earnestly laboured away. I did really want to see the flamingoes, she thought. Maybe if I borrowed Robert Redford from Jane. She closed her eyes. 'Mmmm . . .' she moaned.

'Does it feel good, darling?' Charles muttered into her ear.

'Don't stop,' she said.

By the end of the second week, the whole family were beautifully relaxed and tanned. Rachel was besotted by all the magnificent French vegetables and cheeses available in the local shops. She found she was happy to cook large meals out on a barbeque with huge garlicky salads, fruit, and cheese. 'If only we could always live like this,' she said on one of the last nights. 'I just can't bear the thought of London.'

'I can't wait to get back,' said Dominic. Dominic was

sitting next to a pretty little French girl he had picked up in the town. She clung to his side like a limpet. She didn't speak a word of English.

'Really, Dom? You seem to be having a good enough time. We don't see much of you. What on earth do you two talk about?' Rachel asked.

Dominic exchanged glances with his father. 'Let's just say I'm taking French lessons.' Sarah fell about laughing. Marie-Claire was busy translating. The French girl gave Rachel a contemptuous look.

Later, Rachel was lying on a deckchair next to Charles on the little terrace of the villa. She had been looking at the gorgeous panorama in the skies. 'Charles,' she said, 'they're not sleeping together or anything, do you think? After all, she is only fourteen and Dominic isn't sixteen yet.'

'I don't think it's our business, darling. He's old enough to know what he's doing.' Charles patted her hand. 'Anyway, I've given him a packet of French letters, just in case.' Chip off the old block, he thought. Lucky sod. All I get is a few peeks at Marie-Claire's tits.

Soon they were all squeezed into their air charter seats. 'It's been wonderful, Charles.'

He turned his head and smiled at Rachel. 'I enjoyed the whole thing, Rachel.'

'We've all had a wonderful time. We must go again. Maybe we could go to Spain next time.'

Charles's stomach lurched. He saw Anthea's face. 'Of course we will.'

'Next August then. Let's go for a whole month.' She began to plan out loud.

Oh God, Charles thought as the plane took off, why can't things stay as they are?'

34

The autumn of that year was cooler than usual. The leaves shed from the huge trees in the back garden by mid-November. Anna was by now very pregnant. She telephoned often to talk to Rachel. 'I can feel her kicking, Rachel. It's marvellous, and I feel so much calmer – at peace with myself.'

'I'm glad, Anna. But you know, the baby will probably be a boy.'

'You say that every time. Actually I've been giving it a lot of thought lately, and I don't really mind that much anymore. Somehow, once the baby began to move, I felt as though she or he was really part of me. Do you know what I mean?'

'Yes, I do. It's such a wonderful feeling.' Rachel added half-seriously, 'Do shut up, Anna. You're making me broody.'

They gossiped for a while, and then Anna said, 'I must go. I've got several dogs to groom.'

Rachel put the 'phone down. It rang immediately. 'Claire? What's the matter? You sound tense.'

'Michael's mother has cancer.'

'No – when did you hear that?'

'This morning. Michael's already left for the country.'

'Is it really serious?'

'I'm afraid so. One breast has to go, and they think they should do a hysterectomy, because at her age it's safer to remove the whole lot rather than leave a risk of secondaries.'

'So when does she go into hospital? I must say, Claire, I've never liked the woman, but it does seem awful. She must have had some symptoms.'

'She did, but the silly old cow is so vain she wouldn't agree to any treatment. She was told by her own specialist this morning that she either goes into the hospital and gives herself a chance, or he says she'll be dead in six months. Michael is beside himself.'

'I'll bet he is. You know, Aunt Emily is not at all well. I'm going down this weekend to see her. I know she will die some time, but she's all I have left. I'm dreading it.'

'Funnily enough, Rachel, I always thought I'd be better off when Gloria kicks the bucket, but I've got an awful feeling that Gloria could be even more powerful dead than alive.'

'What a horrific thought.'

'Listen, we'll have lunch next week when you're back. Give my love to the children. Are they okay?'

'Yes, they're fine. Take care of yourself, Claire. See you next week.'

Aunt Emily was propped up in bed when Rachel drove up to the front door. 'Do I look all right?' Aunt Emily looked anxiously at the maid.

'Yes, Ma'am. You look a treat, and you have colour in your face.'

Emily strained to hear Rachel open the front door. 'Oh good. Do you hear, Mary? She's brought Sarah.' She could hear Sarah laughing. 'She's so like her mother.' Within a few moments, the three were laughing and hugging each other. 'You do look well.' Aunt Emily peered at Rachel. 'It must have been your holiday.'

'I'm still brown, even if it has done nothing but rain since we've been back. Yes, we're well. Charles and Dominic send their love to you. Dominic is playing rugger tomorrow, so he couldn't come down.'

'Dominic always stays with Daddy anyway.'

Aunt Emily smiled at Sarah. 'It's only natural for a boy his age.'

Sarah sniffed. 'He's a pig. That's what Dominic is.'

'Stop it, Sarah. You two do nothing but squabble. Anyway, Aunt Emily, how are you?'

'I'm not getting any younger, if that's what you mean, dear. I'm afraid I can't get out of bed for supper, but Cook will bring it up for us. Sarah, why don't you run along to the blue guestroom and make yourself at home. Cook is longing to see you.' Sarah stood up. 'My goodness, you're going to be as tall as your mother.'

Sarah smiled at the old lady. 'I know, it's a nuisance. I'm taller than all the boys, and I've got mum's big feet.'

'Go on, Sarah. Aunt Emily wants to talk business.'

'Okay, okay. I'm going. I'll go and see if Cook needs any help with supper.'

After Sarah had closed the door, there was a silence in the room. It was nearly dusk and Aunt Emily had a small bedside light near her pillows. The brass lamp cast a pool of light around her head. Rachel looked intently into her aunt's face. She noticed how much thinner she had become since her last visit. On her lap was a bed-tray with a large magnifying glass and a book. 'You can still read then, Aunt Emily? I know you were worried last time that your eyes were getting too weak.'

'I read a little, dear, but mostly I have a young girl from the local grammar school come in two or three times a week to read to me. I keep in touch with the news, you know. I listen to the wireless. It's just my legs. I had a slight fall a few days ago and the doctor said to stay in bed for a while.' She looked at Rachel. 'I'm afraid Cook and Mary have to bathe me now. I can no longer manage by myself. I did think of getting a private nurse, but they both said they preferred to look after me themselves.'

'I wish I was near, Aunt Emily.'

'Don't, dear. I'm all right. Really. And when you get to my age, death really is a merciful release.'

'Don't talk like that. Please, Aunt Emily.' Rachel hugged her aunt gently.

'Rachel, you have Charles, and the children, and many good friends. I can't bear to be confined to bed. I know Aunt Bea is waiting for me. I see her all the time now. But I just need to tell you that all the documents for you are in the safe downstairs in the library. You have been well provided for by Bea. I have lived on the interest of the capital, but when I die the house and the money are yours. I have left pensions for Cook and Mary. Other than that, it is all yours.' Aunt Emily lay back exhausted.

'I can't imagine my life without you, Aunt Emily. It was bad enough when Aunt Bea died, but somehow it's your arms I always remember.'

'It is such a joy for me to see Sarah. It's like seeing you as a teenager all over again.' Aunt Emily suddenly smiled. 'Do you remember breakfasts with Bea?'

'Oh I do. They're one of my happiest memories.'

'Go along now and get changed. You must need a wash after such a long journey. I'll have a little nap, and then we'll have dinner.'

'Sounds lovely.' Rachel kissed her aunt on the cheek. 'I love my old bedroom. It still feels like home to me.'

'It is, darling. It's always been there for you.'

'And so have you. That's what's been so marvellous.'

After supper, Aunt Emily obviously needed to sleep. Rachel went down to the kitchen to talk to Cook. 'She's awfully weak now, isn't she?'

Cook, who had been there for many, many years, was a big motherly woman in her late sixties. 'Yes, dear. Your aunt, bless her heart, had a nasty fall.'

'What does the doctor say?'

'What can he say? He says to keep her in bed and keep her quiet.'

'Cook?' Rachel was standing by the old Aga. 'My aunt doesn't really want to live any more, does she?'

'No, my luv. I hear her at night when she can't sleep. She sees your Aunt Bea, you know. She talks to her all the time. She's ready to go, luv.'

Rachel's eyes filled with tears. 'Oh Cook, I do love her.'

'Well, if you take my advice, you'll let her be.'

'You mean tell the doctor to let her die?'

'Rachel,' Cook looked at her very seriously, 'I've worked in hospitals. Do you really want the doctors to put your aunt on life-support machines?'

'No. I see what you mean. It would be awful for her.'

'Your aunt is a very proud woman. She finds it difficult enough now to let Mary and me wash her and help her use the commode.'

'I know. She's very grateful to you.'

'We love her, Rachel.'

'I know you do, Cook.' Rachel flung herself onto Cook's comfortable bosom. 'Oh why does it have to be so awful?'

'Mummy, are you all right?' Sarah came into the kitchen.

'Yes.' Rachel sniffed and dried her eyes. 'I'm just getting used to the idea that Aunt Emily will probably die soon.'

Sarah looked at her mother. 'She's all the family you've got left, isn't she?' Rachel nodded. 'You've got me,' Sarah said.

'I know. Thank God for that.'

That'll be Charles, Rachel thought as the 'phone in the library disturbed the quiet of the house.

'How are you, old girl?' Charles's voice was inappropriately loud.

'I'm afraid Aunt Emily isn't very well, Charles. She could go any day now.'

'Good God. First Michael's mother, now your Aunt Emily. They say it comes in threes . . . You're not upset, are you, Rachel? She's got to go some time, you know.'

'I know that. But I will miss her.' She began to sob.

Sarah came up behind her and put her arms round her. 'Here, give me the 'phone, Mummy.' She took the 'phone out of Rachel's hand. 'Mummy's a bit upset, Dad. Why don't you come down tomorrow?'

Charles cleared his throat. 'Well, ahh . . . I can't actually. You see, I've been asked to cover a government seminar on "Nuclear Reactors in the 'Eighties". So I've got to be at the Dorchester all weekend. I'll telephone twice a day though. Look after her for me, Sarah. There's a good girl.'

'You're never there when we need you.'

'It's not my fault, Sarah. Blame my boss and the government. I'm only doing my job. She isn't going to die this weekend is she?'

'No, I don't think so,' said Sarah, 'but we may not see her again.'

'Must go now, Sarah. Take care of yourself.'

Charles put the 'phone down. He picked up his Gucci suitcase, which was on the floor by the 'fridge in the kitchen. He opened the 'fridge and took out two bottles of chilled white wine.

'Since when was your secretary's name Anthea?' Dominic was lounging against a kitchen door.

Charles looked at him. 'What are you doing tonight, Dominic?'

'Exactly what you're doing, dear Father. Tina Jameson's coming over. While the cat's away . . .' Father and son smiled at each other.

'Good-night, Dominic.'

'Good-night, Father.'

Randy little sod, Charles thought as he left the house. He remembered Alison spread on the floor of the Jamesons bedroom. He revved the Bentley impatiently.

Michael was pacing the floor of his mother's bedroom in Axminster. 'Darling, I'm not going to stop nagging,' he said.

Gloria was lying back against her huge satin pillows. Her long thick hair was lying in strands down her white shoulders. Even in her sixties, she was still a beautiful woman. Her huge blue eyes followed Michael as he strode up and down the room. They had been arguing ever since Michael had arrived before dinner. Now, tired and a little befuddled with wine, she had allowed him to put her to bed. As he helped her into her cream satin nightdress, he couldn't help but notice a slight thickening on her left breast. 'Is that it?' he asked.

She flushed. 'Yes. It feels awful. I feel like I'm already dead,' She began to cry.

Michael gently lifted her small frame into the large double bed and gave her two strong sleeping pills. 'You don't have to die, Mother. The specialist says if you will just have the two operations and some radiation, there is a good chance you will recover.'

Gloria looked at him. 'Can you imagine me with a breast gone? Have you seen those programmes on television when they radiate people? All my hair would fall out. I'd be a freak. You wouldn't like me like that.'

'Mother, I'd love you anyway. You know that. I don't care if you have both breasts off. It doesn't make any difference to me.' He sat on the bed beside her.

'No. I've been thinking about those operations for days. I've only really ever loved your father and you. Nothing else matters much to me. If I die, I don't want you to see me mutilated and hairless. I prefer it this way. I can have a good private nurse who understands pain control, and I can take my time and die gracefully. I never did like the idea of old age anyway. I can't imagine losing my teeth and getting glasses. No,' she sighed, 'I always wanted to be like Tinkerbell.' She smiled suddenly, her old magical child smile. 'I say, Michael, do you remember how you used to be Peter Pan and I'd be Tinkerbell? And you'd have to clap your hands to save me from dying?' Michael nodded. 'Clap your hands for me, darling. Please, Michael. Clap your hands.' She was drifting off into a drug-induced sleep. 'Let me hear you clap.'

Michael obediently clapped his hands. Tears were pouring down his face. 'I can't, Mother. I can't save you.' He stretched out beside her sleeping form, and sobbed.

Rachel and Charles were at Jane's house for drinks on Boxing Day when Dominic rang for Rachel. 'Mother, I'm afraid Aunt Emily died in her sleep a few minutes ago. I told Cook you'd ring back.'

Rachel was almost relieved. 'God bless you, Aunt Emily,' she whispered. She telephoned Cook. 'Cook? I hear Aunt Emily is dead.'

Cook's voice shook. 'Yes, dear. Mary took her morning tea to her a few minutes ago, and she'd passed away. She looks very peaceful. I'm sorry, dear, to ruin your holiday.'

'Don't worry, Cook. I'll come down right away and help with the arrangements. Can you call the doctor?'

'Yes, dear.'

'Tell Mary to make up the bedrooms. I expect Sarah

will come with me now, and Charles and Dominic will be there for the funeral.' She put the 'phone down and went to find Charles.

'. . . Don't think there's much in it these days. The left-wing in England will always be a failure, because they don't understand their own politics. Man's essential nature is capitalist . . .' Charles was addressing an attentive audience.

Rachel touched his arm. 'Charles, can I talk to you?'

'Later, Rachel. Later.'

'No. Now.' She pulled him away from his admirers. 'It's Aunt Emily. She's dead.'

'Oh. I say, you're not going to cry, are you, Rachel? Hang on a minute.' He hurried off to find Jane. 'Jane, Rachel's Aunt Emily has just died. I think she's in a state. Can you do something?'

'She's your wife, Charles.'

'I know, but I'm not much good on these occasions. I hate scenes.'

'I don't think Rachel would ever make a scene. It's not her style.' Charles was wringing his hands. 'Don't be such a big baby.' Jane practically frogmarched him towards the kitchen. 'You stay there and I'll get Rachel.' Rachel was standing by the fireplace. Jane put her hand on Rachel's shoulder.

'Did Charles tell you?'

'Yes. I'm sorry, Rachel.'

'Don't be, Jane. Quite honestly, I did all my crying last time I was with her. She wanted to die. She never really recovered from Aunt Bea's death. It's me I'm sorry for really, I suppose. Where's Charles? He usually disappears if it looks as if there's going to be any sort of emotional scene.'

'I've locked him in the kitchen. Typical. The only scenes a man *can* stand are his own.' Jane laughed. 'Then it's not called a scene; he's "getting in touch with his emotions" or whatever.' Jane pushed open the kitchen door. 'There she is. Charles. Now for God's sake, look after her.'

'I'm sorry about Aunt Emily, Rachel.'

Rachel went across to him. 'It's all right, Charles.

Honestly, I'm okay. I accepted her death when I was last there. We said our good-byes then. Of course I'll miss her, but she's much better off with Aunt Bea.'

'You really do believe in all that stuff, don't you?'

'Yes I do, Charles. And thank goodness. I'm driving down now.'

'Sure you'll be all right?'

'Yes. I'll take Sarah with me.' Rachel paused. 'I think I'd better arrange the funeral for the thirty-first. Is that all right with you?'

Charles nodded. He'd have to tell her at her aunt's house. The next day was New Year's Day. There was no getting out of it. Anthea was adamant.

Once they were back home, he helped her pack her clothes. He kissed her tenderly. 'Drive carefully, darling, and I'll ring you this evening.' As he stood on the pavement waving to her, he thought, It may all work out for the best, you know. I'm all she's got left in the world.

Dominic was waiting in the hall when Charles went back into the house. 'Off to see Anthea again?' he said.

Charles frowned. 'No. You and I are both leaving for Devon tomorrow.'

Dominic made a face. 'I hate funerals. I didn't know her very well anyway. What are you going to do about Anthea? She rings here all the time. One of these days, Mother's going to find out.'

'Well actually, Dominic, I'm going to tell her while we're down there.'

'I wouldn't . . . you don't really know Mother like I do. She's absolutely straight.' Charles shifted uncomfortably. 'Really, Dad, she'll never forgive you. Anthea's not the first by a long chalk, is she?'

'How do you know?'

'I know about Alison. Tina Jameson told me about when you were at one of their orgies.'

'Oh.' Charles walked into the study.

Dominic followed him. 'She'll throw you out, you know.'

'Don't say that, Dominic.'

'You're a fool, Dad. You should have told her ages ago.'

'I know. I just didn't want to hurt her. I do love her, you know.'

Dominic looked at his father. His eyes were very hard. 'You should have thought about that before you went chasing other women. What's Julia going to say?'

'I don't know.' Charles put his head in his hands. 'I really don't know.'

Dominic went over to the drinks tray. 'Do you want a whisky?'

'Yes. Thanks, Dom.'

He handed one to his father and poured one for himself. 'I'll never marry – it's a game for fools. Here's to us: bachelors forever.' Charles tried to smile. 'I'll come down with you, Dad. Maybe the old biddy will have left me some money.'

Charles looked at Dominic. 'Of course, Rachel will be rich now.'

'Not like you to forget a thing like that, Dad. You're getting old.'

Charles later went to sleep trying to imagine how much Rachel would be worth. The house must sell for at least two hundred thou . . . They would have to move, maybe to Surrey. A fresh start, that's what they needed.

35

Aunt Emily was buried next to Aunt Bea. Rachel looked at the coffin as it lay in the ground. Through her tears she felt their presence. The two women were united at last for all eternity. Sarah, nearly as tall as Rachel, stood at her side. The Axminster Cemetery was crowded with villagers. Dominic and his father stood a little way away. They were outsiders, their suits too sharp, and their Yves St Laurent overcoats contrasting with the tweeds and the gaberdines of the country folk. The vicar shook Rachel's hand. 'You know,' he said, 'this was the first Christmas your aunt wasn't down here with a Christmas tree and lights for your Aunt Bea. I used to worry about her in the cold out here. She never missed a Christmas. Will you be selling the house?'

'I don't know. It depends. I would like to keep it as a place in the country. I know Charles would never agree to retire here, but maybe I could keep it at least until the children are gone. Sarah loves it here.'

The vicar smiled. 'I hope you can stay. We are losing all the old families whose roots are in the community, and the new people . . . well, they have no reason to involve themselves. They're here to hunt and fish. God bless you, my child. Come and see me any time.'

'Thank you, Vicar.' She watched him with great affection. He had buried both her aunts, and now he was one of the last links to her life with them.

'Come on, Rachel.' Charles was at her elbow. 'We've got an awful lot to do.'

'Mother,' Dominic looked excited, 'can I have Great Grandfather's old guns? He had a matching pair of

Purdeys, you know, Dad . . . Amazing. The Jamesons shoot. What do you think, Mother?'

Rachel had been looking out of the window of the Volvo. 'I don't know, darling. I haven't really thought about anything like that yet.'

'Leave your mother alone, Dominic.' Charles frowned at him. 'This is no time to harass her.'

Oh hoooh, Dominic thought as he leaned back in his seat. So he *is* going to tell her. It's not like the old man to be so solicitous.

'Thank you, Charles.' She put her hand on his knee.

He took his hand off the wheel and covered her hand with his. 'How do you feel, Rachel?'

She looked up at him. 'Very empty . . . Aunt Emily was always there for me. They both were, but Aunt Emily was always like an open log fire, glowing in the dark in a house in Devon. Whenever I was troubled, I could always sit by that fire in my mind, and stretch out my hands to the flames. Now the fire is extinguished.' She shivered. 'I feel the cold.'

'I've been thinking, you know, Rachel. How about we sell up in London. Sell this house and compromise. We could get a place in Surrey with some land. Then we could have the best of both worlds. You could have your beloved countryside, and I could be within reasonable distance of London?'

Rachel smiled. 'Would you really move out of London for me, Charles?'

He squeezed her hand. 'I'd do anything for you, darling. Anything.'

Cook had prepared a cold supper for the family. Rachel had broken with tradition by not inviting guests back. 'I know they'll understand. I just couldn't go through with it.'

'They will, dear,' Cook assured her.

'Just before you go, Cook, do rest assured that both you and Mary are well remembered in Aunt Emily's will. I would like you to stay here until I make a decision about the house or you decide you want to find another job.'

Cook smiled at her. 'I'm too old for another job, dear. No. Mary and I have decided to retire together at Charmouth. Your aunt said she'd give us enough money for a cottage and there's the old age pension for both of us. We couldn't work for anyone else, not after your Aunt Emily. She was a saint, that woman.' Cook's eyes filled with tears. 'I'm off now with Mary. I'll see you in the morning.'

'What on earth are you going to do with all that stuff? There are cupboards of it.' They had finished dinner, and Charles was poking round the drawers in the Regency side-tables. There were sets of silver knives and forks, cupboards full of silver salvers, candelabra, and other serving objects. 'Look at this,' he exclaimed. He opened a corner cupboard. Rank upon rank of sparkling Irish Waterford crystal wine glasses and tumblers threw diamonds of colour into the air. 'I didn't realize they had so much stuff.' He shook his head. 'It must all be worth a fortune.'

'That's not what you used to say, Charles. You used to think it was all a load of boring rubbish.'

Charles had the grace to look embarrassed. 'Well, it's not actually my style, but I do recognize its value.'

'I love it all.' Sarah was holding a mason's octagonal jug. 'I love this, Mum. Can I have it. Look at the head of the snake.'

Rachel laughed. 'I used to be frightened of that jug as a child. Of course you can have it, darling. Let's leave everything 'til tomorrow. We have several days to sort things out and to make decisions.'

Later that night, Charles and Rachel were lying in bed together. She had her head on his chest. 'I always feel so close to you when we've just made love, darling,' Charles said as he stroked her hair.

She looked at him. 'You're all I've got left now.'

He hugged her. 'I'll look after you, Rachel. Don't worry. Everything will be all right.' Rachel fell asleep in his arms.

Charles held her until the dawn was breaking. He was unable to sleep. He put her down gently on her side, and went for a walk around the house. We can make it together, he thought as he moved from room to room. The house and all the stuff in it is worth a fortune. We could buy a huge house, and even a swimming pool. I could have a flat in London and commute. Rachel won't be all that upset, he reasoned with himself. She'll take a few days to get over it, and then she'll see sense. After all, she's got the children to think of. She can't leave them. He opened cupboards and drawers. God knows where they got all this stuff from. There were sets of dinner services, coffee services, tea services, all lovingly cherished. I suppose that's all they did all day, he thought, remembering the traditional day-to-day running of the house. Suddenly he realized he would miss it. As much as Julia would sniff at the mere mention of Rachel's aunts, he had come over the years to admire the sheer quality of their lifestyle. Indeed, slowly he was gaining an eye for a good piece of furniture or china. Funny old lady, he thought, I'll miss her clucking around the house.

'Breakfast.' Charles came through the bedroom door carrying a large tray with a flower in a small holder.

Rachel opened her eyes and smiled at him. 'Oh, that's marvellous. You shouldn't have, darling. Cook would have done that for you.'

'No,' Charles put the tray on the bed, 'I wanted to surprise you. Anyway, I was up early.'

Rachel lifted the lid of the marmalade pot. 'Lovely, Charles – it's that nice chunky marmalade that Aunt Emily made.'

'I found it in the pantry. She's left you a lifetime of strawberry jam.'

Rachel laughed. 'Isn't it wonderful how that generation of women put all their creative abilities into their homes.'

'They did have money, which helped. It wasn't like that for my mother.'

'Oh I know, Charles. I didn't mean to sound complacent. Julia had a hard time.' She put her arms around Charles who was sitting beside her. The tray was on the end of the bed. 'Do you want to buy Julia a better house?

We'll have the money now.'

'I don't think she'd move, Rachel. She has everything she wants there. She's a creature of habit . . . Rachel? I've got something I want to say to you.'

'What?' Rachel wasn't really listening. She was sitting up in bed with her arms round her knee and her chin resting on her clasped hands. 'Isn't this cosy? Aunt Emily would love to be here with us.'

'Rachel, I have to tell you something.' The urgency in Charles's voice broke through her reverie.

'What is it, Charles?'

He drew a deep breath. 'I've been having an affair.'

Rachel shook her head. 'Oh come on, Charles. That's not funny.'

'I'm not joking.' He got off the bed, came around to her side of the bed, and sat directly in front of her. He pulled her to his chest, and he said, 'I didn't really want to hurt you. Honestly, Rachel. I didn't have any alternative. I wanted to be the one to tell you.'

Rachel's mind went blank for a moment. She just stared at him. 'Rachel.' He shook her. 'Rachel? Are you all right?' She had gone a deathly white colour. Then the tears came. She cried, silently looking at him without blinking. 'I didn't think you'd be this upset.' Charles was confused. 'I didn't ever love anybody but you, Rachel. Honestly. They were all bits of fluff. I never cared for any of them.' Huge tears were running down her face. 'Rachel, say something!' He was getting frantic.

Rachel couldn't say anything. The pain was so intense that she could only rock backwards and forwards. Occasionally she would let out a little mewing sound. Charles was in panic. Why couldn't she behave like other women and scream and throw things at him? He knew how to cope with that. He looked at her. She was like an animal that had been kicked in the stomach. Her long arms were wrapped around her body. She was somewhere in a part of herself that he could never reach. She was back in her grandmother's arms. An abandoned baby. She rocked and cried, holding the pain to her.

'Ma ma,' she whispered. 'Ma ma.'

She's gone crazy, Charles thought. What the hell am I supposed to do? He ran downstairs to the kitchen. 'Cook! Rachel's terribly upset. I think we should call the doctor.'

'No wonder, the poor lamb.' Cook puffed upstairs to Rachel's bedroom. She stood in the doorway. 'Oh dear,' she said. Rachel was still rocking and moaning to herself. Cook bustled over and took the end of her white pinafore and wiped the mucous off Rachel's face. She looked into Rachel's blank eyes. 'Oh dear. Yes, I'll call the doctor right away.'

The doctor was at the house within a quarter of an hour. It was New Year's Day, and the traffic was light. He went straight up to Rachel's room. 'I'll see her by myself, if you don't mind,' he said to Charles. Never did like that man. She should have married one of her own kind, he thought as he stomped across the room. 'Come, Rachel. You know me. It's a sad business losing your aunt . . .' He bent over her. 'Dear, dear,' he muttered out loud. 'You are in a state. I think a sound sleep will help you over this.' He pulled up the sleeve of her night-dress and found a vein. He opened his bag and took out a syringe and an ampoule.

Rachel didn't even know he was there. She was in such a torment of pain. It was so physical a sensation that the whole world had ceased to exist. The drug took effect almost immediately. The doctor stayed with her until her hands fell away from her knees and he was able to ease her into a sleeping position. He drew the covers up under her chin and gently wiped away the tears from her face with his handkerchief. Poor child, he thought. She's taken it badly.

'Anything happened to bring this on?' he asked Charles who was pacing up and down the corridor.

'No, not that I can think of. She did say she felt very alone. Aunt Emily was the last of her relations.'

'She's in a state of delayed shock. We will have to keep an eye on her. I've given her an injection that should keep her out most of the day. If she's still like this by evening, I'll give her another one. Sometimes it's best in these situations to let the body rest so that the grief can be dealt with later. I'll be back at six o'clock this evening.'

'That's very good of you, sir.'

'It's the least I can do for Rachel. I've known the family for a long time. I'll see myself out.' The doctor strode to the front door.

Charles flushed. Bloody country GPs. Think they're gods.

Dominic was standing at the bottom of the stairs. 'So you've told her, huh?'

'Don't *you* start, Dominic. I can understand she's upset, but really it's not the end of the world.'

'It is for her.' Dominic's level gaze held Charles. 'You see, she trusted you, the silly cow. What are you going to say to Sarah?'

'I haven't time to think about that. I just want Rachel to get over it all, and we can start again. We're planning to sell up and buy a house out of London.' He looked appealingly at his son. 'We could all begin again.'

'Don't be stupid, Dad. I don't want to live in some awful suburb. You would only be around for the first few months, and then you'd be off chasing women again. Mother would never be able to trust you again, so she'd go slightly potty waiting for your next lying 'phone call. Face it, Dad. You've blown it. You've blown all our lives.' Dominic's voice was bitter.

'It's not all my fault, Dominic,' Charles looked at his son. 'You won't understand these things until you're older, but your mother had a very odd background. She didn't really ever understand the outside world. She grew up here with two old aunts. What did she ever know about life? Lots of men have affairs and then tell their wives. They go on as usual. It's not such a huge tragedy. After all, I'm staying with her. It's not as if I'm going off and leaving her.'

'Come off it, Dad. She's going to leave you and you know it.'

Charles shook his head. 'She can't leave me. She won't manage without me.'

* * *

The doctor came back at six in the evening. Rachel was awake. She wouldn't speak to anyone, not even Sarah. She stared at the ceiling. She wasn't crying any more. She wasn't even thinking. She was suspended between a wall of pain and a strange peace. The doctor took her pulse. 'I don't know what's going on inside you, Rachel, but a good night's sleep and I'll bet on the old Cavendish spirit returning by tomorrow. Good-night. Sleep well.' The injection took Rachel off into a very far place.

'Dominic?' Sarah was sitting on the edge of his bed. 'What is the matter with Mum? It's not just Aunt Emily dying. Something has happened to her. She knew Aunt Emily was going to die. She looks as if she's had some awful news. I've seen that look on soldiers on television. Like when they're suffering from shell shock. Please tell me, Dominic.'

'Oh, I suppose you'd better know. Dad'll never tell you. Dad told Mother this morning that he's had affairs all their married life.'

Sarah flinched. 'Are you sure, Dominic? Oh poor Mum. Why did he do that?'

Dominic shrugged. 'His latest piece of skirt threatened to tell her, so he had to first. I warned him she'd go bananas, but he knew best. Oh come on, Sarah. Don't you start.'

Sarah's head was bent, and there were tears dripping down her nose on to his counterpane, 'I don't want a father who isn't faithful to his family. It's sordid.'

Dominic looked at her. He felt a stab of compassion for his sister. She always was an innocent child. He put his arms around her. 'It's not that unusual, Sarah. Most men aren't faithful to their wives these days. It's just not fashionable.'

Sarah was sobbing. 'But he's my father. He's not most men.'

Dominic kissed the top of her head. 'Don't worry, Sarah. They'll work something out. Come on. I'll take you back to bed.' Dominic tucked her in and kissed her forehead. 'Sleep well, sis,' he said.

He was walking down the corridor when he saw the light on in the study. He hesitated. Then he thought, There's no point in talking to him. Dad's not going to believe anything 'til it actually happens. What a mess. What an idiot mother is. He felt an unfamiliar tightness in his chest. She shouldn't have to cope with Dad. He needs a woman like Grandmother to keep him in line. He wished fiercely that Julia could be there. She'd cope with it all.

He fell asleep dreaming of his grandmother.

36

Rachel blinked. The sun was shining on the bedroom wall. She stretched out her hand to feel for Charles, and then the pain hit her. He was not there. She lay looking around the room, but now her mind had come out of cold storage, and she knew that the only way she could bear the ache was to get up and keep moving. She got out of bed and got dressed.

Charles came into the room just as she was putting her clothes into her suitcase. 'Rachel,' he said in alarm, 'you're not leaving.' She looked at him and wondered why she had invested him with so many noble qualities. He had drunk himself to sleep in the library. His face was crumpled with self-pity. 'What about me?' he said.

'What about you, Charles? You have a perfectly good mistress. You can always go to her.'

'She doesn't mean anything to me, Rachel. You must believe me.'

'I do, Charles. None of us mean anything to you. That's the problem. How long were you faithful to our marriage, Charles?'

'Does it matter?'

'I want to know.' Rachel stood by the bed cold with anger.

'I suppose about a year.'

'I see. I've decided to go away for a couple of weeks. For the moment I have every intention of leaving you. But I realize that it's too important a decision to make at this moment. So I will spend time on my own and then I will contact you.'

'Where will you go?'

'That's not your business anymore, Charles.' The rage she felt eased the pain. 'You've lied to me all our married lives. What I do now is no concern of yours.'

'But I still love you, Rachel?' He stood looking bewildered. 'I still want to stay married to you. What about the children? Surely you're not going to leave them for two weeks?'

'Why not? They're old enough. Marie-Claire will be there. I'll talk to them on the 'phone every day. Do they know what's happened?'

'Dominic does. He guessed a while ago.'

Rachel's face wrinkled in disgust. 'So my son knew before I did? How about Sarah?'

'I don't know. I haven't spoken to her, Rachel.' Charles tried one more time. 'Please, for the good times we've had, let's try again.' He moved towards her.

She knew if she let him touch her she would be lost, a prey to her own needs for love and affection. She pushed him away. 'It's too late, Charles. You should have thought about all this years ago.'

He stood with his hands helplessly dangling at his sides. 'But, Rachel, you don't understand. It was only sex. It's you I love.'

'I do understand.' Rachel paused at the door. 'It's not the sex I mind. It's the lying. You'll never understand. Never.' She slammed the door hard.

Sarah heard the door bang and came running up to her mother. She saw the suitcase. 'Oh Mummy, don't go. Don't leave me.'

Rachel put her arms around her daughter. 'I'm not leaving you, Sarah.' She hugged her. 'Do you know what happened?' She walked Sarah along the corridor to Aunt Emily's room. They sat on Emily's bed.

Sarah threw herself into Rachel's arms. 'I do. Dom told me last night. I hate him. He's a shit. He's a dirty old man. He's not my father.'

Rachel held her while she sobbed. 'Sarah,' she said, 'I've got to get away by myself, but I'll ring you every night to say good-night. I've got to have time to think. I can't decide when I'm being pushed by your father or by you. I have to think about whether it's good for you, your father, or for me to go on being married.'

'If you decide to divorce, can I stay with you?'

Rachel hugged her. 'Of course,' she said. 'Where's Dominic?'

'He's out in the garden shooting at birds.'

'I wish he wouldn't.' Rachel went to find him.

Dominic was standing over a blackbird. The bird's throat had been torn out by the bullet wound. The eyes were beginning to glaze over. The glossy wings fanned out on the winter lawn. Dominic looked up at his mother. 'I got that bird on the first shot.' His eyes shone.

'Dominic,' Rachel said, 'I'm going away for a couple of weeks. I need time to think.'

Dominic raised his eyebrows. 'You're such a child, Mother. There's nothing to think about. You stay married to Dad, and he'll never change. If you leave him, he won't marry Anthea.'

'Anthea?' Rachel's voice rose. 'Anthea who?'

'Anthea Walters. You know, the one that raised the money for the defence fund of that loony lady.'

'You mean Rose Johnson that shot the man down the road?'

'Yes, her. Anyway, Mother, he won't marry her. I know him much better than you do. He'll move his mother in. Then he can be free again.'

Rachel frowned. 'I suppose you're right.' She looked at her son. 'Dominic, why didn't you tell me?'

He shrugged. 'It's no big deal these days, Mother. Most of the parents I know sleep around. Anyway, I reckoned it was between the two of you.'

'I suppose so. You're right. We shouldn't make it your problem. I'm sorry I asked. Well, I'll telephone every night. Look after Sarah.'

'I will.' Dominic was taller than his mother. He patted her cheek awkwardly. 'Take care of yourself, won't you?'

'I will.' Rachel got into her car. She waved to Dominic as she turned the corner of the drive.

Now that the anger subsided, the pain came back. She stopped at the first petrol station on the M5. While the car was being filled, she went to the bathroom and took two librium. The doctor had given her a small supply. 'Thank God,' she said as she swallowed them. She got into the car and put her foot down. I wonder when I'll feel feelings again? she thought. So far it was mostly rage followed by severe bouts of this awful pain. That's what cancer must feel like, she thought. Most of the journey passed by in a blur.

She came to outside the Savoy. The friendly doorman took her keys. 'Good evening, Madam,' he said. 'It's nice to see you again.'

She looked at him. His by now familiar face was like a beacon in the vast loneliness she was beginning to experience. 'Thank you,' she said. Her suitcases were taken inside. She walked to the desk. 'Is Claire Swann in her suite?'

While the reception desk telephoned the suite, Rachel took a deep breath and looked around. Nothing had changed. The ebb and flow of guests and staff continued to move about under the chandeliers. A piano was tinkling from the cocktail bar. 'No, Madam. Mrs Swann isn't there.'

'Never mind. I will telephone her when I go up.' Rachel took the lift to the suite. She pushed open the door and put on the lights. She walked over to the huge windows which looked out onto the Thames. She was lost in contemplation when her suitcases arrived. She tipped the porter and then relaxed as she heard him shut the door behind him.

The sitting room was full of fresh flowers. She walked over to the fireplace and sat down in one of the armchairs. There was an air of calm in the elegance of the quiet room. Outside she could hear the roar of the rush-hour traffic. She was tired from the drive, and blurred around the edges from the tranquillizers. I'll drink enough to go to sleep, she thought. She went into the bedroom and put on the light. There was the familiar little gold box of chocolate on her pillowslip. They must change them every day, she thought. She went to the 'fridge. She looked through the bottles. Gin, she thought. Lots of it.

After the third miniature had been emptied and drunk, she began to relax her hold on herself. Fortunately, the walls were thick. No one could hear her sobbing. When she finished the gin, she switched to brandy. Finally she staggered from the chair by the 'fridge to the bed. She fell across the bed fully dressed into a deep dreamless sleep.

It was late morning before Rachel woke up. She hardly dared move. She was aware of a thundering roar in her head. She rolled over on to her back and covered her eyes. The lights in the room were still blazing. For a moment she had no idea where she was. Her mouth felt dry and sour. Suddenly she knew she was going to be sick. She struggled to her feet and made her way to the bathroom. Hanging over the white porcelain lavatory, she caught a glimpse of the huge old-fashioned bath with its massive shower rose. She remembered that she was in the Savoy. Thank God for that, she thought between dry heaves. Slowly the nausea subsided and she was able to stand up. She looked at herself in the bathroom mirror. Her face was gaunt and white. I'll have a hot bath and then some coffee, and I'll ring Claire.

She filled the huge bathtub full of hot water. Here I am, she thought, floating about in a scented bathtub, and my marriage has gone bust. For the first time in just over forty-eight hours she felt slightly human. She finished her bath, washed her hair, and ordered coffee and toast.

'Madame, how nice to see you again.' François, the floor waiter, pushed the breakfast table into the sitting-room.

'I only ordered toast and coffee, François.'

'I know, Madame.' He looked very sternly at her. 'Madame is too thin. A good breakfast is necessary for her to begin the day. Madame Swann always say I must look after Madame Hunter.'

Rachel was suddenly curious. 'When did she say that?'

'When she tell me she give you the key. "François,"

she says, "one day Madame Hunter will come by herself. I need you to look after her." "Of course, Madame," I say, "it is an honour." So you see, breakfast is for you.' François pottered about the room, fussing over the details of the table. He sat Rachel down and put the napkin over her lap.

'Thank you, François,' she said. 'You're very kind.' He let himself out. She rose hurriedly to avoid the smell of bacon and eggs, and went into the bedroom with a cup of coffee to 'phone Claire.

'Rachel? How lovely. Where are you?'

'In your suite, Claire. I hope you don't mind.'

'Don't be silly, Rachel. That's why I gave you a key. When did you get there?'

'Claire, did you know? I mean did you guess that Charles was having affairs?'

Claire sighed. 'Oh Rachel . . . so it *was* true. I'd heard rumours, Rachel, but nothing solid. I hoped it would just blow over.'

Suddenly, holding the 'phone, the reality of what had happened between Rachel and Charles hit Rachel with full force. She gasped.

'Rachel?' Claire said. 'Rachel, don't leave the hotel. I'm coming over.'

'What about Michael?' Rachel was breathing carefully. It's like the last stages of labour, she thought. If I can regulate my breathing, maybe it won't hurt so much.

'He's with his mother. I'll be with you in an hour. Promise you won't leave.'

'I haven't got anywhere else to go.' Rachel was crying again. She put down the 'phone.

Rachel was still sobbing an hour later when Claire opened the door. She clung to Claire as if she were drowning. 'Why us?' she kept saying. 'We were such a happy family. What did I do wrong?'

Claire took Rachel by the shoulders and shook her. 'Rachel.' Rachel's attention was caught by the anger in her voice. 'Rachel, you didn't do anything particularly wrong. Charles is the sort of man who's incapable of being faithful to any woman. That's not your fault. Your problem is that you never suspected him.'

'Did you?'

Claire bit her lip. 'I suspect all men, Rachel.'

'I don't want to believe it has to be like that,' Rachel wailed.

'Come on. Pull yourself together.' Claire pushed the hair out of Rachel's face. 'Let's think this out.'

Claire heard François clearing the breakfast table in the sitting-room. She slipped out of the bedroom to see him. 'Madame Hunter est très malheureuse. Son mari a pris une autre femme.'

'Quel bête.' François shook his head.

'François, si je ne sois pas ici, vous la regardez pour moi, s'il vous plait. Si vous êtes inquiet, telephonez-moi immediatement.'

'Oui, Madame. Bien sûr.' François tutted away to himself while he cleared the plates. A good Catholic father of five children, he was horrified by what was happening these days. In his early days at the Savoy, when he was a lad of twenty-five, some thirty-five years ago, there were wives who came to the hotel, and then there were women of ill-repute who were not allowed to set foot in the Savoy. Maybe a mistress or two got by, but now . . . He shook his head. It was better not to think about it. Mind you, he had heard about Monsieur Swann's habits when Madame had a suite up the corridor. What a shame. Such a nice woman. Nothing escaped the notice of the staff at the Savoy. Nothing at all. 'I shall see that Madame Hunter has grapes this evening on her dressing table.' He made a mental note to ask Gérard in the River Room to make sure Madame Swann's table was available for dinner.

'Can I stay for a couple of weeks, Claire?'

'Of course, darling. Stay as long as you like. I have to be at home most evenings to entertain for Michael, but I'm free at weekends. He goes to his mother's, so I can stay with you then.'

'I'll be all right. I just feel like an animal that needs a cave where I can lick my wounds. I can't accept that he lied all these years. It makes everything feel so sordid. I feel such a fool.' She burst into tears again.

Claire held her tight. 'Rachel, it's particularly awful for you because you've never had to suffer much before. It does pass, honestly. Look at me.' She put her face close to Rachel's. 'I promise you, if you can get through the first few weeks, you'll be all right.'

But Rachel wasn't all right. That night, after Claire had left, she walked the floor of the suite driven by such agony that only physical exertion would relieve it. During the day, when Claire had been with her, she had seemed like a soul in torment. After three days, Claire called Jane. Briefly she outlined what had happened. 'The bastard,' Jane said. 'I thought something was wrong. He's got his frigging mother in there, and Sarah looks awful . . . Sure, I'll be in tomorrow. You have the day off.'

'I'm really worried,' Claire said. 'She's getting worse instead of better.'

That night Rachel slipped out of the hotel and walked for miles along the Embankment. She was oblivious to the curious stares of passers-by. She walked unseeingly, her shoulders hunched in her old tweed coat. When she woke up in her bed the next morning, only the blisters on her feet reminded her that she had been out of the hotel.

Jane arrived after she had dropped the children off at school. 'How's Sarah?' Rachel asked after they had hugged each other.

'She's fine. She misses you.'

'I miss her. I talk to them every day on the 'phone. Could you have Sarah to stay if she gets too miserable? She doesn't get on with Julia.'

'Of course. She and Suzanne are such good friends.'

'What am I going to do, Jane?'

'Order me some coffee first.'

Once settled with a pot of coffee on the table in the sitting-room, Jane leaned back in her chair and looked around the room. 'Well,' she said, 'if you have to suffer, this is no bad place to do it in.' Rachel managed a smile. 'That's better. If it was Jerry and he'd been screwing around, I think I'd kill him and then settle down as a widow. No, seriously, Rachel, it all depends on whether you feel you can live with a man you'll never trust again.'

'I know.' Rachel's eyes filled up. 'I know I can't. That's what's so awful. I couldn't bear to let him touch me.'

'Plenty of women do put up with it, you know.' Jane stared at her. 'Getting out means beginning your life again. Both of us have been married since we were very young, and it won't be easy to suddenly find yourself starting all over again.'

'I know, but I don't think I have any choice. If he can lie like that for so many years . . . Anyway, even if he stopped, the damage has been done.'

Jane shook her head. 'Look, sweetheart. When you get down to it, if you get out now, you could begin again. Thirty-six isn't too old. If you go back on a promise and it doesn't work out, you'll find yourself at fifty all washed up. You'll have to make that decision yourself.'

'I know.'

'I got the day off.' Jane looked at Rachel. 'Let's go to a movie.'

Rachel obediently sat through the film. She didn't hear a word of it. She laughed when Jane laughed, but most of the time she was struggling with the pain and with an inner turmoil that was threatening to overwhelm her. When it was time for Jane to say good-bye, Rachel was quite glad to see her go. At least Claire knew betrayal from her own experience with Michael, so she could understand the pain. From Jane she felt an underlying wish that it had been she who was breaking free.

37

Rachel was walking by the houseboats moored by Battersea Bridge when she suddenly pitched forward into a dead faint. Several minutes later, a police patrol car saw her body lying on the pavement. 'Early morning drunk,' said the driver to his partner. 'Let's pull in.' The policemen crouched over her body and shone a torch in her face. Rachel was out cold. 'Call an ambulance. She's not drunk. Could be drugs.'

'We'll take her to Chelsea Women's Hospital,' said the ambulance-driver. 'Any ID?'

'Nothing really,' said the policeman. 'Good coat, but no handbag. Nothing in her pockets.'

'Okay. Put out a missing persons, will you?' The ambulance-driver drove off.

'God knows what gets these women,' the patrolman said to his partner. 'She looked respectable enough.'

'Some boyfriend let her down and she's scared to tell her old man.' The car continued to cruise the silent grey streets.

It wasn't until François decided to check on Rachel at about eleven o'clock the next morning that he discovered she was not there. The little gold box from the night before lay on her pillow undisturbed. He telephoned immediately. 'Madame Swann? I must tell you. Madame Hunter has been out all night. She has not used her bed.'

'Oh dear. Thank you, François. I'll check immediately. Do telephone if she comes in.' Claire 'phoned Jane.

'No, I left her last night at about six. She seemed

okay. We went to a film. She laughed a couple of times. She seemed better.'

Charles was immediately concerned. 'No, I have no idea where she is. She told me she was going away for a fortnight, so I assumed she was with you or with Anna. I hope she's all right. Shall I contact the police?'

'After what you've done, I think it's better if I dealt with it.' Claire's voice was cold.

'Oh, yes. Well, if you think so. But do let me know. After all, I am her husband.'

'You're such a fool, Charles.' Claire put the 'phone down.

'Next of kin?' The young policeman looked up at Claire.

'I suppose it'll have to be her husband.'

The policeman nodded. 'Yes, by law we must contact him.'

'Do you have to tell him where she is?'

'It's like that, is it? Is she battered?'

Claire looked at him. 'No, not that you'd see any bruises, but it's a very middle-class business. He destroyed her soul.'

The young police constable looked puzzled. 'We don't deal with that sort of thing, Ma'am. If she's not in danger from him, then we will tell him where she is. However, if she really doesn't want him to know, I can tell him that she is safe but does not wish to disclose her whereabouts.'

'Thank you.' Claire smiled at him.

Rachel was in no fit state to make a decision about anything. She was still unconscious when the police finally tracked her down to the Chelsea Women's Hospital. Claire arrived a few minutes after Charles did. 'Sorry about that,' the young policeman said to Claire on the 'phone. 'Had to tell Mr Hunter. She looked seriously ill and she's still unconscious.'

'Never mind. Thank you for trying. I'll get there straight away.'

Charles, who hated hospitals, had collected Dr

Burns. 'Don't know what's the matter with her. She went off for two weeks and was found unconscious on the pavement.' Charles looked at the doctor, who was gazing impassively out of the front window of Charles's car.

'Had any marital problems, Charles?' Dr Burns didn't shift his gaze.

Charles cleared his throat. 'No. Not a problem, really. I decided to come clean with her, but nothing that we can't sort out together.'

'Oh, I see. I wondered if that was it. Women tend to be a little emotional about these things. They take it all so personally. I find a few weeks in the Sanctuary in Twickenham usually sorts them out.'

'Really? It's funny, you know, Dr Burns. You're probably right.' He brightened up. 'She's been running about with very unsuitable friends recently. Especially this friend of hers, Claire. Gives her all sorts of rotten ideas. Be much better for her to be in the hands of a professional staff.' They arrived at the hospital.

Dr Burns followed Charles into a small room. Rachel was lying in a white hospital gown with her eyes closed and her hands resting on the counterpane. Charles bent over and kissed her on the forehead. She didn't stir. 'Doctor will be with you in a moment,' the nurse smiled at Charles. 'Don't worry, she'll be all right. Are you the husband?'

Charles nodded. Dr Burns lifted Rachel's eyelids. Charles looked away. A young houseman came into the room. 'Good-morning, gentlemen.'

Charles introduced himself, '. . . and Dr Burns is our family doctor.'

'Ah, good.' The young houseman looked down on Rachel's notes. 'It's all rather odd. There's nothing wrong with her physically. She's pretty fit actually. Her feet are very swollen and blistered, and she's much too thin. I think it's a problem for a psychiatrist, not for us.'

Dr Burns nodded. 'Yes. I agree. She's been a patient of mine for many years. She's had her ups and downs. It's a difficult time for a woman. Children growing up, leaving the nest. Doesn't really know what to do with her time.' He slapped the young doctor on the back. 'A few weeks in the Sanctuary usually puts them back on their feet.'

The young doctor shook his head. 'God, we've got so many like that. We just ship them off. I never see them again.' He looked down at Rachel and shook his head again. 'She seems to be in some sort of catatonic trance.' He sighed. 'Tell her to go easy on the jogging – her feet are in an awful mess.'

'I will.' Charles was already on his way out of the door with Dr Burns. 'Hello, Claire.'

'How is she?'

Charles looked concerned. 'She's not at all well actually. We're moving her to the Sanctuary in Twickenham.'

'For God's sake, Charles, you don't have to do that. The Sanctuary's a mental hospital. Rachel's not mad, she's just upset.'

Dr Burns interrupted. He put his hand on Claire's arm. 'I'm her doctor, my dear, and I feel that Rachel needs a little time to rest. The Sanctuary is very good for women in her condition.'

'Women in her condition?' Claire was almost beside herself. 'Did Charles tell you what he's just done to her? After sixteen years of marriage he tells her he's been screwing like a rabbit. No wonder she's upset. You can't put her in a mental hospital, Charles. It's just too cruel. Let me take her back to the Savoy. They have an excellent doctor on call.' She turned to Dr Burns. 'I'll hire any staff you think fit. Anyone. I can afford it. Please, Dr Burns, don't let her wake up in a mental hospital.'

'There, there.' Dr Burns patted her arm soothingly. 'I've known Rachel for a good many years. I think I know what's best for her. I send many of my patients to that particular hospital. It is excellent.' He turned away. 'Come along, Charles. We have some admission forms to sign.'

Claire went into Rachel's room. She looked down at her unconscious figure. 'Poor Rachel.' She took her hand. 'I love you, you funny old thing.' She began to cry. 'Bloody fool.' She took a handkerchief out of her bag and wiped her eyes. 'I never cry', and she burst into tears again.

'Who on earth was that aggressive woman?' Dr Burns asked Charles as they went to collect the forms to certify Rachel as officially insane and incapable of making her own decisions.

'That's Claire Swann. She's one of those bad influences I've been telling you about. I'm sorry she was so rude. Her husband is a good fellow but he does have his problems with her.'

'Hardly surprising, with an Amazon of a wife like that.' Dr Burns shook his head. 'Ah well, I'm afraid we'll have to get her into the Sanctuary this way, Charles. With influences like that, there's no telling what she might do when she wakes up. I'm afraid you'll just have to make decisions for her, for a while at least.'

'I'd be happy to actually. All this running off is a lot of nonsense. Once we talk some sense into her, she can come home. I'll get some leave from the office so that I can really give Rachel some of my time. We can go away on a holiday, just the two of us. It *has* been hard on her, you know, Dr Burns. I have been away rather a lot. It's been hard on us both really. But then,' he sighed, 'I've had to earn the money to give her the house and the cars and the au pair.'

'Don't reproach yourself, Charles.' Dr Burns put his arm around Charles's shoulder. 'It's a stage many women go through. It's sort of pre-menopausal. She's facing forty soon, you know. It's a sort of watershed in a woman's life. They have to face the fact that they're middle-aged. Life's going to slow down for them. Take my wife, for instance. She had a massive breakdown. I nursed her through it myself.'

'Did you? My God, that was noble of you.'

Dr Burns smiled at him. 'Come on, Charles. Let's get going. I can't stand here chatting all day.'

38

'Rachel . . . Rachel . . .' Someone was leaning over her, calling her name. She kept her eyes closed. She had been in a far place. Now she could hear this muffled voice. It was insistent. 'Rachel, can you hear me?' She remembered the pain. She was afraid it would come back and spring at her like a tiger. She couldn't stand to be so mauled again. 'Rachel . . .'

'Go away,' she murmured. 'Go away.'

The voice wouldn't go away. 'It's all right, Rachel. You can come back . . . You're safe now.'

She opened her eyes. 'Where am I?' She was looking up at a kindly middle-aged man who was leaning over her.

'That's better, my dear.' He sat down in the chair beside her bed. He took her hand and said, 'Don't panic. You're all right. Lie quietly and I'll tell you what happened. You were found unconscious on the pavement near the river. An ambulance took you to hospital, and then your husband, Charles . . .'

The tiger sprang at her. She felt his cruel mouth rip out her heart. She became unconscious again.

'Tell Mr Hunter I'd like to see him after visiting hours,' Dr Pringle said to the nurse. 'Watch Mrs Hunter carefully. It's vital she's not upset at this stage.' He rubbed his tired eyes with his hands. I'll have to haul that woman out of whatever bottomless well she has chosen for her refuge. Otherwise, they'll tie a label round her neck and call it 'Schizophrenia', he thought as he went down the corridor for a coffee break.

* * *

'I think you've been slightly less than honest with me, Mr Hunter.' Dr Pringle's voice was sharp. Charles hung his head. 'So far, all you've told me is that her Aunt Emily died and that she had been depressed.'

'That's quite true.' Charles was indignant. 'She was like a mother to Rachel.'

'Mr Hunter, I don't have much time. What did *you* do to her? She was conscious for a short while this morning, but when I mentioned your name, she lapsed back into unconsciousness. Whatever it was, it's almost too painful for her to bear.'

'Well, I did tell her I'd been having affairs.'

'Mr Hunter . . .' Dr Pringle's voice was ominous.

Charles flushed. 'But I told her that they meant nothing to me and that I loved her. I only wanted to put things right between us.'

Dr Pringle shook his head. 'Do you realize what you did? How soon after her aunt died did you decide to unburden yourself?'

'Well actually,' Charles looked down at the floor, 'it was . . . um . . . it was the day after the funeral.' The doctor's disapproval hung heavily in the air. Charles broke the silence. 'It wasn't my fault. I did it to protect Rachel. You see, this woman Anthea was threatening to tell her. I wanted to tell her myself.'

'I see. Well, Mr Hunter, just for the time being, I suggest that you cease visiting until I can talk to Rachel and see how she feels about it.'

'Fine . . . I'll wait to hear from you then.'

'I'll let you know if there's any news.' Charles fled from the hospital.

'I don't think Dr Pringle likes me,' Charles said that evening to his mother.

Julia was cooking supper in the kitchen. She sniffed. 'Doctors who work in those sorts of hospitals are always a little peculiar.'

'Do you think so? That's a relief. I got worried that it might be me.'

Julia smiled at him. 'Don't be silly, Charles. Why should he dislike you? You've been marvellous. You've practically lived at the hospital all week.'

'She was conscious for a few minutes this morning.' Charles sighed.

Julia looked at him. 'You must be tired, dear.' She called Sarah into the room. 'Please lay the table, dear. We'll eat in the kitchen.'

'Marie-Claire can lay the table,' Sarah objected.

'Don't be rude, Sarah. I asked you to do it. Marie-Claire can eat later. Family's family, I always say.' Sarah shrugged and went to the cupboard to collect the plates. 'Charles, what about Rachel's estate? She's in no fit condition to make any decisions.'

Charles paused. 'I suppose not. Until she's better, I'll have to make them for her. You see, when we signed her in, Dr Burns had to certify her for at least twenty-eight days, because she was found by the river and he was worried that she was suicidal. He expects her to be in the Sanctuary for at least a year.'

'A year?' Sarah stopped laying the table. 'A whole year? I couldn't bear it.' She began to cry.

'Come on, Sarah. Enough of this nonsense. It's for her own good, you know.' Julia's voice was impatient and harsh. 'Really, Charles, she's just like her mother.'

'That clever bitch.' Anthea was furious. 'What do you mean you can't see me?'

Charles said it again very slowly. 'I can't see you, Anthea. My mother is at the house looking after the children, and Rachel is in hospital. She is very seriously ill, and it wouldn't be decent to continue our relationship when she could be dying.' Charles's voice shook.

'Charles, what's so wonderful about Rachel all of a sudden?'

Charles's voice softened. 'You never know how much you love someone until you nearly lose them.' He cleared his throat.

'Bullshit, Charles. But I can wait. Next time you get horny, I'll expect a call.'

You'll be lucky, Charles thought as he put the 'phone

down. Screwing Marie-Claire under his mother's nose was particularly exciting.

'Rachel . . .' It was the voice again.

'No.' Rachel shook her head. 'No . . .'

'Rachel . . .'

'Go away.'

'Come on, Rachel. Just look at me.'

'No . . .'

'You're afraid of the pain, aren't you, Rachel?'

She nodded her head with her eyes tightly closed. The tiger was in the tall grass. She could see the grass moving as it prowled.

'Don't be afraid of the pain.' The voice sounded very confident.

The grass parted. She could see the eyes. They glittered gold. She stood naked in a clearing, her hands across her breasts.

'Talk to the pain.' The voice took on a deep and commanding tone. 'Tell it to come to you.'

Rachel put out her hand. 'Here . . .' she said hesitantly. 'Here . . .' The tiger crouched to spring.

'Go on. Tell the pain you're not afraid.'

'I'm . . . not . . . a . . . afraid . . . of you.' She braced herself for the tiger's jump. The tiger stayed where it was. Rachel got a bit braver. 'I'm not afraid of you.' At that moment, she didn't care whether it jumped or not. What the hell, she thought. 'I'm not afraid of you!' she yelled at the crouched animal. The tiger got to its feet, stretched, and yawned. Rachel opened her eyes. 'The pain's gone,' she said.

Dr Pringle sat back in the chair by her bed. 'Don't try and sit up.' He motioned for her to stay still.

'How long have I been here?'

'Nearly three weeks,' he said. 'You've been conscious some of the time, but it's been hard work getting you back again.'

'It was the pain. It was unbearable.'

'I know. It's like that for a lot of people.'

'Where am I?'

'You're in the Sanctuary.'

Rachel's face changed. 'You mean the mental hospital?'

Patiently Dr Pringle explained once more how she'd got there.

'How long do I have to stay?'

'I don't think for very long. But you are physically and emotionally exhausted. What you need is at least three weeks of uninterrupted sleep.'

'But I've been unconscious for that length of time.'

'I know, but you were struggling internally. I could tell. Here.' He unhooked the blood-pressure chart from the end of the bed. 'Take a look.'

Rachel traced the peaks and valleys of her emotions. 'My God. It got very high.'

'Yes. I was very worried at one point. But,' Dr Pringle smiled at her, 'you're a fighter, you know.'

Rachel smiled wanly. 'I thought I might die. I never believed that anyone could die of a broken heart.'

Dr Pringle nodded. 'Yes, people can. I've seen it happen. Then they write "heart attack" on the death certificate.'

'Dr Pringle, if I let go . . . I mean if I truly let go, I may never get myself back together again.'

'That's what I'm here for, Rachel. Can you trust me?'

She looked at him. 'Yes.' She was quiet for a moment. 'Where's Charles?' She said it very fast, half expecting the tiger again.

Dr Pringle's face brightened. 'You can say his name now without being overwhelmed. Well done, Rachel. Your husband is waiting for me to telephone him. He is anxious to see you with both the children. How do you feel about that?'

'I do have to learn to face him again, don't I?'

Dr Pringle nodded. 'But only if you feel you can handle it. He doesn't make the rules any more. You do.'

'I'm not going to stay married to him.' Rachel looked at the ceiling. 'One thing that awful pain did for me, it sort of cleansed me. I do feel separate from him.'

The doctor smiled. 'That's necessary for you. You have a lot of growing to do, Rachel.'

'I know. I've been a bit like a tortoise. I could always

pull my head into my shell if the going got rough. But there's no shell now.'

'So you will take the plunge?'

Rachel nodded. 'But first I want to see the children, and I want to tell Charles I now no longer consider myself married to him.'

'I'll telephone him. Do you want to see him tonight?'

'Why not. Let's get that over with and then I can go to sleep. Imagine – three weeks of peace.'

'The nurses will wake you up periodically and help you to the bathroom. You will also have three meals a day. There's no need to drug you heavily. I'll have you moved to a sleep ward this afternoon. I find patients much prefer to be together rather than in a room on their own. I have paired you off with a woman called Cici. I think,' his eyes twinkled, 'I think you'll be very good for each other.'

Rachel had to be wheeled into Hope Ward. Her little section contained six beds. There were five other similar units. Thirty-six patients in all.

'Hello, I'm Cici.' Sitting on the bed next to hers was a dark-haired girl with huge brown eyes and a mole that highlighted her luscious mouth.

Nature is kind to some women, Rachel thought, suddenly conscious of her skinny arms. 'I'm Rachel Hunter.'

'Some man dumped you?' She saw Rachel flinch. 'Don't worry. That's why most of us are here.' She grinned, showing perfectly white teeth.

'No. Actually, I'm dumping him.' She felt a great surge of assurance.

'Honestly? That's marvellous.' Cici's face twisted. 'I wish I could dump James . . . Well, put it another way: I *could* dump James. It's the loot I'm after. No James – no money, honey.' She laughed. 'I'm a regular here. When I can't stand him any more, I go off my head and get carted in here. Three weeks' kip and I go out there and cope again.'

'Sounds an awfully drastic way to live.' Rachel peered at her.

Cici looked at Rachel and said, 'You take life far too

seriously. Really, you're halfway through already.'

Rachel couldn't help laughing at herself. 'Are all these women really here because of men?'

'Mostly. Mind you, the other side of the hospital is full of men in there because of women. Anybody else that's left is in the VD Clinic.'

Rachel giggled. 'Cici, you *are* awful.'

'I know. That's why I'm so popular, except with Dr Pringle. He keeps giving me moral lectures.'

'He's an amazing man,' Rachel said, remembering how he tamed the tiger.

'He is. He's the only guy I've ever met who wouldn't let me suck him off.' Cici's face was serious. 'Most men, if you try hard enough, will give in in the end. But not him.'

'Cici, you didn't offer . . .' Rachel looked at her horrified.

'Sure. Why not? He's not God, you know. Mind you, I once had a Catholic priest.'

Rachel gave up. They spent the rest of the afternoon chatting.

The visitors' bell rang and Rachel suddenly saw Charles at the glass door to the unit. He had the children with him. She nervously chewed the end of her plait. Traitor, she said to herself. Judas. He bent over her and kissed her on the forehead. She ignored him.

Sarah flung her arms around her mother. Rachel cuddled her. 'I'm so glad you're awake, Mummy.'

'So am I, Sarah. But I'm only awake for today. Tomorrow I go to sleep for three whole weeks.'

'Does that mean we can't see you?'

'No. You can come and see me at suppertime. I'll be sort of dopey, but I'll know you're there.'

Dominic kissed her cheek. 'Good to see you looking so well, Mother.' He stared round the ward. 'They all look quite normal,' he said to Rachel.

'Of course. They *are* all quite normal. Really, Dom, did you expect us all to have two heads?'

Dominic looked embarrassed. 'You should hear Grandmother on the subject. I expected to see you in a strait-jacket foaming at the mouth.'

'I see Julia hasn't changed much.' Rachel looked at Charles. He dropped his eyes.

'Well in her day mental hospitals weren't the places they are now,' he said lamely.

'Children, would you go to the waiting-room for ten minutes? I want to talk to your father.' When they had gone, Rachel took off her wedding ring and handed it to Charles. 'Funnily enough, Charles, now that I've made that decision, it doesn't hurt so much.'

Charles looked at the ring lying in the palm of his hand. He looked at Rachel's face. 'There isn't any point in arguing, is there?'

'No.' She shook her head. 'No point at all. Call Dominic. I want to talk to him, and then Sarah.'

'All right.' Charles stood awkwardly by the bed. 'I'm sorry it has to be this way.'

'I'm not. It's done now. It's up to me to get on with my life.'

Dominic took the news very casually. 'Is it all right if I stay with Julia, then?'

'I suppose so. I don't want to live in that house again. If she wants to keep house for Charles and for you, that's fine by me. I'll see you often.'

Dominic looked at her. 'I do love you, Mother.'

Rachel hugged him. 'I know you do, Dom. In your own way.'

'I don't care what happens as long as I can live with you.' Sarah was anxiously looking at her mother's face.

'I promise, Sarah. Just as soon as I've had time to get over this, I will get a place for the both of us and for Dom to stay when he feels like it. After all, remember, I'm a rich woman now.'

'No. Daddy has your money because you were put in here by him and Dr Burns.'

Rachel frowned. 'What are you talking about, Sarah?'

'I told you. I heard Daddy telling Grandma that he was in charge of your money now.'

We'll see about that, Rachel thought. 'Doesn't matter

what he says. I promise I'll make a home for you, Sarah. You think about a new bedroom.'

Sarah hugged her mother. 'Do it soon. Grandma's a pain to live with.'

'I will.'

Dr Pringle stopped by her bed to say good-night before he left the ward. 'Am I on an order of some sort or other?' Rachel asked.

'No. I had it lifted this morning. There's nothing wrong with you at all. It just takes time to mend a broken heart.' He smiled. 'Good-night, Rachel.'

'Good-night, Dr Pringle.' Thank God I don't have to put up with being married for money, she thought.

'Good-night, Rachel,' Cici called from her bed. 'Hey. Your old man's a good-looking sod.'

'Yes, but he's still a sod.' Rachel laughed. I do sound hard, she thought. Then the tears came.

Book Three
The Watershed

39

During the three weeks of her sleep, Rachel was only vaguely aware of her visitors. She saw Jane's face at one point. Often she saw Claire and the children. Dr Pringle swam into view. He was holding up her blood-pressure chart and smiling at her. When she was awake, the nurses would take her to the bathroom. 'It's rather like being drunk without a hangover,' she laughed as she lurched down the hall. The days ticked by until the last week, when the dose of pills was slowly decreased. By the Friday morning, Rachel was fully awake.

She opened her eyes and looked around the ward. Cici was grinning from ear to ear. She sat up. 'Right. I'm ready to take James on again.'

Rachel shook her head in disbelief. 'Look, Cici, I've put on weight.' She stood up, and looked down at her legs. 'They're not like matchsticks any more. How fantastic.'

'It's that bloody hospital food. I've been shitting cannonballs for the last three weeks. You could afford to put on weight. I'm going to have to take myself off to a health club to get all the flab off. Yuk. Look at it.' She pinched a fold of skin on her stomach.

'You're voluptuous, Cici, you idiot. You're not fat.'

'You could be beautiful, Rachel.'

'Oh come on, Cici. Don't be silly.'

'No, I'm serious. With a bit of meat on your bones, you'd make a bloody good model.'

Rachel grinned. 'I hate bothering with clothes.'

Cici looked at her. 'Listen. When we get out, I want you to keep in touch with me. You need to loosen up a little. Have fun.'

'Actually, I'd like that.'

'We'll leave James at home and go night-clubbing.'

'Do you really do that?'

'Why not? James is about as much fun as a slice of roast beef. So I tuck him up in bed with the latest copy of *The Economist*, stick his false teeth in a glass beside his bed so he has some company, and off I go. Sometimes on my own. Sometimes with a lover. It just depends how I feel. If you're going to ditch your old man, what you need is a marvellous love affair.' Rachel looked sceptical. 'No, honestly. Puts the roses back in your cheeks and makes you feel like a million dollars.'

'I think I'll wait a bit before I get involved with a man again.' Rachel laughed bitterly. 'I don't want to go from the frying pan into the fire.'

'Don't be so serious, Rachel. All men are the same. The trouble with women is that we take them far more seriously than they take us.'

'Cici, tell the truth. You don't just stay with James for his money, do you? You're the sort of girl that can always attract a rich man.'

'Why do I stay with him then?'

Rachel looked at her appraisingly. 'Because, dear Cici, for all your lectures – most of which I have forgotten, thanks to all those pills – he's your security blanket.'

'Exactly.' Dr Pringle broke into the conversation. 'Cici, my dear, now do you believe me?'

Cici blushed. 'Oh I know, but "My heart belongs to Daddy . . ." ' She didn't finish the line.

'Actually, Cici,' Rachel said, 'you love him a lot more than you'll admit.'

Cici giggled. 'Yeah, you're right. But there's a forty-year age gap between us. I find it difficult to lead an old man's life. Still,' her face softened, 'I've never wanted to be full-time with any other guy. S'funny. I don't mind people thinking I'm after his money. Somehow that seems respectable. But to admit I loved him . . .' she shook her head, 'everyone would be disgusted.'

Dr Pringle looked seriously at her. 'It depends on how much other people's opinions really matter to you, doesn't it?' Cici nodded. Dr Pringle laughed. 'I thought you two would have a lot to say to each other.' He moved on.

'While we're playing at psychiatrists, let me tell *you* something, Rachel.'

'What?' Rachel was lying back on the bed.

'There's part of you that never really liked being married.'

'How do you know that?'

'Well, you're not the usual type of married woman. You haven't mentioned the washing machine or your children once today.'

Rachel immediately felt guilty. 'I haven't, have I? Cici, I think I've always operated on two levels. I did want to be married, but I didn't want the things that marriage did to me. I was so lonely for so many years.' Tears came to her eyes. 'I never could get it all right. If I cleaned the house, I burnt the supper. If I got the supper right, the lavatory blocked.' The tears were running down her face. 'I know I've failed.'

'You didn't fail, honey.' Cici sat down beside her. 'You couldn't win. Look at them.' She made a sweeping gesture with her arm, indicating the women in the ward. 'All of them. At least these women rebel enough to get three weeks' holiday in here. Think of the millions of women behind their front doors all chatting away to their new washing-up gloves.'

Rachel nodded. 'I got like that. I got obsessed with Jimmy Young's recipes. Even if someone dropped by for coffee, I'd have to write the recipe down. It was like if I could write it down, I'd be a good wife and mother for the rest of the day. But if I missed it,' she made a face, 'then the depression would seep in under the doors, through the cracks in the windows. And I'd sit at the kitchen table and watch this brown sticky depression cover the walls and the floor and all the furniture. It was evil stuff, because it lay there waiting. It knew I had to start cleaning all over again. Those were my valium years. It was just coming right when it all went wrong.'

Cici hugged her. 'Rachel, one day you'll find someone.'

'I hope so, but it's just getting used to the fact that it's not Charles.'

'I know how awful it is.' Cici heaved a huge sigh. 'I was married to my first husband for five years. I was sixteen when I got married. I really loved him. It's worse than death, you know. At least if the bastard's dead, you know they're not walking round this earth with someone else.'

Rachel smiled. 'Do you remember the case of Rose Johnson? She shot her lover in the head. It was just a few roads away from our house. Funny thing was, the woman who raised the money for her defence fund was Charles's mistress. I actually told Charles about it and showed him her picture in the paper when it all happened. God, I feel such a fool.'

'Don't worry about it, Rachel. You're not a fool. You don't actually suspect other people of things you don't do yourself. I never suspected my ex, but he cheated me. That's why I've never married James. I just live with him. As far as I'm concerned, he knows I have lovers. But we don't cheat on each other, if you know what I mean. That's what's important.'

Filled with good talk, the day flew by. Rachel was pleased to see Sarah that evening. 'I brought her along tonight.' Jane's face was alight with pleasure. 'It's lovely to see you looking so well.'

Rached kissed her. 'Jane, it's lovely to really see you instead of a blur which I thought was Jane.'

'Sarah?' Jane said. Sarah looked thin and strained. 'Go on, Sarah.'

'Mummy, I'd like to stay with Jane until you're well enough to have me back.'

Rachel looked at Jane. 'That will be at least six months, Jane. Apparently, I've got to take it very carefully for quite a while. We can all leave on Monday morning, the nurses say. I'm thinking of spending the first month with Anna. I'm going to ring her this evening. It's very quiet down at her place. Vera, her mother, is a very nice woman. She's very like my aunts. Also Anna's due to have her baby, so I'd be of some use, as neither of them have any experience. Then I'll probably take another few weeks off. After that, I'm afraid, it's all house-hunting and making a new life for myself. Anyway, Claire says I can stay at her suite in the Savoy while I look for a place.'

'Put like that,' Jane laughed, 'it sounds quite exciting. But really, don't worry. I'll take care of Sarah. It'll be great for me to have someone else's child. They're so much easier than your own.'

'Thanks, Jane. It's enormously kind of you.'

'We women have to stick together. Who knows? I might have to ask for your help one day, though with Jerry I should be so lucky. Keep your hands off Robert Redford now that you're a free woman.'

'Jane, I was going to ask you for another favour. Could you and Sarah pack all my clothes and jewellery and put it in the Volvo? I really don't feel up to dealing with Julia yet.'

Jane nodded. 'Of course we will.'

Rachel's last few days in hospital were made bearable by the hospital routine. Rachel was able to laugh with Cici and to talk to some of the other women in the room. Liz Gordon over in the corner of the room was very much in the same situation as Rachel. 'I can't leave him. I'd have no money, and I don't have any qualifications.' She sobbed for hours. 'We've been married for twenty-five years. He wants to stay married for the church. He's a verger and he never misses a Sunday service. He wants me to accept this relationship with this woman.' She looked hopelessly at Rachel. 'What can I do? If I leave him, I don't even have a roof over my head.'

'At least he still wants you to stay in the house.' A small thin woman was sitting on her bed next to Cici. 'I'm out. I feel just like an old shoebox. A few months ago, Michael, my youngest, was sixteen. Daniel marched into the house at lunchtime – I knew something was wrong right away. He never comes home for lunch – and he told me our marriage was over. He said it had been over for a long time, but he had stayed for the sake of the kids.'

'Don't believe it,' Cici laughed. 'When you hear a man being virtuous, look under the bed for the vice. What he actually did was wait until Michael was sixteen so you could have no claim in law. Also, unless Michael was going on to study, your Daniel won't have to pay a penny for maintenance.'

The little thin woman broke down. 'I don't know what we're going to do, Michael and I. Daniel pays the rent and the tenancy is in his name.'

'Go and see a good lawyer, luv. Here, I'll give you a name,' Cici advised.

Later that night, Cici sat up with Rachel. 'What's happening to you on Monday?'

'I'm going to a friend's house in the country,' Rachel answered. 'Her mother Vera is coming up by train and driving my Volvo down to her place. I don't feel up to driving yet. Do you think you'll have to come in here again, Cici?'

'No.' Cici shook her head. 'Funnily enough, you did more for me than anybody else ever has. I finally feel able to admit that I love James, because you could see through my defences.' She paused. 'My love for him is not disgusting. He's not my father, and I don't need his money. I just need him.' Her face was soft and gentle. 'You're a lovely woman, Rachel. Don't be embarrassed. One day you'll love yourself as much as your friends Claire and Jane and Sarah – people like that – love you. You promise to keep in touch, won't you?'

'Promise.' They kissed each other good-night.

Monday was a beautiful day. Rachel leaned out of the hospital window. She could see the River Thames in the distance. The sunlight touched the bare branches of the trees in the grounds of the hospital. She tilted her face until a stray beam of sun felt warm against her skin. I don't want to leave. The thought frightened her. Of course I'll have to leave, she scolded herself. On this refreshing February day, unseasonably warm for the time of year, Rachel felt the cool wind on her face. She breathed in deeply. Somehow the stuffy central heating in the hospital seemed constant and safe. The world outside was an alien place. Monday, she thought. The children would be going to school and I would be over at Jane's for a cup of coffee. She could see Jane sitting at her kitchen table with the ever-present bottle of valium by her hand. At least Sarah's safe. Suddenly she was crying again. I'm not . . . I'll never be safe again.

A gentle hand touched her shoulder. Matron stood beside her. 'You don't have to leave today, Rachel.' She was a motherly woman.

Rachel hung her head. 'If I don't go now, I'm afraid I'll never leave.'

Matron smiled. 'A hospital can feel like a very safe place. You've lost your safe place, haven't you?' Rachel nodded. The tears were coming faster. 'Let me tell you something. I say it to women who have lost their men or their homes and sometimes their children. The reason why you ended up here is that you invested your safe place in your husband. Am I right?' Rachel nodded again. 'Now you have to start again. Rachel, the only safe place that's of any use to you is the one that you must create inside yourself.'

'I know.' Rachel suddenly remembered a conversation she had had many years ago with Aunt Bea. She now could hear Bea's voice again. 'My aunt warned me, you know, Matron. She said I was always to keep a bit of myself apart.'

'Did she know your husband?'

'Yes.'

'Well, maybe she was more aware of the type of man he was than you realized. If you marry a narcissus, you will always end up wounded.'

'But how do you know? Charles seemed so loving and kind.'

Matron looked at Rachel. 'I made a point of reading your notes. My heart ached for you, Rachel. The same thing happened to me. My first husband was a narcissus and also a compulsive gambler. It took me years to find out. The grief was terrible, but I eventually realized that the important relationship in his life was to his mother. Everything he did was in reaction to her. I was just the whipping post.' She paused, and Rachel could see the suffering etched into lines on her face. 'Sometimes, you know, I think of the women coming in here as wounded birds. They've been dashing themselves against a brick wall again and again, 'til finally they fall, bleeding and exhausted. Most of them try so hard to hang on to what's left of their awful relationships with their men. I see them the first time. Then the second, and after that they usually leave our ward and get into the hands of male psychiatrists, many of whom deeply hate women.'

'I can imagine it. My family doctor's like that. Do you know Dr Burns?' Matron nodded. 'Did you know that he kept sending me to the local VD Clinic because he said I'd picked up an infection? Non-specific urethritis on one occasion, on another I had a discharge. He knew all the time it was Charles.'

Rachel had tackled Dr Burns on his last visit to the hospital two days earlier on the Saturday morning. He tugged at his tie with his beautifully manicured hands. 'Ahem, Rachel dear, it was a matter of professional ethics. I cannot disclose information given to me by a patient. I would betray a professional confidence.'

'Just tell me: what was the discharge?' Dr Burns looked at his fingernails. 'I have a right to know. After all, my own infections are not confidential information, are they?'

'No, but why can't you let well enough alone? It will do you no good dwelling on such an unpleasant subject. What we need to do is to get you better. A little holiday and then back to your family.'

'I'm not going back, so you might as well tell me.'

Dr Burns cleared his throat. 'That particular infection was gonorrhea.'

'Gonorrhea?' Rachel was disgusted with herself and even more with Charles. She said in a tight cold voice, 'I think you are one of the most immoral men I have ever met, Dr Burns. I never want to see you again. Go away.'

Dr Burns left hurriedly. Another hysterical woman, he thought.

So the VD clinic lied as well, Rachel thought after the doctor had left, remembering the smiling face of the doctor there. 'Just a slight yeast infection. Nothing to worry about.' She was lying on the examination table with her feet in the stirrups, thinking, There's something so obscene about lying here with all my clothes on. One end looks perfectly decent, and the other end is exposed for all the world to see. Young interns were moving in and out of the curtain partitions.

She blushed now at the memory. Matron stroked her hair. 'That often happens, I'm afraid. If it's a question of telling a woman that her partner has infected her, the choice is usually to protect the relationship.'

'You mean the man.' Rachel's voice was bitter.

'I'm afraid so, but things are changing. There are many more women doctors. Years ago, long before everyone even started talking about women's rights, I made a commitment with several of my nursing friends to work in places where women were most vulnerable to manipulation by male doctors. Some of us went into psychiatric nursing, and others into maternity hospitals. Unfortunately, since then, everything turned into politics, and the women's movement has done more harm than good in this country.'

'I know. For a while, my friend Anna went through a stage of hating men . . .'

Matron shook her head. 'Hating doesn't change anything.'

'I just hope that it's possible for me to find a man who won't betray me.'

'Don't worry, love. It is possible. I found a man a few years ago. We're very happy together.' Matron went quite pink and she blushed.

Rachel's whole face lit up. 'That's marvellous, Matron. That's the best news I've heard in ages. Even if he's the only man left in a country of dinosaurs, just the fact that he exists is good enough for me. I'm not ready for a relationship with a man yet . . . if ever. But I do need to be able to dream. Thanks, Matron. As long as I know one woman is happy in a relationship, there's hope for everybody else.'

'Remember,' Matron smiled, 'I'm always here, Rachel. If you want to talk to me, just give me a ring. Sometimes you'll feel very down. But remember, for all the bad days there will be good days.'

'I will, and thank you. I must get packed.' Rachel found herself skipping down the corridor. I haven't done this since I was a child, she thought.

'I say, Cici, do you know that Matron's wildly happy with a man? I've been talking to her, and she actually went pink and glowed!'

Cici smiled. 'Yeah, she told me about him. He's twenty years younger than she is.'

'No . . .!' Rachel thought for a moment. 'Did that help you with your struggle over James's age difference?'

'She made me realize how vulnerable James was. I'd always thought in terms of *my* needs, like he might die and leave me. I didn't ever think he was worried that I'd find him too saggy or baggy or revolting or something.'

James came into the unit followed by his chauffeur. Cici jumped up to greet him. Rachel looked at James. 'Darling,' Cici took Rachel's arm, 'this is Rachel Hunter. She's promised to keep in touch with me.'

James smiled at Rachel. What wonderful eyes, Rachel said to herself. He was a small neatly built man. 'That would be lovely, Rachel. Cici needs good friends. I'm a little too old to accompany her to night clubs, but I don't want to cage my wild bird.'

'It's nice to know that you can let her go like that.' At least that's one of Matron's birds that doesn't have to end up mangled, Rachel thought.

James looked serious. 'It's always difficult when a relationship is unusual. I feel bad for you, Cici, when you have to come here.'

Cici took his hand. 'I won't have to any more, James. I'll always come back to see Matron. She keeps my head straight, but I've stopped fighting with the age gap between us. I can love you now and not apologize to anyone.'

The chauffeur blushed furiously and shifted his feet. 'I'll collect the suitcases.'

No one heard him. James and Cici were looking at each other with such love that Rachel was enveloped in the warmth of the moment. Someday . . . Rachel thought.

Vera Compton broke the moment by walking into the room. 'Here I am, Rachel. Are you ready?'

Rachel flung her arms around Vera's neck. 'Vera, how marvellous to see you. Come on. Let's get going. I can't wait to see Anna. Good-bye, Cici. Good-bye, James.' I'll ring Cici just as soon as I get back to London, she promised herself.

40

Rachel had expected to feel strange when she left the hospital. She had warned herself very thoroughly. Dr Pringle's last words were, 'Remember, we are always here.' She was quiet on the drive down to Sherborne. Vera was not a talkative woman at the best of times. She was an excellent driver, but the most healing quality she offered Rachel was her link with Aunt Emily and Aunt Bea.

'I'm sorry about Charles. I know how hurt you must feel.' Vera was hesitant. 'I know I shouldn't probably say this to you, but it may help. Your Aunt Bea was worried about Charles all those years ago. She took an instant dislike to his mother.'

Rachel found herself laughing. 'I bet Aunt Bea said something like "All net curtains and kippers." '

'Yes, actually. It was something like that. She was a good judge of character.' Vera drove with great concentration. 'I'm sorry your aunts are not here now . . . when you most need them.'

Rachel shook her head. 'I thought that for a while, but now I realize that if they were alive and still at home, I'd go back to them and never leave that safe world. Anna needs you now because she will have a child to look after. Also, you've both grown into a sort of a companionable relationship. I was still very much the child of the family. Anna's always been much tougher and more worldly than I have. But then you always were part of the world with your horses and the kennels.'

Vera laughed. 'That was a very *un*natural world, actually, Rachel. I often wonder if I ruined Anna's chances of a normal life.'

Rachel hesitated. 'I don't think so, Vera. Anna's Anna. I've always accepted her just as she is. Remember when she was a horse for years?' Rachel laughed fondly. 'The rest of us pretended, but for Anna it was real. Thanks for coming to get me. I'm very grateful. I know Anna's about due.'

'She's overdue, but I can't resist the opportunity of driving.' Vera sighed. 'I haven't many more years left. I'm one of the oldest drivers in our area – an antique. But I can't exercise the horses anymore, so I have to make do with cars.'

Vera put on the car's tape-deck. *The Archduke Trio* played. Rachel put her seat back in the car. 'That's one of my most favourite pieces of music.' She drifted off to sleep.

Anna was waiting at the door for Rachel. She looked at her friend's white face. 'You've put on weight at last, Rachel,' she joked.

'So have you. Is it an elephant?' Rachel patted Anna's stomach.

Anna led the way into the kitchen. 'You must be exhausted, Mum. That's such a long journey.'

Vera smiled. 'I had a good night's sleep at the Wainwrights. Jenny sends you her love, Anna. It only took about six hours. The traffic was light.'

'I'm afraid I wasn't much help. I slept most of the way.' Rachel sat down at the kitchen table. 'When are you due, Anna?'

Anna shrugged her shoulders. 'I don't know. They keep changing their minds. First they said I was overdue, then they decided they had the dates wrong. Hospitals! If I were younger I'd have the baby at home, but I guess it's wiser this way.'

'Oh Anna, of course it is.' Vera fluttered around Anna's chair.

'It's okay, Mum. I'm not going to expect you to deliver me on the kitchen table.' Anna laughed.

'I've always wanted to be able to say "Quick! Boiling water! Fetch the string!" '

'You will come with me, won't you, Rachel? Mum's going to be there as well. The hospital is very good about that sort of thing.'

Rachel nodded. 'Of course I will, Anna.'

After supper, Vera said good-night and went up to bed. Anna and Rachel cleared away the dishes. 'Come on. Let's go into the sitting-room and put our feet up.' Anna collected a bottle of wine from the wine-rack in the pantry. 'The baby's going to come out with the hiccoughs, but I do find wine relaxing.'

'Do you remember the days when you would only drink pints of bitter?' Rachel said. 'And you were horrid to me because you said my lifestyle was bourgeois? And here you are . . . knitting. Oh Anna, I never thought I'd see the day.'

Anna picked up the little white cardigan. 'I know, but it took me a long time to realize that it's okay for a feminist to do whatever she likes. It's *why* I do it, not what I do. I find knitting very relaxing. To think,' she grinned at Rachel, 'do you remember how I wrote to all those women's magazines and berated them for printing knitting patterns?' She laughed self-consciously. 'This pattern is from a woman's magazine.'

'You always did throw yourself into everything whole-heartedly, while I stood on the sidelines and watched.'

'You don't take so many knocks that way.' Anna looked at Rachel.

'No,' Rachel agreed, 'but it comes to you in the end. Maybe if I'd taken more risks in the early days – I mean with other people and relationships – this wouldn't have happened.'

'Rachel,' Anna's voice was stern, 'it wouldn't have changed anything except maybe you would have realized what a shit Charles was from the beginning. I did.'

'I know. You never really liked him.'

'I didn't just dislike him, Rachel, I hated him.'

'Really? That bad?'

'It's men like Charles who made my friends so hysterical. So many of them were so badly wounded they couldn't do anything but scream with pain. That's why I had to get out of London. All the screaming and crying was translated into such a total hatred of all men that I needed to get away and think for myself. The deadly thing about the Charleses of this world is that they get a deviant delight in kicking a woman's teeth in.'

Rachel nodded. 'Did you know about Anthea?'

Anna looked embarrassed. 'Yes, I did. Only because I was one of the collectors for Rose Johnson. Anthea was obsessed with you.'

'So Charles talked about me to her?'

Anna nodded. 'That's part of the game. I'm sure if you saw Charles now, he'd want to moan about Anthea.'

'I wouldn't have believed you a few weeks ago, but spending some time in the hospital, even if all of us were on sleeping pills, I remember enough of the conversations to see a horrid pattern emerging. You know,' Rachel paused, 'I find it very humiliating to discover that what I thought was a unique relationship was nothing more or less than a sordid episode in a man's life. Charles got his kicks out of sneaking about the world, screwing, and then lying to me. Actually, come to think of it, I don't think he even enjoyed the screwing. I think it was the moment when some fool of a woman said the fatal words "I Love You." Then he would spend the rest of the time kicking her teeth in. How can anyone be so cruel? I even feel sorry for Anthea. By the way, whatever happened to Rose?'

'You were out of it on the pills for all the time the story was on the telly.' Anna made a face and sighed. 'The bother-boots brigade wrecked everything. We begged them not to demonstrate. But they insisted that the cause, not Rose, mattered more. When the judge tried to get into the Old Bailey, they picketed him and they harassed the jury. By the end of the three days, the jury had had enough. They decided that Rose was a calculating extremist like the yelling mob outside. The judge didn't take kindly to banners that read "ALL MEN ARE RAPISTS" and "ALL MEN ARE BATTERERS." He said as much in his summing-up. You can imagine it, can't you?' Rachel nodded. 'Anyway, the jury found her guilty of a criminal charge of murder, and the judge sentenced her to life imprisonment.'

'Did you appeal?'

'We thought about it, but with a mob like that guaranteed to give a repeat performance, what chance did we have? They wouldn't miss an opportunity to demonstrate again. Anyway, Rose was so distraught by the trial. The prosecution read out a letter she had left with Anthea just before she killed Stephen. It sounded like the raving of a maniac. She actually begged us to leave her alone. She says Holloway is a great improvement on real life.'

'You're kidding.'

'No, I'm not. Oddly enough, she says that the war between men and women is so awful now that she likes the peace of Holloway because she doesn't have to struggle with men.'

'I can understand that.' Rachel poured herself a glass of wine. Anna was sitting on the floor with her back against a big chintz-covered sofa. Rachel looked at the familiar walls hung with paintings of racehorses and a few hounds. 'Why didn't you tell me about Anthea?'

Anna frowned. 'I thought about telling you for ages, but then I realized that I'd be doing what I always did for you – I'd be running your life. I'd tell you what Charles had been up to, and then you'd deal with it.' Anna shook her head. 'Believe me, it was much harder to sit on the side lines and wait for him to tell you. I knew he was going to have to tell because Anthea kept crowing about it, so it wasn't for long. I was afraid actually that if *I* told you, you'd forgive him and go back. The way it happened, I mean because he had to actually confess, I think made it much harder on you, but you did have to make a decision on your own.'

'You were right,' Rachel said. 'You know, it's funny. One phrase of his stuck in my mind. He said that it was only me that he loved, and then he said "All of the other women were merely fluff." I didn't think about it much at the time, but just lately I realized that if he can write off all those women so easily, there wasn't much hope for me anyway. Funnily enough, when I do see pictures in the newspapers of yelling, shrieking women, I feel confused. Part of me absolutely hates what they do on behalf of women, and they scare an awful lot of women away. But there's part of my soul that now understands their pain and is leaping about under the banners completely out of control. My banner says: "ALL MEN ARE BASTARDS." '

Anna grunted. She put her hand on her belly. 'Ohhh. My stomach gets so tight.'

Rachel, curled up on the sofa, leaned over and put her hand on Anna's stomach. 'Wow! It's a footballer.'

'Girls play football too,' Anna retorted. Anna returned to the subject. 'If I had a banner now, I suppose I'd like it to have something optimistic on it, like "LOVE PEOPLE." '

Rachel grinned. 'We're switching roles, Anna. It used to be you who went on about men.'

Anna shrugged. 'I've worked through a lot of things in my life, and I'm comfortable with myself now. Quite honestly, I had to face the fact that I couldn't go around blaming all men for the sins of the world when there are women like Julia turning out sons by the millions all over the world.'

'If you think Julia's awful, you should see Michael's mother.'

'No thanks. I'm not going to waste my time even thinking about them. I'd like to be like my mother, still buzzing about the roads in a car at eighty, organizing stud farms. She's amazing really. They don't make them like that anymore.'

'I suppose women like my aunts were so independent because for many years they had to do without men. They were all away during two world wars. So really, when you think about it, they were little girls during the First World War when women had to leave their homes to run the country. And they were young women when it happened again.'

'Maybe we'll have a selective bomb that wipes out men for long enough that women are forced to take responsibility for themselves. During that time we can clone to keep the human race going. Then, after several hundred years, men can be reintroduced into the world.' Anna sat upright. 'Mind you,' she said, 'men could take one look and freak and refuse to come back.'

Rachel smiled. 'At the moment, I don't much care. It seems that after all these years, when I'm in trouble, all my friends that I can lean on are women. Especially you, Anna. I can't explain how amputated I feel. It's like one half of my body has gone missing. I never realized that being a couple means just that – you do most things in two's. I find myself still thinking "I must tell Charles that", or "I wonder what he's having for supper." The days aren't too bad, but the nights are still dreadful.'

Anna put her hand on Rachel's knee. 'Oh God, Rachel. There's a sort of universal pain attached to bad relationships. I can only tell you that it does get better. If you can grit your teeth and throw away the valium, it gets better faster. Are you taking pills?' Rachel nodded. 'If you can't manage without the pills, it sort of takes longer, but the pills dull the edge of the pain. Whatever you do, you can't dodge any of it. It's there. I used to think it was like a horse in a circus. They hold up a huge burning hoop and the poor horse would have to leap through it. Only I had to go through and would get suspended in the middle of the fire.' She shook her head. 'But I realized that I kept doing it to myself. Time and time again. Woman after woman. I hope you don't do that.'

'I couldn't. . . I couldn't put myself through this again.'

'Good. It's just not worth it. If a good relationship comes along, I'll be more than happy, but until then, I care too much about myself to compromise.'

'You've sorted out a lot about yourself, Anna. Would you ever consider a relationship with a man?'

'I don't know. I tend to think of people as people more than as a man or a woman these days.'

'My God. It's nearly three o'clock, Anna. You should be in bed.' Rachel hauled Anna to her feet. 'Come on. You're going to need all your strength for when you're in labour.'

The first week passed by uneventfully. Rachel lay in the small guest-room feeling completely disorientated. It was one thing to be a guest with a home and a family to go back to, but quite another when you were a homeless guest. At times she would go to the kitchen to make a cup of coffee and start with surprise. For a moment she would be transported into her own kitchen. There, by her hand, was the red coffeepot. On the windowsill her avocado plants grew their glossy green leaves, catching the sun that streamed through the kitchen window. Abruptly, the scene would fade and she would find herself clutching the old kettle that sat on Vera's white Aga. Tears would run down her face.

Anna was like a rock for her to cling to. She never had to apologize, and Anna never once told her to pull herself together. Rachel drove Anna around Sherborne because Anna was too pregnant to drive. On the first day in the local supermarket, Rachel lost sight of Anna and found herself standing in the middle of a world full of moving creatures, not one of which looked even vaguely human. She began to scream until she felt Anna's arms around her and saw her concerned face.

'I don't know what I'm going to do with myself, Anna.' She was driving carefully back to the house.

'You may not realize it, Rachel, but each day it will get better.'

'I do hope I'm doing the right thing. Sometimes I wonder if I should go back just for the children's sake. Do I have the right to bail out of a marriage having brought two children into this world?'

'Do you think that if you go back anything will change?'

'No. In my heart of hearts I know nothing can ever be the same between Charles and me. We don't even believe in the same things.'

'Well then. Stop struggling with thoughts of going back, and think of the future.'

They arrived back in the house in time for the second post. There was a letter from Manny for Rachel:

> 'Ruth wrote to me a few weeks ago and told me that you have left Charles.'

Trust Julia to put it that way, Rachel thought in a flash of annoyance.

'I know you well enough to realize that it would be a final decision on your part because you took your marriage vows so seriously. I realized that Charles was a very unhappy and confused man the last time we were together at William's funeral. Sometimes, when everything looks bleak, it is a good idea to give oneself a present. How about making an old friend very happy and paying me a visit in New York. I have a lovely loft in Greenwich Village. I am taking a sabbatical from the Temple to write a book, so I have plenty of time on my hands. Please do seriously consider my invitation.

'Love, Manny'

'Anna, it's a letter from Manny. He wants me to go to New York. Do you remember him? He used to be an old friend of Charles's in Bridport. He became a rabbi and lives mostly in America.'

'No, I don't know him, but I do think it's a super idea. Just as soon as you feel emotionally strong enough to cope with the journey, you should go.'

Rachel was delighted. It would be lovely to see dear gentle Manny again, she thought.

That night Anna went into labour. It was long and hard. Vera and Rachel took turns in the labour ward. Towards the end, the doctor decided to use forceps to pull the baby out. 'Fuck off,' said Anna. 'You're not touching my baby with those things.'

The doctor looked at Anna. 'I'm only saving the baby any possibility of foetal distress,' he said primly.

Anna let out such a roar that he left the room. 'Quite right,' the midwife said approvingly. 'He just wanted to get off duty. You're doing just fine, Anna.'

For the last few moments of the baby's birth, Vera was holding Anna's arms and Rachel had her hands around the back of Anna's head. 'Go on, push!' Rachel was shouting.

Vera was quite beside herself. 'We're winning, darling! Anna, we're coming down the home stretch! Two to one it's a boy!' And suddenly he was there. 'It *is* a boy, Anna.'

Anna lay back exhausted. 'Is he all in one piece?'

'He's beautiful. Oh Anna, look at his huge feet.'

Anna grinned at Rachel as she took the baby from the midwife and plonked him on Anna's stomach. The baby started rooting for her nipple. Anna raised herself on one arm and put the baby beside her on the delivery table. She was half laughing and half crying. 'He's gorgeous. Mummy, look at his eyelashes.' She shook her head. 'It's so unfair. Boys always get them, don't they, Rachel?'

'Yes.' She remembered looking at Dominic when he was a few hours old. Well at least this baby won't have a weak mother like me and a domineering grandmother like Julia, she thought.

'I don't suppose we can tell if he's going to have a good seat for a horse yet, can we?'

'Mummy, give him a chance.'

'Oh I will.' Vera beamed at everyone.

'Time to go home.' The midwife popped her head around the door.

Rachel drove Vera back to the house. 'This is one of the happiest days of my life.' Vera looked shyly at Rachel. 'I know I'm not one for showing much emotion. We weren't allowed to in my day, but I must say, Anna is everything I could want in a daughter. I know that might sound strange, coming from an old-fashioned woman such as myself, but in spite of her rebellions, she is a lovely, warm, loving woman, and I feel privileged to live with her.'

'You're both lovely.' Rachel stretched out her hand. 'Vera, if anything happens to you, you know that I will take care of Anna.'

Vera sat very quietly in the car for a moment. 'Thank you, Rachel. You're a very sensitive woman. That is exactly what I was going to ask you to do for me.'

There was no keeping Anna in hospital. By the time Rachel got into town and did a bit of shopping for Vera, Anna was packed and ready to leave. Rachel had only counted on visiting Anna, but when she arrived at the hospital Anna immediately said, 'Bloody concentration camp. Come on, Rachel. Get me out of here.' She had the baby tucked under one arm. 'I kept my own clothes,' she said defiantly to the senior sister, 'because I reckoned you wouldn't be able to run a place without making everybody's life hell.' She glowered at another nurse who was hovering in a distracted fashion by the door.

'You can't leave, Mrs Compton.' The senior nurse was barring the door.

Anna pushed her aside. 'It's *Miss* Compton, and I'm going *now*,' she growled.

'Your baby will die.'

Anna turned on her. 'He'll die here with all your regulations. Wheel him here . . . wheel him there . . . keep him in a room full of other screaming babies. What exactly do you think he'll die of?'

'Hypothermia,' the nurse spluttered.

'Have you ever heard of central heating, Nurse?'

The nurse had the grace to look embarrassed. Anna charged down the hall with Rachel after her. 'You'll have to wait for the doctor,' the nurse called out.

'Fuck the doctor,' screamed Anna. In a few minutes they were in the car. Anna grinned at Rachel. 'That was like a commando raid,' she said with some satisfaction.

Rachel was puffing. 'Anna, you're supposed to take it easy.'

Anna snorted. 'I spent from six a.m. this morning to ten a.m. listening to the other women in the ward discussing their kitchen freezers. Then they discussed what sort of nappies they were going to use. After that, there was a scintillating debate on powdered milk, followed by a competition on whose husband had the best car. I thought I'd go potty. Then, I had to stake out the whole floor before I could find the baby. Some bloody nurse had wheeled him off in the middle of the night. When I found him he was screaming and tearing at his face. Poor baby. But those women, my God, it was like being locked up in a mad house.'

'I was one of those women once, Anna.'

'As bad as that?'

Rachel nodded her head. 'If you live in a world of toddlers and small children with a husband away all day, your world shrinks and shrinks until you don't feel confident enough to talk about anything except the kitchen sink. It's not like that for everyone, but it was for me.'

'Thank God, I may not be a respectable member of society, and there may be lots of groups and Home Office committees to bar people like me from having babies in the future, but at least this baby isn't going to have a rabid mother sinking her teeth into him with boredom and sucking his life's blood to give her enough energy to measure the dimensions of her refrigerator yet again.'

Rachel laughed. 'You do exaggerate, Anna. But yes, your baby is lucky. Dom had a hard time between Julia's malignant spoiling and my valium-encrusted lifestyle. If I did it again I would never live in a house with just a man. Not when you're bringing up children. That's when you most need people.'

Anna hugged the baby to her breast. 'Tupperware,' she murmured faintly to herself.

'Hello, darling.' Vera was quite unperturbed.

Anna laughed. 'You guessed.'

Rachel looked at the kitchen table. Vera had laid three places. Anna shook her head. 'You're incredible, Mother. Let's have a naming session. I had a girl's name picked out. I was going to call her Joanna, but I tried not to think of a boy's name. Silly really. When it comes down to it, it doesn't make any difference at all.'

The three of them spent lunch discussing names. 'How about "Giles"?' Vera suggested.

'No,' said Anna, 'too posh.'

Vera finally said, 'What about "Sam"?'

'That's it!' said Anna. 'Just "Sam". I'll go and get him. I can hear him yelling from here.'

Slowly Rachel recovered a fragile sense of balance. Some days she could manage without weeping at all. Other days, a line in a book or a scene on television, or just two people holding hands in the road, was enough to set her off again. But slowly the pain was becoming bearable. She spoke to Sarah every night and occasionally to Dominic if he was in. Julia asked about her furniture. 'I'll discuss that with Charles when I'm back from New York.'

She heard the outrage in Julia's voice. 'New York?'

'Yes. I'm going to live it up for a while,' Rachel said sweetly. 'I'll be staying with Manny.'

Julia put the 'phone down. 'I don't know what's happening to that silly girl. She's going to New York, you know, Charles.'

Charles frowned. 'She's not in a fit state to go anywhere. I've told Dr Pringle that if anything happens to her, I shall hold him personally responsible. Imagine, lifting my committal order. Totally irresponsible. She will squander all her money and then land back on me.'

Charles telephoned Manny that night. 'I hear Rachel is going to stay with you, Manny.'

'Oh, it's you, Charles. Yes. I've invited her to stay. I thought she could do with a break.'

'You know she walked out and left me?'

'Yes. That's all Ruth said.'

'I think I must warn you – she's not very stable. She's been in a mental hospital.'

Manny laughed. 'Oh come on, Charles. There's nothing wrong with Rachel that getting away from you and that mother of yours won't cure.'

'I don't know what you mean.'

'I'll tell you then. I've been meaning to say this for years, but there has never been a suitable opportunity. Charles, you have become a first-class shit.'

'I'm not . . .' Charles was hurt. 'I was just trying to put you in the picture.'

'I can paint my own pictures, thanks, Charles. I don't know what you did to Rachel, but it must have been bad. She took her marriage very seriously.'

'I do want her back, Manny.'

'I have a feeling it's too late, Charles.'

'So do I.' Charles put the 'phone down. He felt like crying. It's not fair, he said to himself. He's *my* friend.

* * *

'Anna,' Rachel was cuddling Sam, 'I think I'll go up to London next week and stay with Claire. Then I'll get a ticket for New York.' She looked at the baby who was having a hard time keeping his eyes uncrossed. 'I do feel much better.'

Anna looked at her. 'You're coming along very well. It's been three months now, hasn't it? And you're still here. I wondered at first if you would go back to Charles.'

'I know you did, but the one thing that made it all so final is that I realize that I do want to live on my own and do something for myself. I could have died in Charles's arms, a picture of a happy wife, but inside I was almost dead anyway. Now, not in forty years time. I'm luckier than most women. I'm due to inherit a lot of money so I can afford a comfortable lifestyle. Most women who take a gamble like this do it in one room on Social Security with a child or two.'

'Most women with an illegitmate baby don't have a mother to welcome them home.' There was a silence.

'You're not going to put "Turkey Baster" as Sam's father's occupation, are you?' Rachel grinned at Anna.

'I thought about it,' Anna laughed. 'Julian wants his name there so that Sam will know he had a father. He's thrilled. He says he's always wanted a son. Actually, he's putting money into an account for Sam's education, and he's sending me some for the housekeeping. He should be coming down soon to see him. He's a very nice man actually. I hope Sam inherits his brains. He's very clever.'

'Well he's certainly got somebody's brawn,' said Rachel as Sam waved his fat little fists enthusiastically.

41

Claire was looking as beautiful as ever. She was waiting for Rachel in the Foyer, the cocktail area of the Savoy. She had on a magnificent pair of emerald square-cut earrings. They flashed green lights into her hazel eyes. 'Where on earth did you get those?' Rachel asked.

'From Michael. It's sort of an "I'm sorry" present. I've bank vaults full of those sort of gifts.' She looked sadly at Rachel. 'He's with his mother nearly all the time now. The end is near. She really wouldn't fight the cancer, so she's dying fast. It's awful to see what it's doing to Michael. He feels so helpless. He sits with her in a huge rocking-chair in her bedroom. He has her wrapped in a blanket. And he just sits there whenever she's conscious, and rocks backwards and forwards and sings to her. I can't bear it. I do try and go down for the weekends, but they're both locked away in their own worlds. I'm really worried about what he's going to do with himself when she dies. I feel so helpless . . . and useless. Meanwhile he gives me expensive gifts. Anyway, enough of my troubles. How are you?'

Rachel looked across at Claire. 'I honestly think I'm beginning to get over it. I don't know what the first signs are, but I can laugh again.'

Claire nodded. 'That's certainly a major landmark. Let's have a celebration lunch.'

'What plans have you made, Rachel?' They were having coffee after their lunch in the River Room.

Rachel was feeling very relaxed. She raised her brandy glass and said, 'Well, I decided to sell the house in Devon. I'll put all the furniture in storage. I've actually put the house in the hands of agents down there. Knight, Frank, and Rutley also have it in London, though I hope a local person buys it. The vicar will be awfully distressed if yet another big house becomes a weekend shooting lodge. When I get back from New York, I should start looking for a place to live.'

'What sort of place?'

Rachel smiled. 'You've no idea, Claire, how much time I've taken just thinking about it. Somehow, when I find myself a place to live and when I've moved in, it's almost as if I've decided to join the adult world. Do you know, I've never had to pay a bill in my life? The most responsible thing I've ever done is the weekly shopping. If Charles was away, he'd leave all the bills neatly laid out on the desk. The cheques were left blank and all I had to do was fill in the amount. The thought of all that responsibility terrifies me.'

Claire laughed. 'It won't take long. I always ran my parents' disastrous bills. Borrowing off Peter to pay Paul, and then owing money all over the village, gave me a huge distaste for administering the stuff. That's why I like it here. I don't have to worry about a thing.'

'It does have its attractions. I couldn't afford to live here permanently, but I've always got you.' Rachel grinned. 'Imagine, in those early days at Exeter when we were too broke to go to the cinema. We never guessed we would end up like this.'

'Oh *I* did. I always knew I'd end up rich.' Claire smiled. 'You were always a silly romantic.'

'I suppose so. Claire, do you think you could help me look for a place?'

'I'd love to. While you're in New York, I'll get some lists from house-agents together. Which area do you fancy?'

'I don't know . . . I'd like to be within walking distance, say five minutes, of the river. Maybe around Chelsea. I'm comfortable there. It's not fashionable any longer.'

'Okay. Let's go up to the suite and have a rest. I've

arranged for several guests to join us for dinner this evening. It's good for you to socialize.'

Just as Rachel was ready to go down to dinner the telephone rang. 'It's for you, Rachel,' said Claire.

The voice on the other end was aggressive. 'Is that Rachel Hunter?'

Puzzled, Rachel said, 'Yes, but I don't think I know you.'

'I'm Anthea Walters.'

'Oh . . . oh, yes.' Rachel remembered the pretty looking woman in the newspapers. 'How did you know where I was?'

'Charles told me. That's what I want to talk to you about.'

'Oh . . .' Rachel paused. 'There isn't much to say, is there?'

'Yes there is. I need your help.'

Rachel found herself smiling. 'You need my help? I think you've managed very well so far.'

Anthea's tone changed. 'Please . . . I won't take up much of your time. I know I don't have the right to ask you even to speak to me, but I'm so miserable.'

Rachel shook her head. Poor woman, she thought. 'All right, Anthea. I'm flying to New York the day after tomorrow, but I could meet you for lunch in the Grill downstairs.' She sensed Anthea's relief on the other end of the 'phone.

'Thank you, Rachel. Good-bye.' Anthea's tone was humble.

'I say, Claire, that was Anthea. She wants to see me. I wonder what she wants?'

Claire snorted. 'Strategies to capture Charles. I expect he's playing a new game with her and she can't cope. That's when those sort of women turn up on the ex-wife's doorstep.'

Rachel nodded. 'You're probably right, but I do feel sorry for her – for anyone caught up with Charles.'

'You look fantastic, Rachel.' Claire smiled at her.

Rachel looked at herself in the mirror that hung over the fireplace. 'Do I?' She looked at her reflection. Her hair was hanging softly to her shoulders. Thanks to the weeks of good food and rest, she was looking healthier than she had been for years. Staying with Claire at the Savoy gave her the unbelievable luxury of spending hours of leisure, time to spend exclusively for herself. As a result, her nails were long and manicured. Her hair, thanks to Jean in the hairdressers on the ground floor of the hotel, was red-brown and glowing. 'I'll always be too thin.' She did a little pirouette in the centre of the room. 'You taught me all I know about clothes and make-up, Claire.' She was wearing a dark green silk kaftan with a rope of pearls.

'You learn fast,' said Claire. 'Come on, they'll be gathering downstairs.'

'Is Michael coming?'

'I don't know.' Claire's face tightened. 'He spoke to me yesterday. He'll come if the doctor says it's okay. He's terrified of not being there when old Gloria dies.' They were going down to dinner in the lift. Suddenly she clutched Rachel's arm. 'I'm desperately afraid he'll kill himself when she dies.'

Why does Claire always let down her defences in the most impossible places, Rachel wondered. The little box was packed with people. She thought, What the hell, and put her arms around Claire. 'Just you make sure you're there when Gloria dies. If you're there, Michael wouldn't do that to you.'

Claire smiled weakly. 'I hope you're right, Rachel. I really hope so.'

The lift doors opened. People started streaming into the hall. A Frenchman was staring after them as they left the lift. Quel dommage, he thought. Le vice anglais. Such a waste of two lovely women. He shook his head.

The Scott-Montcriefs, old-time friends of Claire's, were already waiting in the Foyer. Claire introduced Rachel. 'Pauline and George, I want you to meet Rachel Hunter.'

Rachel winced at the name Hunter. Inwardly she swore, That's not my name any longer. It belongs to Charles and his bloody mother. She smiled at Claire.

'Actually, I've decided to go back to my own name. I've just left my husband,' she said, turning to George and Pauline, 'and I feel a hypocrite using his name. Meet Rachel Cavendish.'

Claire raised her eyebrows. 'Good for you, Rachel. Cavendish always was a much nicer name.'

'I know how difficult it is.' Pauline was immediately sympathetic. 'Was he your first?'

Rachel laughed. 'And the last.'

Pauline looked at George. 'I said that too – and now here I am on my third – and last.' George growled at her affectionately. Pauline laughed. 'I suppose Scott-Montcrief is a much better last name than Schwartzkopf, my first ex, or Bloom. You'll find it difficult when you change chequebooks. You'll keep writing Hunter.' She sighed 'George gets furious when I call him Jerry.'

'Jerry . . . at least Jerry died, darling. It's when you call me Lenny, and he lives only two streets away.'

Pauline patted his hand. 'Imagine, after all those years, poor Lenny is still waiting for me to come back.'

Rachel shivered. 'I can't imagine,' she said. 'I hope Charles doesn't.'

They were joined by a sleek impeccably dressed young man. 'This is Liam O'Ryan, Rachel,' said Claire. 'He works in the same department as Michael.'

Rachel put her hand into his. He held it for a moment longer than necessary. Rachel blushed. She looked at Claire who smiled wickedly. Liam said, 'Claire said you were fun, but she didn't say you were beautiful.'

'Watch Liam,' Claire warned, 'he has half of London in love with him, and the other half sucking tranquillizers.'

'It's my Irish blarney.' Liam smiled at Rachel.

In spite of herself, Rachel responded to his arrogant obvious charm. They were just going in for dinner when Michael arrived. God, Rachel thought, he looks dreadful.

Claire kissed Michael's cheek. 'She's unconscious,' Michael said. 'The doctor says she'll be all right for the next few days. I'll go into the office tomorrow.'

Claire squeezed his hand. 'Darling, you look so tired. Do you want to stay with me tonight?'

Michael was threading his way through the dining-tables beside her. 'Really, Claire?'

'Yes, really.'

He sighed. 'Thank you.'

They all settled themselves at the table. How lovely to be in the River Room at the Savoy with an attractive man, Rachel thought, eyeing Liam. Suddenly she was sorry she was leaving for New York.

By the time the trolley, piled high with fresh fruit and chocolate puddings, had been wheeled to the dining-table, Rachel was feeling giddy with wine and laughter. Even Michael's drawn face had relaxed. Pauline was telling outrageous stories about well-known people. 'They call him "Herpes Henry" because he lasts forever. Once he attaches himself to a woman he won't go away.'

Rachel's eyes widened. 'But he's a priest. I've seen him on television.'

Pauline grinned. 'It's all that flagellation.'

'Enough, Pauline,' George insisted.

Liam looked at Rachel. 'Nothing is what it seems.'

Rachel looked down at her beautiful new nails. 'I know,' she said.

'Do I detect a heart that has recently been broken?' Liam looked sympathetically at her.

'Yes, but I'm getting over it.'

'What you need,' Liam said leaning forward, 'is a beautiful romantic affair with someone like me.'

Suddenly Rachel was very glad she was going to New York. 'I'm leaving the day after tomorrow for New York.'

Liam lowered his eyes. 'Leaving? Just as our paths crossed in the universe? Think again, my beautiful Rachel with those wonderous deep brown eyes.'

Rachel shifted uncomfortably in her chair. 'Oh Liam, have some pudding.'

'I want to feast on your meringues, gorge on your delightful chocolate mousse, and dive headfirst into your bowl of fresh strawberries.'

'Liam,' Claire interrupted. 'What *are* you saying to Rachel?' Rachel was laughing helplessly. 'Don't say I didn't warn you, Rachel. Liam is dangerous to any woman under ninety years old.' Liam leered at Claire. 'Take that look off your face, Liam. It doesn't work with me. I know you too well.'

Liam sighed. 'Only woman in London absolutely impervious to my charm. That's why I adore her. Promise me, Rachel,' he clasped his hands earnestly to his chest, 'promise you'll have dinner with me tomorrow night.'

Rachel hesitated. 'But . . .'

Liam's voice rose. 'Rachel, you must have dinner with me.' People from other tables were beginning to stare. A sudden hush descended on the room.

'Liam, it's my last night before flying to New York.'

Liam let out a loud mock wail. 'Please, Rachel. Please,' he begged. The whole room turned and stared at her. By now Liam had grabbed the flowers from the table and was kneeling at her feet. 'Please, Rachel. Say yes . . . please.'

Rachel looked around the River Room. There was no way out. Liam had her trapped. Everyone in the room was waiting to see what would happen next. 'Oh, all right, Liam.' The whole room clapped. Rachel didn't know where to put herself. She was blushing furiously.

Liam got to his feet. He plucked the tiger lily from the flowers and gave it to Rachel. 'A token of my affection,' he said, and lightly kissed the top of her head.

'Mr Swann? The telephone, sir.' The head waiter, who had known Michael for years, made it his business to relay the call himself. He knew, as did all the staff, that Gloria was dying. His finely attuned sixth sense told him that this was the end.

The nurse sounded panicked on the phone.

'I must go,' Michael said when he came back to the table. 'Nurse says she's called the doctor. Mother's much worse.'

'I'm coming too, Michael.'

He looked steadily at Claire. 'No, it's best if I do this on my own.'

'You'll need me to keep you awake. It's a long drive to Axminster.'

Michael could see Claire was determined to go with him. 'All right. I'll have the car brought up. I'm sorry,' Michael looked round the table, 'Rachel, do look after the others for us.'

'Of course.'

Claire had already left to pack a few things. Michael walked swiftly out of the dining-room. Pauline shook her head. 'Gloria – now there's a powerful woman. My last mother-in-law was like that. I thought it was only Jewish mothers.' She made a face.

'It's universal,' Rachel said.

'But it doesn't have to be terminal. My second husband died ten days after the old bag. Massive heart attack. The doctor said her death literally broke his heart.' She paused. 'We are lucky with your mother, George.'

George grinned. 'Scottish matrons are too busy running damp draughty castles to worry about their sons. Anyway, I was brought up by the gillies on the estate.'

Pauline looked at him fondly. 'He's the least confused man that I know. Give him a dog, his gun, and access to a river for fishing, and he's perfectly happy.'

George shrugged. 'I can't see what's wrong with that?'

'Actually,' Pauline laughed, 'it took three marriages for me to realize that there *is* nothing wrong with that. I kept looking for this sensitive aware new being – "the fully liberated man".'

'What happened?' Rachel leaned forward intently.

'Well, my first husband was gentle, sensitive, and aware. He even shared my make-up, but I couldn't fancy him after a while. He was into pink silk nightshirts. I think it was the way he always wore his little pinny and blue rubber gloves to wash up that did it. The second one understood me to death. It got very boring in the end . . . all that meaningful silence. George doesn't understand me at all. Do you, darling?'

George smiled at her. 'I'm content just to love you.'

'There, you see?' Pauline smiled at Rachel. 'I don't

understand what George gets out of standing up to his testicles in icy water or chasing some poor fox for miles on a resentful horse. But then, it doesn't matter.'

George put his hand on Pauline's arm. 'Before you take over Rachel's life, we'd better get going. Rachel, do telephone as soon as you have any news about Gloria.' He scribbled down the number.

Pauline kissed Rachel on the cheek. 'Come and see us when you get back. I'm a mine of information about marriage.'

'You certainly do seem to have got it right this time.'

Pauline beamed. 'I'm lucky.'

Rachel watched them leave the nearly empty dining-room. The waiters were quietly clearing away the dirty crockery. The pace in the room had changed from the bustling waiters weaving their way in and out of the tables supervised by the various senior staff, to a quiet hum from the last few occupied tables. 'I suppose,' Liam interrupted her reverie, 'there's no chance of seducing you tonight?' He wiggled his eyebrows. 'See?' he said, pointing to them, 'they're all shook up.'

'At the risk of disappointing your eyebrows, I really must decline.' Rachel was pleased with herself.

Liam nodded his head. 'That's just my eyebrows asking. Just wait 'til you feel the full force of my magnetic personality.'

'Sounds wonderful, Liam, but I must go up now. It's late.' They were now the last couple in the dining-room.

'How about a little brandy and a delicious cup of coffee . . . Listen . . .' Liam put his hand behind his ear. 'Hark,' he said, 'They're playing our song.' From the Foyer, Rachel could hear the piano. Liam was humming, '. . . when they begin the beguine.'

'No coffee,' said Rachel firmly.

'I'll see you to your door.'

'No thank you, Liam. I can do that myself.'

'Don't you trust me, Rachel?' He looked hurt.

She smiled. 'I'll see you tomorrow.' It's me I don't trust, she thought.

Liam walked with her to the lift. 'You're quite right not to trust me,' Liam said as the lift door opened.

'Once past the first floor of a building, I turn into a sexually depraved monster.' He kissed her on the mouth. It was a firm affectionate kiss. 'Good-night, my beautiful Rachel. I will telephone tomorrow with details of some enchanted glade. I'll bring my pan-pipes and you bring a jug of wine.'

She smiled at him as the doors closed. He did look a bit like Pan, she thought.

When she reached her bedroom, she looked at herself in the mirror. I do look nice, she thought. She looked yet again in the mirror. Her face was flushed and her eyes sparkled. He said I was beautiful. She took off her clothes and walked across to the bathroom. She stood under the bright lights and laced her hands behind her head. 'Not bad,' she muttered. 'Not bad at all.' The bathroom mirror reflected her shining eyes and her pointed nipples. 'He said I was beautiful.' She leaned forward and kissed her reflection.

She fell asleep thinking of all the new people in her life. Cici will be thrilled about Liam. She slipped into a deep relaxed asleep. And for the first time since it all happened, she did not think about Charles at all.

42

Claire and Michael drove through the night. Michael's face was ashen. Claire began conversations, but he was not listening. They stopped for cups of coffee. Even then, Michael was silent. Claire realized that he was already anticipating his mother's death. She felt helpless. They arrived in the early dawn. The shadows around the graceful Georgian house were beginning to release their grip. As soon as the car pulled up to the front door, the nurse came out onto the drive. 'Quick, Mr Swann. She's sinking fast.'

Michael threw himself out of the car. He raced up to Gloria's bedroom. Claire followed him. She was cut off by the abrupt slam of the bedroom door. I'd better leave him alone, she thought. She went down to the library to wait.

Michael went over to the bed. The relief nurse was sitting beside Gloria. All the lights in the room had been extinguished except for the light that illuminated the Chagall on the wall opposite her bed. 'My magic painting,' Gloria would call it. Even in pain, she loved to lie looking at the tumbling cows and cockerels in the blue, blue sky. 'I can feel the sun on my face when I look at that picture,' she would say to Michael.

He would smile at her and gently brush her long hair away from the shrivelled sunken face. Gently he would bend to kiss the dry cracked lips. 'When you're better, darling, we will find the sun.'

Gloria's eyes would sparkle and she'd be away. Together they would plan adventures – an audience with the Pope, give thanks at Lourdes, breakfast on the roof of the Hotel Forum in Rome, a consultation with the Oracle at Delphi. 'Shall we take the ferry to Crete?'

Michael would rock her softly in the rocking-chair. 'I think by that time we'll be a little tired. Let's agree to fly.'

She would snuggle into his breast. 'All right, darling. You know best.'

Tonight he realized there were no adventures to be planned. He lifted Gloria off the bed. The relief nurse tried to object. 'Get out,' he said. Tenderly he wrapped her emaciated little body in a blue cashmere blanket and carried her over to the rocking-chair by the window. The wooden shutters were open. The grey morning light flooded into the window. Michael called Gloria softly. 'Mother. Mother.'

For a moment Gloria's eyes lit up. 'Michael. My Michael . . .' she whispered.

Tears rolled down his face. 'Oh Mother, don't leave me. Please don't leave me.' His body was racked with sobs.

'Never leave you, Michael. Never . . .' She slipped into total darkness.

About an hour later her breathing changed. Then for a moment her face filled with light. She opened her eyes and looked directly at Michael. 'I'll always be here, Michael. Always.' She looked like a young and vibrant girl again.

Michael held her close. 'Always and forever, Mother,' he said.

She gave a deep sigh. 'Blue sea,' she murmured. 'Deep blue sea.' Then she stopped breathing.

Michael's sobs could be heard all over the house. 'Don't leave me! Oh God, don't let her leave!'

The servants stood still, some in the kitchen, some in the dining-room. The senior nurse ran for the 'phone. 'Doctor, come quick. Mrs Swann has gone.'

Claire sat in a chair in the library. She had her arms wrapped around her body for comfort. Tears for Michael were falling down her face. I can't help you. I can't help you, Michael. She was praying. 'Dear God, keep him sane. Please, dear God.' She hadn't prayed for years.

The whole house reverberated with the agony of a man who had lost the only thing he lived for. The pain was like a tornado, howling, and shaking the chandeliers. The pain tore down the narrow corridors in the attic. It banged doors and shrieked at windows. Then, spent, all that was left of the pain was a white-faced man sitting in a rocking-chair, crying over the little hunched woman lying dead in his arms.

'Let me take her.' Dr Rosen put his hand on Michael's shoulder. 'Come on, Michael.'

They had grown up together. Michael had tormented John Rosen at school.

John lifted Gloria from Michael's arms. 'Come and help me.' Michael followed John to the bedside. John put the still figure gently down on the bed. 'There,' he said. 'Look, Michael. She's at peace.' Michael obediently looked down at his mother She did indeed look like a small child. Her face was smooth and her hands were clasped as if in anticipation of a gift from Michael. 'Do you see, Michael? She is free from any pain. Sometimes death is a release.' Michael nodded. 'Michael?' John's voice became sharp. 'Michael.' Claire heard the doctor's voice. He was shouting at Michael. 'For God's sake, Michael, come back.' When Claire burst into the room, he was slapping Michael's face. He looked desperately at Claire. 'We'd better call a psychiatrist.'

But it was too late. That part of Michael which made him a human was gone. Away and free, he travelled the realms with his mother. Hand in hand they lived in the blues of Chagall and in the autumnal mists of a Turner landscape. All Claire had left was a polite, functioning husk.

'It's all I had anyway really,' she said to Rachel on the 'phone, and she began to cry. 'At least he didn't kill himself.'

'Shall I cancel New York and come down?' Rachel was very concerned.

'No, I think we're better off alone. Maybe it's just shock. But Rachel, his eyes . . . they're empty. It's like looking into a dark room with a brick wall behind it.'

'Claire, don't worry too much at this stage. Remember when I was out for ages. Everyone dies a little when they're hurt.'

'That's the problem, Rachel. Ever since John Rosen left, Michael's been perfectly normal. He's on the other 'phone now, making arrangements with the undertaker. You would think he was talking about a complete stranger.'

'Poor Claire. I'm sure he'll join the living again later.'

'Rachel, do me a favour and ring the Scott-Montcriefs. Tell them to ring all our friends. I'd rather they had the news by 'phone than just seeing it in *The Times*.'

'All right, Claire. I'll do that right away.'

'Thank you.'

'I wish I wasn't so far away from you.' Rachel was worried. 'I'll ring tomorrow to say good-bye. Take care, Claire. A big hug from me.' Rachel put the 'phone down. She shook her head. I hope Michael does come back. She remembered distant landscapes. Then she remembered the tiger. Go away, she said fiercely.

She took a look in the cupboard. I'll wear my black dress, she thought. She smiled to herself. I never thought I'd see the day when I would dress for effect. She ran a deep hot bath. The smell of the Savoy bath oil filled her nose. She lay back looking at her toenails. Even my feet look quite nice with nail-polish. She looked at her pubic hair lying like a half-submerged island between her legs. Liam, she thought. But first Anthea . . . I wonder what she wants?'

Anthea was very direct. She was a little taken back by Rachel's newly acquired self-confidence. Gone was the scrawny, nail-biting housewife whose progress was predictable from morning to night. Instead, the men in the American Bar all looked up when Rachel walked through the door. Anthea had already ordered herself a drink at the bar. She saw Rachel coming across the room, and was suddenly aware of her own studied neatness.

Rachel, dressed in a slim-fitting grey dress with two diamond earrings, slid on to the stool beside Anthea. 'Hello,' she said, smiling at Anthea. Her huge brown eyes rested warmly on Anthea's bitter face. 'I recognize you from the newspapers.'

Anthea frowned. 'What a farce. I think I did more harm than good.'

Rachel shook her head. 'No. It wasn't you. It was those lunatic ladies. How is your friend?'

Anthea smiled. 'Last I heard, she was studying for a degree in zoology. She said she chose zoology instead of sociology because human beings weren't worth saving anymore. And when the world comes to an end, it won't be because of a bomb, but because men and women will have abandoned each other.' Anthea laughed. 'Rose's got a dose of religion as well. She reckons God'll wipe out the human race and stick to animals.'

Rachel looked seriously at her. 'Actually, Anthea, she's not as daft as she sounds.' Rachel looked around the room. It was full of pinstriped men all braying at each other. She shuddered. Rachel hated the Grill. It was very much a male watering hole. However, she had chosen to have lunch there so as to preserve the peace of the River Room for herself. 'They're dinosaurs,' she said to Anthea.

'They're all we've got,' Anthea replied. She lit a cigarette and offered one to Rachel. 'Do you smoke?'

'I used to, and I used to enjoy it. But it gave me up when I went into hospital. No thanks.'

'Rachel,' Anthea blew out a large puff of smoke. 'I've got to talk to you.'

'Your table, Madame,' the waiter interrupted.

'Thank you,' said Rachel. Anthea stubbed out her cigarette, and the two women walked past tables full of men.

Their greedy lustful eyes followed Rachel and Anthea to their table. 'Nice pair of legs on the blonde,' Rachel heard one of the men say as they passed by.

'I'm a tits-man myself,' said his partner. Their

raucous laughter could be heard above the lunchtime chatter.

Anthea began to talk as soon as they were seated. 'I know its not very usual to go and see a man's wife.'

Rachel looked at her coolly. 'But Anthea, that's what you threatened to do for the last year. Charles would never have told me if it hadn't been for you.'

Anthea's voice was aggressive. 'Well, you didn't really want him anyway.'

Rachel looked surprised. 'Is that what he told you?'

'It's true, isn't it? Look at you. You're a different person. When you were with Charles you were a scarecrow.'

Rachel smiled. 'Yes, but I didn't know I didn't want him. Don't be angry with me, Anthea. I have an awful lot to be grateful to you for. If it weren't for you, I'd probably have stayed with Charles until the day I died.' She paused. 'No . . . I don't think I'd even have lasted that long. I think I'd have ended up in a mental hospital forever, locked away in a back-ward, babbling to myself, never really understanding what went wrong.' She looked at Anthea. 'Honestly, Anthea, I really am grateful.'

'You mean you really don't want him?'

'Please, Anthea, do have Charles. He needs someone to take care of him. He's not nearly as tough as he makes out.' She sighed. 'Julia's awfully bad for him . . . for all of them really.'

Anthea looked at Rachel. 'You see, I can't pin Charles down, because he says you're going to come back to him.'

Rachel shook her head. 'I promise you I'm not. I couldn't. It wasn't you that I minded. It was the lies.' She laughed. 'Anyway, it's not all Charles's fault. I guess I'm unmarriageable.'

Anthea's mouth tightened. 'I'm not. I want to be married. I very much want to be married to Charles.'

Rachel shook her head. 'I don't believe this conversation.'

Anthea suddenly softened. 'It's good of you, Rachel . . . to see me I mean. It's funny. I've been obsessed by you for nearly three years. It's no fun being the "other woman", you know.'

Rachel touched Anthea's arm. 'I can imagine. It must have been awfully difficult. Was it you on the 'phone?'

Anthea nodded. 'I'm sorry about that. I was desperate at that time.'

'So was I. You see, I'd known for years that something was wrong. I can't explain except to describe it as a kind of hollowness. There was a huge gap in me anyway. That was nothing to do with Charles. That was to do with me. I didn't have a normal family, so I sort of made myself up. Mostly out of bits and pieces of who Charles said I was.' She made a wry face. 'He certainly didn't think much of me. But underneath that false me who had a perfect husband, two children, and a Volvo, there was a huge unmarked continent.' She grinned at Anthea. 'That's what's so exciting. Once I let go of the made-up bits, I'm free to explore myself.' She thought of Liam. 'It's all turning out to be great fun.'

'You're lucky.' Anthea's voice was bitter. 'You've had your children. But time's running out for me. I don't fancy doing what many of my friends have done. Having children on your own is a poor substitute for having a man to look after you all those vulnerable years. Anyway,' she made a face, 'the poor kids don't ask to be born bastards.'

Rachel winced. 'I was a bastard.' She looked at Anthea.

'Oh, I . . . sorry . . . I didn't . . .'

Rachel shook her head. 'No. It's an awfully ugly word, but you are right. I had a dreadful time coming to terms with the fact that my father probably just saw me as a quick orgasm in the middle of the night in a potato field. Here I sit, I'm half American, you know.'

Anthea looked surprised. 'Really?'

'Yes. My father was some unknown pilot.' She leaned back in her chair. 'Anyway, that's enough about me. Do you want coffee?'

'Yes, please.' Anthea lit a cigarette.

Rachel thought for a moment. 'Look, I'll give you a

letter for Charles. I'll tell him we've had lunch together and that I've made it quite clear to you that there is no question of me going back. Claire's lawyers say that we can have a perfectly simple divorce. As I don't want anything from him, except my furniture and bits and pieces that belonged to my aunts, there's no problem. We can share joint custody of the kids. All we have to do is send the relevant bits of paper to the clerk of the court, and then go and see the judge so that he's sure we've made proper provision for the children. And bingo – it's all over.'

Anthea sighed. 'Your bit's so easy. What about me?'

Rachel laughed. 'I can't order him to marry you, Anthea. But Charles does like his creature comforts. Julia supplies most of those.'

Anthea dropped her eyes. 'I think the au pair does the rest.'

Rachel looked at Anthea. 'Marie-Claire? Yes, I suppose so. It keeps it in the family, and Julia doesn't even have to wait up for him.'

Anthea looked anguished. 'What happens if he marries Marie-Claire? Lots of men do.'

Rachel shrugged her shoulders. 'Well, Anthea, you must admit that if you're going to play around with married men who are cheating on their wives, you have to accept the same thing can happen to you.'

'It's not a question of playing around with married men, Rachel. There aren't any other kinds of men around. If they're single, they're gay. I don't fancy being a fag hag, though plenty of my friends do it. Or . . .' she heaved a sigh, 'they're such awful wrecks nobody will marry them. Or they're already married. Not much of a choice really.'

Rachel looked at her watch. 'Good Lord. It's nearly three o'clock. I must pack, Anthea. I'm going out tonight.'

'Lucky you. I'm sitting by the 'phone.'

Rachel finished her coffee. 'That used to be me . . . I mean sitting by the 'phone, waiting for Charles to call.' Rachel escorted Anthea to the door. She saw her into a taxi. 'Good luck,' she said as she said good-bye.

Anthea smiled grimly. 'I'll need it.'

On her way back into the hotel Rachel stopped by the kiosk in the lobby and bought a *Cosmopolitan*. She took the glossy magazine upstairs with her. Funny, she thought, I never thought I'd have anything in common with all those articles. *Home and Garden* never mentioned seducing men.

She was still reading the magazine, sitting by the 'phone in her bedroom, waiting for Liam to telephone. From about seven o'clock she had felt the elation and the excitement draining away. She looked at her little carriage clock on the dressing-table. It was now eight o'clock. He's not coming, she thought. The maids had been in to turn down her bed. She threw the magazine across the room. Slowly she walked into the sitting-room and looked at herself in the mirror. The gold sheath of her dress glittered under the sitting-room lights. She took down her hair which she had so carefully styled that afternoon. She looked at her face framed by her dark thick locks. 'Bloody fool,' she said. She went into the bedroom.

Suddenly the tiger pounced. It came from nowhere. Not even a warning. She shrieked and rolled on the bed. 'Charles, Charles,' she called for help. She cried for the familiar safety of his arms. Their bed. Their lives together. Hours later, she stood by the window looking at the Thames gliding by. The water always reassured her. She imagined the barges of Elizabeth I floating slowly down the centre of the river. She could see them full of gorgeously dressed courtiers, the flash of diamonds, the music. The Thames was eternal for her. She shivered in the cold night air. There was no going back. She managed a wry smile. Anyway, if I went back now I'd have to join the queue. She did not much fancy sharing Charles with Anthea and Marie-Claire.

I'll sleep on the plane, she thought. I wonder if I'd said 'Yes' to Liam last night, would he have 'phoned tonight? She shrugged her shoulders. Too bad . . . and to think (she found herself a little shocked), to think that I put Mitsuko behind my knees. She blushed. *And* between my legs, she admitted. Oh Rachel, what would Reverend Mother say? She found herself laughing. She suddenly felt enormously hungry.

'Could you send me a bottle of Dom Perignon and a chicken salad?'

The night waiter wheeled in Rachel's supper and lowered his eyes discreetly in case Rachel was not alone. However, Rachel was quite alone in the sitting-room, curled up with her magazine. Such a pity, the waiter thought with a sigh, to see such a beautiful woman all alone.

When he left, she sipped the champagne. I know a lot about food and wine now, she thought, but almost nothing about relationships. She flicked over the pages of the magazine. Mmmm . . . That mayonnaise sounds lovely . . . 'Forty Exercises to Improve Your Orgasms,' she read aloud. 'It's not orgasms I'm short of,' she muttered. The chicken was lightly spiced and so tender it melted in her mouth. 'It's men . . . real men.' She looked at the bottle of champagne sitting in the bucket by the table. 'A toast,' she said, raising the glass. 'New York,' she said standing up. She looked at her reflection. She was still wearing her evening dress. A lovely dark-haired woman in the mirror stood with her glass raised. They saluted each other. 'To New York.'

43

When Rachel arrived in New York, her American half felt that she was coming home.

'Manny,' Rachel said as she stood in his kitchen, 'you could live in your 'fridge. It's huge.'

Manny laughed. 'As a dull old bachelor, that's what I like about living in America. Everything is huge. Larger than life, really. Even the stuff in the kitchen makes my mother's kitchen look antiquated.'

Rachel was rummaging around in his kitchen drawers. 'What on earth is this?' She waved a plastic object at him.

'That's a spaghetti spoon. You hook the spaghetti, and it catches on all those prongs.'

'You mean no more chasing it around the kitchen sink?'

Manny laughed. 'That's the general idea. You know, Rachel, you're much better than I thought you'd be. I was prepared to pick up a nervous wreck from the airport.'

Rachel smiled at him. 'Actually, Manny, I think I came down with such a crash that I sort of sorted out a lot about myself very quickly. It was almost as if I knew I was either going to come together, or I'd spend the rest of my life leaking out little bits of agony like old dolls used to leak sawdust. Plenty of women didn't put themselves together.' She paused. 'Lots of them waited for Matron or Dr Pringle . . . or just anyone to glue them back into one piece.' She shook her head. 'I knew all along it would have to be me. Mind you, I had Anna and Claire . . . and you.'

'Listen. Let me take you out to lunch. There's a really

comfortable restaurant across the road.'

Rachel looked at him. 'That's nice of you, Manny, but I'd rather just get used to being in your flat.'

'It's not a flat, Rachel.' Manny laughed affectionately. 'American is a completely different language. Actually, this is called a "loft". Originally, all this area off Washington Square was full of warehouses. These huge areas were used for storage. Then the trendies moved in, followed by the hippy-dippy 'sixties, and suddenly they became terribly fashionable.'

'Manny, don't tell me you're a trendy rabbi!'

Manny shrugged. 'I love this loft. You see, I realized at the Jewish Theological Seminary that I couldn't cheat and hide as a homosexual behind my religion. So I took a vow of celibacy.' Rachel nodded sympathetically. 'It's not easy for a rabbi. You see, rabbis, unlike priests, are supposed to be married. So I'm always being fixed up by members of the congregation with a nice Jewish princess.' He laughed. 'You'll restore my reputation among my congregation. Anyway, I'm not going to get married or have children. I get quite a good salary from my new congregation because this particular temple draws from a very mixed area here. You have the young bankers, lawyers, and doctors all in these lofts, and then you have the really poor families in awful one-room apartments, squeezed against each other, a few blocks down. So I make my living-style my relationship.'

Rachel wandered from the huge airy kitchen into the massive sitting-room. 'It's beautiful, Manny.' She looked at the polished wood floors. Persian prayer carpets lay like jewels on the floor. Huge sofas breathed comfort against the walls. An old Dutch cooking stove jutted out of the wall, the blue and white tiles contrasting with the cream of the armchairs. 'It's so peaceful.' Rachel walked over to the large French windows. 'Can I go outside?'

'Yes. I've strengthened the fire-escape.'

Rachel opened the double-glazed windows. The roar of New York frightened her. She came in again. 'Manny, it's so alive out there.'

Manny nodded. 'That's another reason I love it. If I'm depressed I just stand out there and feel the exuberance of that huge sprawling city. I can't stay depressed for long. I tell you what, Rachel, I'll order a pizza for you now, and have them deliver it. It's a real experience. They don't make them like that in England. I think it's the sweat.'

'I've never really liked pizzas,' Rachel said, 'but I'll trust you.'

'That was amazing.' Rachel wiped her mouth. She felt her stomach. 'I must have put on at least five pounds.'

Manny looked at her across the table and smiled. 'Wait 'til you try dinner.'

He spent the rest of the afternoon taking pleasure in creating a lovely surprise for her. 'No, don't get in the way, Rachel. It's your first evening in New York, and I want to make it a memorable one.' He banished her to his spare bedroom. 'Get unpacked and take a shower.'

Rachel loved the room immediately. She looked out of the window. Small dots were scurrying around the streets below her. It's really dirty, she noticed. She looked back at the room. The furniture was heavy and solid. Her bed was made of cherrywood. She ran her hands over the richness of the carving. The cover was patchwork. Simple blues and greens. The writing-desk against one wall was plain pine. A Victorian chaise-longue completed the room. Where are the cupboards, she wondered. That must be the bathroom. She pushed the door. Gosh. What luxury. Manny had provided bath oil and lots of big thick cream towels. *There* are the cupboards. Rachel saw a complete wall of hanging cupboards and shelves.

I do love bathrooms, she thought. The floor was tiled with marble. Rachel suddenly felt much in need of a shower. The aeroplane had left a sour smell to her skin.

She realized as the water bit into her body that she had just found an amazing new toy. That's what Jane was talking about. She grinned. It does feel good. She had unhooked the shower head and was pointing it between her legs. She wondered if she should go on.

No, she thought. I'm too tired. I'd probably fall asleep at the dinner table. But if I don't find a man, I'll get one of these when I get back to London, she promised herself. Maybe, she thought hopefully, I can have both.

'Oh Manny. It's really lovely.' Rachel was standing in the doorway. Manny had faithfully recreated an English dining-room. It took Rachel back to meals with Aunt Bea and Aunt Emily. Her eyes filled with tears. Manny had already lit the candles. The Sheraton dining-table glowed in the soft light. The chairs, with their Regency striped brocade, sat stiffly in order.

Manny smiled at her. 'I do love this room. You know, as a little Jew-boy at school, I always swore that one day I'd live somewhere where at least I'd be tolerated, and also that I would have a room like this.'

'Those paintings are gorgeous.'

Manny looked at the quiet peace of the English countryside. 'That's the way I like to remember England,' he said. 'Those are done by a little-known school of Norfolk painters. By "little known",' he added hurriedly, 'I mean not as well-known as Constable, for example.' He'd remembered just how much each one cost.

'Try the gefilte fish,' Manny said over dinner.

Rachel had already finished her first course of borscht with sour cream. 'It looks awful.'

Manny giggled. 'Tact was never one of your virtues, Rachel.'

She wrinkled her nose. 'I know. Anyway, you still giggle.' She tasted the round ball of fish on her wedgewood plate. 'Actually it's nice.' She looked at Manny, surprised.

'Good. I'm glad you like it. New York is full of wonderful Jewish delicatessens.' They chattered away to each other for the rest of the meal, eating their way through plates of blintzes and kugel.

After dinner, Rachel lay on one of the big sofas in the sittingroom. Manny was sprawled on the floor with his head on a soft velvet cushion. They were listening to

Beethoven. There was a peace broken only by the sound of the dishwasher in the kitchen. 'I thought,' Manny began, 'I thought I'd have to listen to hours of tales about Charles.'

Rachel looked at him. 'Don't worry. I did all that to Anna, and to a certain extent Claire.' She moved her head and looked at Manny. 'I'm here for myself. I don't need a refuge any more. I want to have a really good time.'

'You shall, my dear. Come on. Bedtime. Tomorrow we'll hit the town.'

Rachel yawned. 'Tomorrow I would like to do all the tourist things there are to do.'

'Okay,' Manny said. 'We'll do it all.'

'I never want to see another skyscraper as long as I live. Oh, my feet.'

Rachel slipped off her shoes under the table.

Manny smiled.

'You did say *everything*.'

Rachel scowled. 'I didn't mean all in one day. We've done . . . let me see . . . the Statue of Liberty, Fifth Avenue . . .' She sighed. 'Just imagine – me, Rachel Cavendish, at Tiffany's and the Lincoln Center . . .'

'We're going back there tomorrow,' said Manny. 'I've asked a couple of friends to join us. I got tickets for *La Bohème*.'

Rachel clasped her hands. 'I've never been to an opera before. Charles didn't like that sort of thing. How wonderful! Oh, Manny. Look at the view from up here.' They were sitting at a window table in the Rainbow Room, high above Rockefeller Plaza.

Manny followed Rachel's gaze. 'Yes, we're sixty-five floors up.'

'It's all like a magic fairy land. Bloomingdale's chocolate department, the World Trade Center – all those busy little helicopters. They looked like bees landing on their huge concrete flowers.' She gave a long sigh. 'I never realized how provincial I was. Those New York women are terrifying.' All around them she noticed women were talking loudly, spilling cigarette ash everywhere, and gesticulating widely.

'They are a little over-powering.' Manny agreed. 'They're all ferocious business women that you see in a place like this.'

'But where are the men?'

Manny looked around. 'I see what you mean. These sort of women don't actually have men around. They all fled to the hills years ago. If they are with a man, it's usually because the man is gay.'

Rachel looked again. There was a sprinkling of rather solid-looking married men with what could be wives – Probably mistresses, she thought – and many more very feminized men. On the whole, the women were dining either alone or with each other.

'You have to remember,' Manny explained, 'women in this country got into the job market long before English women.'

Rachel looked at him. 'God, Manny. I hope this doesn't happen in England.'

Manny raised his eyebrows. 'It will. Most men won't deal with these so-called "liberated women".'

Rachel nodded. 'That's true. Certainly of someone like Charles. Oh Manny,' she turned to him suddenly, 'why on earth do you have to be gay? It's such a waste. You'd be a wonderful husband and such a good father.'

Manny's eyes were clouded with pain. 'I think in my case it was more to do with my relationship with Ruth.' Both Rachel and Manny had been drinking Tom Collins, a speciality of the restaurant. Manny was on his third. 'You can't imagine how claustrophobic my relationship was. When my father was away on business, she used to sleep on the spare bed in my room. I realized when I was about thirteen that even the smell of her in the room in the morning excited me. I'd go into the bathroom and sit there with this damn erection. Finally,' he looked at Rachel, 'I locked her out one day. She was very hurt, but I couldn't tell her why. I stay away from her as much as I can.'

Rachel looked puzzled. 'But she didn't mean any harm. I always remembered how loving she was.'

'That's it. That's exactly the problem. She did love

me, and she would have been horrified . . .' He corrected himself, 'She would be horrified now if she knew I was a homosexual. She's still hoping for a rebitzin as a daughter-in-law. That's what a rabbi's wife is called. And grandchildren.' Manny broke off as the waiter brought their steaks.

'I've never tasted meat like this.' Rachel dug her teeth into her steak. 'Just look at the size of it. Anyway, Manny, go on. Why do you think she was so possessive?'

Manny gave a short laugh. 'Lots of women are like her. She was very powerful, very bright, and very bored. She and Julia made a pretty terrifying couple.'

Rachel was thinking of Charles. 'You know, Manny, I don't think Charles even likes women very much.'

Manny thought about it. He swallowed a mouthful of steak and said, 'It's hard not to be afraid of other women when it was your own mother who first betrayed you.'

'What do you mean?' Rachel sipped from her Tom Collins.

'Just that. I suppose my mother found my father very boring. All he could think about was business, so she turned to me. First she was a mother to my child, and then she was a lover to my emerging man. That's where I feel the anger. A mother would kiss her son with love, not longing.'

There was such pain in Manny's voice that Rachel changed the subject. They took a yellow cab to Washington Square and walked back to the loft from there. Rachel was frightened. The cab-driver gave a long and lurid account of several recent murders in the area. Steam wafted round her ankles from the manholes in the road. Vagrants shuffled by, clutching paper bags full of alcohol and their secret belongings. Everywhere the pavement was covered in old cardboard boxes. She was glad when they turned the corner of Beaker Street. Manny opened the door.

'Come on. Only six flights,' he said. Rachel puffed her way up the stairs. 'I'll make you some Irish coffee and bring it to you in bed,' Manny called from the kitchen.

'All right. That would be lovely.' Rachel went into her room and put on her nightdress. She was sitting up in bed with her knees under her chin when Manny carried the two silver goblets over to the bed. They sat amicably together, sipping the strong whiskey and coffee. 'You've got the cream right. I can't ever do that,' Rachel said. Manny looked suddenly very tired and very vulnerable. Rachel finished the drink. She looked very steadily at him. 'You can spend the night in my bed, Manny.' She sensed his upset over his recent confession. He was a very private man. She smiled. 'I'm not at all a predatory woman. We can just cuddle each other.'

Manny looked at her. 'I was hoping you'd ask.'

He look off his clothes quite unselfconsciously and slid into her bed. They lay with their arms about each other. Manny began to cry. 'It's all right,' Rachel whispered. 'I'm here.' Soon they were both fast asleep, locked in each other's arms.

Rachel woke before Manny. She got quietly out of bed and went into the kitchen. She looked in the 'fridge. She took six croissants out of a bag. She made a pot of coffee and carried the tray into the bedroom.

Manny was awake. He looked like a vulnerable small boy. 'Do you know, Rachel,' he said, his eyes big with surprise, 'you're the first woman I've ever spent the night with.'

Rachel laughed. 'Well, you're only the second man. Was it awful?'

'Don't be silly, Rachel. Just to cuddle up to another human being who cares is a miracle.'

Rachel nodded her head. 'I do miss that. I'm used to sleeping next to a warm breathing body.' She put the tray on her bedside table and climbed back into bed. Manny helped himself to a croissant. Rachel lay back and breathed out deeply. 'Maybe a day will come when men and women can get into bed together and relax.'

Manny looked wistful. 'Maybe a time will come when people can get into bed with each other without demanding anything from each other. You know, Rachel, it's not sex I miss so much. I can always have a wet dream. It's much more the need for a warm loving partner.'

'I know what you mean. I miss that too. Now that I'm suddenly on my own, I feel great icy drafts of loneliness.' Rachel bit into her croissant. 'Sometimes if I'm walking down the street, I feel an unaccountable fluttering inside. It's like a trapped bird trying to get out. Then it feels as if the sky is going to fall on my head. I usually bolt into a shop.' She laughed. 'People must think I'm mad.'

'No. Lots of people feel like that. I comfort many of my bereft congregants. You describe exactly what they feel, only they use different images. It was lovely to be comforted by you, Rachel.' They smiled at each other. 'What shall we do today?'

Rachel thought. 'I'd like to just explore around the Village.'

'All right. I'll go and shower, and we can go. Have a rest this afternoon because we'll be late tonight.'

'Oh yes . . . the opera.'

They spent the day poking around the many rather tatty shops in the district. 'Oysters,' said Rachel. She dragged Manny into the small raw-fish bar. 'They're much cheaper than in England.' They sat with a bottle of Pouilly Fuissé and two dozen large, sea-swollen oysters. 'Perfect,' Rachel breathed. 'Just perfect. Here I am, in the middle of Greenwich Village, eating oysters.' She had two large carrier bags full of Big Apple T-shirts and jeans for Sarah and Dominic.

Rachel found herself sitting in the grand opera auditorium in the Lincoln Center. By the time Mimi had coughed her way into an early grave, Rachel was incoherent. 'Manny,' she sobbed, 'you didn't tell me people paid large sums of money just to be racked with grief.'

Leah , one of Manny's friends, put her arms round Rachel. 'Hush,' she said, half laughing, 'I thought the English were supposed to be cold and unfeeling.'

Rachel gave a long unladylike sniff. She mopped at her eyes. 'I've only got to look at the *Reader's Digest* and I howl. As for *Lassie* . . .' she shook her head, 'I have to be carried out.'

'Then I guess we're lucky this time. Here. Take my kleenex. You've saturated yours.'

'Thanks, Leah.' Rachel looked at her appreciatively.

Leah was a very striking-looking woman. She was fashionably thin with a huge hook nose and thick jet-black hair. But it was the fire in her eyes that caught Rachel's attention. Although her eyes were deep-set, they were not small. Rather, they slanted upwards. The expression on Leah's face caught Rachel's heart for a moment. There was such tenderness in her gaze. Rachel looked down at her mangled handkerchief. Somewhere a distant memory stirred.

44

A few days later she was lying in Leah's arms. 'I know what it is,' Rachel said to Leah. 'I've always been looking for that moment when I used to lie beside my Aunt Emily when I was a little girl.' She sighed. 'Life has never been as simple or as safe since then.' She raised herself on one elbow. 'Leah, I don't remember much of what happened last night.' Rachel was embarrassed. 'I'm not used to American cocktails.'

Leah laughed and stretched. 'Well, darling,' Leah was lying naked on top of her duvet, 'after dinner, everyone left. You told Manny you wanted to stay and talk to me. So Manny went home, and then you asked me to make love to you.'

Suddenly it all came flooding back. Rachel grinned. 'Yes. Now I remember. We were laughing a lot.'

Leah smiled back. 'You had a terrific climax.' Leah shook her head. 'Then you opened your eyes, looked at me very seriously, and said, "Thank God for that." I asked you what you meant. You were almost asleep. You just managed to say, "I'm prick-related", and then you began to snore.'

Rachel was mortified. 'Leah.' She leaned forward and kissed her on the mouth, 'Honestly, I didn't mean to hurt you.'

Leah pushed her away gently. 'You didn't hurt me, Rachel. I do understand. You were probably married to a man who spent his time insisting that you were either frigid or a "dyke", as he would put it, if you didn't come across. It happens to lots of women. How do you feel this morning?'

'Great, funnily enough.' Rachel sat up. 'I've always

wondered what it would be like to make love to another woman. Now I know.'

'What *was* it like?' Leah asked, amused.

'Like doing it myself, but much less lonely. I like the softness of your breasts, but . . .' she hesitated.

'You can tell me, Rachel. We're friends first, remember?' Leah took Rachel's hand.

'I missed the otherness of a man. I mean, I felt as though a large component – I think that's the word – was missing.'

Leah nodded. 'That's how I felt when I was married. For years I struggled with a feeling that what I shared sexually with my husband was too compatible. I was looking for an "otherness" in someone else.' Leah put her hands behind her head. Her dark olive body lay in a fluid line along the yellow duvet cover. 'I tried other men, even during our marriage, but it was never there. Finally we ceased making love all together. Then I met Kate.' Her face softened at the memory. 'Then I really knew what love was.'

'What happpened to Kate?' Rachel asked.

'She died.' Leah looked across the room to the photograph of her lover. 'She was a publisher. I met her through my husband. We fell in love. It wasn't at all a fashionable relationship in those days like it is now.' She shook her head. 'I lost custody of my two kids because the judge said lesbians could not be fit mothers.' Her voice shook at the memory of holding on to Kate in the busy courtroom. She was screaming 'Give me back my kids!' The two solemn-faced teenagers looked at her with disgust.

'Well, at least that's all over now. Both kids spend a lot of their time here, but they were bitter for years. Still, Kate was a wonderful ten years of my life. She'll be dead two years this Thanksgiving.'

'Do you know why you prefer women?' Rachel asked.

Leah leaped to her feet. 'Hang on. I'll get a cigarette.' She came back into the room smoking a Marlboro. 'I spent years on that question, but when it comes down to it, I don't think I care. Kate was my choice. Not because she was a woman. She could have been a man.

There was something in Kate that was unique for me. She felt the same about me. It was entirely unimportant to us what shape our genitals happened to be. That's what made it so hard for us to bear other people's perception of our relationship. It was ours – private and personal.' She sounded angry.

'What about gay groups?'

Leah stopped and looked at Rachel. 'You can't take personal relationships and make them into a political movement. It doesn't work. Look what's happened between men and women.' Rachel rolled her eyes. Leah laughed bitterly. 'The great hope here in America was that men would change alongside women, and new relationships would be forged that would allow women their rightful space in the world. Here all that's happened is that men are so hostile to women and so threatened, that most women who have achieved independence find themselves alone. Or, and I'm not altogether happy about this, they turn to each other for comfort, and then agree that men are the enemy. There *is* no enemy, Rachel. Do you understand that?'

Rachel laughed uncomfortably. 'I'm finding it hard not to be bitter and angry with Charles.' To say nothing of Liam, she thought.

'Think, Rachel. You chose Charles and I'll bet for all the wrong reasons. Women can't corral a man to build their nests and then holler when they don't change.'

'Why should they change? Charles doesn't have to lift a finger. He's got his mother, Anthea, and the au pair at his beck and call.' Rachel snorted. 'He doesn't even have to blow his own nose.'

'Yes, but who provides the support system to nurture his disgusting narcissism?'

'Other women, I suppose.'

'Exactly. There isn't much hope for men until women put their own house in order. That means every woman. Too many of our sisters charged around organizing the world, and forgot the huge turd in their backyard with the six-pack in his hand.'

'You're right,' Rachel laughed. 'Still, Leah, you know, I do want a warm loving relationship with someone. After last night, I realize that I'm basically attracted sexually to men, not women.' She stopped to think. 'Actually, although I realize I'm not gay, it cleared up a lot of negative feelings about myself. Again, they were just Charles's feelings about me. But I do realize it's wiped out retreating into a gay commune or something like that as an option. That does make me feel lonely. Because I do find, Leah, that I much prefer the company of women. Very few men are as interesting or as honest.' She suddenly missed Jane.

'Poor men,' said Leah. 'They're such emotional cripples. But it's no good for us to kick away their crutches. They'll have to give them up themselves. Come on, Rachel. We New Yorkers talk too much. Enough philosophizing. Let's get up. I'll take you for a walk in Central Park. We'll meet Manny for lunch. I know a wonderful restaurant in China Town. Here, I'll lend you a pair of jeans and a sweater.'

Rachel found herself avoiding Manny's inquiring gaze. The three of them were sitting at Peng's on East 44th Street. 'Try the minced squab and water chestnuts,' Manny said.

'No, I think Rachel should have the Dragon and Phoenix dish.' Leah said firmly.

'What's that?' Rachel asked.

'It's a special dish made from chicken and lobster.'

'But,' Manny looked innocently at Leah, 'I know Rachel would like the little bamboo basket that goes with the squab.' Rachel nodded.

Leah laughed. 'I give in, but I get to choose the wine.'

To think I've shared a bed with Manny and made love to another woman, Rachel said silently to herself.

Leah looked amused. 'Dreaming, Rachel?'

Rachel blushed and hoped Leah couldn't read her mind: I do feel odd sitting here with Leah fully clothed when just a few hours ago we were naked in bed, she thought. She felt very close to both Manny and Leah.

The restaurant was crowded. Rachel couldn't get used to the noise. 'Do all Americans shout like this?' Rachel asked Manny.

'No, Rachel. It's New Yorkers.'

'We all do a lot of yelling,' Leah butted in.

'And interrupting,' Manny teased. 'Really, Leah, you'll have to learn some English reticence.'

Leah shook her head. 'Look, Manny, I'll admire your fine old historic buildings, but not your emotionally constipated countrymen.' She shuddered. 'I spent a summer in England once. It rained all the time . . .'

'Not *all* the time.' Rachel was laughing.

'And,' Leah continued, 'I was propositioned in an art gallery by a man with no chin and buck teeth.'

'Really?' said Rachel. 'I'd have thought you would have frightened an Englishman to death.'

Leah laughed. 'Imagine having a good screw with someone who says, "I say, how about a spot of lunch?" ' She shook her head. 'I thought it only happened in the movies.'

'Unfortunately it isn't just in old films,' Rachel said dryly. 'Our English public-school system really does produce a sort of strange eunuch. It's improved since I was at school, but honestly, Leah, you can't imagine what an awful upbringing it is for a small boy. At least the French and Italians are all allowed to shriek, but we have to keep everything bottled up. Women in England are terrified of being called aggressive or loud. Maggie Thatcher's called "the Iron Maiden", and she hardly ever raises her voice. She once admitted she cried. The newspapers were horrified.'

'That's why I choose to live in New York.' Manny looked at Rachel. 'Now can you see why?'

Rachel nodded. 'It's like being in a champagne bottle here.' She was getting mildly drunk. 'I feel like one of the little golden bubbles bouncing along with hundreds of other little bubbles.'

'Hey, what do you want to do this afternoon?' Leah asked.

'What about Times Square?'

'Oh Rachel,' Manny protested, 'honestly. It's not one of the nicest places in the world. It's worse than Soho in February.'

'Doesn't matter. You have to remember that almost

my entire knowledge of the outside world was created in the cinema at Lyme Regis. Most of those films were American. We didn't jitterbug at the malt-shop, exactly. We had rock and roll in the gym with a nun to see that nothing got out of hand.'

Leah laughed. 'In my day it was padded shoulders and Russian tea rooms.'

'That's a good idea,' Manny said. 'Let's go. I want to show Rachel *the* Russian Tea Room.' He looked at Rachel. 'It's right next to Carnegie Hall.'

'Lovely, but I must get home in time to ring Claire and the children.'

'Do it tomorrow. You rang yesterday. Remember?' Manny reminded her.

'To tell you the truth, Manny, I'd forgotten. I had rather a lot to drink.'

'You can say that again,' Leah agreed. All three of them laughed.

Times Square was as tatty as Rachel had imagined. 'I don't care,' she said, looking at Leah. 'Here I am, standing by the Times Tower. You can't imagine what that feels like. I always wanted to be Doris Day, you know.' Rachel pushed the end of her nose upwards with her finger. 'I used to spend ages trying to get my nose to look like a little snub American nose.'

'You look more like an English pug when you do that,' Leah joked.

'Leah, I just realized. I've left my evening dress at your place. I'm wearing your jeans and we're going to the Russian Tea Room tonight. I'd better get my act together, as you say in New York.'

'Okay. Let's go back to my place,' said Manny. He hailed a cab.

Manny offered to make tea for both women. While he was in his kitchen, Leah put her arms around Rachel and looked at her very seriously. 'How do you feel now, Rachel?'

'A bit odd,' Rachel confessed. 'I feel sort of confused . . . I suppose going to bed with another woman was always considered beyond the pale in my life. If Charles was really furious, the worst insult he could think of would be to call me or any of my friends a lesbian. Actually, it was usually "dyke", or "faggot" if he was angry with a man. It's difficult to do something that felt loving and warm . . .' She paused. 'I want you to know, Leah, it wasn't just therapy for my soul. Being with you last night gave me back a lot of good feelings I had about myself as a child before I met Charles.'

Leah smiled gently. 'Don't keep apologizing, Rachel. Everyone has to define their own sexuality for themselves. The problem is that far too many people refuse to take that responsibility. Instead, they look themselves up in books or watch films. I thought I was Lauren Bacall for years, and it was okay to get slapped about by men.'

Manny came in carrying a lovely Japanese teapot. 'I always wanted to be James Dean,' he said.

Leah took her arms from around Rachel and sat down on the sofa. 'Given the circumstances,' she said, 'I'll let Manny be mother and pour.'

Manny grinned. 'I thought you didn't like stereotyped role-play.'

Rachel laughed. 'Shut up, you two. You're like an old married couple.'

'We go back a long way, don't we, Manny?'

He nodded. Rachel looked at them. 'I hope I'll aways know that you both are in New York, and even if I can't see you often, in my mind's eye I can be with you when I want to. You know, when I get back to London I'm going to get a flat. Something like this would be ideal for me, and you're both welcome to stay.'

Leah made a face. 'I can't stand England. I told you, it's too cold. I keep wanting to pinch the passers-by just to get a reaction. I must be the only American who doesn't swoon over the idea of London. But thanks, anyway. I'll bear it in mind. There's nothing like six weeks of rain for improving my writing techniques.'

Manny and Leah got into a long literary argument. Rachel was soon bored. She went into her room and lay down to sleep. I can't wait to tell Claire, she thought.

She imagined Anna's face. She imagined Reverend Mother's face. And then she fell asleep.

The rest of the time passed in a haze. If Manny was busy, Leah took Rachel out. Sometimes all three of them were together. On one never-to-be-forgotten occasion, Leah took both Manny and Rachel to dinner with some friends. The man, Paul Horowitz, was a well-known writer. His wife Emily was 'into art'. Rachel had never seen paintings quite like it. 'What is that?' she asked Emily.

'It's a prick.' Emily beamed. 'See? It's by Franz, a friend of mine. She intended to portray male domination. See? That's the White House.'

'Ah yes.' Rachel peered closely. She could see the building nestling among the hair of the scrotum.

'Leah, do you remember the ideological struggle we had deciding whether the prick should be circumcized or not?'

Leah laughed. 'Thank God most of us grew out of that phase.'

Rachel was curious. 'Who won?'

'Oh Franz did.' Emily was a big woman with a warm laugh. 'Come on, Rachel. Let's go into dinner.'

Rachel had almost forgotten the outside world existed. So far, she had been whirled around New York by an energetic Leah or gentle kindly Manny. The three of them lived among the seething people of New York using the crowd as a backdrop in their pleasure of each other's company. Suddenly Rachel realized, as she sat at the immaculately laid table, that her magic time was nearly over. The world wasn't made up of Annas, or Claires, or Mannys, not even Leahs. The world was really ninety-five per cent populated with people like Paul Horowitz.

'We've been very worried here about your Labour Party,' Paul announced. 'I've been watching your left wing.' He paused. 'The only solution for your country is a socialist government that will effectively redistribute the wealth of the nation.'

Rachel looked apprehensive. 'Oh I hope not,' she said. 'All my money is inherited.'

Paul's nostrils flared. 'Do you vote Conservative?'

'I don't vote.' Rachel became flustered. 'I don't do anything about politics. I sort of know that there's a right and a left, and the rest are rather nasty and best left in the woodshed.' She laughed selfconsciously.

Paul and Emily looked at her. 'Come on, Paul,' Leah burst in, 'keep your political opinions to yourself. You're a closet Republican anyway. How much were these crystal glasses?' She held up an exquisite Georgian wine goblet.

Rachel spoke before Paul could answer. 'I should say about a hundred and twenty pounds each in England. That particular design is very rare.' Rachel looked at Paul. 'Did you get a complete set?' Paul nodded. 'Then you can double the price.'

'A hundred and twenty pounds . . . each?' Manny whistled. 'That's a lot kreplach.'

The evening lumbered to its end. It seemed that Paul and Emily knew everyone there was to know in New York, and that they spent most of their time eating in restaurants and going to the theatre. Paul was sitting next to Rachel, so at one point in the evening he was forced to make conversation with her. Manny and Leah were locked in combat with Emily over a new book on feminism, and Rachel, who had heard enough feminism from Anna to last a lifetime, was grateful for an opportunity to relax.

'Do you like New York?' Paul was speaking very quietly. Rachel had to bend her head to hear him. She smiled and nodded amiably. 'You're a very beautiful young woman, you know.' He was not smiling. 'Beautiful young women don't have to know anything about politics – just how to please a man.' Rachel sat up. Paul continued. 'Now, I know how to please a woman.' He stared at her. 'I make sure that Emily has an orgasm every night. What do you think of that?'

Rachel was stumped. I really can't say 'how bloody boring' at his own dinner-table, she thought. 'I think I'd like some more wine,' she said at last. She proceeded to get very drunk.

Manny and Leah had to carry her to the taxi. Rachel

was hooting with laughter. 'What's so funny?' Manny asked as he propped her up in the taxi.

'Paul gives Emily an orgasm every night . . . Poor Emily.'

Leah smiled. 'What Paul doesn't know is that Emily has a girlfriend.'

Manny looked at Leah. 'Franz?' he said. Leah grinned. 'So he never guessed about the picture?'

'Nope. It cracks me up.'

Rachel looked at Leah. 'Does everybody cheat?'

Leah shook Rachel gently. She could hear Rachel's laughter was about to turn to tears. 'Almost everybody, Rachel. Don't be so hard on the world and yourself. People don't cheat because they're bad, They're mostly sad.'

'I suppose so.' Rachel clutched her head. 'I think I'm going to be sick.' Leah held her hand against Rachel's forehead as they crouched in the gutter. Manny was hovering about.

The cab-driver looked disgusted. 'Gimme the fair. I'm not taking no drunk dames in my cab.'

'I'm awfully sorry, Leah.' Rachel was retching.

'Don't give it a thought,' Leah said. 'Lean over a bit more – that's what friends are for.'

Rachel looked up at the Christmas decorations. The whole atmosphere of the Russian Tea Room delighted her. 'How lovely to have Christmas all year round!' she exclaimed.

'Have the Siberian Pelmeny. They only serve it today,' Manny said.

It was Rachel's last night in New York. A farewell dinner at the Russian Tea Room was her choice, because she had so enjoyed her first dinner there. Manny was sipping an exotic drink. 'What's that?' Rachel asked.

'It's a Harvey Wallbanger.'

'I do love American cocktails.'

'I want a borscht blinis.' Leah ordered for them all.

One of the Cossack barmen came over to their table. 'I look at you, beautiful lady,' he said to Rachel, 'I think

I make a cocktail for your lovely mouth.' Rachel smiled. 'Ah!' The barman threw out his arms. 'What teeth! What smile! Like the madonna . . .' He gestured at Manny and Leah. 'What love I feel in my heart for such beauty.' He shot off to the bar. 'I come back!' he yelled over his shoulder.

'Is he really Russian, Leah?' Rachel looked a little anxious.

'He's an Italian with a Russian accent. Don't worry, darling. They all behave like that.' She smiled at Rachel.

In a moment the ebullient waiter was back. 'What's your name?' he asked Rachel.

'What's yours?' She asked warily.

'Giorgio,' he beamed at her.

'Rachel Cavendish.' She warmed to his smile.

'Drink,' he said as he placed a cocktail glass in front of her.

She sipped it. 'That's lovely, Giorgio.' She handed the glass to Leah to taste.

'Cavendish Cocktail,' Giorgio announced to the whole restaurant. The diners fell silent. People were staring at Giorgio. He raised the glass. 'New cocktail – we all drink to most beautiful woman in New York.' Rachel was covered in confusion. Everyone was staring at her. Leah and Manny were amused.

'How does it feel being Belle of the Ball?' Leah asked.

'Very odd,' Rachel replied. 'I've been a nobody for years. Giorgio,' she said, 'how do you make my drink?'

'Strawberry liqueur for your lips,' he smiled at her, 'vodka for your pure fire, fresh orange juice for your innocence.'

Rachel was laughing. 'Oh come on, Giorgio.'

He grinned. 'I slice a strawberry and put crushed ice.' Suddenly he let out a huge roar and began to dance wildly between the tables. The other barmen and waiters joined in. Several diners left their seats and the restaurant was full of swirling, singing people.

Only in New York, thought Rachel.

Leah smiled and put her hand on Rachel's arm. 'We'll miss you,' she said.

A lump came into Rachel's throat. 'Leah, you'll never know how much you've done for me.'

Leah nodded. 'I believe people's paths cross each other. You can do another person good or evil. The difficulty for most of us is learning to let go.' She smiled.

Rachel nodded. 'I'm still having a struggle. I've got rid of Charles physically, but emotionally he's still around, mostly disapproving of me, I'm afraid.'

Leah shook her head. 'You needed his disapproval for a long time, Rachel, if you think about it. Lots of women let their husbands disapprove of them, because if they feel worthless, they don't have to fight their way out of that particular hole. I was like that for years.'

'Sometimes it's rougher fighting your way out than just giving in and going on,' Rachel said. She sighed. 'If Charles hadn't told me, I'd still be in Richmond. It's an ill wind . . .' She was interrupted by Giorgio.

'Dance, beautiful lady! Dance!' He swung her off her feet.

45

Claire had sent a Savoy limousine to collect Rachel from Heathrow Airport. Rachel sank thankfully into the thick upholstery. She looked out of the windows. I never realized how ugly the drive from the airport into London is, she thought. Suddenly she felt sad that people who flocked to England should see London like a beautiful woman wearing a dirty petticoat. Never mind, she comforted herself. The Savoy is its own city. Once I'm inside, I'll feel safe again. She was surprised at how vulnerable she had felt once she left the warm company of Manny and Leah.

The man next to her on the aeroplane had persistently asked questions until Rachel had turned her back on him. Thank God I can afford first class, she had thought. She remembered how cramped she once was with Charles and the children on their flight to France. Idly she wondered if she should wear a ring on her wedding finger. It would save me from louts like this, she thought. But then she remembered the freedom she had felt when she handed the ring to Charles. No more slavery. She looked at her finger, still indented from years of wearing the thick gold band.

I belong to me now, she thought as the car slid into the courtyard of the hotel.

'Welcome back, Madame.' The doorman took her suitcases and followed her into the reception area. What a change, he thought. Five months and the little mouse had become a princess. He was particularly fond of Rachel. He beamed at her. 'Nice weather for the time of year,' he said.

Rachel smiled, remembering Leah's dictum that English men were emotional cripples. 'I missed you all very much,' she said.

The doorman's eyes misted over. He cleared his throat with embarrassment. 'Thank you, Madame,' he said as he pocketed his tip. Women, he thought as he returned to his place outside the front door. Never know what they're going to say next. He stood impassively staring into space. She missed me, he thought. He failed to nag the new doorman.

Hello? The old man's getting soft in the head, the younger man thought. I'll have his job soon. He darted into the traffic signalling for a taxi.

Claire was in the sitting-room reading when Rachel let herself into the suite. 'Darling! You look marvellous!'

'Do I!' Rachel glanced at the mirror above the fireplace. 'I've had such a good time, Claire. I feel as if I've been away for ages. New York was like running away with a circus.' She stopped and looked at Claire. 'You look awful. Is Michael any better?'

Claire shook her head. 'It's too soon to tell, but I think he'll recover as far as the rest of the world could tell. But for me, or people who knew him well, part of him – the Michael we all knew – died that day. He's given up the Foreign Office and he says he's going to live down there.'

'What are you going to do, Claire?'

Claire thought for a while. 'I'll stay will him, Rachel. As long as I can stay here when I need a break, I'll be okay. I can't stay buried in the country. Michael can occupy himself hunting and fishing, but I'm not the sort of woman to enjoy country life. Michael and I are used to each other.' She smiled a thin wintery smile.

Rachel knelt by Claire's chair. 'Don't you miss being loved? I mean hugged and kissed?' She remembered the warmth she felt from Manny and Leah. 'I can't do without it, Claire. I need to feel love for someone. I know Charles didn't love me back, but I need to give love unconditionally. I can see it now,' Rachel laughed, 'I'll end my days with four smelly poodles and a teacosy on my head.'

Claire smiled. 'I'm not like you, Rachel. I never did feel as passionately about life or about Michael. We care for each other, and that's good enough for me. Sometimes, if I see a particularly good painting or a perfectly cut diamond, I do feel a surge of emotion; but people,' Claire shook her head, 'I gave up on them when I was a little girl. Not you of course, Rachel,' Claire said hurriedly. 'You've always been different. Actually,' she smiled at Rachel who was stretched out beside her, 'you're good fo me. You and all your messy feelings. They bring me down to earth.'

Rachel crossed her arms under her head. 'Feelings,' she snorted. 'It's going to take me months to sort out this present lot. Do you know, I slept with a woman when I was in New York?'

Claire's eyebrows arched. 'Did you, Rachel? What was it like?'

'Lovely,' Rachel said. She sighed. 'You know, Claire, it would be so easy just to pack men in and live with someone like Leah. It's not anything to do with the sex. It's more to do with comfort.' She paused. 'If Leah and I were together, we fitted. I noticed especially when we were doing things like cooking. If Charles was in the kitchen, he was always in the way. If he wasn't in the way, I'd be careful I wasn't standing on his ego. Looking back, I realize life for me was a minefield. No wonder I bit my nails.'

Claire nodded. 'I've often thought I'd like to make love to another woman. Funny, you'd have thought it would be me not you that would have at least tried it. I've done most things in my life. Maybe I'm frightened of what I'd find out about myself. I need my fortress.'

'Actually, it cleared up a lot for me. Sad, in a way. The idea of living with a lover who was a woman was always a comfort. But I realized that night with Leah that I actually find a man's body more erotic.' Rachel shifted her position on the floor.

'I think I'm always looking for Aunt Emily,' she sighed. 'Her breasts were so safe.'

Claire was sitting upright in her chair. Her face was

grey with strain and her fists clenched. 'At least you had an Aunt Emily,' she said.

The next four months were hectic. Claire and Rachel combed the streets of Chelsea looking for a flat. Rachel sold the house in Devon for £268,000. She auctioned off most of the contents, which brought her another £100,000. She finally decided to buy one of the rather gloomy cavernous flats in Beaufort Street. 'It does have four bedrooms. It doesn't cost the earth like the modern flats, and I can see the river if I hang out of the window by my toes,' she told Anna on the 'phone. 'How's Sam?'

'He's sprouting teeth and he yells a lot,' Anna said. 'Hurry up and buy the flat. I'm dying to come and see you. Julian has asked me to let him have Sam for a weekend, so I can have time off and be a human again.'

Rachel laughed. 'I told you. It's a full-time job. Remember all the times you used to nag me about being a boring housewife?'

'Shut up, Rachel. I don't need to be reminded.' She laughed. 'You know, I found myself telling the kennel maid that Sam was eating carrots. Me . . . having nothing to talk about but my child's eating habits. I always swore I'd kill myself before I did a thing like that. Mum's lucky. She just potters in and out and loves Sam. I have to deal with the two ends of him that leak.' Her voice softened. 'But you know, Rachel, he's got a fabulous smile. Shit, I can hear him now. Must go, Rachel. He's fallen over.'

Rachel smiled as she put the 'phone down. She remembered Ashley Road and the times she had to put the 'phone down in a hurry. That precious link to the outside world. She ran her fingers through her hair. No crumbs now, she thought. She still couldn't see a tin of baked beans on a shelf without shuddering. Still, there were good memories. Just after the children were bathed and ready for bed, their clean little faces shining, their little fat hands reaching for a kiss. She smiled to herself.

* * *

Even Dominic was pleased with the flat. 'Dad said you'd buy something too expensive.' He looked around the empty kitchen. 'It's a bit dark, but it's very central. I might stay sometimes. It's a bore getting out to Richmond late at night.'

Sarah was clattering in and out of the bedrooms. 'Mummy, can I have this one?'

Rachel looked at her. 'No, Sarah. That's my room. It's the biggest. I can see the river from that window. Why don't you have the one next door?'

Sarah made a face. 'I want the big room.'

'Sarah,' Rachel's voice was firm, 'it's my flat and that's my bedroom. Okay?'

Sarah looked at her. 'Okay. Can I have a rocking-chair?'

'Of course.' Rachel smiled.

'Won't it be fun?' Sarah looked at Rachel. 'Can Giles stay?'

'Of course, darling.' Rachel was thinking of the curtains.

'I mean for the night in my bedroom.'

Rachel was startled. 'Do you mean you want him to sleep in your bed?'

Sarah nodded. 'I can at his house.' Sarah paused. 'Grandma would die if she knew . . . Everyone's doing it, Mummy. Really.'

'Sarah,' Rachel was upset, 'do you mean to say you've slept with Giles?'

Sarah lowered her eyes. 'Not yet, but he has asked me.' She looked defiantly at her mother. 'Dr Burns gave me the pill.'

'Did he?' Rachel's mouth was set.

Sarah walked across the room to where Rachel stood. 'I would have told you, Mum, but you were in America, and Giles was insisting.'

'Oh Sarah.' Rachel pulled her daughter into her arms. 'Do you really want to make love with Giles?'

Sarah looked at her mother. 'Not really, but he won't stay if I don't, Mum. There's always old "Juicy Lucy". She'll let anyone have her.' She sighed. 'It makes life difficult for girls like me. Anyway,' Sarah brightened up, 'I don't have to worry about it now because I want to live with you. I can't stand living at home any longer. Grandma's an awful pain. Marie-Claire fights with her all the time, and Dad just ignores it. Actually, I think he enjoys them fighting for his attention. Then there's Anthea . . . You know, I feel sorry for her, Mum. She's really lost out. I heard Dad scream down the phone at her.'

'Did he?' Rachel was interested. 'What did he say?'

'He said, "There'll be no Mrs Hunter. Don't you understand that?" She doesn't, poor thing.'

Rachel shook her head. 'There's no reason for your father to remarry. From all accounts, he's having the time of his life.'

Sarah nodded. 'There's always a list of 'phone calls from women waiting to hear from him.'

'I'll bet.' Rachel felt a sharp stab of pain. 'Anyway, you can move into the Savoy if you like 'til the flat is ready. There's a spare bed in my room.'

Sarah hugged her mother and ran into the sitting-room. Dominic was measuring the window for Rachel. 'I'm going to live with Mum from now on,' Sarah told Dominic.

'Huh. You're as disorganized as she is.'

'I heard that, Dominic!' Rachel yelled from the bed-room. She walked quickly into the sitting-room. 'I'm not at all disorganized!' Rachel found herself furiously angry. 'Don't you think it's time you looked at me as I am now, and not as your father knew me ages ago?'

Dominic shifted uncomfortably. 'Don't get hysteri-cal, Mother.' Rachel shrugged her shoulders and walked out of the room.

'By the way,' said Dominic as he got out of the car to catch the train to Richmond, 'can I have a key to the flat?'

'No,' said Rachel. 'It's my flat. Sarah will have a key because she's living with me, but you can ask when you want to stay.' She looked at her son. 'You see, Dominic, people can change. I've changed. I don't need your disapproval. Until you learn – maybe you never will –

that there are lifestyles other than your own, you don't have any right to impose yourself on me.'

Dominic wasn't listening. I wonder what they put in those pills in that loony-bin, he thought.

'Do I have to go to Daddy's for Christmas?' Sarah was sitting on the end of Rachel's bed in the new flat.

'No, not if you don't want to, darling. But it will be very quiet for you here. I've asked the Gelbs from next door for the meal on Christmas Day, and Jane is coming with Jerry and the children for Christmas Eve.'

'I don't care,' Sarah said. 'I'll see him Boxing Day. Christmas Day is one gigantic fuss.'

'Not this year.' Rachel smiled. 'Anna will be staying for a few days after Christmas, and I'm going to a party with Claire on Boxing Night. Maybe you can stay with Charles and come home here the next day.'

'He won't be in. Especially not on Boxing Night.' Sarah sighed. 'Dom will go with him, and I'll have to stay with Julia. But,' she smiled, 'you haven't been out for ages. It'll do you good, Mum. You're going to get housebound.'

Rachel giggled. 'I love being housebound. Do you realize, Sarah, that this is the first time I've been able to have a place of my own?' She flung herself back on the pillows. 'It's been heaven. My bedroom, in my flat . . .'

She still couldn't get used to putting the key in the lock and walking into the flat and being alone. Some days it was exhilarating. She would walk through the luxurious silence, savouring the moment when she would open her bedroom door. There, warmly awaiting her arrival, stood her books in neat rows above her bed. Usually an empty coffee cup stood quite unashamed by her bed, and the morning newspapers sprawled on the thick white carpet. Other days would be filled with pain and loneliness. The walk to the bedroom would seem endless. The coffee cup and the newspapers – guilty reminders of her disordered lifestyle. Without Charles's lists, she constantly forgot to buy the lavatory paper. If she remembered the lavatory paper, she forgot the butter.

Worst of all were the bills. The gas bill was in league with the electricity bill. They would switch envelopes when she wasn't looking. The bank statements were incomprehensible, and her investment portfolios she consigned to the dustbin. Mr Gardiner, from the Midland Bank, was surprisingly understanding. 'Miss Cavendish,' he said, 'don't be so upset. You're not the first person or the last to find all these documents confusing. Really.' Rachel felt immediately comforted. 'And,' he continued, 'just a many men are incompetent when it comes to keeping track of their money as women. Don't let it worry you. I'll keep an eye on your shares, and I will telephone you if you need to buy or sell.' She smiled at him. 'That's better.'

Rachel walked back to the flat. What a nice man, she thought. Her confidence was now restored. She telephoned the central-heating firm. Why is it, she thought as she waited for the 'phone to be answered, that I can cope with a real disaster now, but a leaking radiator seems like the end of the world?'

46

Sarah was at school the day the central-heating man called. 'Live on your own, love?' he said, tinkering with the radiator.

'No. I live with my daughter.' At first Rachel had responded to his chatter. She was lonely. 'Shall I make you a cup of coffee?' she asked.

He was soon sitting at the kitchen table. 'Another cup would go down well.' By this time, he made her thoroughly nervous. Ron, as he introduced himself, laced his thick fingers around the cup. 'Must be lonely, all day by yourself.'

'Oh no. I have very good neighbours.'

Ron looked at her meaningfully. 'How about the nights?'

'My daughter is home.' Rachel said stiffly.

'Don't you miss a little bit of the old . . .' He clenched his fist and made a lewd gesture.

Rachel flushed. 'Really, I think you'd better leave.' Ron rose to his feet. He walked towards her. Rachel was transfixed with terror. 'No,' she said. 'Don't.'

'They all say that, the first time.' He seized her in a bear-like hug and bent her backwards. His thick fleshy lips enveloped her mouth. He stuck his tongue down her throat. Rachel was too busy struggling to notice his right hand at her skirt. He had his fingers inside her pants.

Just then the 'phone rang. He pulled himself away. 'Shit,' he said, fumbling with his trousers.

Rachel ran to the 'phone. 'What's the matter, Rachel?' Jane said. 'You sound as if you've been running up the stairs.' Rachel burst into tears. 'Come on, Rachel.

Don't cry. Tell you what. I've got the day off. I'll come over.'

'No! No. Don't do that. I'll come to you.' Rachel slammed the 'phone down and ran to the door.

'Hey!' Ron was waving a piece of paper at her. 'Hey! You haven't paid the bill!'

Rachel ran down the stairs sobbing hysterically. She remembered his tobacco-stained teeth and his foul breath. She was still shaking when her taxi dropped her off at Jane's house.

Jane paid the taxi-driver and took Rachel into her house. 'Here,' Jane said, giving her two pills.

Rachel pushed her hand away. 'No. I've made a vow. I'll never suck another tranquillizer. Hug me, Jane. Hug me.' She needed to feel warm undemanding love.

Jane hugged her. 'Oh Rachel,' was all she could say when Rachel finished telling her about Ron.

'Was it anything I did wrong?' Rachel looked at her anxiously. 'I mean I might have unconsciously asked him for it.'

Jane shook her head. 'Don't be such a sap, Rachel. He didn't have any right to touch you. Don't make his lousy behaviour your responsibility.'

Rachel sighed. 'You're right. I'm giving up guilt for New Year.'

'Here. Have a cup of coffee.'

Rachel looked at Jane. 'Is there something worrying you?'

Jane was chain-smoking, as usual. 'I wasn't going to tell you, Rachel. You've got enough problems of your own, but,' Jane smiled, 'I realize that you're the only person I can tell.' She blushed and suddenly the years fell away from her face. Her eyes sparkled and she giggled.

Rachel looked at her. 'Another man?'

'How do you know?' Jane was astonished.

Rachel laughed. 'You lit up like a Christmas tree. I wondered why I didn't see much of you this summer. Who is he?'

Jane hung her head. 'It's Liza's teacher.'

'You mean John Fields? The art teacher at her

college? The one she's always talking about?' Jane nodded. Rachel whistled. 'He's gorgeous.' Jane was blushing furiously. 'What about Jerry?'

Jane shrugged. 'That's the problem. John wants me to leave Jerry . . . But every time I get myself all ready to go, Jerry does something nice and I fall apart. And then there's the kids. They love their father. I don't see them wanting the family to split up. Anyway, I don't see how I can divorce Jerry. He hasn't done anything wrong except bore me to death. I can just see the judge: "Boring your partner to death, Madam, is hardly a cause for divorce." Well it should be.' Jane's fists were knotted. 'Terminal boredom should come after "Unreasonable Behaviour". Do you know,' she suddenly switched moods, 'I've gone back to buying pretty clothes? Here.' She stuck her arm under Rachel's nose. 'Smell. *Shalimar*. Like it?'

Rachel grinned. 'I'm sorry for Jerry, but I'm thrilled for you.'

'I've got to make a decision one way or the other,' Jane said. 'The suspense is killing me. I don't like cheating on Jerry. It's not in my nature. So,' she lit another cigarette, 'I've decided to either give up John and go back to being a faithful housewife – in which case I'll insist we go back to the States, I couldn't hack trying to live here with John so close – or, I'll ask Jerry for a divorce.'

Rachel looked at Jane. 'Could you really go back into the trap again?'

Jane rolled her eyes. 'Sometimes I think no, and then I think "Well, at least it's a mink-lined trap." Life with John wouldn't be easy. He doesn't get much of a salary, and,' she frowned, 'I don't expect the kids will want to come with me.'

'But you'd be far happier with John. At least he looks like a kind, warm, loving man. I know Jerry loves you, Jane, but he is married to his job.'

'I don't know. I really don't, Rachel. I'll tell you on Christmas Eve. Okay?'

Rachel got to her feet. 'I must get back to the flat, Jane. I left that man in there. He's probably stolen the silver.'

'Do you want me to come with you?'

For a moment Rachel was tempted. 'No thanks, Jane. It's nice of you to offer, but I'm trying to discipline myself to be independent.' She laughed. 'I try and do something independent each day. Like go for a walk by myself, or go to a restaurant and have a meal by myself. I'm not very successful though. I guess I'm not independent by nature. I've always envied Claire, you know. She just naturally does things on her own. She goes to parties by herself. She went to Rome this summer.' Rachel sighed.

Jane kissed her good-bye. 'I know how you feel. I'm a lost cause. Even though I sound like an aggressive independent American, I hate doing things by myself. See you on Christmas Eve.'

'Mummy.' Sarah was helping Rachel clear up the kitchen on Christmas Day. 'That was the nicest Christmas Day I've had since I was little.'

'Really, Sarah?' Rachel was pleased. 'I enjoyed myself very much indeed.' Rachel smiled at Sarah. 'I'm not exhausted. Usually by now I'd be stinking of turkey grease and I'd have a raging headache.'

'But the Gelbs are lovely people, and it meant we could spend all day lounging around in our night-dresses watching television. I've always wanted to do that . . . and to have the telly on during dinner,' Sarah said gleefully. 'We've always had to miss the Christmas film.'

Rachel laughed. 'I can see myself remaining a cantankerous old lady. I couldn't give up all these freedoms.'

'Did you miss Daddy at all?'

'Part of me does. After all, we shared so many Christmases. Some were good times. Getting the Christmas tree from the Crab Tree Lane, choosing the stilton at Fortnum's . . . Lots of things, really. But,' and she smiled, 'it's a big "but", Sarah, I realize that an awful lot of that time I was dreadfully unhappy. That wasn't me all those years. I was a robot.'

'Jane looks like that,' Sarah observed. 'Jake says she's probably having an early menopause.'

'She's much too young, Sarah. No, Jane's just having a few problems.'

'Jake said he was afraid his parents might break up like you did. Jake said he'd kill himself.'

'I know he did.' Rachel's face tightened. 'Selfish little sod.'

'Mummy,' Sarah looked at Rachel . . .

Rachel remembered Jane's desperate face in the kitchen on Christmas Eve. 'I can't do it, Rachel. They all need me.'

'But do they love you?' Rachel had asked.

'Does it matter? It's sort of love. Anyway, Jerry's agreed to go home.'

'Oh Jane.' Rachel hugged her. 'I'll miss you.'

'. . . Sorry, Sarah.' Rachel pushed the button on the dishwasher. 'I didn't meant to sound sharp. I'm just glad you didn't say that to me when I was leaving Charles.'

'That's different, Mum. He – I'm calling him Charles from now on. I can't think of him as a father – Charles had loads of affairs. Besides, he didn't approve of you very much. Jerry loves Jane an awful lot. He does everything he can to please her.'

Except talk to her, Rachel thought. 'I know, Sarah. Now you get your things together for tomorrow. I'll drop you just before lunch.'

Sarah stretched. 'Oh God. I'll have to get up for breakfast, and Grandma'll sniff and say I developed bad habits.'

'What does Charles say about you calling him by his first name?'

Sarah laughed. 'He prefers it. He says people think he's out with a new girlfriend. Do you want me to call you Rachel?'

'No,' said Rachel. 'I'm your mother. You need one of those.'

47

Rachel was lying in her own bed with a blinding headache. Oh no, she thought, I must have had too much to drink. She groaned. Suddenly she heard a loud snore. Who on earth is it? she asked herself. She had a half-remembered vision of herself crashing down the corridor carefully trying to negotiate herself into the bedroom and then collapsing on the bed. She then had an even sharper vision of two bare bodies writhing about on the bed, followed by the body on top panting like a train, and then collapsing on top of her. She couldn't at the moment put a head to the body or a name to the face. Oh my God, she thought. This is awful. She lay in the darkness with her eyes shut. It's no use. I've got to pee. She slid quietly out of the bed and stood upright. The ceiling immediately fell on her head. 'Ow,' she moaned, holding her hands over her ears.

The figure on the other side of the bed sat up. 'Are you all right?'

'I'm stopping my brains from leaking out of my ears.' The figure laughed. Rachel winced. 'Don't make a noise.'

'I'll get you some coffee. Where do you keep your aspirin?' The figure sounded very confident. (He must do this quite often, Rachel thought.) 'Close your eyes,' he said. 'I'm going to put on the light.'

'No, don't. I haven't got any clothes on.' Rachel leaped back into bed.

'It's a bit late for all that modesty act.'

The light snapped on, and Rachel found herself staring at a fair-haired, blue-eyed young man. 'My

God. How old are you?' Rachel was horrified. He looked about the same age as Dominic.

'I'm twenty-four.' He frowned. 'What's that got to do with it?' Rachel slid under the covers. 'It's all the fashion now – older woman/younger man thing.'

'Well, it feels like cradle-snatching to me.'

'It didn't last night.'

'I can't remember last night.'

'Well, I can . . . Anyway, this isn't the sort of conversation we should be having now.'

'No?' Rachel asked. Rachel removed the sheet from her face. 'What should we be doing?'

The man stretched. 'It's confession time. You tell me about your husband, and I'll tell you about my herpes.'

'Herpes?' Rachel said with panic in her voice.

'Calm down. I'm in remission. You're safe. Anyway, it's not nearly as dangerous as it's made out to be. We just can't screw if I get blisters.'

'Oh.' Rachel didn't know what to say.

'First of all,' the young man sitting beside her said with a winning smile, 'let's introduce ourselves. I'm Peter. Who are you?'

Rachel thought of giving him a false name. No point, she thought. He knows where I live. 'I'm Rachel Cavendish.' She put out her hand. Peter shook it cheerfully.

'Well,' he said, glancing around the room. 'You've got a nice place here.'

'Do you do this often?' Rachel was curious.

'As often as I can.' Peter laughed. 'Haven't you ever had a one-night stand before?'

'Oh don't. It sounds so awful.'

Peter jumped out of bed. 'Wait 'til I get you coffee, lots of aspirin, and a big breakfast.' He grinned. 'You'll feel great.'

'By the way,' he yelled from the kitchen, 'there's no Mr Cavendish about to return with a shotgun, is there?'

'No,' Rachel yelled back.

While Peter was in the kitchen, Rachel stood under the shower in the bath. She had to pull her thoughts together. Sarah was going to be back soon. What would she think if she found a man? Not only a man, but a much younger man, in her mother's bed? Maybe she could get Peter out before then. She realized that she had absolutely no idea how Peter had got into her flat, let alone her bed. The party, or what she could remember of it, was the usual Hampstead affair. Claire, she now recalled, was dancing with Jerome, an old friend of hers. Peter, Rachel realized, was the host's son. 'My God,' she murmured. 'He wasn't even supposed to be there.'

'I saw you come in.' Peter was munching a large slice of toast as Rachel walked out of the bathroom. 'Most of my mother's friends look like withered toads, but when I saw you, I decided to chat you up.'

Rachel laughed in spite of herself. 'Peter . . .' he looked so unabashed and extremely pleased with himself, 'do you often chat up older women?'

'All the time.' He grinned. 'They're much more fun than girls. Besides, they don't want to get married. You don't, do you?' He was suddenly anxious. Rachel shook her head. 'And they usually have their own place. Mind you, I've never had a woman as fabulous as you, Rachel.'

'Honestly?' Rachel looked at him. 'You're just saying that.'

'No, I'm not. You're truly beautiful, and last night you were very funny.'

'When last night?' Rachel asked suspicously.

'When we were dancing. Do you remember the Cossack dance you did?'

'No.'

'Well everyone else will. We broke enough glasses.'

'Oh my God,' Rachel wailed.

'You know, for someone your age, you're very naive.'

'I know.' Rachel nodded. 'But I'm learning.' Very fast, she thought.

'Let me stay, lovely Rachel.' Peter leaned towards her. 'Please let me stay.'

Rachel, full of toast and coffee, smelled his clean warm body. It's been a long time, she thought. 'All right,' she said.

Peter put the tray on the floor and then pounced on her.

They rolled around on the bed. 'Hey! You're strong!'

Rachel was sitting astride him. 'You mean for a woman my age?' Rachel panted. Peter heaved her onto her back and began to kiss her fiercely. Rachel's body filled with an aching need for release. Her mind babbled away incessantly. Suddenly the mind gave in and shut up. 'Do that again, Peter,' she moaned. He obligingly did. They both climaxed together. Then they fell asleep in each other's arms, like the survivors of a shipwreck.

Rachel woke up to the sound of Sarah in the kitchen. Hurriedly she put on her bathrobe to go out and warn her. She was mid-sentence when Peter padded out. 'Hello,' he said amiably. 'I'm Peter.'

Sarah went red and looked at her mother. 'He's not your own age,' she blurted out.

Peter smiled. 'No, she's more like my age.' Rachel stood helplessly in the middle. Sarah walked out and slammed the door. Peter sighed. 'She'll get over it. She's not used to sharing you, is she?'

'No. I'm not used to sharing myself any more either.' Rachel looked at Peter.

'That's why I'm the perfect answer,' Peter congratulated himself. 'I'm not one of the usual rent-a-dick mob who go around screwing bored women, but I do like to have fun. We can just hang out together. I'll bet you don't go out much.'

'I don't actually,' Rachel admitted.

'All right. I'll institute a Rachel Cavendish Improvement Programme. First thing tomorrow, I'll be around and we'll spend the day looning.' Rachel raised her eyebrows. 'Yes. It's my recipe. The three Ls: Looning, Loafing, and Laughing. Now, tomorrow I'll bring you a present, and you can get me a present.'

Rachel frowned. 'I have no idea – what would you like?'

'We'll go to Turnbull and Asser; and I'll choose. Okay? You haven't asked where I'm spending the night.'

'Should I?' Rachel sounded surprised.

'Yes, you should. Because I've got a woman I live

with. I can't just throw her out because I've found you.'

'Are you faithful to her? I mean usually?'

'Not very, but then, neither is she.'

'I'd like you to tell her about me.' Rachel was serious. 'I'm quite happy to have fun with you, Peter, but I don't want to hurt her.'

'All right, all right. I promise I'll tell her.'

Rachel smiled at him affectionately. 'The lovely thing about good sex is that it makes everything flow so smoothly. I feel harmonious now.'

'You look lovely, Rachel. Sex suits you.'

'I know. I've missed making love. I'd almost got to the point where I thought it was me and my right hand forever.'

Peter laughed. 'You've got *me* now.' He hugged her. 'I'll tie your right hand behind your back.'

Rachel sniffed her fingers. 'I can still smell you.' She pushed him off. 'No, Peter . . . don't. I must talk to Sarah.'

Sarah was unrepentant. 'Everybody will laugh,' she said, pacing up and down her room.

Rachel shrugged. 'I don't mind about "Everybody" any more, Sarah. I spent far too much of my life caring about what people think.'

'Are you going to let him move in?' Sarah stood anxiously waiting for an answer.

'No, darling.' Rachel shook her head. 'Peter's a friend and a lover, but he's far too young. I don't mean because of his age. How grown up you are usually has nothing at all to do with age. Peter is great fun, and I know he'll be good for me. I need to get out.'

Sarah relented. 'Well, as long as he doesn't move in permanently . . . I guess I can share you.' Rachel hugged her.

Peter knew everyone there was to know in London. He wore Rachel on his arm like a treasured flower. She, in turn, blossomed. Since she had left Charles, she had become aware of herself as a person, but with Peter's unabashed love and sexuality, she now flourished fully. They chased each other across Kensington Gardens and stood by the statue of Peter Pan. 'That's me,' Peter said proudly. Rachel bought a first edition of *Peter Pan in Kensington Gardens* for him. They spent weekends in small villages sniffing out old pieces of silver. Peter bought Rachel a pair of Georgian sugar tongs. For Rachel, it was a drowsy, sun-drenched summer, whatever the rest of England felt about the weather.

When it was hot, they lay in Holland Park on a blanket. 'Stop it, Peter. I'm too old to neck in public.'

'I'm not.' Peter continued to browse on her shoulder.

Rachel laughed. 'Really, Peter. Do you ever think of anything except sex?'

Peter looked solemn. 'No. Food, maybe. But then that's just another form of sex. Actually everything you do is sexual if you do it the right way.' He suddenly dived at Rachel.

'Stop it!' she shrieked. He pulled the blanket over both of them. 'No, Peter. Don't be silly. We'll get arrested.'

Peter giggled. 'Then they'll have to take my pecker as evidence.' He was struggling with Rachel's bikini pants. 'Better come quietly, Rachel darling. The longer you struggle, the more likely we are to get caught.'

She could feel his tongue between her legs. She lay back. The now familiar warm bubbling pleasure invaded her. What would Reverend Mother say? was the last thought before she plunged into an ocean of bliss.

Claire was amused. Rachel took Peter to Axminster for a weekend. Fortunately, Peter could fish and was a passable shot, so Michael was happy to take him off across the endless moors with the dogs.

'That man's not there, you know.' Peter was floating in the bath. 'I must have collected half a ton of Devon soil.'

Rachel looked at him. His hair was plastered to his head. He looks just like a seal, she thought. 'I know, Peter, but I did warn you.'

'Poor Claire,' Peter said earnestly.

Rachel sighed. 'It's her choice. I've often talked to her about Michael, but she prefers to stay with him. At least he's given up other men since his mother died.'

Peter looked up at Rachel. 'Do you know that he sleeps in a room full of pictures of her?'

Rachel nodded. 'That used to be *her* room.'

The next afternoon, Rachel and Claire were having tea on the sweeping lawn that surrounded the house. 'English bees buzz quite differently from Greek or Italian bees,' Claire observed. 'They have a particularly restrained English buzz.' Both women paused to listen. It was an unusually hot day. The two marmalade cats lay like discarded sandwiches on the flagstones. Even the dogs were too hot to chase them away. 'I know.' Claire sat up. 'English bees buzz in unison. Now, if you were in Greece, Rachel,' she laughed, 'each bee carries on like a lunatic.'

'I'd love to go to Greece or Italy, or anywhere for that matter.'

Claire looked at her. 'Well, why don't you?'

Rachel grinned and stretched. 'I suppose I'm having such a good time here. You know, I don't quite trust happiness yet. Life at the moment feels like a shiny bubble with all those lovely iridescent colours.' She laughed. 'I'm afraid it'll go "pop" and I'll be left with just an empty bubble bottle.'

'No, you won't.' Claire leaned towards her. 'Whatever happens between you and Peter, you'll be all right. You're not the same person you were.'

'It's funny, you know,' Rachel poured some more tea, 'I always thought it was me. I mean, I thought I was a bad lover, but after being with Peter, I realize that it was never me at all. Charles was awful.' Rachel was indignant. 'He made something that's wonderful and fun into a depressing duty.' She grimaced. 'Ugh. When I think of all those years . . .'

Claire took her hand. 'At least you know now.'

Rachel saw the pain on Claire's face. 'Are you still celibate, Claire? I can't imagine life without making love.'

Claire smiled. 'Well, I tried affairs years ago, mostly to pay Michael back, but I didn't enjoy them very much. All that sneaking around either turns you on or off. For me it was definitely off. So really I chose to be celibate.'

Rachel looked at her in surprise. 'You mean really celibate, like not even your own fingers?'

Claire nodded. 'Actually, there's so much nonsense written about sex these days. Celibacy is a perfectly comfortable way of life. I really never much enjoyed sex anyway.' Claire wrinkled her nose fastidiously. 'All that mess and smell of fish. I don't think about sex at all. I just get on with my life. I'm off to New York next week. Harry Winston's are selling a diamond that interests me.'

Rachel's eyes lit up. 'Will you take a parcel to Leah for me?'

'Of course I will.'

'I do miss her,' Rachel sighed. 'It's funny how you can meet someone for a couple of weeks and feel as if you've known them all your life. Last time I 'phoned, she said Manny was going to live in Israel for good. She's coming to stay with me early next year. Everybody's moving.' Rachel suddenly felt sad. 'I said goodbye to Jane last week.'

Claire lit a cigarette. 'How was she?'

'Awful. She cried and cried. All I could do was hold her. I can't understand why she didn't leave Jerry. John really loved her – Jerry just needed her. It's awful to think that she'll go back to America. Jerry will commute and Jane will sit in her kitchen with the valium bottle.' Rachel shook her head. 'I can't understand it.'

Claire looked up at the bright blue sky. 'I can.' Her voice was resigned. 'You know, Rachel, it takes more courage to get out than it does to stay in. People grow attached to their chains.'

'I suppose so. I'm glad I'm free.'

'Just remember, Rachel, you had money. Jane didn't have anything. Love on an artist's salary could soon peter out.'

Rachel frowned. 'If a man and woman truly love each other, then nothing can destroy that.'

Claire threw back her head, laughed, and slapped Rachel's knee. 'Rachel, I thought you'd given up all that romantic nonsense. Men and women don't love each other – they can barely tolerate each other. Show me one happy couple.'

Rachel thought very hard. 'Well, I know happy individuals, like Anna and her mother.'

'Exactly. Usually it's a man or a woman who has found a way of life that really suits them. And usually that means they are on their own.'

'Stop it, Claire. You're depressing me.'

'All right. I won't be the one to burst your bubble. Come on. Let's go up and get changed for dinner. Cook has created an amazing new recipe for salmon.' The sound of their voices trailed behind them as they walked across the flagstones. One of the dogs stretched and shattered the silence with a snarling attack on one of the marmalade cats.

48

The music roared. The party was awful. Rachel was prepared to write the evening off as a total waste of time until she bumped into Cici. 'Rachel!' Cici called out as she made her way through the crowd. 'How lovely to see you. What are you doing here? Are you a friend of Tony's?'

'No, I came with Peter. Tony's a friend of his. I'm so glad to see you again.' She hugged Cici. 'I felt so guilty for not contacting you.'

'Never mind. I can see you've been busy.' Cici eyed Peter. He smiled back at her. 'Let's have lunch tomorrow, Rachel.'

Rachel looked at Peter. 'Are you free?' Rachel asked.

'I'm always free,' said Peter, grinning at Cici.

'Okay,' said Rachel. 'How about the Blue Anchor at Hammersmith Bridge?'

'Lovely,' said Cici. 'See you then.' Cici floated off into the crowd.

'Wow. She's stunning,' Peter said to Rachel.

'Yes. She's also great fun.' Rachel laughed. 'She kept me going in hospital.'

'What was she doing there?'

'Oh, it's a long story. She married a man who is about eighty now.'

'Eighty? How disgusting!'

Rachel looked at him. 'Peter? I thought we agreed age had nothing to do with a good relationship.'

'What does she do for sex?'

'I think she has lovers, but basically she loves James and would never leave him.'

'Haven't I seen you somewhere before?' Rachel followed the voice to a stocky rather shy man. 'I don't usually accost strangers,' he said apologetically, 'but I feel I know you from somewhere.'

Rachel looked at him. She shook her head. 'You must be mixing me up with someone else.'

'I'm sorry. I do have an awful memory for names, but I always remember faces. Let me introduce myself. My name is Adam Treherne. Do you live around here?'

'Yes. I'm Rachel Cavendish, and I live at number 4 Beaufort Street, Chelsea, London SW6, England, the World,' she recited.

Adam laughed. 'I used to write that sort of thing on my exercise books at school.' He sighed. 'I do hate being in London when the weather is so good.'

'I know. It's so hot at night.'

'Where do you come from?'

Rachel smiled. 'I was brought up in Upottery.'

'Really?' Adam brightened. 'I'm from North Devon. We lived on Hartland Point.' His eyes clouded. 'I'm going back there just as soon as I can get a job.' He grinned. 'I'm a doctor for my sins, but I want to be a GP in a country practice.'

Peter came up behind Rachel. He put his arms around her and nuzzled her neck. 'This is Adam, darling.' Rachel unwound his arms.

'Hello.' The two men stared at each other.

He's rather nice, Rachel thought.

'Sorry, Adam. Must drag her away. We've got to go home.'

Adam shrugged. 'Ah well, I hope our paths cross again, Rachel.'

'I hope so too,' Rachel said over her shoulder as Peter led her off by the hand. 'It's a ghastly party, but we don't have to leave now, Peter.'

'He fancies you,' Peter said sharply.

'Do you think so?' Rachel was pleased.

'I know so.'

Cici met Peter and Rachel at the Blue Anchor the next

day. She had her current lover wrapped round her like a boa constrictor. Saul was very black and very angry. 'Come on, Poopsie,' Cici said, 'don't be so horrid.' Saul growled, and several people nearby left their seats. 'I promise I won't do it again.'

'What did you do, Cici?' Rachel couldn't wait to find out.

'Oh nothing. Saul gets very jealous. That's all.'

'Cici . . .' Rachel laughed. 'Come on. Tell.'

'Well, there was just a slight hitch in timing.'

'Ya, and I kicked his arse so hard he won't sit down for a week.'

'Naughty boy.' Cici slapped his wrist. 'You mustn't kick ambassadors' bottoms. You'll get deported back to St Lucia.'

Saul smiled at the memory of his island. 'Hey you! Peter, get the ladies a drink!' he ordered.

'Certainly.' Peter went up to the bar.

Rachel dragged Cici into the ladies' lavatory. 'Where on earth did you find Saul?'

Cici grinned. 'He works for the GPO, so I don't even have to leave the house.' She giggled. 'I just have the 'phones mended rather a lot.'

'Cici, you haven't changed.'

'Never will. You've done well for yourself. Peter's gorgeous. You look great, Rachel.'

Rachel laughed. 'I feel great.'

Not far away, Adam was also sitting in a pub with several of his friends. Rachel's face haunted him. He knew he had seen her somewhere before. Just then a jogger came puffing up to the bar. Feet. That was it: feet. Now he remembered. Swollen and bruised feet. Yes. Suddenly he remembered a very different Rachel lying unconscious on his ward at the Chelsea Women's Hospital. Pleased with himself, he ordered another beer. As he picked up the pint mug and buried his mouth in the foam, he suddenly felt an intense longing for Rachel. The feeling would not leave him. It chased him all the way home to his tiny flat in Fulham and nagged him until he put down his book and went out into the street.

He ordered a dozen red roses from Mrs Wright at the local florists. 'Address it to Miss Cavendish, No. 4 Beaufort Street, London SW6, England, the World.'

Miss Wright looked surprised. She had known Adam for years. He wasn't one for sending roses to strange women, but she kept her thoughts to herself. She sighed when he left the shop. 'He's got it bad,' she said to her husband.

'What's he got?'

'You wouldn't know if I told you,' she snapped.

'Don't bovver then.' And he slammed the door.

'There's flowers for you.' Sarah had a teasing note in her voice.

Rachel went to the sink in the kitchen. She smiled. 'A dozen red roses.' She didn't know anyone who would be seen dead sending anything so corny. She put them into a vase. 'Must be Adam,' she thought when she saw the address. She remembered his intense blue eyes. The card simply said:

'If we can't be lovers, let's be friends.
'Adam'

'I told you he fancied you,' Peter said when he telephoned to say good-night.

'Don't worry, Peter, I'd like him as a friend, especially now that Claire is almost always in Axminster. We Devonians stick together.'

Peter snorted. 'You can't say the same thing about St John's Wood.'

Rachel laughed. 'Anna's going to be here for the next few days, and I'll be busy, but I'll see you next week.'

'Okay. I'll ring you next Thursday, Rachel. Maybe we can go away for the weekend.'

'That sounds lovely.' Rachel put the 'phone down. The roses stood in the corner of the room glowing. Rachel walked over to the vase. She touched the thick fleshy petals. 'They are beautiful.' She drowned her nose in the sweet corrupt smell. 'Ummmm . . .' She sat down and wrote Adam a note:

'Dear Adam,
'Friends would be lovely.
'Rachel'

Anna bounded through the door. She whooped up the hall and threw herself on Rachel's bed. 'No nappies, no potties, no turds! Three days off!' She hugged Rachel. 'You are my refuge, my only refuge . . .' she sang.

Rachel winced. 'Well, your singing hasn't improved.'

Anna grinned. 'No, but then you always were jealous.'

'How's Julian with Sam?' Rachel asked later as she was laying the kitchen table.

'Good as ever. He's just as competent as I am. He suggested that we share a flat because he really adores Sam, and Sam loves him. But,' Anna shook her head, 'I don't know, Rachel. He has an awful time with his lovers, and I don't want him to screw Sam up. I'd like Sam to at least live most of his young life in a peaceful household.'

'That makes sense to me.' Rachel was busy stirring the casserole.

'Sam has got a father, and he does stay with him a lot. Julian doesn't have lovers around when he has Sam. It's a deal we made.' Anna laughed. 'Poor Julian. He always falls for ghastly little twerps who beat him up and then steal from him. I keep telling him he ought to be a social worker if he wants to reform people. I do worry, Rachel. Life isn't going to be easy for Sam. A lesbian for a mother, and Julian a homosexual.'

Rachel tasted the stew. 'Actually, Anna, when you get right down to what makes people happy and loving, it's always the same answer: being really loved. I know my leaving Charles caused the children a lot of pain, but we both love them in our own way. I honestly believe that every case is individual. Some straight couples should never have children. The same goes for some gay couples. It depends on the quality of the loving. In fact, I can give much more time to Dom now, and I'm much better at dealing with him, than I ever was when I was the perfect wife and mother.'

Anna nodded. 'I love my time with Sam. I'm happier now than I have ever been. I'm lonely, but I don't want to take on a relationship with another woman who professes to be gay, and then wrecks my life because all she is doing is acting out her own damage and using me as a refuge. No, I decided I'll wait until I find someone who has really made me their choice. I don't want to be like Julian – a sort of emotional dustbin.'

Rachel leaned against the refrigerator. 'At the moment I'm having lots of fun. It won't last forever, but I know that I can live by myself quite contented. When Sarah takes off, I'll sell up and go back to Devon and potter.'

'Pottering has always been your major hobby,' Anna teased.

'Hey, I meant to tell you,' Rachel was giggling, 'Peter and I were at a party, and this very famous anthropologist got drunk and gave us an awful lecture. He said that when older women turn to younger men, it's the end of civilization as we know it. I felt so responsible for the whole of civilization, I couldn't screw for two days.'

'Seriously, Rachel, the anthropologist didn't follow his argument right through, but he did have a point. What women are saying is that if all that is available is men like Charles, then of course younger men – who have grown up in a much more enlightened time – will be an obvious choice. It won't destroy civilization,' she grinned, 'but enough of those relationships, with men opting out of being pushed into professions and choosing to live and work from home, and BANG! There goes patriarchy.'

'I say,' Rachel was impressed, 'Anna, you really are very clever. Did you think that up yourself?'

'No. I'm in touch with women in America. They're writing about women. They call women like us "New Age Women".'

'Do they? What does that mean?'

'Well, it simply means that you take responsibility for yourself.'

Rachel stood still. 'That sounds so obvious.'
Anna looked at her. 'How long did you let Charles take the responsibility from you?'
'All my married life, I suppose.'
Anna nodded. 'Most women dump themselves on men as soon as they can.'
'I'll never do that again.' Rachel thought of Jane. 'I'd much rather be a New Age whatever than a feminist.'
Anna laughed. 'You never understood feminism, Rachel. You were too busy burrowing away on the back shelf of life.'
'Cupboards of tins of cat food,' Rachel agreed.
Anna sighed. 'All that anger was necessary. Without it, everything would slide back and we'd be begging doctors for contraceptives.'
Rachel thought of Dr Burns. 'Oh God. That would be awful. What do New Age Women do about men? I can't bear all this feminist hatred.'
'New Age Women don't do anything about men.'
'You mean nothing? No making love?' Rachel was appalled.
Anna shook her head. 'Now listen, Dumbo. It's quite simple.'
'Let me get a gin. I think better with ice and lemon. What do you want?'
'I'll have a brandy and soda.'
Rachel took the bottles from the drinks cabinet in the sitting-room. No red roses, she thought. She took a guilty look at them. They still glowed comfortingly.
'Now,' said Anna, 'don't interrupt like you usually do.'
'Okay.' Rachel sipped her gin.
'Most women who were in the movement with me now agree that we have to get on with our own lives, right? So I chose a woman for my doctor, and a woman accountant. I've drawn a blank on a woman bank manager. There aren't any in my area. But we see this as only temporary. Eventually, there will be sufficient women around for us not to have to discriminate. As far as relationships with men go, well,

it's not a problem for me. But many of my friends who do relate to men just gave up and stuck to chastity. Of course, there are men out there who want to be part of a New Age movement. That's fine.'

Rachel relaxed. 'You mean if a man really does want to join, he can?'

'It's not that kind of movement, stupid.' Anna finished her drink. 'It's more of an attitude. You're not asked to do anything, you just have to live it every day. I tell you, it's damn difficult.'

'But,' Rachel's face lit up, 'that's the first time I've heard you agree that men can also be included.'

Anna smiled. 'I wouldn't want to live in a world that excluded Sam, would I?' She sighed. 'At the moment, everything is in a turmoil. The old-style feminists spend all their energies on hating men. You only hate when you're still attached.'

Rachel nodded. 'I know. I hated Charles for months, then I realized that it was tying me to him. So I gave it up.'

'That's right. The more modern part of the movement wants to work with men – all men.'

'I think that's doomed to failure really.'

'Yes, it's far too early. There's not enough women in positions of power.'

'I don't want to be powerful. I just want to be happy.'

'That's fine,' Anna said, 'but there are other women who do want to have a voice in the government for instance. You can give them a hand.'

'I suppose so. I don't even vote.'

'Oh Rachel, you're impossible. I'm not going to ruin the evening with any more politics. You should stop me. It's just that I don't have anyone to talk to at home. Vera, bless her heart, can't understand why women have any problems.'

Rachel laughed. 'Well, she's always been responsible for herself. Come to think of it, everybody thought Aunt Bea was totally responsible for Aunt Emily, but actually, looking back, they were both equally responsible.'

When Rachel got into bed that night, she thought about Anna. Oh dear. I'm just not good at joining anything, she thought. But I will vote. She went to sleep trying to remember who she should vote for. She didn't much like any of the parties.

49

A distraught Dominic telephoned Rachel on Anna's last day in London. 'Dad's dead,' he said.

Rachel's face went white. 'Oh no, Dominic.'

Dominic was trying not to cry. 'They were doing a story in Borneo and the helicopter went down. Oh Mum . . .' Suddenly he could control himself no longer. 'I need you, Mum.'

'I'm coming. I'll find Sarah, and I'll be right over.'

Anna said, 'Is it bad news?'

'Yes. Charles is dead. A helicopter crash. Poor Dom.' There were tears running down her face.

She was still crying when she found Sarah. 'Well at least we can shift the old bitch back to Bridport.' Sarah sat up in the car with a look of steely satisfaction.

'Don't talk like that, Sarah. It's not necessary.'

Sarah looked at her. 'Why are you crying? I thought you didn't like Dad.'

'I'm not crying for him,' Rachel said defensively. 'I'm crying for Dom.' But she was surprised to find that she cried for Charles for many days to come.

The house on Richmond Hill was full of mourners. Almost everyone from the newspaper was there. Television cameras and reporters were set up outside the house and at the cemetery. The five dead men were heroes – men who had died valiantly for their country in search for truth.

Rachel felt absolutely stupid. She stood on the lawn in front of the house with one arm draped over Dominic and the other around Sarah. Julia was standing beside Dom. 'Look at the camera,' Julia said through her teeth.

Rachel remembered the house a few streets away. That time it was Anthea . . . poor woman, Rachel thought. Marie-Claire had taken flight as soon as she heard of Charles's death. At least she's young enough to start again, Rachel thought. But Anthea . . .

'Mrs Hunter?' The reporter's voice was lugubrious. 'Tell us how it feels to be married to a dead hero.' Rachel was at a complete loss for words. She moved her mouth. Her lips flapped together. Nothing came out.

We got a right dud here, the reporter thought. I'll try the old bag behind. 'I believe you're Charles Hunter's mother?' Julia nodded. Great, the reporter thought. A crying granny . . . 'What do you feel about your son's death?'

Julia raised her head. 'My son always was and always will be a hero to me and to his family, who were devoted to him.' Tears ran down her cheeks.

Rachel looked at her sideways. She even cries tidily, Rachel thought.

The four of them stood like animals in a zoo while cameras clicked. Lenses zoomed. 'I saw a report in a gossip column.' A pushy *Mirror* reporter was determined to do her job well. 'The press cuttings said you were separated from your husband. Would you care to comment on this, Mrs Hunter?'

Rachel opened her mouth to answer. Julia interrupted before Rachel spoke. 'Mrs Hunter,' she said to the assembled press, 'was living away from the family on the advice of her doctor.' She put her arm around Rachel's shoulder. 'She unfortunately had to spend several weeks in a mental institution. She needed the time to convalesce.'

'Do you think, Mrs Hunter,' it was the *Express* this time, 'that the strain of his wife's illness had anything to do with the crash?'

Julia paused for a moment. 'No,' she continued smoothly. 'I think Charles was too professional to let personal feelings intrude in his life of service to the public.'

The old cow, she's been rehearsing. Rachel was furious.

Inside the house, Julia spoke to Rachel. 'I trust you will keep the fact that you left Charles to yourself. I don't expect you to disgrace the family anymore. That young man of yours is nowhere about, I hope?'

Rachel shook her head. 'No. I've been too busy with the children. Besides, he didn't know Charles.'

Julia sniffed. 'Just remember, you owe it to Dominic to behave yourself. After all, you are still Mrs Hunter.'

Rachel made a face. 'I suppose I am legally. How awful.' Julia's mouth tightened.

Claire came up to Julia and offered her condolences. She pulled Rachel aside. 'I'm sorry he's dead, Rachel, but I can't help thinking that here he is, a hero – he'd have liked that – but what he really would have loved would have been to die of a heart attack while he was inside some glamorous blonde.'

Rachel giggled. 'I thought of that too.' She sighed. 'It's such a farce.'

'How's Julia taking it?'

'Very badly.' Rachel looked across the room at Julia. 'She cries mostly when she thinks no one can hear her. Funnily enough, Anna seems to be able to talk to her. Julia's even stopped referring to Anna as "that queer girlfriend of yours".' Rachel smiled.

Manny pushed his way through the crowd. 'Manny!' Rachel was thrilled. 'How wonderful!' She hugged him enthusiastically.

'This *is* Charles's *funeral*,' Julia hissed as she swept by.

Rachel bit her lip. 'Are you all right?' Manny asked Rachel.

'Yes, I am, oddly enough. I grieved for the old days, for the Charles I thought he was. And now I'm over it.'

'Leah's in the hotel. She came with me.' Manny looked at the crowd. 'My God, Charles knew a lot of people . . . Anyway, we're staying for a while and then she's coming with me to Israel just to settle me in.'

'Great. Listen,' Rachel pulled him closer, 'just as soon as we can, let's get out of here after the funeral. We'll get Leah, and you both move into the flat if you want. I'll see if Dom wants to come back with us, and we can just relax.'

Manny smiled. 'I'll cook kasha – it's good funeral food.'

Suddenly, everything was over. The lawn cleared as if by magic. All that was left of the press were little piles of cigarette butts. The cars filled with people and they drove to the church. Again the cameras rolled and the photographers clicked like agitated grasshoppers. Rachel held Sarah very close while the coffin went into the ground. She was crying for all the funerals she had attended: for William, for Aunt Bea, for Aunt Emily, and now for Charles. Dominic was holding Julia who was weeping hysterically. Rachel knew that Manny was standing behind her. She was surprised to hear him sob. She turned to him. His delicate face was contorted. 'We had such fun on our bikes,' he whispered.

Rachel nodded. 'There were good times.' She felt tears fall.

Just before Rachel left the house in Richmond, Dominic took her into Charles's study. 'Mother, I've talked to Dad's lawyer. Dad didn't bother to alter his will. You're the chief beneficiary and there is provision for Julia.' He was sitting in Charles's chair with his feet on the desk. Suddenly he became a young boy again. 'What I want is for you to let me live here with Julia. Please, Mother. All my friends are here and I like living with Julia.' He lowered his eyes. 'I don't think we get on well enough for me to live with you.'

Rachel looked at him. 'Actually, Dominic, I can live with your disapproval, so don't feel embarrassed about it. I haven't even thought about the future, but as far as I'm concerned, I don't need any of Charles's money or this house. You can certainly stay here with Julia, and as soon as you and Sarah are old enough, I'll see that the money gets turned over to you both. I'm sure that's what Charles would have wanted.'

'Great!' Dominic leaped to his feet enthusiastically. 'I can have Dad's bedroom?'

Rachel nodded. 'I must go now. Are you sure you don't want to come to the flat tonight?'

'Quite sure. I feel I ought to stay with Julia.'

She stroked the back of his neck. 'You really are a kind boy, Dom.'

He smiled. 'I'm the man of the family now, aren't I?'

'I suppose so.' Rachel laughed and went to find Manny.

Dominic looked for Julia. 'It's all okay. I've cleared it with Mum. You can stay.'

Julia's nostrils flared at the thought of living as tenant in a house owned by Rachel. 'Don't go out to a night club or anywhere you can be seen with that gigolo,' Julia said to Rachel as Rachel was leaving.

'He's not a gigolo, Julia. He has more money than I do.'

'And as little sense.'

Rachel sighed. She was still furious with Julia. She shrugged her shoulders. She's lost the only thing she's ever cared about, I suppose. Rachel comforted herself with Julia's loss.

'Dominic, where are you going?' Julia asked later that evening.

'Out,' Dominic said. 'Dad wouldn't want me to stay in and mope.'

Julia sat alone in the house. She was mending Dominic's jeans. Every so often she would wipe a tear from her face.

Dominic was licking cocaine off Tina Jameson's nipples. 'We can use my room as soon as the fuss dies down.'

'Won't your grandmother object?' Tina asked him.

'She can't,' Dominic smiled. 'It's my place now.'

50

Leah was delighted to see Rachel. 'Only for you, honey. Only for you.' She hugged Rachel. 'London's just as awful as I remember. The hotel . . .' she shuddered.

Claire, who stopped by for a drink with Michael, said, 'If I'd known you were coming you could have used my suite at the Savoy. We're going back to the country tomorrow. Do move in if you're uncomfortable at your hotel or too crowded here.'

Rachel laughed. 'Leah, as much as I want you to stay here, you'll do nothing but grumble. Anyway, if you stay in the suite, I'll be in most of the time anyway. It's my home from home.'

'The Savoy?' Leah cocked her head on one side. 'I could get to like London.'

'Me – a poor Jewish boy – in the Savoy? Oy,' said Manny.

'Peter?' Rachel's voice was full of sleep.

'Have you seen the newspapers?' he asked.

'No. We're all flat out this morning.'

'I've been 'phoning for the last week, but you're always out.'

'I know, Peter, I'm sorry. I've been charging around like a lunatic.'

'When can I see you?' Peter's voice was anxious. 'I want to talk to you.'

'Well, I'm busy today. Is it urgent?'

'Fairly.'

'Okay. Come by at about ten o'clock tonight. I'll be in by then. What did the newspapers say?' Rachel was curious.

'Oh yes. Well, most of them went on about his lovely mother and that you were just out of a nut house.'

Rachel had to laugh. 'Julia was very clever. She didn't want anyone to know that Charles was less than perfect. She pulled it off . . . Damn.'

'What's the matter?'

Rachel suddenly remembered Anthea. 'Can you make it tomorrow night?'

'All right.'

'I really must go and see how Anthea is, Peter. I feel so sorry for her.' She blew kisses into the 'phone and put it gently down.

Anthea was drunk, and not particularly pleased to see Rachel. 'You won in the end.' Anthea was holding a bottle of whisky. 'Come round to see if I'm taking pills? Well I'm not.'

Rachel walked into the little white carpeted sitting-room. She saw a pile of newspapers on the table. 'Honestly, Anthea. If you read all that fine print, it's all about Julia. I'm just written off as a woman convalescing from a spell in the loony bin. You know what English people are like about mental hospitals. Everywhere I've been today, people whisper and point. I can hear them.' She made a face. 'I got quite paranoid by teatime.' Indeed, Rachel had given up trying to shop at all and fled for a soothing cup of tea at the Savoy.

'Dreadful,' François the floor waiter had said when he saw Rachel. 'I hope Madame remembers that the Royal Family also suffers.' Rachel felt amused and comforted.

'Please, Anthea. I ended up in hospital, and if you don't watch your drinking, you'll end up an alcoholic. Are men really worth that amount of pain?' Anthea slumped into a chair. 'Anyway,' Rachel crouched beside her, 'I'm not going to live in that house or touch his money. Except,' she hesitated, 'I don't want you to think of this as charity, but there is a great deal of money, so I wondered if you would accept a small legacy. I think you should have a really good holiday.'

Anthea started to object. Rachel pressed on. 'Look,

Anthea, what made my misery bearable was money. New York made me realize how much more there was to life than just this. Please take the money and spend it.' She looked shrewdly at Anthea. 'After all, I bet you spent all the money you had on Charles over the last three years.'

Anthea nodded. 'Yes. I did.'

Rachel shook her head. 'He had very expensive habits. Come on. It's yours anyway.'

Anthea stood up. 'I wish I could hate you, or make it all your fault.'

Rachel laughed. 'I know. I tried to hate you once, but I gave up. I'm not a very good hater.' She wrote out a cheque and handed it to Anthea.

'Ten thousand pounds?' Anthea looked at Rachel. 'I can let my flat and go to live in Greece for a year. I've always wanted to do that.'

'Do it then. Ring me when you get back.'

'I will. I promise.' Rachel hugged Anthea and left. Anthea went back into the flat and looked at the slight stain on the carpet in the sitting-room. She remembered that night, and she cried for Charles.

Peter was direct. 'While you've been busy, I've been seeing Cici.'

'Oh. I see.' Rachel was hurt. 'You mean seeing Cici, as in looking, or have you been sleeping with her?'

'I've been sleeping with her.' Rachel turned her back to him. The roses need to be thrown out, she thought. Peter took her by the shoulders. 'I had to tell you because I don't want to lie to you.' He looked seriously at her. 'I normally lie, you know. It doesn't make any difference to us.' He laughed bitterly. 'After all, you made me tell old Angela when we first met, and she packed up and left.'

Rachel shook her head. 'Actually, Peter, I'm not into sharing like that. I'm a bit too old. Or unliberated, if you like. I think you're better off with Cici.' She could see the relief in Peter's eyes. She gently steered him to the front door. 'We had a marvellous time. I'll always be grateful to you for making me laugh again.' She kissed him. 'Cici is great fun, but don't hurt James.'

'I won't,' he promised. He bent down and kissed Rachel. 'I'll give you a ring sometimes.'

'Do that.' Rachel closed the door and leaned against it. She took a deep breath and got to the kitchen. She took out a bottle of brandy and went into the bedroom. She began to drink. Halfway down the bottle, the pain hit her. 'Shit,' she said and doubled up. 'But enough brandy dulls the pain.' She lay curled up on the bed.

'Hello, old friend,' she said out loud. She took another swig, and another. Finally she had enough to risk letting the pain out. Thank God Sarah's spending the night with Jane, she thought. Alone in the flat, she could let it out in roars and howls. She writhed on the bed until finally the great beast departed. She stood up and then was sick. She immediately felt better. 'Now,' she muttered, 'a long hot bath and then a few days in bed.'

I could teach other people, she thought. Getting over Peter equals one bottle of brandy, two hours of howling, one hot bath. She cleaned up the vomit. Two days in bed with everybody fluttering about, and I should be through. She was looking for the bath oil. Damn. I've run out. She went into the sitting-room. Carefully she carried the dead roses into the bathroom. She filled the bath with the petals. Then she poured in baby oil. She lay in the perfumed hot water until her toes were wrinkled and white. Finally she dried herself and went into the bedroom.

She was on her second day of bed rest when Adam called. 'I didn't telephone when I saw all that stuff in the newspapers because I thought you'd be inundated. But now would you like me to visit you? People usually need their hand held by a kindly friend after a funeral.'

'I do need a friend.' Rachel burst into tears.

'All right. Tell you what – I'll be there in about half an hour.'

Rachel put the 'phone down. 'Sarah,' she said. 'Adam is coming round to see me. Can you let him in?' Rachel went back to bed.

'For a woman your age, you do pull them, Mum.'

Rachel didn't hear her. She was busy deciding about whether to change out of her old nightie. 'No,' she decided, 'if he's going to be a friend, he might as well see me at my worst.'

Adam brought her another dozen red roses and a box of chocolates. Rachel laughed. 'You'll give me a bad reputation, you know, Adam. Roses and boxes of chocolates are romantic, and romance is out of fashion.'

Adam smiled. 'I can't help it. I like romantic things, like open fires and chintz curtains.'

Rachel nodded. 'Actually, so do I.'

'You know, I did meet you before, Rachel.'

Rachel raised her eyebrows. 'Where?'

'You were unconscious at the time. When the police found you by the river, they brought you to the Chelsea Women's Hospital as an emergency. I was a houseman there.' Adam saw her face change. He patted her hand. 'Don't worry. You're all right now.'

'I know,' she said and she smiled her huge sweet smile.

I could swim forever in those eyes, he thought.

Just then, Leah and Manny arrived. 'Manny, Leah, this is Adam.'

'You don't waste much time,' Leah muttered in Rachel's ear as she leaned to kiss her.

Rachel lay back on her bed. She stretched like a cat. 'Not this time, Leah . . . Adam and I are going to create history. For once, there will be a friendship between a man and a woman that will be untainted by sex, jealousy . . .' She looked at Adam.

'Competition,' he added.

'Yes, what else?' Rachel couldn't think of anything else.

'What about me?' Manny looked hurt. 'I'm your friend.'

'I know. But Manny, we don't have to forswear sex, do we?'

'True. Well, I'll give it a week.'

'Manny, don't be so cynical.'

'All right. Three days.'

* * *

It was, in fact, two months before Rachel broached the subject of sex.

The weeks flew by. He's like a comfortable pair of gumboots, Rachel thought after returning from a weekend at his cottage in Devon.

Manny was still incredulous. He kissed Rachel goodbye at Heathrow. 'You sure he's not . . .' Manny flapped his wrist, 'one of us?'

'Sure,' Rachel said firmly.

Leah hugged her. 'Listen, honey. He's okay. And guess what?'

'What?' Rachel looked at her.

'I think London's fabulous.'

'Come on, Leah. You didn't leave the Savoy.'

'Who needs to leave the Savoy?' She hooted with laughter. 'I never ate so much in my life. And the people . . . incredible. Say thank you to Claire for me.'

'I will.' Rachel waited at the airport until the plane was in the air.

Sam took to Adam immediately. Anna watched them playing together. 'Well, he's an improvement on Peter, Rachel,' Anna grudgingly admitted.

Rachel laughed. 'Actually I've never met anyone quite like him.'

'You're in love with him.' Anna looked at Rachel in amusement.

'I'm not.'

'Oh yes you are.'

'Then if this is "in love", why does it feel so tense?'

'Because you might lose him,' Anna shrugged. 'Another woman, a train, a bus . . .'

'Oh don't, Anna. I couldn't bear it.'

'There you are. That's love. You mark my words: I'm looking at a Mrs Treherne in the making.'

'You must be joking. No, I'm not ready for any permanent involvement. I doubt I'll ever be. With anybody.'

'Face it, Rachel. You're going to marry him. I can tell. Mind you, you could have done worse for yourself, I suppose.'

'Thanks very much, Anna. But it's not like that. You'll see.'

Anna laughed. 'No, Rachel. *You*'ll see.'

Rachel couldn't believe that Adam had never made even the slightest attempt at a pass. To begin with, she had found it relaxing to be with a man who just enjoyed her company. But after three weeks, she began to get worried. Maybe he just doesn't fancy me, she thought.

She took Adam down to Axminster to visit Claire. Adam was very good with Michael. He talked business and politics. Michael actually smiled. 'For a man of thirty, he's very well read,' said Claire.

Rachel nodded. 'His mother died when he was young, so he grew up in his father's library. He always wanted to be a doctor like his father. Now he's looking for a job in North Devon. I'll miss him, you know, Claire. He's so easy to be with. I've never felt so comfortable with anyone before.' In fact, she had to confess to herself, she didn't like seeing him leave in the evening. She went to bed in a hazy glow just from a good-night kiss. 'Silly cow,' she said to herself in the mirror.

'I have a present for you,' said Adam a few days later. He was standing at the front door to Rachel's flat with only his head peering in.

'How exciting,' said Rachel. 'What are you waiting for? Come in and give it to me.'

'Hang about. It's more difficult than that. I've had to heave it all the way up the stairs.' He turned around, lifted something heavy, and then backed his way through Rachel's door with his arms full.

'Oh Adam. It's lovely,' Rachel said, looking at the heavy wooden globe.

'It used to be my father's. A real relic, you know. It's very old. Most of the world was British then.' Together they carried the globe and put it in the corner of Rachel's sitting room. The polished wood was covered in pink patches denoting England's far-flung Empire.

Rachel made coffee, and the two sat on the floor in front of the globe admiring its beautiful and detailed painting. 'I used to spend hours,' said Adam, 'just turning it slowly round and imagining where I'd go.'

'It must have been wonderful,' said Rachel.

'Well, it was all right, I suppose. A bit lonesome, but I enjoyed it.'

'No, I don't mean that. I mean it must have been wonderful back then. All those places you could go in those days. I could have travelled by boat to India, and then taken the train to Simla. I've always loved the idea of travelling.'

Adam laughed. 'I'm afraid I've become awfully mundane since my childhood fantasies. Terribly English. I must seem a bit boring to someone who has actually been to New York.'

Rachel smiled. 'Adam, you're never boring. I don't think I've ever talked to anyone so much in my life, not even Anna. You know, we don't get much time for ourselves, what with Sarah at home. This is the first time we've been alone for ages.'

'I know,' Adam sighed. 'Since we met, life seems to rush by. Come on. If we go now there's still time for a walk before it's dark.'

They walked along the Embankment underneath the tall autumn trees. 'Look at those trees,' said Rachel. 'The leaves are just on the turn. I love that moment between the deep green and then the tinge of yellow.'

Adam wrinkled his nose. 'I can smell the beginning of autumn. It would be even nicer if we were in Devon. This time of year smells like crumpled earth and woodsmoke.'

Rachel laughed. 'You know, they will have harvested the wine in France by now.'

Adam looked at her. 'You've got itchy feet, haven't you?'

Rachel nodded. 'I suppose so. I told Claire a while ago that I'd love to go to Greece, or maybe Italy. I've always wanted to see Rome. That's probably the convent influence. We were taught that if you saw the Pope, somehow it made you holy.'

'Well,' Adam stopped walking, 'we could go if you want to. I think we could only make it as far as Rome though. I only have two weeks holiday left. But if you want to get away from everything, I would love to go with you. If you want me to, I mean.'

Rachel looked at his face. 'Oh Adam. I'd really love to go, and I'd love to travel with you. Just think, we can stay at the Hotel Bernini-Bristol in Rome. It has five stars. Claire is always telling me about the rooms. They sound fabulous.'

'Rachel,' Adam's face was stern. 'Rachel, *we* can't stay in the "Hotel Bristol-whatever-it-is". I can't afford to. I'm not a private specialist. The National Health Service doesn't expect its GPs to stay in five-star hotels.'

'Oh.' Rachel hesitated. 'But I can pay, Adam. Honestly. I have lots of money.'

Adam shook his head. 'No thanks. I don't want to feel like a gigolo, and if you paid the bills I'd feel awful. I know it's old-fashioned, but I can't help it. I'm perfectly happy to go with you. In fact, I can't think of anything I'd like more, but we have to go the cheapest way possible.'

'Well then, I suppose we could take the Volvo and stay in cheap hotels.'

'Actually,' Adam said with a smile, 'how about camping?'

'Camping?' Rachel frowned. 'I've never camped before. But it might be all right. What do you think?'

Rachel threw herself into the Rome adventure with a passion. Claire shrugged when Rachel told her on the telephone. 'Oh God. If he's too proud to take your money, you could at least stay in the hotel yourself and let him camp among the cow-pats.'

'Come on, Claire. I'm not so spoiled that I can't spend a few nights in a tent.'

'Well I am,' Claire sniffed. 'Mind you disinfect yourself before you come to see me again. Take lots of tummy stuff and a hat pin. Italian drains are terrible, and the men pinch.'

The night before they were due to leave, Anna telephoned. 'Are you all packed?'

Rachel looked at her two bulging suitcases. 'Yes. I must admit, I was a little uncertain about what to take. So I've included one of everything. Adam is taking care of all the camping equipment.'

'One tent or two?' Anna asked slyly.

'Two, I think. I haven't really asked.'

'One's more cosy,' Anna teased.

'Oh Anna. I told you. This is platonic. Anyway, I must go. I've got masses to do.'

'Okay. Have fun.'

Rachel picked up her suitcases and vainly tried to close the catch. 'Damn,' she swore, 'I'll have to get Sarah to sit on it . . . One tent or two?' She suddenly found herself wishing very much that it would not be two tents. I'd be scared on my own, she thought.

Rachel was quiet most of the way to Dover. 'What are you thinking about?' Adam asked.

'Oh, I don't know. I hope Sarah is all right with Julia. I don't worry so much these days. She's old enough to cope with Julia, and Dominic is becoming less horrible, and . . .'

'Rachel, what's really on your mind?'

'Well, I suppose it's more that we might not hit it off, and you'll dump me in some isolated spot, and I won't know how to get home.'

'Oh Rachel, you really don't have much faith in men, do you?'

Rachel dropped her head. 'I had such a hard time with Charles, I'll take ages to trust any man again.'

'I can wait,' said Adam. 'I promise I'll never do anything to hurt you. Ever.' He put his big capable hand on Rachel's knee. 'You will learn to trust me. I promise.'

'How do you know?' Rachel smiled.

'Because . . . I'm a hundred per cent trustworthy. Like British wool.'

'You won't go running off after a French *femme fatale* as soon as we're on the other side of the channel?'

'Rachel,' Adam chuckled, 'there's only us in this beautiful wide world. Other people are just an illusion.

Oh look,' Adam pointed. 'There's the sea.'

Within an hour they were on board the Sea-Link ferry. Slowly the ferry pulled out to sea. Rachel hung on to the railings gazing at the blue-grey waves. Adam stood beside her looking back at the Dover cliffs. 'Now I understand how our men must have felt during the War,' he said. 'They really are white for miles.' Sea gulls glided suspended over the ship.

'What's that beautiful ship over there?' Rachel pointed to a palatial white boat.

'That's the *Britannia*, the Queen's ship. Look. Can you see the flag? That means she's on board, God bless her.'

Rachel laughed. 'You really are patriotic.'

'I know. I still stand up when anybody plays *God Save the Queen*.'

'I'll confess: I always listen to her speech at Christmas.'

'So do I. I suppose you could say I'm just a fuddy-duddy conservative.'

'Conservative, maybe. But certainly not fuddy-duddy.' Rachel pulled his arm. 'I'm starving. Come and buy me something to eat.'

A few hours later, they landed in Calais. 'Oh God,' said Rachel. 'Claire warned me that Calais was awful. We should have landed in Boulogne.'

'Never mind.' Adam was busy trying to remember to stay on the right side of the road.

A huge lorry bore down on them, hooting furiously. '*Merde!*' shouted the driver, shaking his fist.

Rachel cringed. 'What did you do wrong?'

'What did *I* do wrong? It's *him*, the idiot! He shouldn't be driving so fast . . . Sorry, Rachel. I didn't mean to snap. Driving is all back to front here.' They drove on in a tense silence.

The campsite was bleak and packed with travellers on their way back to England. 'You sit in the car and I'll have the tents up in a minute.'

Rachel experienced a moment of intense unhappiness. Two tents after all, she thought as she watched Adam through the car window.

'Oh bloody hell!' Adam was sucking his hammer-struck finger.

'I thought you said you were good at this,' Rachel laughed.

'I am . . . usually. Look, why don't you go for a walk, and by the time you get back, both tents will be up.'

'Ah,' Rachel teased, 'but will they look as good as those over there?' She pointed to two pristine tents with immaculately laid out provisions.

'Of course,' Adam said. 'Go and do something useful, like check out the lavatories.'

Rachel wandered in the general direction of the shower block. When she got there she decided to have her first pee on French soil. 'What on earth is that?' she said to a woman who was washing her hands in a sink.

'That's a squat-loo. You'll be lucky if you sit down again anywhere on the continent. I've been constipated for the last two weeks. See where those shoe marks are? Well, you face the door, squat down, and fire. If you miss you drown you shoes . . . or worse.'

Rachel shook her head. 'I think I'll wait.'

The two women laughed. 'You'll have to give in sooner or later. That's what camping is all about.'

Rachel walked back to see how Adam was faring. 'Adam, did you know about the squat-loos?'

'Yes,' he said. 'I've been told by friends. You'll get used to it. Anyway, you can dig out the food now, and I'll set up the stoves.'

Rachel retrieved the food and the cooking utensils from the car.

'There you are,' said Adam, standing proudly over the outdoor kitchen he had fashioned.

'What, those silly little blue things? I can't cook a meal on a stove like that.'

'Yes you can. I've done it lots of times. Don't worry. I'll help you.'

Rachel was silent.

'Rachel,' Adam put his hand on her shoulder, 'what's the matter?'

Rachel's eyes filled with tears. 'I feel so useless. I didn't do any of the driving, and now you have to help me cook. I'm really no good at camping, or anything, come to think of it.'

'Don't be an idiot, Rachel. Camping and cooking on these tiny stoves takes some getting used to. Look, we're both tired. Why don't we forget about cooking tonight and find a restaurant? There's one right here on the campsite. And then tomorrow we can worry about home-cooking.'

'Okay,' Rachel cheered up. 'I'm dying to try French food.'

The restaurant was cavernous and empty. The tourist season was ending, and 'Madame' was in a furious mood. '*Eh, que voulez-vous?*'

Adam answered in fluent French, and Madame softened. Adam ordered steak and chips. 'I think it's wisest to stay away from the rest of the menu,' he said to Rachel. 'This place isn't too clean.'

Rachel agreed. 'It smells of garlic and armpits. But, I suppose, that's France.' Madame brought two plates with an enormous steak on each. 'The salad is lovely,' said Rachel. 'But thank God we're in different tents. I'll have garlic-breath for a week.'

'Mmm,' said Adam. 'This steak is lovely.'

When Madame returned with the bread Adam complimented her on the food. She melted completely. '*Cheval*,' she said with pride.

'*Cheval?*' Rachel stopped chewing. 'You mean "horse"?'

Madame nodded, beaming. '*Oui*. 'orse.'

'Ugh,' choked Rachel.

Adam went on eating. 'Tastes great.'

'*Merci, monsieur*,' said Madame as she walked back to the kitchen, wiping her fat red hands on her apron.

'Oh Adam, you can't seriously eat a horse?'

'Why not? I eat deer. I've even eaten a badger. Why not a horse?'

'Because . . . well, horses are different. They're like dogs.'

'They eat dogs in China.'

Rachel found herself becoming very angry. 'You're

just another insensitive lout. I'm going back to the tent. Good night.'

Adam sat still as Rachel stormed out of the restaurant. He looked at the steak sitting lifelessly on his plate. Suddenly he saw the warm brown eyes of his father's mare. 'Damn,' he thought. 'I'm so hungry.' Madame came bustling up. Adam explained that his friend was unwell and that he must go to see to her.

Madame gave a very Gallic shrug. 'Ah, monsieur. She is not your friend. She very special. *Non*?'

Adam laughed. 'No,' he said, shaking his head. 'We are just friends.'

Madame winked. 'Not for long, monsieur,' she said. 'Not for long.'

When Adam arrived back he found Rachel's tent tightly zipped. Rachel could hear him fumbling about outside. She was still furious. 'I'm going home tomorrow, Adam!' she shouted through the canvas. 'This isn't going to work. I nearly fell down the hole in the lavatory, I don't like lying on the ground, and there's a huge spider in my tent. I'm not the camping type. You have to be a masochist to enjoy it.' She paused to hear Adam's reply; all she heard was him still moving about. 'What are you doing out there?'

'Come out and see.'

Rachel considered remaining in a sulk, but it was only nine o'clock and she didn't want to sleep yet. 'All right,' she said, 'but I'm still going home in the morning. Anyway, where is all this comfort you promised me?'

'This is comfortable,' said Adam.

'Maybe for someone your age it is, but not for me. You forget, I'm a middle-aged woman now, and I'm too old to go sleeping on the hard ground and peeing in some bottomless pit.'

'My God. You talk about yourself as if you already have one foot in the grave.' Adam handed her a steaming mug of coffee and a huge lump of French bread thick with butter. 'Here.' He patted the ground beside him. 'Sit down by the lamp next to me, and we can work out how we can make you more comfortable.'

Rachel took a sip of coffee. 'Ummmm. That's marvellous. What's in it?'

'Fundador. Very cheap Spanish brandy, but it's very gentle and mixes perfectly with coffee and condensed milk. After several cups of that you'll sleep like a top.'

Rachel cupped her hands around the warm mug. 'Wonderful.' She smiled at Adam. 'Maybe we can work it out. But first of all, we have to buy a portable lavatory. I can't go through all that again.'

'I promise,' Adam laughed. 'We'll go to a camping shop tomorrow.'

Suddenly Rachel was tired. 'I must go to bed, Adam.'

'Good night,' he said as he leaned forward and very gently kissed her on the mouth.

She felt a question in the kiss, and she was bemused by the brandy. She didn't know how to answer. 'Good night, Adam,' she said.

The next morning Rachel crawled out of her little tent into a lovely bright sunny day. Adam already was stowing away his belongings in the car. 'How did you sleep?' he asked.

'Wonderfully. I must take a shower.'

'Go ahead. I'll deal with your tent and make some coffee.'

'Great. If you look in the boot, there's bread and marmalade.' Rachel slung her towel over her shoulder and started for the shower block. She felt curiously light, as though she could take off and fly any second. Odd, she thought, this must be the first time I've been on my own without any responsibilities in my life. She liked the feeling. After a lengthy shower and a hair-wash she sauntered back to the car where she saw Adam meticulously cleaning up after the night before. 'Here,' she said. 'Give me the washing-up. I need to feel useful.'

'You are useful, twit. I just want you to have a complete rest.'

Rachel laughed. 'You spoil me.'

'You deserve it. We had better get moving. We need to drive a long way today.'

Rachel studied the map as they drove. 'I'll drive on the motorways,' she said.

'You don't have to drive,' Adam assured her.

'I must,' Rachel said firmly. 'I'm not going to let myself be driven everywhere. I let Charles do that, and very soon I didn't have the confidence to drive anywhere by myself.'

'Rachel, don't see everything in terms of Charles. I'm not a bit like Charles, am I?'

'I suppose not.' Rachel grinned. 'But I can tell you don't like women drivers.'

'No, that's not true. I don't like anyone but me to drive. I love driving. When I was a child I always wanted to be a doctor or a long-distance lorry-driver.'

'You were quite a lonely kid, weren't you?'

Adam nodded. 'Yes. My father was always very busy, but I had my books. Then I learned to play the piano. I played for hours. I was lonely, but happy to be alone, if you know what I mean.'

'Oh I do. Being on my own at times is vital to me. It's a good job we have two tents, so we can give each other space.'

'Yes, and I can tell by now when you need time to yourself.'

Soon they were driving on the road which circled Paris. Rachel was like a child. Her eyes shone, and she hung out of the window pointing out various buildings. 'There's Sacre Coeur!'

Adam laughed. 'Rachel, we'll get killed if I don't concentrate.'

The traffic roared around them. Rachel was busy deciphering the various road signs. 'I'm afraid my French is not as good as yours.'

'Never mind. Just keep looking out for signs to Lyon. Okay?' And they plunged into yet another tunnel.

Eventually they left Paris behind, and the countryside became more peaceful. Rachel loved the service stations with their plentiful cheeses and their racks of wine. 'Why can't it be like this in England?'

Adam thought for a moment. 'I suppose English people don't much care for comfort. Sad, really. I must say, I am very impressed so far.'

They grinned at each other. By nightfall the weather was in a foul mood. 'Let's stop at Chalon-sur-Saône.'

Rachel was reading from her camping book. 'The town sounds lovely and the campsite is by the river.'

'Okay, but I think we will have to go to a restaurant for dinner. It looks like rain.'

'Please let me take us out tonight,' Rachel said. 'I feel like a real French meal. I want to try snails. Do you?'

'No. Definitely not. I never want to try snails or frogs' legs.'

'Okay, none for you. But, Adam, please let me pay. Do say yes. Then we can order anything we like and not break our budget.'

'Rachel, you just spent a fortune in the camping shop, and then you bought an eiderdown and masses of pillows.'

'I know, but if I'm going to camp I need to be comfortable. Anyway, I do have lots of money now. I was very poor when Charles and I first married, but now I'm lucky, and I want to enjoy it.'

Adam frowned. 'It's still difficult for me to accept money from a woman, you know.'

'I'm not *a* woman,' Rachel reminded him, 'and I don't see why it's all right for women to take money from a man but not the other way around. Does it really matter who has the money?'

'I suppose not, if it's a couple who love each other and who work together. But I do think it matters when one of the couple doesn't pull their weight and just sponges off the other.' By this time they were in the middle of the town.

'You're not sponging off me. It's just that I'm famished. Now let's just get there and not go on about it. Look for Mercure Avenue de l'Europe . . . Oh, there it is over there.' She pointed ahead.

They parked the car and walked into the crowded restaurant. As they stood in the doorway waiting for the manager to lead them to a table, the entire room fell silent. It took Rachel a few seconds to realize that all eyes were focused on them. Suddenly various tables broke into rapid French. 'That can't be her son . . . he's a little too old?'

'Ah, but she is beautiful,' a man said loudly on Rachel's right.

'Beautiful women don't usually need to keep young men,' his wife snapped.

Rachel knew sufficient French to follow most of the comments. 'I feel like a freak,' she whispered to Adam.

'At least you look like a clean freak. I didn't even take a shower this morning. We really should have put on some nicer clothes, you know.'

'Adam, for some reason I don't think it's our clothes they're all staring at.'

'No? Oh, I see what you mean. Yes, I suppose you could be right.'

'Oh really, Adam.'

'Don't worry, darling.' Adam grinned. 'Let's give them something to really talk about.' He put his arm around her waist as they followed the manager to the table and all eyes followed them.

'You'll have to grow a moustache. You don't even look thirty.'

'I'll age well this way,' Adam joked. The room was going about its business again.

'I must say, you're cool about the whole thing. Don't you mind that they all think you're a kept man?'

'No.' Adam shook his head as he opened his menu. 'I only mind if I feel I am, or if you feel I am. The opinion of the rest of the world doesn't matter to me at all.'

'That's wonderful, Adam,' Rachel laughed. 'It's taken me ages to give up worrying about what other people think.'

Adam put his hand over hers. 'Don't ever worry again. I'll always be around to tell you you're okay. You don't ever have to feel alone.'

Rachel smiled. 'Thanks, Adam. That's a great comfort.'

'Madame, monsieur, qu'est-que vous desirez?' The waiter smiled at them both.

'Snails,' Rachel said to Adam.

'All right, if you insist.' Adam ordered snails followed by coq-au-vin. 'At least that doesn't sound too foreign,' he said.

'And a bottle of "Les Amoureux",' Rachel said to the waiter.

'Bon, Madame,' said the waiter.

'I don't know anything about wine,' Adam said after the waiter had collected their menus.

'I do,' Rachel said. 'Claire taught me, and the wine waiter at the Savoy continues to teach me. You'll love this wine. I promise. It's a lovely bottle and a good year.'

The snails were delicious. Rachel chewed on the slightly rubbery lumps and dipped her bread in the thick brown sauce. 'I like the sauce,' said Adam, 'but I can't quite get used to eating snails.'

'Why not? You eat horse, so why not snails?'

'Not any more, I won't.'

'I'll reform you yet.' Rachel smiled. They ended dinner with fifty-year-old brandy. The liquid was pale and gentle. They left the table in a warm glow created by excellent food and wine. 'That was lovely,' Rachel said to Adam.

'Hm,' he said nearly asleep.

Later, after Adam had managed to set up the tents in the darkness and the fog which lay heavily beside the river Saône, Rachel lay alone in her tent. She was comfortable at last on a heap of blankets and thick French pillows, knowing that in the back of the car she had a magnificent bright blue portable lavatory. Her only problem was working out how to use it in her tent without Adam hearing her. I'll worry about that tomorrow, she thought.

The next morning she awoke to a thunderous explosion. 'Adam, what on earth are you doing?'

'Shitting,' he replied. 'I was going to let you christen the loo, but my snails were anxious to vacate.'

'Oh, Adam. You'll wake up the whole campsite.'

'Then I'll sing loudly.' Adam broke into a rousing chorus of *Tit Willow*. Rachel laughed helplessly on the floor of her tent. 'You know you're friends when you can fart in front of each other,' Adam said cheerfully.

'I suppose so.' Rachel grew quickly shy. 'I'll get there eventually, but it will take me time. Charles never farted.'

'Never?' Adam was incredulous. 'Poor man. Missing one of life's most pleasurable experiences.'

'Oh stop it, Adam.'

By this time Adam was out of his tent and was getting the kettle to boil. 'No, really. I'm quite serious. Far too many of my patients who are city-bred are too fastidious about the basic things in life to be healthy either physically or sexually.' He stretched. 'Fortunately, I've never had a problem.'

Rachel suddenly felt an urge to climb out of her tent and hug this warm lovely man. Adam was kneeling on the ground, his blond hair falling over his forehead. He looked up and caught her eye. His eyes were intensely blue and they held a fire that Rachel had never seen before. 'Adam,' she said.

He turned away and lit the stove. 'Yes?'

'Oh, nothing . . . Where are we going today?'

'Through the Mont Blanc tunnel and down into Italy.'

The moment had passed, but Rachel was aware of a power in Adam, a quiet confidence regardless of events, that made him deeply attractive to her. Did he find her sexually attractive, she wondered.

Adam was loading the car in a daze. How am I ever going to manage this trip without holding her? he asked himself. Lying in his tent he had been awake most of the night. What did a thirty-year-old penniless GP, earning £9,000 a year, have to offer a beautiful, sophisticated, rich woman like Rachel Cavendish? 'I mustn't rush anything,' he had said to himself again and again during the months he had known her. 'She's been so badly hurt. She needs to know that she can trust absolutely,' he counselled himself. But his body refused to obey his mind's instructions, and his dreams were full of passionate romantic embraces with Rachel. Occasionally he would wake up and nearly cry with disappointment when he found her not in his arms. Sometimes in the car the air would be electric between them, and both of them would crack jokes to relieve their feelings.

Climbing up and up through the thickly wooded mountain passes that divided France from Italy, both of them marvelled at the scenery. The drive was at times perilous for two people so unused to the French lorry drivers, who liked to play death games around tight corners. Adam stayed calm, and Rachel grew to trust him completely. He had no need to drive aggressively, and his reflex actions were excellent. 'You're a good driver, you know,' she said after a particularly hair-raising experience.

'Yes, I know. I did six months in a casualty ward, and patched so many torn bodies that I swore I'd never take risks. And you're a much better driver than you think you are, you know, Rachel.' Rachel squirmed. Adam smiled. 'You still can't take a compliment, can you?' Rachel looked at her fingers and blushed. 'Right then,' said Adam. 'Let's sing.'

'And did those feet in ancient time
walk upon England's mountains green?'

Rachel joined in.

'And was the holy lamb of God
on England's pleasant pasture seen?'

Rachel loved Adam's voice. It was a deep velvety bass. They sang all the way into Italy, through the border, and down the wide roads into the yellowish brown lights and shades of Tuscany. 'I feel at home in Italy,' Rachel said. 'The people are warm and the women's waists are wide. They look as if they love their men and their children.'

They camped in Aosta on a spotlessly clean campsite. After Rachel had telephoned Sarah and Dominic to see that they were safe, she walked back to their car, finding their neat little tents set up with care in the glow of the Italian sunset. 'I'm quite used to being with you,' Rachel said to Adam as they sat over the little gas stove, eating a wine-soaked stew.

'And I love your cooking.'

Rachel made a face. 'I'm afraid it was a bit watery.'

'Rachel,' Adam's voice was sharp, 'stop it. Don't always set yourself up as a victim. If the stew was too watery, I would tell you. You must stop this awful habit of putting yourself down. I know you only do it to stop anyone else doing it to you first, but I'll never put you down. I don't want or need to hurt you.'

'I know.' Rachel looked at him. 'It's difficult for me to believe that you really are not going to turn on me.'

'I promise, Rachel. I promise. Let's get to bed. We have to make it to Florence tomorrow.'

Adam wanted to see the Uffizi Gallery. Rachel found the noise and the bustle almost too much to bear after the peace of their own company. The gallery, to be fair, had magnificent paintings, but they were hung in a jostling confused mass, all vying for attention. 'You go on looking,' she said to Adam who was spellbound, 'and I'll lean out and look at the city.'

Adam took off into the many small rooms that formed a bewildering honeycomb in the centre of the gallery. Rachel leaned out of the heavily shuttered windows which were opened to the evening breeze. The red and orange tiled roofs gave a soft colour to the city. The browns and pale purples of the evening mingled with the crowds that paraded in the streets along the River Arno. 'What a mixture Adam is,' Rachel thought. 'So much of him is a solid plain Englishman, but underneath he is so warm and gentle with such a love of music.' She turned to look for him and smiled as he came hurrying towards her.

'I haven't kept you, have I?' he said.

'No. I love that view out of the window. Look.' They stood side by side. Adam put his arm around her waist.

'Wonderful,' he said. 'I'm really happy.' He smiled down at her.

'So am I.' Rachel agreed. She waited.

'Come on. Let's get back to the campsite before it gets dark,' Adam said.

Rome was everything Rachel had hoped for. Even Adam, normally so unflappable, was torn between trying to negotiate the car through the erratic and dangerous traffic, and feasting his eyes on the gorgeous exuberant statues that lined the roads of the city. On their first evening there, they found a small restaurant with a few chairs on the pavement. They ordered veal in red wine with plump juicy black olives. 'Heaven,' pronounced Rachel.

Adam wiped his chin with a huge crisp linen napkin. 'Let's run away and never go back.' His eyes glittered. 'We could find a small white-washed villa with grape-vines.'

'Oh yes,' Rachel interupted, 'and we can keep chickens. I've always wanted to keep chickens.'

Adam laughed. 'Rachel, chickens are stupid animals. Let's have a pig.'

'All right. We can have both, and in the meantime we could grow all our own food, and officially leave the rest of the world to get on by itself. Oh Adam, wouldn't life be wonderful?'

Adam filled his glass with wine. 'It would, Rachel, but you'd get bored with just me.'

'No I wouldn't, Adam. You're never boring. I love being with you.'

On the way back to the campsite, they stopped the car underneath the massive walls of the Coliseum. Rachel shivered. 'You can feel all those people who died in there mauled by the lions.'

Adam took her hand as they walked back to the car. 'Rome is such an odd city,' Rachel said. 'Parts of it feel so violent, and other parts are so steeped with religious feelings.' As Adam drove to the campsite, Rachel watched the statues on the Via Venite glow whitely in the moonlight. The streets were deserted. 'I can see why they call Rome "the Eternal City".'

Adam smiled. 'This is the first time the place has been quiet all day. I can't get used to the silence. I've never known people scream at each other like they do here. Rome's more like the "Eternal Fish-wife".'

Rachel laughed.

Damn, she thought, lying in her tent a few hours later. I haven't cleaned my teeth . . . I could very easily get used to being a gypsy. She fell asleep dreaming of Adam.

Rachel was immediately disappointed when she found that the statue of the Virgin Mary cradling her dead son was shielded by a wall of glass. She so much wanted to touch the white marble. They stood in St.

Peter's Basilica, both spellbound by the beautifully carved 'Piéta'. A great well of sadness formed in Rachel's heart. She blinked away her tears. Adam fumbled for a handkerchief. 'I can't bear the way Mary seems so resigned to Jesus's death,' said Rachel as she wiped her eyes.

'Well, she knew her son had a destiny to fulfill. So I suppose she could accept his death.'

'You know, Adam, of all life's tragedies, to lose one's child must be the worst that could happen.'

'I don't really know because I haven't had any. But when one of my patients is a small child and dying, I know that I find it hard to be objective.'

'I can hear a mass being sung over there. Let's go and listen.'

Holding hands they walked in a haze of wonder. All around them, in gold and silver lay centuries of worship to God. Huge black marble tombs housed the relics of wealth and circumstance. People moved in silence. Heads bent as rosaries slipped through fingers. The clear high soprano voices were underscored by the depth of the basses. The sounds curled upwards and mingled with the cloud of incense over the High Altar, disappearing into the secret corners of the gilded roof. Adam and Rachel joined the circle that stood around the High Altar. Rachel found herself praying intently. 'Let him love me,' she prayed. She looked at Adam's still face.

His eyes were closed. 'Dear God, don't let me do anything to hurt her.'

The mass came to an end, and the bells suddenly rang all over the basilica. Adam and Rachel joined the throng of people who moved towards the front doors. The Swiss Vatican guards gently herded the people out onto the steps of the Vatican. Rachel felt as though she and Adam were floating across the courtyards and out into the still warm, pale gold of the evening sunset. Finally they came to rest at a little restaurant called Mario's. 'Tomorrow we go home,' Adam reminded her.

'I know.' Rachel shook her head. 'I can't believe that we've had such a magic time together. I would like to go on travelling together forever.'

Adam laughed. 'One thing we do know now – we both are good travellers. I can't think of any better test than spending this much time alone together.'

Rachel nodded. 'You know, you and I don't ever really get cross or fight, do we?'

Adam raised his eyebrows. 'No. If I got tense or angry with you, I know we can always talk about it, and then it's over.'

Rachel was expertly twirling her spaghetti around her fork. 'Life was so different with Charles. He needed a daily diet of arguing. In the end, I was nearly as bad as he was. I never want to repeat that mistake. Sometimes I'm really frightened that I'll choose the same sort of man again.'

Adam shook his head. 'No you won't, Rachel. I'll see to that.' He spoke the words with such force that Rachel looked surprised. 'Anyway, I must load the car tonight. We can get an early start tomorrow.'

Mario came and leaned on their table. 'Everything all right?' he asked.

'Wonderful,' they both said in unison.

'*Bene, bene,*' he said with a huge Italian smile, 'for a couple so in love. May the wine make your bed soft tonight. *Buona sera.*' He nodded and went off to write up the bill.

The journey back to England was a jumbled blur of campsites and picnics by the roadside; garlicky Italian sausages with bread, and plum tomatoes on the Italian border; artichokes, oysters, and French bread on the way through France. Bottles of excellent wine from each region washed away the dust and the dirt from the *Route Nationale.* By the time they reached Calais, Rachel knew she was dreading the moment when she would have to say goodbye.

'I can put you on the Exeter train,' she said as the boat docked at Dover.

'All right. I'd love that.' Adam was busy buying the tickets at the window on the boat. 'Rachel, I want you to come down to the cottage next weekend.'

'I'd love to. I hoped you'd ask.'

Adam hugged her very hard and then kissed her on

the forehead. 'Thank you for a marvellous holiday.'

Rachel smiled. 'Let's go to Greece next.'

A whistle blew. 'All passengers proceed to disembark.'

Rachel felt strange to be back in England. She missed the sensual warmth of Europe. England felt like a poor and shabby sister. Rachel put Adam on the train. As it pulled away she caught a last glimpse of his face, and then just a hand waving. She walked back to her car and burst into tears. All through the next week she felt as if a whole part of her were missing.

Rachel arrived at the cottage on Friday night. It had taken her all week to decide to tackle Adam. He can only say no, she reasoned. They had finished dinner and were sitting by the fire. 'Adam, I've been thinking . . .'

He was reading. 'Um?' He didn't look up.

'I was wondering. Can friends ever be lovers?'

Adam shut the book with a bang. 'Rachel, what about our agreement?'

Rachel looked down at her lap. 'Well, that *was* months ago.'

Adam grinned. 'I've been waiting for you to ask.'

'You mean you do want to be lovers?'

Adam suddenly became very serious. 'Only if you marry me.'

Rachel sat with her mouth hanging open. She stuttered. 'Adam, nobody gets married these days. At least not 'til they've lived together for a while.'

'I know. I've lived with a few women myself, but I'm not interested in part-time commitments. I want to marry you. Not live with you. I want a solid commitment that both of us will work at our marriage, and thrive and prosper for the rest of our lives. I also want to keep bees, so I can go out every night and tell them how happy we are.'

Rachel was desperately confused. 'But I don't want any more children. You won't have a son.'

Adam shrugged. 'I don't want children. I want you.'

'I don't want anyone in my bed all the time. One thing

I've learned is to keep a bit of time for myself.'

'We can have an extra bedroom for when you want to be alone. I promise I won't crowd you.'

'I hate washing up.' Rachel was running out of excuses.

'I'll wash up if you cook.'

Rachel looked at him. 'Do you really want to marry me? Honestly?'

'Stay there.' Adam left the room. She could hear him out in the garden. Suddenly he was back. He beamed at her through a wild mass of weeds and flowers. 'Here,' he said as he got down on one knee. 'Will you, Rachel Cavendish, marry me, Adam Treherne?'

Rachel knelt on the floor beside him. 'Oh yes. I will, I will.'

Adam took a small velvet box from his pocket. 'I've been waiting to give this to you.' It was a simple solitaire diamond. He slipped the ring onto her finger. The room was quiet except for the crackling of the fire. Adam began, 'Wilt thou, forsaking all others, keep thee only unto us, so long as we both shall live?'

Rachel joined in. 'To have and to hold from this day forward, for better for worse, for richer for poorer, in sickness and in health, to love and to cherish, till death us do part.'

'My darling Rachel,' Adam said. 'With this ring I thee wed.' He kissed her gently on the lips.

'Oh Adam.' Rachel looked at him. Tears were running down her cheeks. 'For ever and ever, Adam?'

He put his arms around her. 'For ever and ever, Rachel.'

Later that night, Rachel lay contentedly beside Adam, listening to his gentle snores. 'My God,' she suddenly thought, 'what am I going to tell Anna?'

THE END

JUDITH KRANTZ
MISTRAL'S DAUGHTER

Maggy, Teddy and Fauve – they were three generations of magnificent red-haired beauties born to scandal, bred to success, bound to a single extraordinary man – Julien Mistral, the painter, the genius, the lover whose passions had seared them all.

From the '20s Paris of Chanel, Colette, Picasso and Matisse to New York's sizzling new modelling agencies of the '50s, to the model wars of the '70s, *Mistral's Daughter* captures the explosive glamour of life at the top of the worlds of art and high fashion. Judith Krantz has given us a glittering international tale as unforgettable as *Scruples*, as spellbinding as *Princess Daisy*.

0 552 12392 7 £2.95

CORGI BOOKS

Golden Hill

SHIRLEY LORD

Set on the exotic island paradise of Trinidad, *Golden Hill* tells the story of three families whose destinies interweave to shape the history of the island. It is a passionate story of love and hate, lust and greed, malice and envy in which the members of the three families struggle and clash violently against the background of the depression, World War II, and the island's fight for independence.

"*Golden Hill* is indeed golden and glorious. I don't know when I've enjoyed a novel as much. It is insanely romantic and at the same time historically fascinating. It is as sensuous as a Caribbean night and the characters are memorable"

David Brown, co-producer of *Jaws*

0 552 12346 3 £2.50

CORGI BOOKS